Miss Read, or in real life Dora Saint, was a school teacher by profession who started writing after the Second World War, beginning with light essays written for *Punch* and other journals. She then wrote on educational and country matters and worked as a scriptwriter for the BBC. Miss Read was married to a schoolmaster for sixty-four years until his death in 2004, and they have one daughter.

In the 1998 New Year Honours list Miss Read was awarded an MBE for her services to literature. She is the author of many immensely popular books, including two autobiographical works, but it is her novels of English rural life for which she is best known. The first of these, *Village School*, was published in 1955, and Miss Read continued to write about the fictitious villages of Fairacre and Thrush Green until her retirement in 1996. She lives in Berkshire.

D0488764

Books by Miss Read

NOVELS

Village School * Village Diary * Storm in the Village
Thrush Green * Fresh from the Country
Winter in Thrush Green * Miss Clare Remembers
Over the Gate * The Market Square * Village Christmas
The Howards of Caxley * Fairacre Festival
News from Thrush Green * Emily Davis * Tyler's Row
The Christmas Mouse * Farther Afield
Battles at Thrush Green * No Holly for Miss Quinn
Village Affairs * Return to Thrush Green * The White Robin
Village Centenary * Gossip from Thrush Green
Affairs at Thrush Green * Summer at Fairacre
At Home in Thrush Green * The School at Thrush Green
Mrs Pringle * Friends at Thrush Green * Changes at Fairacre
Celebrations at Thrush Green * Farewell to Fairacre
Tales from a Village School * The Year at Thrush Green
A Peaceful Retirement

ANTHOLOGIES

Country Bunch * Miss Read's Christmas Book

OMNIBUSES

Chronicles of Fairacre * Life at Thrush Green
More Stories from Thrush Green
Further Chronicles of Fairacre * Christmas at Fairacre
A Country Christmas * Fairacre Roundabout
Tales from Thrush Green * Fairacre Affairs
Encounters at Thrush Green * The Caxley Chronicles
Farewell, Thrush Green * The Last Chronicle of Fairacre

NON-FICTION

Miss Read's Country Cooking * Tiggy
The World of Thrush Green
Early Days (comprising A Fortunate Grandchild &
Time Remembered)

Miss Read

Village Affairs
Village Centenary

Village Affairs
First published in Great Britain by Michael Joseph Ltd in 1977

Village Centenary
First published in Great Britain by Michael Joseph Ltd in 1980

This omnibus edition published in 2009
by Orion Books Ltd
Orion House, 5 Upper St Martin's Lane
London WC2H 9EA

An Hachette UK company

A CIP catalogue record for this book is available
from the British Library.

ISBN 9781407221267

Printed in Great Britain by Clays Ltd, St Ives plc

www.orionbooks.co.uk

Village Affairs

To
Anthea and Mac
With love

CONTENTS

* * *

PART THREE

Fate Lends a Hand

PART ONE

The Rumours Fly

* * *

1. Forebodings

It is an undisputed fact that people who choose to live in the country must expect to be caught up, willy-nilly, in the cycle of the seasons.

Spring-cleaning is done to the accompaniment of the rattle of tractors as they drill up and down the bare fields outside. Lambs bleat, cuckoos cry, blackbirds scold inquisitive cats, while upstairs the sufferers from spring influenza call hoarsely for cold drinks.

Summer brings its own background of sights and sounds and the pace of village life quickens as fêtes follow cricket matches, and outings, tennis parties and picnics crowd the calendar.

There is not quite so much junketing in the autumn, for harvest takes pride of place, and both men and women are busy storing and preserving, filling the barns and the pantry shelves.

It is almost a relief to get to winter, to put away the lawn mower, to burn the garden rubbish, and to watch the ploughs at work turning the bright corn stubble into dark chocolate ribs ready for winter planting, while the rooks and peewits flutter behind, sometimes joined by seagulls when the weather is cruel elsewhere.

For each of us in the country, our own particular pattern of life forms but a small part against the general background of the seasons. If you are a schoolmistress, as I am, then the three terms echo in miniature the rural world outside. The Christmas term brings the arrival of new children to the school, harvest festival and, of course, the excitement of Christmas itself.

The Spring term is usually the coldest and the most germ-ridden, but catkins and primroses bring hope of better times, and summer itself is the crown of the year.

It is good to have this recurring rhythm, this familiar shape of the year. We know – to some extent – what to expect, what to welcome, what to avoid.

But there is another aspect of country life which is not so steady. There are certain topics which crop up again and again. Not, to be sure, as rhythmically as primroses and harvest, but often enough over the years to give us a little jolt of recognition. There is the matter of the village hall, for instance. Is it needed or not needed? And then there is the parlous state of the church organ and its eternal fund. And Mrs So-and-so is expecting again for the twelfth – or is it the thirteenth? – time, and something must be done about her house, or her husband, or both.

It is rather like watching a roundabout at a fair. The galloping horses whirl by, nostrils flaring, tails streaming, and then suddenly there is an ostrich, strange and exotic in its plumage among the everyday beasts. The merry-go-round twirls onward and we begin to sink back again into our pleasant lethargy when, yet again, the ostrich appears and our interest is quickened once more. So it is with these topics which disappear for a time whilst we are engrossed with everyday living, and then reappear to become the chief matters of importance, our talking points, things which have startled us from our normal apathy and quickened our senses.

Just such a recurring topic is the possible closure of Fairacre School. I have been headmistress here for a number of years, and talk of closing it has cropped up time and time again, diverting attention from the Church Organ Fund and the village hall as surely as the ostrich does from the horses. Naturally, after a week or two, the excitement dies down, and we continue as before with feelings of relief, until the next crisis arrives.

The cause varies. The true difficulty is that our numbers at the school scarcely warrant two teachers. One-teacher schools are considered undesirable, rightly, I think, and have been closing steadily in this area. Every now and again, the word goes round that Fairacre School really only needs one and a half teachers, and this half-teacher problem cannot be overcome, although one has the pleasing fancy that a great deal of ruler-gnawing in county offices goes on while the matter is being given consideration.

Usually, Providence steps in. A new family of six children appears, and is joyously added to the register. Cross parents refuse to send their young children by bus to the next village, or some other benign agency gets to work, and the matter of Fairacre School's closure is shelved once more.

I had become so used to the ostrich appearing, that I confess I could scarcely distinguish him from the galloping horses.

Until one evening, when Mr Annett, the headmaster of neighbouring Beech Green School, startled me with his disclosures.

As well as being a headmaster, George Annett is choirmaster of St Patrick's, Fairacre. On Friday evenings he drives over from Beech Green, a distance of some three miles, to officiate at choir practice.

For a small village we have quite a flourishing choir. Two of the stalwarts are Mr Willet, part-time caretaker of the school, sexton, grave-digger and general handyman to the whole village, and Mrs Pringle, our lugubrious school cleaner, whose booming contralto has been heard for long – far too long, according to the ribald young choristers – resounding among the rafters of St Patrick's roof.

On this particular Friday, George Annett called at the school house where I was busy putting away the week's groceries and trying to recover from the stunning amount I appeared to owe for about ten everyday items.

'Have a drink,' I said. 'I reckon I need a brandy when I see the price of butter this week.'

'A spot of sherry would be fine,' said George. 'Not too much. Can't arrive at church smelling of alcohol, or Mrs P. will have something to say.'

'Mrs Pringle,' I told him, with feeling, 'always has something to say. And usually something unpleasant. That woman positively invites assault and battery.'

'Heard the latest? Rumour has it that my school is being enlarged.'

'I've heard that before. And Fairacre's closing, I suppose?'

George studied his sherry, ignoring my flippancy. His grave face sobered me.

'It rather looks like it. The chap from the office is coming out next week to see me. Don't know why yet, but this rumour has reached me from several sources, and I believe something's in the wind. How many children do you have at the moment?'

'We're down to twenty-eight. Miss Edwards has fifteen infants. I have the rest. Incidentally, she's going at the end of term, so we're in the throes of getting a new appointment.'

'No easy task.'

'No. I expect we'll have to make do with a number of supply teachers until next term when the girls are appointed from college.'

George Annett put down his glass and rose to his feet. 'Well, I'll let you know more when I've seen Davis next week. I can't say I want a bigger school. We'll have the upheaval of new building going on, and a lot of disgruntled parents who don't want their children moved away.'

'Not to mention disgruntled out-of-work teachers.'

'You won't be out of work for long,' he smiled. 'Perhaps you'll be drafted to Beech Green?'

'And where should I live? No doubt the school and the school house would be sold together pretty quickly, and I certainly can't afford to buy either. I'm going to need a sub from the needlework tin, as it is, to pay for this week's groceries!'

George laughed, and departed.

I might have ignored this rumour, as I had so many others, if it had not been for Mrs Pringle.

She arrived at the school house on Saturday morning with a

nice plump chicken, of her own rearing, in the black oilcloth bag which accompanies her everywhere.

'Have a cup of coffee with me,' I invited.

'I don't mind if I do,' replied Mrs Pringle graciously.

I recalled a forthright friend who used to reply to this lacklustre acceptance by saying: 'And I don't mind if you don't!' But, naturally, I was too cowardly to copy her.

I took the tray into the garden, Mrs Pringle followed with the biscuit tin. Spring at Fairacre is pure bliss and I gazed fondly at the almond blossom, the daffodils and the faintest pink haze of a copper beech in tiny leaf.

'I see you've got plenty of bindweed in your border,' said Mrs Pringle, bringing me back to earth with a jolt. 'And twitch. No need to have twitch if you weeds regular.'

It sounded like some nervous complaint brought on by self-indulgence – a by-product of alcoholism, perhaps, or drug addiction. However, the sun was warm, the coffee fragrant, and I did not intend to let Mrs Pringle deflect me from their enjoyment.

'Have a biscuit,' I suggested, pushing the tin towards her. She selected a chocolate bourbon and surveyed it with disapproval.

'I used to be very partial to these until they doubled in price pretty nearly. Now I buy Osborne. Just as nourishing, and don't fatten you so much. At least, so Dr Martin said when he gave me my diet sheet.'

'A diet sheet?'

'Yes. I'm to lose three stone. No starch, no sugar, no fat, and no alcohol – though the last's no hardship, considering I signed the pledge as a child.'

'Then should you be eating that biscuit, and drinking coffee with cream in it?'

'I'm starting tomorrow,' said Mrs Pringle, taking a swift bite at the biscuit.

'I see.'

'You've heard about our school shutting, I suppose?' said the lady, her diction somewhat blurred with biscuit crumbs.

'Frequently.'

'No, the latest. My cousin at Beech Green says they're going to build on to Mr Annett's school, and send our lot over there in a bus. Won't suit some of 'em.'

A vague feeling of disquiet ran through me. Mrs Pringle was so often right. I remembered other dark warnings, airily dismissed by me, which had been proved correct as time went by.

Mrs Pringle dusted some crumbs from her massive chest.

'Some seems to think the infants will stay here,' she went on, 'but I said to Florrie – that's my cousin at Beech Green, and a flighty one she used to be as a girl, but has steadied down wonderful now she's got eight children – I said to her, as straight as I'm saying to you now, Miss Read, what call would the Office have to keep open all that great school for a handful of fives to sevens? "Don't make sense," I said, and I repeat it now: "It just don't make sense."'

'No indeed,' I agreed weakly.

'Take the heating,' continued Mrs Pringle, now in full spate. She held out a large hand, as though offering me the two tortoise stoves in the palm. 'Sacks of good coke them stoves need during the winter, not to mention blacklead and brushes and a cinder pail. They all takes us taxpayers' money. Then there's brooms and dusters, and bar soap and floor cloths, which costs a small fortune—'

'And all the books, of course,' I broke in.

'Well, yes,' said Mrs Pringle doubtfully, 'I suppose they needs *books*.' She spoke as though such aids to learning were wholly irrelevant in a school – very small beer compared with such things as scrubbing brushes and the other tools of her trade.

'But stands to reason,' she continued, 'that it's cheaper for all the whole boiling lot to go on the bus to Beech Green, though what the petrol costs these days to trundle them back and forth, I shudders to think.'

'Well, it may not happen yet,' I said, as lightly as I could. 'We've had these scaremongering tales before.'

'Maybe,' said Mrs Pringle, rising majestically, and adjusting the black oilcloth bag over her arm. 'But this time I've heard it from a good many folk, and when have our numbers at Fairacre School ever been so low? I don't like it, Miss Read. I feels in my bones a preposition. My mother, God rest her, had second sight, and I sometimes thinks I take after her.'

I devoutly hoped that Mrs Pringle's premonition meant nothing, but could not help feeling uneasy as I accompanied her to the gate.

'You wants to get rid of that bindweed,' was her parting shot, 'before it Takes Over.'

That woman, I thought savagely as I collected our cups, always has the last word!

By Monday morning my qualms had receded into the background, as they had so often before. In any case, everyday problems of the classroom successfully ousted any future threats.

Patrick had been entrusted with a pound note for his dinner money and had lost it on the way. He was tearful, fearing awful retribution from his mother.

'It was in my pocket,' he sniffed, mopping his tears with the back of his hand. 'All scrunched up, it was, with these 'ere.'

He produced four marbles, a stub of pencil, a grey lump of bubble gum and a jagged piece of red glass.

'You'll cut yourself on that,' I said. 'Put it in the wastepaper basket.'

He looked at me in alarm. A fat tear coursed unnoticed down his cheek.

'But it's off my brother's rear lamp,' he protested.

'Well, put it in this piece of paper to take home,' I said, giving in. 'And put all that rubbish on the side table. Now *think*, Patrick. Did you take the pound note out of your pocket on the way?'

'Yes, he did, miss,' chorused the class.

'He showed it to me,' said Linda Moffat. 'He said he betted I didn't have as much money.'

'That's right,' agreed Ernest. 'And it was windy. Blowing about like a flag it was. I bet it's blown over the hedge.'

'And some old cow's eaten it.'

'Or some old tramp's picked it up.'

'Or some old bird's got it in its nest.'

At these helpful surmises, Patrick's tears flowed afresh.

'You must go back over your tracks, Patrick, and search,' I told him. 'And someone had better go with him. Two pairs of eyes are better than one.'

Silence descended upon the class. Arms were folded, chests stuck out, and expressions of intense capability transformed the countenance of all present. What could be better than escaping from the classroom into the windy lane outside?

'Ernest,' I said, at last.

There was a gust of expelled air from those waiting lungs, and a general slumping of disappointed forms.

Ernest and Patrick hastened from the room joyfully, almost knocking over Joseph Coggs who was entering with a bunch of bedraggled narcissi. He looked bemused.

'I bin and brought you some flowers,' he said, holding them up.

'My auntie brought them on Saturday, but my mum says they'll only get knocked over, so you can have them.'

'Well, thank you. Fetch a vase.'

When he returned, I added: 'You're late, you know, Joseph.'

His lower lip began to droop and I feared that we should have yet another pupil in tears.

'A policeman come,' he said.

Everyone looked up. Here was real drama!

'From Caxley,' faltered Joseph. Bright glances were exchanged. This was better still!

'He wanted to see my dad, but he was in bed. My mum give me these flowers and said to clear off while she got Dad up. The policeman's waiting in our kitchen.'

'Well, there's no point in worrying about that,' I said reassuringly. 'Your mother and father will see to it.'

The class looked disappointed at the dismissal of such an enthralling subject. What spoilsports teachers are, to be sure!

By the time prayers had been said, a hymn sung and the rest of the pupils' dinner money safely gathered into my Oxo tin, the hands of the great wall clock stood at a quarter to ten. Patrick and Ernest were still at large in the village, and no doubt enjoying every minute of it.

'We're having a mental arithmetic test this morning,' I announced, amidst a few stifled groans, 'and I shall want someone to give out the paper.'

At that moment, there was a cry from the back of the room, and Eileen Burton stumbled down the aisle with a bloodied handkerchief clapped to her streaming nose.

This is a frequent occurrence and we all know what to do.

'Lay down, girl!' shouted one. I should like to have given – not for the first time – a short lecture on the use of verbs 'to lie' and 'to lay', but circumstances were against me. As it was, I fetched the box of paper handkerchiefs and assisted the child to a prone position by the stove.

'Shall I get the cold water?'

'Do she need a cushion, miss?'

'She wants a bit of metal down her neck, miss.'

I fetched the cutting-out scissors, a hefty chunk of cold steel, and put them at the back of her neck, substituting, at the same time, a wad of paper tissues for the deplorable handkerchief. Eileen remained calm throughout, accustomed to the routine.

We left her there, and set about the test.

'Number down to twenty,' I told them. Would we never get started?

There was a clanging noise as feet trampled over the iron scraper in the lobby. Ernest and Patrick entered, wind-blown and triumphant, Patrick holding aloft a very dirty pound note.

'We found it, miss!' they cried. 'Guess where?'

'In the hedge?'

'No.'

'In the duck pond?' shouted someone, putting down his pen.

'No.'

'In your pocket after all?'

'No.'

By now, pens were abandoned, and it was plain that the mental arithmetic test would be indefinitely postponed unless I took a firm hand.

'That's enough. Tell us where.'

'In a cow pat. So stuck up it was, it couldn't blow away. Weren't it *lucky*?'

They thrust the noisome object under my nose.

'Wipe it,' I said faintly, 'with a damp cloth in the lobby, then *bring it back*. Don't let go of it for one second. Understand?'

By now it was a quarter past ten and no work done.

'First question,' I said briskly. Pens were picked up, amidst sighing.

'If a man has twelve chickens,' I began, just as the door opened.

'And about time too,' I said wrathfully, expecting Ernest and Patrick to appear. 'Get into your desks, and let's get some work done!'

The mild face of the vicar appeared, and we all rose in some confusion.

2. NEWS OF MINNIE PRINGLE

The Reverend Gerald Partridge has been vicar of this parish for many years. I have yet to hear anyone, even the most censorious chapel-goer, speak ill of him. He goes about his parish duties conscientiously, vague in his manner, but wonderfully alert to those who have need of his sympathy and wisdom.

In winter, he is a striking figure, tramping the lanes in an ancient cape of dramatic cut, and sporting a pair of leopard skin gloves, so old that he is accompanied by little clouds of moulting fur whenever he uses his hands. It is commonly believed that they must have been a gift from some loving, and possibly beloved churchgoer, in the living before he came to Fairacre. Why otherwise would he cling to such dilapidated articles?

Fairacre School is a Church of England School, standing close to St Patrick's and the vicarage. The vicar is a frequent visitor, and although I have heard the ruder boys mimicking him behind his back, the children are extremely fond of him, and I have witnessed them attacking a stranger who once dared to criticize him.

'I'm sorry to interrupt,' he said, 'but I was just passing and thought I would have a word with you.'

'Of course.'

I turned to the class. 'Turn over your test papers and write out the twelve times table,' I directed. Long-suffering glances were exchanged. Trust her to want the twelve times! One of the nastiest that was! Their looks spoke volumes.

'What on earth is the matter with that child?' asked the vicar,

13

in a shocked tone, his horrified gaze upon the prone and bloodied figure of Eileen Burton.

'Just a nose-bleed,' I said soothingly. 'She often has them.'

'But you should have a key,' cried Mr Partridge, much agitated, 'a *large* key, to put at the nape of the neck—'

'She's got the cutting-out scissors—' I began, but he was now
too worried to heed such interruptions.

'My mother always kept a large key hanging in the kitchen
for this sort of thing. We had a parlour maid once, just so
afflicted. What about the key of the school door? Or shall I run
back to the vicarage for the vestry key? It must weigh quite two
pounds, and would be ideal for the purpose.'

His face was puckered with concern, his voice sharp with
anxiety.

At that moment, Eileen stood up, dropped the paper handkerchief in the wastepaper basket, and smiled broadly.

'Over,' she announced, and put the scissors on my desk.

'Take care, dear child, take care!' cried the vicar, but he
sounded greatly relieved at this recovery. He picked up the
cutting-out scissors. 'A worthy substitute,' he conceded, 'but it
would be as well to get Willet to screw a hook into the side of
one of the cupboards for a key. I can provide you with one quite
as massive as this, I can assure you, and I really should feel
happier if you had one on the premises.'

I thanked him, and asked what it was he wanted to tell me.

'Simply a rumour about the school closing. I wanted you to
know that I have had no official message about such a possibility. I pray that I may *never* have one, but should it be so, please
rest assured that I should let you know at once.'

'Thank you. I know you would.'

'You have heard nothing?'

'Only rumours. They fly around so often, I don't let them
bother me unduly.'

'Quite, quite. Well, I must be off. Mrs Partridge asked me to
pick up something at the Post Office, but for the life of me I

can't remember what it is. I wonder if I should go back and ask?'

'No doubt Mr Lamb will know and have it waiting for you,' I suggested.

Mr Partridge smiled with relief. 'I'm sure you're right. I will call there first. No point in worrying my wife unnecessarily.'

He waved to the children, and made for the door.

'I won't forget to look out a suitable key,' he promised. 'My mother would have approved of having one handy at all times. First aid, you know.'

The door closed behind him.

'First question,' I said. 'If a man had twelve chickens—'

Although I had told the vicar that I was not unduly bothered by the rumours, it was not strictly true. Somehow, this time, as the merry-go-round twirled, the ostrich had a menacing expression as it appeared among the galloping horses. Perhaps, I told myself, everything seemed worse because I had heard the news from several sources in a very short space of time.

After school, I pottered about in the kitchen preparing a salad, which Amy, my old college friend, was going to share that evening. She had promised to deliver a pile of garments for a future jumble sale, and as James, her husband, was away from home, we were free to enjoy each other's company.

Apart from a deplorable desire to reform my slack ways, Amy is the perfect friend. True, she also attempts to marry me off, now and again, to some poor unsuspecting male, but this uphill job has proved in vain, so far, and I think she knows, in her heart, that she will never be successful.

It was while I was washing lettuce that Mr Willet arrived with some broad bean plants.

'I saw you'd got some terrible gaps in your row, miss. Bit late perhaps to put 'em in, but we'll risk it, shall us?'

I agreed wholeheartedly.

He departed along the garden path, and I returned to the sink.

'*No rose in all the world*' warbled Mr Willet, '*until you came.*'

Mr Willet has a large repertoire of songs which were popular at the beginning of the century. They take me back, in a flash, to the musical evenings beloved of my parents. Mercifully, I can only remember snippets of these sentimental ballads, most of which had a lot of 'ah-ah-ah'-ing between verses, although a line or two, here and there, still stick in my memory.

'*Dearest, the night is over*' (or was it 'lonely'?)

'*Waneth the trembling moon*' and another about living in a land of roses but dreaming of a land of snow. Or maybe the other way round? It was the sort of question to put to Mr Willet, I decided, when Amy arrived, and Mr Willet and the ballads were temporarily forgotten.

'Lovely to be here,' sighed Amy, after we had eaten our meal. She leant back in the armchair and sipped her coffee. 'You really do make excellent coffee,' she said approvingly. 'Despite the haphazard way you measure the beans.'

'Thank you,' I said humbly. I rarely get praise from Amy, so that it is all the more flattering when I do.

She surveyed one elegant hand with a frown.

'My nails grow at such a rate. I always remember a horrifying tale I read when I was about ten. A body was exhumed, and the poor woman's coffin was full of her own hair and immensely long finger nails.'

'Horrible! But it's common knowledge that they go on growing after death.'

'A solemn thought, to imagine all those dark partings on Judgement Day,' commented Amy, patting her own neat waves. 'Well, what's the Fairacre news?'

I told her about the school, and its possible closure.

'That's old hat. I shouldn't worry unduly about that, though I did hear someone saying they'd heard that Beech Green was to be enlarged.'

'The grape vine spreads far and wide,' I agreed.

'But what about Mrs Fowler?'

'Mrs Fowler?' I repeated with bewilderment. 'You mean that wicked old harridan who used to live in Tyler's Row? Why, she left for Caxley years ago!'

'I know she did. That's why I hear about her from my window cleaner who lives next door to her, poor fellow. Well, she's being courted.'

'Never! I don't believe it!'

Amy looked pleasantly gratified at my reactions.

'And what's more, the man is the one that Minnie Pringle married.'

This was staggering news, and I was suitably impressed. Minnie Pringle is the niece of my redoubtable Mrs Pringle. We Fairacre folk have lost count of the children she has had out of wedlock, and were all dumb-founded when we heard that she was marrying a middle-aged man with children of his own. As far as I knew, they had settled down fairly well together at Springbourne. But if Amy's tale were to be believed, then the marriage must be decidedly shaky.

'Mrs Pringle hasn't said anything,' I said.

'She may not know anything about it.'

'Besides,' I went on, 'can you imagine anyone falling for Mrs Fowler? She's absolutely without charms of any sort.'

'That's nothing to do with it,' replied Amy. 'There's such a thing as incomprehensible attraction. Look at some of the truly dreadful girls at Cambridge who managed to snaffle some of the most attractive men!'

'But Mrs Fowler—' I protested.

Amy swept on. 'One of the nastiest men I ever met,' she told me, 'had four wives.'

'What? All at once? A Moslem or something?'

'No, no,' said Amy testily. 'Don't be so headlong!'

'You mean headstrong.'

'I know what I mean, thank you. You rush *headlong* to conclusions, is what I mean.'

'I'm sorry. Well, what was wrong with this nasty man you knew?'

'For one thing, he cleaned out his ears with a match stick.'

'Not the striking end, I hope. It's terribly poisonous.'

'*Whichever* end he used, the operation was revolting.'

'Oh, I agree. Absolutely. What else?'

'Several things. He was mean with money. Kicked the cat. Had Wagner – of all people – too loud on the gramophone. And yet, you see, he had this charm, this charisma—'

'Now there's a word I never say! Like "Charivari". "Punch or the London" one, you know.'

Amy tut-tutted with exasperation. 'The point I have been trying to make for the last ten minutes,' shouted Amy rudely, '*against fearful odds*, is that Minnie Pringle's husband must see something attractive in Mrs Fowler.'

'I thought we'd agreed on that,' I said. 'More coffee?'

'Thank you,' said Amy faintly. 'I feel I need it.'

The fascinating subject of Mrs Fowler and her admirer did not crop up again until the last day of the spring term.

Excitement, as always, was at fever-pitch among the children. One would think that they were endlessly beaten and bullied at school when one sees the joy with which they welcome the holidays.

Miss Edwards, who had been my infants' teacher for the past two years, was leaving to get married at Easter, and we presented her with a tray, and a large greetings card signed by all the children.

The vicar called to wish her well, and to exhort the children to help their mothers during the holidays, and to enjoy themselves.

When he had gone, I contented myself with impressing upon them the date of their return, and let them loose. Within minutes, the stampede had vanished round the bend of the lane, and I was alone in the schoolroom.

I always love that first moment of solitude, when the sound

of the birds is suddenly noticed, and the scent of the flowers reminds one of the quiet country pleasures ahead. Now, freed from the bondage of the clock and the school timetable, there would be time 'to stand and stare', to listen to the twittering of nestlings, the hum of the early foraging bees, and the first sound of the cuckoo from the coppice across the fields.

Spring is the loveliest time of the year at Fairacre, when everything is young, and green, and alive with hope. Soon the house martins would be back, and the swifts, screaming round and round the village as they selected nesting places. Then the swallows would arrive, seeking out their old familiar haunts – Mr Roberts' barn rafters, the Post Office porch, the loft above the vicar's stables – in which to build their nests.

Someone had brought me a bunch of primroses as an end of term present. Holding the fragrant nosegay carefully, I made my way through the school lobby towards my home across the playground, full of anticipation at the happiness ahead.

The door scraper clanged. The door opened, and Mrs Pringle, her mouth set grimly, confronted me.

'Sorry I'm a few minutes late,' she began, 'but I'm In Trouble.'

'In Fairacre, this expression is commonly used to describe pregnancy, but in view of Mrs Pringle's age, I rightly assumed that she used the term more generally.

'What's wrong?'

'It's our Minnie,' said Mrs Pringle. 'Up my place. In a fair taking, she is. Can't do nothing with her. I've left her crying her eyes out.'

'Oh, dear,' I said weakly, my heart sinking. Could Amy have heard aright?

I smelt my sweet primroses to give me comfort.

'Come to the house and sit down,' I said.

Mrs Pringle raised a hand, and shook her head.

'No. I've come to work, and work I will!'

'Well, at least sit on the bench while you tell me.'

A rough plank bench in the playground, made by Mr Willet, acts as seat, vaulting horse, balancing frame and various other things, and on this we now rested, Mrs Pringle with her black oilcloth bag on her lap, and the primroses on mine, in the hedge dividing the playground from the lane, a blackbird scolded as Tibby, my cat, emerged from the school house to see why I was taking so long to get into the kitchen to provide her meal.

'That man,' said Mrs Pringle, 'has up and left our Minnie. What's more, he's left his kids, and hers, and that one of theirs, to look after, while he gallivants with that woman who's no better than she should be.'

'Perhaps he'll come back,' I suggested.

'Not him! He's gone for good. And d'you know who he's with?'

'No,' I said, expecting to be struck by lightning for downright lying.

'You'll never guess. That Mrs Fowler from Tyler's Row.'

I gave a creditable gasp of surprise.

'The scheming hussy,' said Mrs Pringle wrathfully. A wave of scarlet colour swept up her neck and into her cheeks, which were awobble with indignation.

'It's my belief she knew he had an insurance policy coming out this month. After his money, you see. Well, it wouldn't have been his looks, would it?'

I was obliged to agree, but remembered Amy's remark about the plain girls and the young Adonises at Cambridge. Who could tell?

'But, top and bottom of it all is – how's Minnie to live? Oh, I expect she'll get the Social Security and Family Allowance, and all that, but she'll need a bit of work as well, I reckons, if she's to keep that house on at Springbourne.'

'Won't he provide some money?'

'That'll be the day,' said Mrs Pringle sardonically. 'Unless Min takes him to court, and who's got the time and money to bother with all that?'

Mrs Pringle's view of British justice was much the same as her views of my housekeeping, it seemed, leaving much to be desired.

'If she really needs work,' I said reluctantly, 'I could give her half a day here cleaning silver, and windows, and things.'

Mrs Pringle's countenance betrayed many conflicting emotions. Weren't her own ministrations on my behalf enough then? And what sort of a hash would Minnie make of any job offered her? And finally, it was a noble gesture to offer her work anyway.

Luckily, the last emotion held sway.

'That's a very kind thought, Miss Read. Very kind indeed.'

She struggled to her feet, and we stood facing each other. Tibby began to weave between our legs, reminding us of her hunger.

'But let's hope it won't come to that,' she said. I hoped so too, already regretting my offer.

Mrs Pringle turned towards the lobby door. 'I'll let you know what happens,' she said, 'but I'll get on with a bit of scrubbing now. Takes your mind off things, a bit of scrubbing does.'

She stumped off, black bag swinging, whilst Tibby and I made our way home.

3. Could it be Arthur Coggs?

The policeman from Caxley, who had called upon the Coggs household, was making inquiries, we learnt, about the theft of lead in the neighbourhood.

Scarcely a week went by but the *Caxley Chronicle* reported the stripping of lead from local roofs around the Caxley area. Many a beautiful lead figure too, which had graced a Caxley garden for generations, was spirited away under cover of darkness, lead water tanks and cisterns, lead guttering, lead piping, all fell victim to a cunning band of thieves who knew just where to collect this valuable metal.

It so happened that the Mawnes had an ancient summer house, with a lead roof, in their garden.

Their house had been built in the reign of Queen Anne, and the octagonal summer house, according to Mr Willet, who considered it unsafe and unnecessarily ornate, was erected not long afterwards, although it was, more likely, the conceit of some Victorian architect. It was hidden from the house by a shrubbery, and nothing could have been easier for thieves than to slip through the hedge from the fields adjoining the garden to do their work in privacy.

The lead was not missed until a thundery shower sent cascades of water through the now unprotected roof into the little room below. A wicker chair and its cushion were drenched, a water colour scene, executed by Mrs Mawne in her youth, became more water than colour overnight, and a rug, which Mr Mawne had brought back from Egypt on one of his bird-watching trips, and which he much prized, was ruined. Added to all this was the truly dreadful smell composed of wet timber and the decaying bodies of innumerable insects, mice, shrews and so on, washed from their resting places by the onrush of rain.

Fairacre was shocked at the news. It was one thing to read in the pages of the respected *Caxley Chronicle* about lead being stolen from villages a comfortable distance from their own. It was quite another to find that someone had actually been at work in Fairacre itself. What would happen next?

Mr Willet voiced the fears of his neighbours as he returned from choir practice one Friday night.

'What's to stop them blighters pinching the new lead off the church roof? Cost a mint of money to put on. It'd make a fine haul for some of these robbers.'

A violent storm, some years earlier, had damaged St Patrick's sorely. Only by dint of outstanding efforts on the part of the villagers, and never-to-be-forgotten generosity from American friends of Fairacre, had the necessary repairs been made possible. The sheets of lead, then fixed upon much of the roof, had formed one of the costliest items in the bill. No wonder Fairacre folk feared for its safety, now that marauders had visited their village.

'They wouldn't dare to take the Lord's property,' announced Mrs Pringle.

'I don't think they care much whose property it is,' observed Mr Lamb from the Post Office. 'It's just how easy they can turn it into hard cash.'

'My sister in Caxley,' replied Mrs Pringle, still seeking the limelight, 'told me the most shocking thing happened all up the road next to hers.'

'What?' asked Mr Willet. The party had reached the Post Office by now and stopped to continue the conversation before Mr Lamb left them.

Twilight was beginning to fall. The air was still and scented with the flowers in cottage gardens.

Mrs Pringle looked up and down the road before replying.

Her voice was low and conspiratorial. Mr Willet and Mr Lamb bent their heads to hear the disclosure.

'Well, these lead thieves came one night and went along all the outside lavatories, and cut out every bit of piping from the cistern to the pan.'

'No!'

'They did. As true as I'm standing here!'

'What! Every house?'

Mrs Pringle shifted her chins uncomfortably upon the neck of her cardigan.

'Not quite all. Mr Jarvis, him what was once usher at the Court, happened to be in his when they reached it, so they cleared off pretty smartly.'

'Did they catch 'em?'

'Not one of 'em!' pronounced Mrs Pringle. 'Still at large, they are. Quite likely the very same as took Mr Mawne's lead off the summer house.'

'Could be,' agreed Mr Lamb, making towards his house now that the story was done. 'Thought I heard as Arthur Coggs might be mixed up with this little lot.'

'Now, now!' said Mr Willet, holding up a hand in a magisterial gesture. 'No hearsay! It's not right to go accusing people. Us doesn't know nothing about Arthur being connected with lead stealing.'

'He's connected with plenty that's downright dishonest,' rejoined Mr Lamb, with spirit. 'Dammit all, man, he's done time, he's a poacher, he's been had up, time and time again, for stealing. And he ought to be had up for a lot of other things, to my mind. Wife-beating for one. And dodging the column for another. Why, that chap hasn't done a day's work for weeks, and all us old fools keeps him by giving him the dole and the family allowances. Makes my blood boil!'

'We knows all that,' agreed Mr Willet, taking a swipe at a passing bat with a rolled-up copy of Handel's *Messiah*. 'But you just can't pin everything that's crooked on Arthur Coggs.'

'Why not?' asked Mrs Pringle belligerently. 'More times than not you'd be right!'

And on this note the friends parted.

Human nature being what it is, there were far more people in Fairacre who shared Mrs Pringle's view than Mr Willet's.

Arthur Coggs was the black sheep of the village, and his wife greatly pitied. He was supposed to be a labourer, although his neighbours stated roundly that labour was the last thing Arthur looked for. He occasionally found a job on a building site, carrying a hod, or wheeling a barrow slowly from one place to the next. But he rarely stayed long. Either he became tired of the work, or more often, his employer grew tired of paying him to do nothing.

The greater part of his money went on beer, and he was a regular customer at the Beetle and Wedge in Fairacre. He and his family had once occupied a tumbledown cottage, one of four in Tyler's Row, now made into one long attractive house occupied by a retired schoolmaster from Caxley and his wife.

The Coggs family had been rehoused in a council house which was fast becoming as dilapidated as their last abode. Mrs Coggs, with a large family to cope with, and very little money with which to do it, struggled to tidy the house and garden, but never succeeded. Over the years she had grown thinner and greyer. Her highest hopes were that Arthur would stay sober, and that he would provide more housekeeping money. So far, her hopes had not been realized.

Now and again, Arthur would appear to have money in his pocket and this she felt certain was the result of some dishonest dealings. Arthur had appeared in the Court at Caxley on many occasions, and his list of previous convictions, handed up for the Bench to study, included such offences as theft, receiving goods knowing them to have been stolen, shoplifting, burglary and house-breaking.

Mrs Coggs knew better than to question Arthur about any unusual affluence. A black eye, or painful bruises elsewhere would have been the outcome. But experience had given her some cunning and she had sometimes been able to abstract a pound note or some change from his pocket, when he was fuddled with drink.

Pity for Arthur's wife had prompted several people in Fairacre to employ her dissolute husband over the years. Mr Roberts, the local farmer, had taken him on as a farm hand, only to find that eggs vanished, one or two hens disappeared, as well as sacks of potatoes and corn. The other men complained that they were doing Arthur's work as well as their own and they were right. Mr Roberts dispensed with Arthur's services.

Mr Lamb had tried to employ him as a jobbing gardener, but again found that vegetables were being taken and the jobs set him were sketchily done, and the local builder's patience snapped when he caught Arthur red-handed, walking home with a pocketful of his tools.

The plumber at Springbourne, whose soft heart had been touched by the sight of Mrs Coggs and her four children all in tears one morning as he passed through Fairacre, was moved to take on Arthur for a week's trial. By Wednesday he discovered that a considerable amount of copper piping had vanished, and Arthur was sacked once again.

Virtually, he was unemployable, and soon realized that he was far better off collecting his social security allowance and other moneys disbursed by a benevolent government, and indulging his chronic laziness at the same time.

He was known to be in tow with some equally feckless and dishonest men in Caxley and, in fact, Arthur frequently acted as look-out man when the more daring of the gang were breaking-in. His wages for this kind of work were in proportion to the loot obtained, but always far less than the share each burglar received.

'You didn't take much risk, chum,' they told him. 'Piece of cake being look-out. You can reckon yourself lucky to get this bit.'

And Arthur agreed. As long as it helped to keep him in beer, there was no point in arguing.

For a while, immediately after the discovery of the loss of Mr Mawne's roofing lead, Fairacre folk were extra careful about making their homes secure. People actually shut their front doors on sunny days, instead of leaving them hospitably open for neighbours to enter. They began to hunt for door keys, long disused, and some very funny places they were found in after the passage of time. Mr Willet, after exhaustive searching, admitted that he found his front door key at the bottom of a biscuit tin full of nuts, bolts, screws, hinges, padlocks, latches, tacks, brass rings, and other useful impedimenta vital to a handyman.

His neighbour found his on top of the cistern in the outside lavatory. The two Misses Waters, Margaret and Mary, who had a horror of burglars but so far relied on a stout bolt on both back and front doors, now scoured their small cottage in vain for the keys they had once owned. It was Margaret who remembered eventually, at three o'clock one morning, that they had hidden them under the fourth stone which bordered their brick path, when they were going away for a brief holiday some years earlier. At first light, she crept out, and unearthed them, red with rust. She remained in a heady state of triumph all day.

Mr Lamb, it seemed, was the only householder in Fairacre who locked up and bolted and barred his premises methodically every night. But then, as people pointed out, as custodian of the Queen's mail he'd have to see things were done properly or he'd soon get the boot. No one gave him credit for his pains, and to be honest, Mr Lamb was sensible enough not to expect any. But at least he was spared the searching for keys, for his own hung, each on its hook and carefully labelled, ready for its nightly work.

For a time, even the children caught the fever and became aware that it was necessary to be alert to dishonesty. One Caxley market day, Linda Moffat and Eileen Burton arrived each with a door key on a string round their necks.

'My mum's gone on the bus to buy some material for summer frocks,' said Linda, 'and she may not be back when I get home.'

'And mine's gone to buy some plants,' announced Eileen. 'Ours never come to nothing.'

'If they never come to nothing,' I said severely, 'then they must have come to something. Say what you mean.'

The child looked bewildered. 'I did, miss. Our seeds never come—'

'*Your seeds did not come up*,' I said, with emphasis.

'That's what I said.'

'You did not say that,' I began, and was about to embark, for the thousandth time, on an elementary grammar lesson, when Mr Willet intervened. He had been listening to the exchange.

'Your mum's seeds never come up,' he said forcefully, 'because she used that plaguey compost muck out of a bag. She wants to mix her own, tell her, with a nice bit of soft earth and dung and a sprinkle of sharp sand. Tell her they'll never come to nothing in that boughten stuff.'

I gave up, and turned to the marking of the register.

It came as no surprise to the good people of Fairacre when they heard that a week or two after the visit of the police to the Coggs' house Arthur Coggs was to appear in Court charged, together with others, with stealing a quantity of lead roofing, the property of H.A. Mawne Esq.

At the time of the theft, the *Caxley Chronicle* had given some prominence to the affair, enlarging upon Mr Mawne's distinction as an ornithologist, and reminding its readers that the gentleman had frequently contributed nature notes to the paper's columns. News must have been thin that week for not only was Mr Mawne given an excessive amount of type, but a photograph was also included, taken by one of the younger staff against the background of the depleted summer house.

Even the kindest readers were at a loss to find something nice to say about the likeness, and the subject himself said it looked to him like an explosion in a pickle factory, adding tolerantly that maybe he really looked like that and had never realized.

'There's three other chaps,' Mr Willet told me. 'Two of 'em is Bryants – that gipsy lot – and the third's a real bad 'un from Bent. I bet he was the ringleader, and that poor fool of an Arthur Coggs told him about the roof here. I still reckons we ought to keep watch on the church, but the vicar says we must trust our brothers.'

'He's a good man,' I commented.

'A sight too good, if you ask me. "There's brothers and brothers," I told him. I wouldn't want any of them four for brothers, and I wouldn't trust them no further than that coke pile, idle thieving lot.'

'We don't know that they're guilty yet,' I pointed out.

'I do,' said Mr Willet, picking up his screwdriver.

Later, I overheard a conversation in the playground as I strolled round holding my mug of tea. It was a glorious May morning. The rooks cawed from the elm trees as they went back and forth feeding their hungry nestlings, and the children were sitting on the playground bench, or had propped themselves against the school wall, legs outstretched, as they enjoyed the sunshine.

Joseph Coggs sat between Ernest and Patrick, all three oblivious of the condition of their trouser seats in the dust.

'Saw your dad in the paper,' said Ernest.

'Ah,' grunted Joseph.

'Bin pinchin', ain't he?' said Patrick.

'Dunno.'

'That's what the paper said.'

Joseph scratched a bite on his leg and said nothing.

'That's what the copper come about,' said Ernest to Patrick.

'Is he in prison?' asked Patrick conversationally of Joseph.

'No,' shouted Joseph, scrambling to his feet. His face was red, and he looked tearful. He rushed away towards the boys' lavatories, obviously craving privacy, and I approached his questioners.

They gazed up at me innocently.

'You should stand up when ladies speak to you,' I told them, not for the first time. They rose languidly.

'And don't let me hear you upsetting Joseph with questions about his father. It's none of your business and it's unkind anyway.'

'Yes, miss,' they replied, trying to look suitably chastened.

One or two of the other children hovered nearby, listening to my brief homily, and I was conscious of meaningful glances being exchanged. It was difficult to be critical. After all, the Arthur Coggs affair was the main subject of spicy conjecture in their homes at the moment, and it was hardly surprising that they shared their parents' interest.

That afternoon when the sun was high in the heaven, and the downs were veiled in a blue haze of heat, I decided that a nature walk was far more beneficial to my pupils than a handiwork lesson.

As the sun was so hot, we kept to the lanes, in and around the village, which are shaded by fine old trees. The hawthorn hedges were sprouting young scarlet shoots, and in the cottage gardens the columbines were out. The children call them 'granny's bonnets', and they are exactly like the beautifully goffered and crimped sun bonnets that one sees in old photographs.

Some of the lilac flowers were beginning to turn rusty, and the old-fashioned crimson peonies were beginning to droop their petals in the heat, but the scent was heavy, redolent of summer and a whiff of the long days ahead.

The children straggled along in a happy and untidy crocodile, chattering like starlings and waving greetings to friends and relations as they passed.

Fairacre, I told myself, was the perfect place to live and work, and early summer found it at its most beautiful. I stopped to smell a rose nodding over a cottage gate, and became conscious of voices in the garden. Two neighbours were chatting over their boundary hedge.

'And if it isn't Arthur Coggs, then who is it?' asked one.

I sighed, and let the rose free from my restraining hand.

Every Eden seemed to have its serpent, Fairacre included.

4. Mrs Pringle has Problems

With the departure of the infants' teacher, Miss Edwards, we were back in the familiar circumstances of looking for a second member of staff.

As it happened, only two new children arrived for the summer term, both five-year-olds, making the infants' class seventeen in all. Altogether we had now thirty children on roll, and although this might sound a laughably small number to teach compared with some of the gigantic classes in over-crowded urban primary schools, yet there were considerable difficulties.

I struggled alone for two weeks before a supply teacher could be found.

It meant a proliferation of groups working in the one class-room, and an impossible situation when one tried to play games, or choose a story or a song, which could be enjoyed by five-year-olds and eleven-year-olds at the same time. I always feared that some accident might happen, when the sole respon-sibility rested on me to get help and to look after the rest of the school at the same time. It was a worrying time and I was mightily relieved when Mrs Ansell arrived to share the burden.

She was a cheerful young woman in her thirties whom I had met once or twice at teachers' meetings in Caxley. She had a young son of two, and had not taught since his birth, but her mother lived nearby in Caxley, and was willing to mind the child if Mrs Ansell wanted to do occasional supply teaching.

All went well for a fortnight, and the children were settling down nicely under their new regime, when the blow fell. She rang me one evening to say that her mother had fallen down in the garden and damaged her hip. She was in Caxley hospital, and of course quite unable to look after Richard.

I expressed my sympathy, told her we could manage, and hung up.

Now what, I wondered? Supply teachers are as rare and as precious as rubies. Most of those local few who were in existence lived in Caxley and preferred to attend the town schools. I had been lucky enough to get Mrs Ansell because she particularly wanted to teach infants, liked country schools, and had her own car.

'I shall have to ring the Office again in the morning,' I told Tibby gloomily. 'And what hope there?'

Tibby mewed loudly, but not with sympathy. Plain hunger was the cause, and I obediently dug out some Pussi-luv and put it on the kitchen floor. I then supplied my own supper plate with bread and cheese.

It was while I was eating this spare repast that I thought of Amy. She has helped us out on occasions, and there is no one I would sooner have as my companion at Fairacre School.

'Are you in the middle of your dinner?' was Amy's first remark.

'It's only the last crumb of bread and cheese,' I assured her.

'Is that all you have had?'

'Yes. Why?'

'I really do think you should be a little less slapdash with your meals,' said Amy severely. 'And on your lap, I suppose. It's ruination to the digestion, you know, these scrambled snacks.'

'Well, never mind that,' I said impatiently, and went on to tell her our troubles.

'Could you?' I finished.

'I could come on Monday,' said Amy, 'not before, I'm afraid, as I'm helping Lady Williams with the bazaar for the Save The Children Fund on Friday.'

'Come and save my children instead.'

'And it can't be for long,' went on Amy, 'as I have Vanessa coming some time next month.'

'But you could come for a week or two?'

'Probably three weeks. James is off to Persia on some trade mission or other, and then to Australia, I believe, unless it was New Zealand. They're so close, one gets confused.'

'I believe they are thousands of miles apart, and they get pretty stroppy about being muddled up. It's like the Scandinavian countries, isn't it? Do you know which is top and bottom of that craggy looking piece of coastline?'

'No, I don't. But I remember it was always a great help to trace the outline on the way home in the train. The movement was invaluable round the fiords.'

'You are a darling to come,' I said, reverting to the main topic. 'I'll ring the Office in the morning and get things straight, and let you know the result. It really is murder trying to cope alone. One grazed knee or a pair of wet knickers is enough to stop us all in our tracks.'

'Never fear,' cried Amy, 'help is on its way!'

'The relief of Mafeking,' I told her, 'will be nothing to it.'

Jubilantly, I hung up.

The Office gave its blessing to my arrangements, and we all awaited Amy's coming with varying degrees of pleasure.

My own feeling was of unadulterated relief. The vicar, who has a soft spot for Amy, said it would be delightful to see her again, and how very generous she was with her time when one considered that she had a husband and a house to look after.

Mr Willet was equally enthusiastic. 'I can ask her about those pinks cuttings I give her,' he said. 'Always a bit tricky pinks are, if the soil's not to their liking. I'd dearly love to go over to Bent to keep an eye on 'em, but I don't want to push meself forward.'

I said I felt sure that Amy would welcome his advice, and he retired to the playground humming cheerfully.

Mrs Pringle greeted the news with modified rapture. Amy is too well-dressed, drives too large a car, and altogether has an aura of elegant affluence which Mrs Pringle disapproves of in a teacher. I think she feels that anyone as comfortably placed as Amy should do a little voluntary work for some deserving charity, but to take on a teaching job smacks too much of depriving some poor wretch of her rightful dues.

Since taking to her slimming diet, Mrs Pringle seemed to be even more martyr-like than usual. She received the news of Amy's arrival on Monday with a resigned sigh.

'Best get both gates wide open,' she said, 'for that great car of hers. I take it you'll tell the children to keep off of it? It's a big responsibility havin' an expensive motor like that on the premises, and I haven't got eyes in the back of my head.'

I reassured her on that point.

'And last time she come, she didn't eat no potatoes I noticed. Now that's a bad example to the children. We tells 'em to eat up all they've got, and then they sees their teachers pickin' and choosin'. Just drop a word, Miss Read. She's your friend after all.'

'How's the dieting?' I asked, hoping to change the subject.

Mrs Pringle's gloom deepened. 'That Dr Martin's getting past it. Fairly snapped my head off when I went to get weighed, just because I've only lost two pounds in a month! I told him straight: "Well, at least I've *lost* it. There's no call to get so white and spiteful. Anyone'd think I'd *put on* two pounds"! He calmed down a bit then, and made me write down all I'd eaten since Sunday.'

'Could you remember?'

'Most of it. And when I give him the list, he shouted out so loud that Mrs Pratt's baby started hollering in the waiting room.'

'Why, what was wrong?'

'You may well ask. He shouted: "I said no cakes, no bread, no potatoes, and no sugar"! And I said to him: "How's a body to drink tea without sugar? And what's tea time without a slice of cake? And what's a dinner plate look like without a nice little pile of potatoes?" He never answered. Just went a bit pink, and hustled me out, telling me to do what he'd said. No sense to him these days. Too old for the job, if you ask me.'

'But he's right, you know. You won't lose weight unless you cut out all those lovely fattening things.'

'I don't call them *fattening*,' said Mrs Pringle, with immense dignity. 'They're *sustaining*! A woman what works as hard as I do needs nourishment. The days I've given up me bread and that, I've felt proper leer. Me knees have been all of a tremble. With this job to do, let alone my own home, I needs the food.'

There seemed little to add. Mrs Pringle shuffled off, limping slightly, a sure sign that her bad leg was giving trouble, as it always does in times of stress.

As she went, I noticed she did up a button on her cardigan which had burst from its buttonhole under excessive strain. The two pounds had not been lost from that portion of her anatomy obviously.

Come to think of it, I pondered, watching her massive rear vanish into the lobby, it would be difficult to say just where she had lost those pounds.

The hot weather continued, showing May in all her glory. In my garden the pinks began to break, shaking their shaggy locks from the tight grey cap which held them.

On the front of the school house, the ancient Gloire de Dijon rose, planted by one of my predecessors, turned its fragrant flat-faced flowers to the sunshine in all its cream and pink splendour.

The hay crop looked as though it would be heavy this year, and the bees were working hard. A field of yellow rape made a blaze of colour across one of Mr Roberts' stretches of land, and it was this, I suspect, that attracted so many bees to the area.

The copper beech was now in full leaf, and the box edging to the garden beds gave off its peculiar aromatic smell as the noonday sun drew out all the delicious scents of summer.

The school room door was propped open with a large knobbly flint, turned up by the plough in the neighbouring field. The sounds and scents wafted in, distracting the children from their work, so that I often took them all into the grass under the trees, and let them listen – or not – to a story. The daddy-long-legs floated round us in the warm air, small birds chattered and squeaked in the branches above, and only the sound of Mr Roberts' tractor in the distance gave any hint of the village life which was going on around us. They were lovely sessions, refreshing to body and mind, and we always returned to the classroom in a tranquil state of mind.

Amy arrived on Monday morning, wearing a beautiful pale pink linen suit, but with her usual foresight had brought with her a deep rose-pink overall to ward off such infant room hazards as sticky fingers, spilt milk, and chalk dust.

Some of the children knew her already, and it was not long before her calm efficiency had made friends of them all. I closed the infants' room door with a sigh of relief, and set out to catch up with many neglected lessons with my older children.

Things went swimmingly all week until Friday morning.

'Guess who I saw at the bus stop in Caxley,' said Amy, trying to adjust her hair by the reflection from 'The Light of the World' behind my chair.

'Haven't a clue,' I replied.

'Why don't you have a mirror somewhere? I see there isn't one in the lobby either. Where do you do your hair?'

'At home.'

'But surely, when you've been in the playground on a windy day, you – and the children, for that matter – need to tidy up.'

'We manage.'

'By just leaving things, I suppose,' said Amy. 'It's too bad of you, you know. The children should be set an example of neatness. And did you know that the hem is coming down on that frock?'

'I had a suspicion. There was an ominous tearing sound when I caught my heel in it this morning, but no time to investigate.'

'Dreadful!' murmured Amy, more in sorrow than anger. She does try so hard to improve me, with practically no success.

'You were telling me,' I said, 'about someone at the bus stop. Miss Clare?'

'At eight-thirty in the morning? Don't be silly.'

'Who then?'

'Mrs Fowler and Minnie Pringle's husband, whatever he's called.'

'What? Waiting for the bus to Springbourne?'

'It looked remarkably like it.'

I pondered upon this snippet of news. 'Do you think they might be going to collect his children from Minnie's?'

'It would be a jolly good thing if they did,' said Amy forth-rightly, 'but I doubt it. They've managed quite happily without them, as far as one can see, so why suddenly want a family reunion now?'

'It certainly seems odd,' I agreed. 'Perhaps Mrs Pringle will be able to throw light on the matter.'

Sure enough, when Mrs Pringle arrived for her after school duties, it was quite apparent, from the important wobbling of her chins, that she had great news to impart.

'Well, I've got that Minnie of mine back again. I've left her grizzling in the kitchen and the children are in the garden. I've dared them to put a foot on the flower beds, unless they want to be skinned alive. I can't say fairer than that to them.'

'What's the matter this time?' I asked. Amy who had picked up her handbag ready to depart, put it down again and perched on the front desk to observe the scene.

Mrs Pringle looked at her with some dislike, but aquiver as she was with her momentous news, she decided to ignore her presence and tell all.

'That man had the cheek to come out to Minnie's this morning, with that woman who's no better than she should be, and I'll not soil my lips by repeating her name, and ask for his furniture back.'

'But can he? Isn't it the marital home, or whatever they call it in Court?'

'Whether he can or he can't,' boomed Mrs Pringle, 'he's done it. And that Mrs Fowler—'

'With whose name you wouldn't soil your lips,' I remembered silently.

'Well, she was at the bottom of it. It was that cat as put him up to it. And her nephew had his van waiting by Minnie's gate to put the stuff in. All planned and plotted you see. And off they drove, leaving our Minnie without a frying pan in the house.'

'Nothing at all?' I said horrified.

Mrs Pringle tutted with impatience.

'No, no, they never took *the lot*, I'll give 'em that, but they took two armchairs, and the kitchen table, and no end of china, and the upstairs curtains, and some cooking pots and the frying pan, so of course Minnie and the kids have had no dinner.'

I could not quite see why the frying pan was the only utensil needed to cook the family's food, but this was no time to go into all that, and I was beginning to feel very sorry for poor luckless Minnie, and for Mrs Pringle too, when her next remark cooled my sympathy.

'So it looks to me, Miss Read, as Minnie will be very glad to take up your offer of some work. She's got all that stuff to buy anew, and money's very tight anyway. I told her to come up and see you to arrange things some time.'

'Thank you,' I said faintly. It was an appalling prospect, and I cursed myself for ever making such an idiotic suggestion. I avoided meeting Amy's gaze. She appeared to be struggling to hide her very ill-timed amusement. Like Queen Victoria, my amusement was nil.

'Well, I'd better get on with my tidying up and then hurry back to see what damage them little varmints of Minnie's have done. When shall I tell her to come?'

'She'd better come one evening,' I said. 'There's no hurry, tell her, and if she gets a post elsewhere I shall quite understand.'

Amy suffered a sudden fit of coughing which necessitated a great deal of play with her handkerchief. At times, she can be very tiresome.

'Right!' said Mrs Pringle, shaking out a clean duster from her black oilcloth bag. 'I'll let her know. But I wouldn't trust her with glass, if I were you, or any china. She's a bit clumsy that way.'

She went into the infants' room and vanished from our sight.

'Come and have tea with me,' I said to Amy.

'No, I really must get back, but I couldn't possibly leave before knowing the outcome of this morning's activities.'

We walked out into the sunlit playground. Overhead the swifts screamed and whirled, and the air was deliciously fresh after the classroom.

'Looks as though I'm saddled with that ghastly Minnie,' I remarked.

'You should have been firm from the outset,' replied Amy.

'I didn't get much chance,' I protested. 'She practically told me she was coming. What on earth could I do?'

'You could have said that you had offered the job to someone else, and it had been accepted.'

'What? In Fairacre? Be your age, Amy! Everyone knows I

haven't a job to offer! It's as much as I can cope with having Ma Pringle bullying me about the house. I don't want more.'

'You should have thought about that earlier,' said Amy primly. 'I'm always telling you how you rush headlong into things.'

'Well, don't keep rubbing it in,' I retorted crossly. 'It's quite bad enough having to face the possibility of Minnie wrecking my home weekly, without enduring your moralizing.'

Amy laughed, and patted my shoulder.

'What you need is a nice husband to protect you from yourself.'

She slid into the driving seat.

'That I don't,' I told her, through the car window. 'I've quite enough troubles already, without a husband to add to them.'

Amy shot off with an impressive turn of speed, and I waved until my maddening old friend had disappeared round the bend in the lane.

5. HAZARDS AHEAD

One Friday evening, George Annett called in on his way to St Patrick's. I could see at once that he was the bearer of bad tidings.

'There's definitely something in the wind,' he said, in answer to my queries. 'I've had several chaps from the Office measuring the school and offering me a temporary classroom to be erected across the playground, complete with wash-basins and lavatories.'

'When?'

'No one can say definitely. Obviously, they're just making sure I can cope with the extra numbers. It may never happen. You know how these things hang on.'

'I remember Dolly Clare telling me that poor Emily Davis, who was head at Springbourne, had this closure business hanging over her for nearly ten years.'

'There you are then! Don't get steamed up yet. But I thought I'd let you know the latest. Had any luck with applicants for the teaching post?'

'Not yet. Amy is coping for a little longer, then it will be another supply until the end of term, if I'm lucky.'

George laughed, and rose to go across to his duties. 'You will be.' He patted my shoulder encouragingly. 'Cheer up! I'd take a bet on Fairacre School remaining as it is for another thirty years.'

'I wonder. Anyway, there's a managers' meeting soon, and perhaps we'll learn something then.'

'Ask Mrs Pringle what's going on,' shouted George, as he went down the path. 'She'd be able to tell you.'

At that moment the lady was approaching, also on her way to choir practice, and had obviously heard the remark.

I was amused to notice George's discomfiture, as he wished her 'Good evening' in a sheepish fashion.

The night was hot, and I could not sleep – a rare occurrence for me.

There was a full moon, and the room was so light that it was impossible to lie still, and equally impossible to draw the curtains on such a torrid night.

The longer I stayed awake, the more I worried. What would become of me if the school closed? I had no doubt that I should be treated honourably by the education authority. Whatever teaching post I was offered would provide me with my present salary, but that was the least of my worries.

Not for the first time, I blessed my single state. I had only myself to fend for, and I thought of other teachers who were widowed with young children, or those who supported aged parents, or invalid relatives, and whose salary had to be stretched much farther than my own. Amy often told me that I led a very selfish life and perhaps it was true, but when one was faced with a situation such as that which I now contemplated, there were compensations. No one depended on me. No one offered me disturbing advice. No one would blame me for any decision I took, however disastrous it turned out to be.

I left my hot and rumpled bed, and hung out of the window. The shining rose leaves glittered in the bright moonlight. The sky was clear, and the evening star hung low over the village, as brilliant as a jewel.

Here was the heart of my grief. To leave this – my well-loved school house, and its garden, shady with trees planted by other teachers, long dead, but remembered by me daily for their works, which still endured.

I could truthfully say that I relished every day that I spent in

Fairacre. It was not only a beautiful place, backed by the downs, open, airy, and dominated by St Patrick's spire thrusting high above the thatched and tiled roofs around it. It was also a friendly place, as I soon found when I had arrived as a newcomer some years earlier.

The thought of leaving Mr Willet, Mr and Mrs Partridge, the Mawnes – even Mrs Pringle – was unbearable. My life was so closely bound with theirs, in fact, so closely woven with all those living in the village that I should feel as weak and withered as an uprooted plant if circumstances forced me to go.

As for the children, to part with them would be the hardest blow. I loved them all, not in a sentimental fashion but because I admired and respected their sound country qualities. I loved their patience, their docility, their efforts to please. Certainly, at times, these very virtues exasperated me. Then I would find them unduly slow, complacent and acquiescent, but when I took stock I had to admit that it was often impatience on my part which roused my wrath. How could I ever leave them?

I returned to my bed, and now it was practical matters which bedevilled me. Why on earth hadn't I bought a house for myself, instead of living in a fool's paradise in the school one? The times I had thought about it – and the times Amy had admonished me on the same subject – were beyond counting.

But somehow, I had let matters drift. I had never seriously thought of leaving Fairacre, apart from the odd urge to make a change which sometimes hit me in the spring. Even then, just reading the advertisements in the *Times Educational Supplement* had usually been enough to quench my brief ardours. To slide gently from middle age to retirement in Fairacre seemed such a serene and mellow way to face the future. Of course, I realized that one day, when I had left, someone else would live in my dear house and teach in the school, but it all seemed so far away that I was lulled into a dream-like state of bliss.

Now had come the rude awakening. It was E.M. Delafield, I believe, who said that she wanted seven words on her tombstone:

'*I expected this, but not so soon.*'

They echoed my own thought absolutely.

All the cocks in Fairacre were crowing before I fell into an uneasy sleep.

It was the following evening, when I was making plans for an early night, that I saw, with horror, the untidy figure of Minnie Pringle coming up the path.

I think it is uncommonly sensible and prudent of Minnie to buy her clothes at local jumble sales, and I have often recognized old garments of mine among her wardrobe. But what irks me is the way she wears them without the slightest attempt to adapt them to her skinny figure.

She is particularly fond of a dilapidated fur coat which was once Mrs Mawne's. It is a square garment, made from square pieces of moulting fur. A great many squares are parting from their neighbours, and as the whole thing swamps Minnie, it would have seemed reasonable to remove one row of squares to make it fit, or at least to mend the slits and tie a belt round it. As it is, Minnie's hands are hidden about six inches up the sleeves, the hem, which is coming undone, reaches her calves, and the rest of the tent-like object swings about round Minnie's frame like a scarecrow's coat on a broomstick.

On this occasion, as the evening was warm, I was spared Mrs Mawne's ex-coat, for Minnie was wearing a shiny mauve blouse over a wrap-around skirt whose pattern seemed vaguely familiar to me. On her bare feet were black patent evening sandals with high heels ornamented with diamanté studs.

I braced myself for the interview and invited her in.

'Auntie says as you could do with some help,' began Minnie, once settled in an armchair.

'Would two hours a week suit you?'

I had given some thought to this problem of my own making, and had decided that, with some contriving, I could find her work within her limited ability which would not conflict too obviously with Mrs Pringle's duties. It was going to be a delicate matter trying to keep her off her aunt's preserves, such as cleaning my few pieces of silver and washing the kitchen floor with as much care as one would sponge a baby's face, and I guessed that my efforts were probably doomed to failure at the outset. But surely, in two hours even Minnie could not do much harm.

Also, two hours of work were really all I could afford to pay on top of Mrs Pringle's weekly dues. I awaited Minnie's reaction with mixed feelings.

Minnie scratched her tousled red locks with a silver-varnished nail of inordinate length.

'Same pay as auntie?' she inquired at length.

'Yes.'

'OK. What wants doin'?'

'I'll show you in a minute,' I said, feeling that we were going along rather fast. 'When can you come? I gather you have some work already.'

'You can say that again,' said Minnie, lying back and putting her sandals on the coffee table. 'I goes to Mrs Partridge Mondays – the vicar fixed that.'

My heart bled for poor Mrs Partridge, at the mercy of her husband's Christian charity. The havoc Minnie could cause in that fragile collection of old glass, Hepplewhite chairs and china cabinets made one shudder to contemplate.

'Then I goes to Mrs Mawne on Wednesday morning, but that's all scrubbin'. Mr Mawne don't want no one to touch his butterfly drawers and stuffed birds and that, though I offered to give 'em a good dusting. He's a funny chap, ain't he?'

I forbore to comment, but my opinion of both Mr and Mrs Mawne's good sense rose considerably.

'And Thursday evenings I does out the hall, 'cos Auntie says she's getting a bit past it, and the committee gentlemen said it was all right for me to do it, though I don't know as I shall stick it long.'

'Why not?'

'Mucky. Bits of sausage roll and jam tart squashed between the floor boards, and the sink gets stopped up with tea leaves.'

'Don't they use tea bags?'

Minnie's mouth dropped open. She looked as though she had been coshed. I began to feel alarmed, but at last she spoke.

'Cor!' she whispered. 'You're a marvel! I'll tell 'em that! It's the cricket tea ladies as does it, I reckons, though them scouts and cubs isn't above mucking things up in spite of them oaths they take. Tea bags is the answer. Of course it is.'

I said I was glad to have been of help, and wondered how soon I should be ostracized by all those who managed the village hall kitchen.

'Is that all the work you do?'

'I has to keep my own place tidy at Springbourne,' said Minnie, looking suddenly truculent.

I hastened to apologize. 'Of course, of course! I meant any more work in Fairacre.'

Minnie sat up, removed her sandals from the table top, and surveyed her grubby toe nails.

'I likes to keep Saturday free.'

'Naturally. I shouldn't want you to give up your weekends. What about Friday afternoons?'

'I shops on Fridays.'

'Wednesday then?'

'Auntie comes up here Wednesdays.'

'Oh, of course. Tuesday any good?'

'I goes to Springbourne Tuesdays, 'cos it's double Green Shield Stamp day at the shop.'

'What's wrong with Monday?'

'The vicar.'

I was beginning to get desperate. Did Minnie want work or did she not? Heaven alone knew I would be happy to dispense with her services, but having got so far I felt I must soldier on. I changed my tactics.

'Well, Minnie, when *could* you come?'

'Friday afternoon.'

I took a deep breath. 'But I thought you said you went shopping on Friday.'

'Not till six o'clock. It's late night Caxley.'

I controlled a sudden desire to scream the place down.

'Very well then, let's say from two until four on Friday afternoon. Or one-thirty to three-thirty, if that suits you better.'

'Is that harpast one?'

'Yes,' I said weakly. Whoever had had the teaching of Minnie Pringle deserved deep sympathy, but not congratulation.

There was silence as Minnie scratched her head again, and thought it out. 'Well, that's fine and dandy. I'll come up harpast one and do two hours, and go at – what time did you say?'

'Harpast – *half past* three,' I said faintly. 'I shall be back from school soon after that.'

'What about me money then?' She sounded alarmed.

'I shall leave it on the mantelpiece,' I assured her, 'just as I do for Mrs Pringle. Now, come and look at the work.'

I proposed that she took over window-cleaning and the upstairs brasswork, and bath and basins. This meant that she would be out of Mrs Pringle's way, and could not do too much damage.

I showed her where the dusters and cleaning things were kept, and she looked doubtfully at the window-cleaning liquid.

'Ain't you got no meths and newspaper? It does 'em a treat. Keeps the flies off too.'

I said shortly that this was what I used, and that I disliked the smell of methylated spirits.

'My uncle drinks it,' she said cheerfully. 'Gets real high on it. They picks 'im up regular in Caxley, and it's only on meths!' She sounded proud of her uncle's achievements.

We returned downstairs.

'You want the grandfather clock done? I could polish up that brass wigger-wagger a treat. And the glass top.' There was a gleam in her mad blue eyes which chilled me. '*Never* touch that clock!' I rapped out, in my best school-marm voice.

'OK.' said Minnie, opening the door. 'See you Friday then, if not before.'

I watched her totter on the high heels down the path, still trying to remember where I had seen that skirt before.

'Heaven help us all, Tibby,' I said to the cat, who had wisely absented herself during Minnie's visit. 'Talk about sowing the something-or-other and reaping the whirlwind! I've done just that.'

I felt the need for an early bedtime more keenly than ever. Just before I fell asleep, I remembered where I had seen Minnie's skirt before.

It had once been my landing curtain. I must say, it looked better on Minnie than many of her purchases.

Notice of the managers' meeting arrived a few days after Minnie's visit. It was to be held after school as usual, on a Wednesday. There was nothing on the agenda, I observed, about possible closure of the school. Could it be village rumours once again?

The vicar called at the school on the afternoon following the receipt of our notices. He was in a state of some agitation.

'It's about the managers' meeting. I'm in rather a quandary. My dear wife has inadvertently invited all the sewing ladies that afternoon, so the dining-room will be in use. The table, you know, so convenient for cutting out.'

'Don't worry,' I said. 'We could meet here, if it's easier.'

We usually sit in comfort at the vicar's mahogany dining-table, under the baleful eye of an ancestor who glares from a massive gilt frame behind the chairman's seat. Sometimes we have met in the drawing-room among the antique glass and the china cabinets.

'And the drawing-room,' went on Mr Partridge, looking anguished, 'is being decorated, and everything is under shrouds – no, not *shrouds* – furniture covers – no, *loose* covers – no, I don't think that is the correct term either—'

'Dust sheets,' I said.

His face lit up with relief. 'What a *grasp* you have of everything, dear Miss Read; no wonder the children do so well! Yes, well, you see my difficulty. And my study is so small, and very untidy, I fear. I suppose we could manage something in the hall, but it is rather draughty, and the painters are in and out, you know, about their work, and like to have their little radios going with music, so that I really think it would be *better*, if you are sure it isn't inconveniencing—'

'Better still,' I broke in, 'have it in my dining-room. There's room for us all.'

'That would be quite perfect,' cried the vicar, calming down immediately. 'I shall make a note in my diary at once.'

He sighed happily, and made for the door. 'By the way, no more news about the possible closing. Have you heard anything?'

'Not a word.'

'Ah well, no news is good news, they say. We'll hear more

perhaps on Wednesday week. I gather that nice Mr Canterbury, who is in charge of Caxley Office, is coming out himself.'

I thought that sounded ominous but made no comment.

'No,' said the vicar, clapping a hand to his forehead. 'I don't mean *Canterbury*, do I? Now, what is that fellow's name? I know it's a cathedral city. Winchester? Rochester? Dear, oh dear, I shall forget my own soon.'

'Salisbury,' I said.

'Thank you. I shall put it in my diary against Wednesday week. I shouldn't like to upset such an important fellow.'

He vanished into the lobby.

'It's more likely,' I thought, 'that the important fellow will upset us.'

6. The Managers' Meeting

Amy's last week at Fairacre School arrived all too soon, and I was desolate. She was such good company, as well as being an efficient teacher, that I knew I should miss her horribly.

'Well, I'd stay if I could,' she assured me, 'but Vanessa arrives next week, and I hope she'll stay at least a fortnight. She's rather under the weather. There's a baby on the way. Or *babies*, perhaps!'

'Good heavens! Do they think it will be twins?'

'The foolish girl has been taking some idiotic nonsense called fertility tablets, so it's quite likely she'll give birth to half a dozen.'

'But surely the doctors know what they're doing?'

'Be your age,' said Amy inelegantly. She studied the lipstick with which she had been adorning her mouth. 'I must have had this for years. It's called "Tutankhamen Tint".'

'It can't date from that time.'

Amy sighed. 'The Tutankhamen Exhibition, dear, which dazzled us all some years ago. Everything was Egyptian that year, if you remember. James even bought me a gold necklace shaped like Cleopatra's asp. Devilish cold it is too, coiled on one's nice warm bosom.'

'I'm glad about Vanessa's baby,' I said. 'I'll look forward to knitting a matinée jacket. I've got a pattern for backward beginners that always turns out well. Is she pleased?'

'After eleven in the morning. Before that, poor darling, she is being sick. Tarquin is terribly thrilled, and already planning a mammoth bonfire for the tenants on the local ben, or whatever North British term they use for a mountain in Scotland.'

'He'll have to build six bonfires if your fears prove correct.'

'He'd be delighted to, I have no doubt. He's a great family man, and I must say he's very, very sweet to Vanessa. They seem extremely happy.'

She snapped shut her powder compact, stood back and surveyed her trim figure reflected murkily in 'The Light of the World'.

'I think I might present Fairacre School with a pier-glass,' she said thoughtfully.

'It would never get used,' I told her, 'except when you came.'

We went to let in the noisy crowd from the playground.

Mrs Pringle's slimming efforts seemed to he having little result, except to render her even more morose than usual. I did my best to spare her, exhorting the children to tidy up carefully at the end of afternoon school, and putting away my own things in the cupboards instead of leaving them on window sills and the piano top, as I often do.

Luckily, in the summer term, the stoves do not need attention, but even so, it was obvious that she was finding her work even more martyr-making than before. I was not surprised when she did not appear one morning, soon after Amy's departure, and a note arrived borne by Joseph Coggs. He pulled it from his trouser pocket in a fine state of stickiness.

I accepted it gingerly. 'How did it get like this, Joe?'

'I gotter toffee in me pocket.'

'What else?'

'I gotter gooseberry.'

'Anything else?'

'I gotter bitter lickrish.'

'You'd better turn out that pocket!'

'I ain't gotter—'

'And if you say: "I gotter" once more, Joseph Coggs, you'll lose your play.'

'Yes, miss. I was only going to say: "I ain't gotter thing more." '

He retired to his desk, after putting his belongings on the side table, and I read the missive.

Dear Miss Read,

Have stummuck upset and am obliged to stay home. Have had terrible night, but have taken nutmeg on milk which should do the trick as it has afore.

Clean clorths are in the draw and the head is off of the broom.

Mrs Pringle

I called to see my old sparring partner that evening. She certainly looked unusually pale and listless.

'I'm rough. Very rough,' was her reply to my inquiries. 'And there's no hope of me coming back to that back-breaking job of mine this week.'

'Of course not. We'll manage.'

Mrs Pringle snorted. 'But what I mind more is not doing out that dining-room of yours for the managers tomorrow.'

'I'll do it. It's not too bad.'

She gave me a dark look. 'I've seen your sort of housework. Dust left on the skirting boards and the top of the doors.'

'I don't suppose any of the managers will be running their fingers along them,' I said mildly. 'Has the doctor been?'

'I'm not calling him in. It's him as started this business.'

'How do you mean?'

'This 'ere diet. Drinking lemon juice first thing in the morning. That's what made my stummuck flare up.'

'Then leave it off!' I cried. 'Dr Martin wouldn't expect you to drink it if it upset you!'

'Oh, wouldn't he? And the price of lemons what it is too! I bought a bottle of lemon juice instead. And that's just as bad.'

She waved a hand towards a half-empty bottle on the sideboard, and I went to inspect it. It certainly smelled odd.

'Is it fresh?'

Mrs Pringle looked uneasy. 'I bought it half-price in Caxley. The man said they'd had it in some time.'

'Chuck it away,' I said. 'It's off.'

The lady bridled. 'At fifteen pence a bottle? Not likely!'

'Use oranges instead,' I urged. 'This is doing you no good, and anyway oranges are easier to digest.'

She looked at me doubtfully. 'You wouldn't tell Dr Martin?'

'Of course I wouldn't. Let me empty this down the sink.'

Mrs Pringle sighed. 'Anything you say. I haven't got the strength to argue.'

She watched me as I approached the sink and unscrewed the bottle. The smell was certainly powerful. The liquid fizzed as it ran down the waste pipe.

'One thing,' she said, brightening, 'it'll clean out the drain lovely.'

It was certainly a pity that Mrs Pringle had not given the dining-room the attention it deserved, but I thought it looked quite grand enough to accommodate the managers.

There are six of them. The vicar is Chairman and has been for many years, and the next in length of service is the local farmer Mr Roberts.

When I first was appointed I was interviewed by Colonel Wesley and Miss Parr, both then nearing eighty, and now at rest in the neighbouring churchyard. Their places were taken by Mrs Lamb, the wife of the postmaster, and Peter Hale, a retired schoolmaster from Caxley, who is very highly regarded by the inhabitants of Fairacre and brings plenty of common sense and practical experience of schooling to the job.

The other two managers are Mrs Mawne and Mrs Moffat, the latter the sensible mother of Linda Moffat, the best dressed child in the school. She is particularly valuable, as she can put forward the point of view of parents generally, and is not too shy to speak her mind.

On Wednesday we had a full house, which is unusual. It is often Mr Roberts who is unable to be present and who sends a

message – or sometimes puts an apologetic face round the door – to say a ewe or cow is giving birth, or the harvest is at a crucial stage, and quite rightly we realize the necessity for putting first things first, and the meeting proceeds without him.

As well as the six managers Mr Salisbury arrived complete with pad for taking notes. I had a seat by him, with my usual brief report on such school matters as attendance, social activities and the like. Also in evidence were the log book of the school and the punishment book – the latter with its pages virtually unsullied since my advent.

The vicar made a polite little speech about the pleasure of using my house for the meeting. The minutes were read and signed and I gave my report.

There were the usual requests to the Office for more up-to-date lavatories and wash-basins. The skylight, which had defied generations of Fairacre's handy men to render it rainproof, was mentioned once more, and Mr Salisbury solemnly made notes on the pad. We fixed a date for our next term's meeting, and then settled back for Any Other Business.

'Is there any message, in particular,' asked Gerald Partridge, 'from the Office? We have heard some disquieting rumours.'

'Oh?' said Mr Salisbury. 'What about?'

'Might close the school,' said Mr Roberts, who does not mince words.

'*Really*?' cried Mrs Moffat. 'I hadn't heard a thing! Now that I get my groceries delivered I hardly ever go to the shop, and it's amazing how little one hears.'

'I've taken to going into Caxley for my provisions,' said Mrs Mawne conversationally. 'I can't say I enjoy these supermarkets, but when soap powder is ten pence cheaper it makes you think.'

'And bleaching liquid,' agreed Mrs Moffat, 'and things like tomato ketchup.'

'I make my own,' broke in Mrs Lamb. 'We grow more tomatoes than we can cope with, and it's no good trying to freeze them, and bottled tomatoes are not the same as fresh ones, are they? If you are interested, I've a very good recipe for ketchup I can let you have.'

The ladies accepted the offer enthusiastically. The vicar wore his resigned look. Most of our village meetings get out of hand like this, and he is quite used to waiting for these little asides to resolve themselves.

Mr Salisbury, tapping his expensive pen against his expensive false teeth, looked rather less patient, and cast meaningful glances at the Chairman.

Mrs Moffat had just embarked on a long and somewhat confused account about pickling walnuts when the vicar rapped gently on the table and said kindly: 'Order please, dear ladies, I think Mr Exeter has something to tell us.'

Mr Salisbury, taking his new name in his stride, put down the pad and assumed an expression of disarming candour.

'Well, I don't quite know just *what* you have been hearing at Fairacre, and I can assure you that the Office would always consult with the managers of any school as soon as the possibility of closure cropped up.'

'And has it?' asked Mr Roberts.

'There is always some chance of really small schools becoming uneconomic,' began Mr Salisbury cautiously.

He's been through this hoop many times before, I thought to myself. How far would he commit himself today?

'Fairacre's not really small,' said Mrs Mawne.

'I like a small school anyway,' pronounced Mrs Moffat.

'Much more friendly,' agreed Mrs Lamb.

'There are certain disadvantages,' said Mr Salisbury. 'Lack of team games, for instance. No specialist teachers on the staff for certain subjects. Older children get deprived.'

'*Deprived*?' squeaked Mrs Lamb. 'Our children aren't *deprived* are they, Miss Read?'

'I hope not,' I said.

'But what about Fairacre?' persisted Mr Roberts. 'Are you sharpening the knife for us?'

'Nothing will be done without your knowledge and cooperation,' repeated Mr Salisbury.

'But it's on the cards?' asked Peter Hale quietly. 'Is that it?'

'Numbers are going down steadily,' replied Mr Salisbury. 'We have to assess each case on its merit. Certainly, Fairacre is costing us a lot of money to maintain and the children might well be better off at a larger school.'

'Such as Beech Green?'

'Such as Beech Green,' agreed Mr Salisbury.

'When?' said Mr Roberts.

Mr Salisbury put down his pen and tilted back in his chair. I hoped that the rear legs of my elderly dining-room chair would stand the strain.

'It might be years. It all depends on numbers, on getting staff – a problem you are facing at the moment – and the feelings of managers and parents of the school.'

The vicar was looking unhappy. 'But what about Miss Read? It is unthinkable that she should have her school taken from her.'

There was a rumble of agreement round the table.

Mr Salisbury smiled at me. I felt like Red Riding Hood facing the wolf.

'Miss Read's welfare is our concern, of course. There would always be a post for her in the area. That I can promise you.'

'But we want her *here!*' wailed Mrs Lamb. 'And we *don't* want our school to close!'

'Absolutely right!' said Mrs Mawne. 'People in Fairacre simply won't stand for their children being uprooted, and carted away in buses like so many – er, so many—'

'Animals?' prompted Mr Roberts helpfully.

'No, no, not *animals*,' said Mrs Mawne testily. 'Animals don't go in buses! What I mean is, we won't have it. We'll never let Fairacre School close.' She looked round the table. Her face was red, her eyes bright. 'Agreed?'

'I do for one,' said Mr Roberts. 'I never heard such a shocking thing in my life. The idea of some of our little tots being hauled off to Beech Green fair gives me the shudders. This school's served the village for a hundred years, and I don't see why it shouldn't go on doing so for another hundred.'

'Hear! Hear!' said Mrs Lamb.

Mr Salisbury scribbled something on his pad, then looked up. 'Well, Mr Chairman, I have noted the objections of the managers, though I must point out that no decision of any kind has been taken by the committee about Fairacre School.'

'I hope nothing will ever happen to disturb the *status quo*,' said the vicar. 'We are all extremely happy with our little school. We should be deeply distressed if anything were done to close it, and we rely upon you to keep us informed of any developments.'

Mr Salisbury nodded agreement, and began to put his things together.

The vicar glanced at the clock. 'If that is all our business then nothing remains for me to do but to thank Mr Wells for coming here today and to remind you of the date of the next meeting.'

Mr Salisbury smiled at us all, shook my hand warmly and departed.

'He'd better not try any funny business with our village school,' said Mr Roberts, watching the car drive away. 'And don't you bother your head about all that nonsense, Miss Read. We're all behind you in this.'

'Indeed we are,' said the vicar.

'They closed Springbourne though,' said Mrs Moffat thoughtfully.

'Took 'em ten years,' observed Mr Roberts. 'A lot can happen before they think of Fairacre again. In any case, we can all have a damn good fight over it, and I bet we'd win. The parents would be with us, that I do know.'

One by one, the managers left, until only Mr Partridge remained with me.

'We don't seem to have gone very far with this business,' he remarked, 'but at least it has been mentioned, and I think that is a good thing. He seems a good fellow, that Mr Wells – Winchester, I mean—'

'Salisbury,' I interjected.

'*Salisbury* yes, *Salisbury*. I feel he would act honourably and not do anything without letting us know first.'

'So I should hope.'

'Don't upset yourself about it, dear Miss Read. I cannot believe that it would ever happen here.'

'Let's hope not,' I said. I really felt that I could not discuss the wretched business any more, and I think the vicar sensed this, for he patted my shoulder encouragingly, and made his departure.

I felt more shaken by the meeting than I would have admitted to anyone. My mouth was dry, my knees wobbly. I tottered into the garden and sat on the seat.

Everything around me burst with healthy life. Sparrows flashed from plum tree to cherry tree. A peacock butterfly flapped its bejewelled wings from a daisy top. The pinks gave out their heady scent. The rose buds opened gently in the warm air. Even Tibby displayed every sign of well-being, with her stomach exposed to the sun, and her eyes blissfully closed.

Only I, it seemed, was at odds with my surroundings. Their very beauty emphasized my own malaise. Should I ever come to terms with this horrible nagging uncertainty? Would it be better to take the bull by the horns, and apply for another post now? If I kept putting it off I should be too old to be considered by other managers. Perhaps I was too old already? How old was Emily Davis, I wondered, when she first heard that Springbourne was going to close? How long did Mr Roberts say that was hanging over her? Ten years? The suspense could not be borne.

At least, I told myself, no one need know yet about the shadow coming nearer. Enough to let the rumours die down, as they were doing quite comfortably, before stirring them up again like a swarm of angry bees.

I went indoors, at length, and tried to busy myself with bottling gooseberries, but the operation did not get my whole attention. I was glad when Mr Willet knocked at the back door and asked if he could borrow my edging shears.

It was a comfort to exchange a few general remarks with him on the state of our gardens, and the surprising need for rain at this time of year.

I accompanied him to the gate.

'All right if I bring these 'ere cutters back in the morning?' he asked.

'Fine,' I told him. 'I shan't be doing any gardening tonight.'

'I'd have an early night if I was you,' he advised me. 'You looks a bit peaky. I hears they brought up that school closing business again at your meeting. Bit of a shock, no doubt, but you put it out of your head.'

I was too stunned to reply.

He smiled kindly upon me. 'Us'll rout anyone who tries to shut up our school! You can bet your last farthing on that!'

He strode down the lane, my edging shears across his shoulder like a gun.

'There goes a militant Christian,' I said to Tibby, 'but how on earth did he know?'

7. TROUBLES NEVER COME SINGLY

Now that Amy had gone to attend to her other commitments, I was left to cope alone once again.

Luckily, it would be only for one week – or so the Office told me. After that, help was at hand in the form of Mrs Rose who had been headmistress of a small school near by. That school had been closed for some two years, and Mrs Rose was now euphoniously termed 'a peripatetic teacher'.

This meant that she moved from school to school, sometimes helping children who found reading difficult, and sometimes acting as a supply teacher when staff was short.

I viewed her advent with mixed feelings. She was over sixty, and was in this present job because she was in the last stages of her forty years' service. Her health was not good, and she was a martyr to laryngitis.

On the other hand, she was of a gentle disposition, anxious to fit in, open to suggestions, and generally amenable. And, in any case, the mere presence of another human being – even one as frail as Mrs Rose – on the other side of the glass partition, was a great comfort and support.

In the meantime, I soldiered on and was relieved, in a way, to have the school to myself in order to try to come to terms with the dreadful possibility of becoming, like Mrs Rose, a teacher without a school of my own.

Despite my airy dismissal of rumours on so many earlier occasions, this time I had an uncomfortable feeling that change was in the wind. Something in Mr Salisbury's manner at the managers' meeting made me fear the worst, and I was surprised to find how upset I was.

Normally, I slept for nine hours, drugged with work and good downland air. Now I took an hour or more before drifting off, as I tossed and turned trying to decide what to do. Even my appetite suffered, a most unusual symptom, and I found myself nibbling a biscuit with cheese rather than facing a square meal in the evening. What Amy would have said if she could have witnessed my more than usually casual eating habits, I shuddered to think.

Now and again, I found myself trembling too. Good heavens, was I becoming senile into the bargain? Fat chance I should have of landing another teaching post if I appeared before strange managers with my head shaking and possibly a drop on the end of my nose!

It was all extremely unnerving, and I was grateful for the children's company in my alarming condition.

There were other disquieting factors. The weather had turned cold and blustery, despite the fact that June had arrived. We could have done with some heating from the tortoise stoves, but that, of course, was out of the question.

Then Minnie Pringle's presence about the house on Friday afternoons was distinctly unsettling. On the first visit, she had managed to drop a jar of bath salts into the hand basin, smashing the former and badly cracking the latter.

Also, in a fit of zeal, she had attacked my frying pan with disinfectant powder kept for the dustbin, and some steel wool, thus effectively removing the non-stick surface.

'I thought as it was Vim,' she explained, in answer to my questioning.

'But it says DISINFECTANT POWDER on the tin!'

'Can't read them long words,' said Minnie truculently.

'But you can read "Vim", can't you? And this tin didn't have "Vim" written on it.'

'Looked the same to me,' replied Minnie, and flounced off,

tripping over a rug on the way, and bringing the fire-irons into the hearth with a fearful crash.

I fled into the garden, unable to face any more destruction. So must victims of earthquakes feel, I thought, as they await the next shattering blow.

It was during this unsettled period that the case of Arthur Coggs and his companions was heard at Caxley.

As they appeared in Court on market day, several people from Fairacre were interested spectators, among them Mr Willet. He had travelled in by bus to pick up some plants from the market, and having two hours to spare before the bus returned, decided to witness the fate of the four accused.

Mr Lovejoy, the most respected solicitor in Caxley, was defending all four, as he had done on many previous occasions.

'And an uphill job he'll have this time,' commented Mr Willet to me. 'They had the sauce to plead Not Guilty, too.'

'Perhaps it's true,' I said.

Mr Willet snorted, puffing out his stained moustache. 'Want to bet on it? Anyway, old Colonel Austin was in the chair, and he read out a bit, before they got started, about committing 'em to Crown Court if they was found guilty. Something about their characters and antecedents, whatever that means. But it made it plain that they could get clobbered for more than six months, if need be, and I'd stake my oath that's where they'll end up. All four's got a list as long as my arm, as everyone knows.'

'A man is innocent,' I said primly, 'until he is proved guilty.'

'Them four,' replied Mr Willet, 'are as innocent as Old Nick hisself. My heart bleeds for that chap Lovejoy trying to white-wash them villains. It'd turn my stomach to do a job like that. I'd sooner dig Hundred Acre Field with a hand fork, that I would!'

On Monday morning, Mrs Rose arrived in good time, in a little car, shabby and battered enough to win approval from Mrs Pringle, in whose eyes it appeared a very suitable form of transport for teachers. Amy's large high-powered beauty had always offended Mrs Pringle's sense of fitness. She opened the gates for Mrs Rose's vehicle with never a trace of a limp, or a word of complaint. Clearly, Mrs Rose was accepted, and that was a great relief to me.

She looked frailer than ever, and also decidedly chilly in a sleeveless cotton frock.

'I'd no idea it would be so cold,' she said, clutching her goose-fleshed arms. 'It is *June*, after all!'

'It's always colder up here on the downs,' I told her, 'and these old buildings are pretty damp. We grow quite a good crop of toadstools in the map cupboard when the weather's right.'

She was not amused. I hastily changed my tactics.

'Come over to the house,' I urged, 'and we'll find you a cardigan. It will be too big, I fear, but at least you will be warm.'

Tibby greeted us effusively, no doubt imagining that the

morning session had gone by with unprecedented speed, and it was now time for a mid-day snack.

Mrs Rose paused to take in my accommodation and furnishings before coming upstairs with me.

'I used to have a nice little house like this,' she mourned.

I felt very sorry for her, and slightly guilty too. I certainly was lucky, that I knew. All the old fears of losing my home came fluttering back as we mounted the stairs. I did my best to fight them off.

I set out a selection of woollen garments, and she chose a thick Shetland wool cardigan which would have kept out an arctic wind. It would certainly mitigate the chill of Fairacre School in June.

Her eyes wandered over the bedroom as she did up the buttons.

'You have made it so pretty and snug,' she said enviously. 'I had much the same curtains when I was in the school house at Bedworth.'

'I always admired the garden when I passed that way,' I said hastily, trying to wean her from her nostalgia. 'The roses always seemed so fine in that part of the country. Clay soil, I suppose. What sort of garden do you have now in Caxley?'

I could not have done worse.

'I've no garden at all! Just a window box in my upstairs flat. I can't tell you how much I miss everything.'

The sound of infants screaming in the playground saved me from commenting.

'I think we'd better go back,' I said, leading the way downstairs, 'or we may find spilt blood.'

But all was comparatively calm, and I led Mrs Rose inside to show her the infants' room, and to introduce her to Mrs Pringle.

That lady was leaning against the doorway, upturned broom in hand, looking rather like Britannia with her trident, but a good deal less comely. She bowed her head graciously to Mrs Rose.

'We met at Mrs Denham's auction sale,' she reminded the new teacher. 'I remember it well because you bid against me for a chest of drawers.'

Mrs Rose looked nervous.

'Not that you missed much,' continued Mrs Pringle. 'Even though it was knocked down to me at four pounds. The bottom drawer jams something cruel, and them handles pulls of in your hand. We've had to glue 'em in time and time again.'

I thought, once again, on hearing this snippet of past history, that life in a small community is considerably brightened by such memories as this one of a shared occasion. Some of these joltings of memory are caused by pure happiness – others, as in this present case, owe their sharpness to a certain tartness in the situation. Obviously, Mrs Pringle's bad bargain had caused some rankling since the day of the ladies' battle for the chest of drawers.

'Miss!' shouted Ernest, appearing on the scene. 'Can I ring the bell, miss? Can I? Can I ring the bell?'

'Yes, yes,' I replied. 'And there's no need to rush in here as though a bull were after you.'

I ushered Mrs Rose into the infants' room as the bell clanged out its message to my tardy school children still in the fields and lanes of Fairacre.

The *Caxley Chronicle* carried a full report of Arthur Coggs' case that week, and eagerly devoured it was by all his neighbours in Fairacre. There is nothing so comforting as reading about others' tribulations. It reminds one of one's own good fortune.

The prosecution's most weighty piece of evidence, in more senses than one, was the entire piece of lead roofing which was carried into Court by six sweating policemen.

A plan was handed up to the Bench, and the magistrates were invited to compare the shape of the roof displayed on the paper before them, with that of the lead, now being unrolled and stamped into place beneath large feet, on the floor below.

After old Miss Dewbury's plan had been put the right way up for her by a kindly fellow-justice, the magistrates gave their attention to the matter with more than usual liveliness.

Amazing how they come to life, thought Mr Lovejoy, when a few pictures or objects to play with are handed up! Glazing eyes sparkled, sagging shoulders were braced. Could it be that addresses given by prosecution and defence sometimes bored the Bench? Not, thought Mr Lovejoy seriously, when he addressed them. He had a turn of phrase, he fancied, which commanded respect as well as attention to his cause, but possibly some of his learned colleagues were less fortunate in their powers. (Mr Lovejoy, it will be noted, was without humour.)

Certainly, there was a surprising likeness between the plan and the cumbersome evidence on the floor. The lead undoubtedly came from a small building with an octagonal roof like Mr Mawne's. It had been found, the magistrates were told, hidden under a pile of sacks in the Bryant brothers' outhouse. They looked suitably impressed.

Mr Lovejoy, on the other hand, looked calm and faintly disdainful. His eye fixed on the pitch-pine ceiling of the Victorian court house, he was clearly rehearsing his speech which would show that a person or persons unknown had humped the lead, from a source equally unknown, and dumped it upon the Bryants' premises with the intention of getting them into their present unfortunate position.

The case ground on for the rest of the morning, and continued after the lunch break. Witnesses were called by the indefatigable Mr Lovejoy, who testified to the fact that the accused had been in their company, regularly each evening, whilst imbibing, in a modest fashion, as befitted their unemployed state, at local hostelries.

At four o'clock Miss Dewbury was nudged into wakefulness, the accused men were told that the charge against them had been proved, and the prosecutor handed up long lists of previous convictions for the Bench to study.

The Chairman, Colonel Austin, after a brief word with his colleagues, then committed them in custody to the Crown Court for sentence, just as Mr Willet had prophesied, and they left the Court escorted by two policemen.

Mr Lovejoy shuffled his papers together, bowed politely, and hurried after his clients.

'That is the business of the Court,' announced the clerk, 'and the business of the day is over.'

'And only just in time,' observed old Miss Dewbury as she departed. 'I put a beef casserole in the oven at lunch time, and it must be nearly dry by now.'

'Never like sending chaps to prison,' grunted Colonel Austin to his male colleague, as they reached for their hats, 'but what can you do with four like that? How many times have we seen 'em, John?'

'Too many,' replied his friend, 'and we'll see them again the minute they're out!'

In Fairacre, reaction to the Court's decision was mixed. Most agreed that Arthur Coggs was only getting his just deserts, and speculated upon how long the Judge would give all four when the time came. But more were concerned about the effect of Arthur's absence on his wife and family.

'She'll be a damn sight better off without him around,' said Mr Willet. 'What good's he to her, poor soul? She'll get the social security money to herself now, instead of watching Arthur swilling it down his throat at the Beetle. Besides, she won't get knocked about. Make a nice change for her, I'd say, to have a peaceful house for a time.'

To my surprise, Mrs Pringle took another view.

'She'll miss him, I'll be bound, bad lot though he is. A woman needs a man's company about the house.'

'I can't say I've missed it,' I observed. 'And I could well do without Arthur Coggs' company, at any time.'

'Yes, well,' admitted Mrs Pringle, 'there's some as lead an *unnatural* life, so their opinions don't altogether matter.'

'Thank you,' I said. My sarcasm was ignored, as Mrs Pringle followed her train of thought.

'I knows he keeps her short of money. I know he raises his hand to her—'

'And his boot,' put in Mr Willet.

'And I knows his language is plain 'orrible when he's in liquor, but then she's used to it, and used to having him around the place. She'll be terrible lonely with him gone.'

Several other people echoed Mrs Pringle's comments, but the general feeling was that Mrs Coggs must be relieved she was safe from physical assault, at least for a year or more. A number of inhabitants went even further in their concern, among them Gerald Partridge the vicar, who spoke about the family to me.

'I am right in thinking that the Coggs children get free dinners?'

I reassured him on this point.

'And their clothing? Shoes and so on. Are they adequately provided for? I should be only too happy to give something, you know, if it could be done without causing distress to poor Mrs Coggs. She has enough to bear as it is.'

I said that I tried to keep an eye on that side of things, and had been lucky enough to get Mrs Moffat and other generous parents to hand down garments that were little worn directly to Mrs Coggs, instead of sending them, in the usual way, to our local jumble sales.

'She won't be too badly off,' I promised him. I could not bear to see his gentle face puckered with anxiety. 'And now Arthur is out of the way, I believe she will take on more work.'

'Yes, indeed. Mrs Mawne is having her there for a morning. I gather that Minnie Pringle insisted on dusting some very precious glass cases housing some of Mr Mawne's rarer birds, and two were broken, most unfortunately. Mr Mawne was a little put out about it, and fired the girl on the spot.'

Later I was to hear from Minnie's own lips, the exact words used by her irate employer – short, brutal, words of Anglo-

Saxon origin – which, I felt, had been put to their proper use under the circumstances.

'Well, I'm glad to know Mrs Coggs has got the job,' I said. 'It will give her an added interest as well as more money. But don't worry too much about her. The social security office will see she is looked after, and really she's so much better off without that ghastly husband.'

The vicar looked shocked. 'Strong words, Miss Read, strong words! He is one of my flock, remember, even if he has strayed, and I can only hope that his present afflictions will make him change his ways.'

'That'll be the day,' I said.

But I said it when the vicar had departed.

PART TWO

Fairacre Hears the News

* * *

8. A WELCOME DIVERSION

One summer afternoon, soon after the vicar's visit, I had a surprise call from Amy and Vanessa.

The children had just run home, glad to be out in the sunshine, and I was just about to make tea.

Vanessa, a niece of James, Amy's husband, was always attractive, but now, in pregnancy, had that added lustre of skin and hair which so often goes with the condition. I said, truthfully, how radiant she looked.

'But *enormous*!' protested Vanessa, holding out her arms sideways, the better to display her bulging form. 'I'd no idea one could stretch to this size. All those women's magazines chat away about letting out skirts a few inches, as time goes by! My dear, *look* at me! This is a shirt which was too big for Tarquin, who stands six feet four as you know, and even this is getting tight. I'm thinking of hiring a bell tent.'

'A dirndl skirt's the answer,' said Amy, 'with a huge smock over it. Or a kaftan, perhaps.' She gazed at Vanessa with a thoughtful smile. 'There's no denying that one really does need a waist for most clothes.'

'Well, I hope to have one again in a few weeks' time,' replied Vanessa, settling her bulk on the sofa.

'Put your feet up,' I urged.

'Too much effort, darling. I really don't recommend this baby business. Don't attempt it.'

'I should get the sack if I did,' I told her.

'Which reminds me,' said Amy, 'what news of Fairacre School closing?'

I felt Amy could have been a little more tactful, but forbore to comment upon it.

'Not much, but something's in the wind. George Annett has been asked to send in lists of equipment he would need if another class were added to his school – or possibly two classes.'

'It does sound ominous.'

'It does indeed. But there's mighty little one can do until I hear something more definite. It seems silly to try for another post when I'm so settled here, and in any case, all this may come to nothing.'

Amy fixed a steady gaze upon me. 'Poor old dear,' she said, so sympathetically that I was glad to turn away from her and busy myself with pouring tea.

'Vanessa is staying for a whole week,' she went on, 'and I wondered if you would come over for dinner one evening?'

'You know I'd love to,' I said, carrying a cup to the recumbent figure on the sofa. Vanessa struggled to a more upright position.

'I'll just lodge it on this bulge,' she said with a dazzling smile. 'It really comes in quite useful, this extra shelf. I shall miss it. Sometimes I think I shall give birth to at least *three* babies.'

'Don't the doctors know?'

'My own, who is a sweetie, says twins. The other chap, a top-flight gynaecologist, won't commit himself, but then he's terribly cautious. Always worrying about his hypocrites' oath, I think.'

'*Hippocrates*, Vanessa!' exclaimed Amy. 'Really, when I think of the money spent on your education and see the result, I shudder!'

'I have a cosy little argument with him sometimes,' continued Vanessa unabashed, 'just to stretch his mind, you know. "If I had a tumour on the brain, which meant I was a living vegetable, don't you think you should put me gently to sleep?" I ask him. Of course, he gets in a terrible fluster, and talks about this old hypocrites' oath he took when he was a beardless boy, and we both thoroughly enjoy a little abstract thinking after all the dreadfully coarse back-and-forth about bowels and heartburn.'

Vanessa sighed, and the teacup wobbled dangerously.

'I must say it will be quite a relief to know how many. Luckily, I've been given enough baby clothes for a dozen. Tarquin's mother is a great knitter, and does everything in half-dozens. Even *binders*! I don't think babies have them now, but I haven't the heart to tell her. She's also presented me with a dozen long flannel things, all exquisitely feather-stitched, which have to be pinned over the baby's feet to keep it warm. I can't see the monthly nurse using those.'

'You're having it at home then?' I said.

'Good heavens, yes! All the family's babies have to be born in the castle, and the piper waits outside – for days sometimes – ready to play the bagpipes to welcome the child.'

'I'd have a relapse,' I said. 'To my Sassenach ear "The Flowers of the Forest" sounds exactly like "The Keel Row".'

'Well, don't let Tarquin know,' advised Vanessa. 'The sound of the bagpipes brings tears to his eyes.'

'He's not the only one,' I told her, rescuing her empty cup.

On the Saturday following Amy's visit, I was invited to attend a lecture by Henry Mawne. It was to be held in the Corn Exchange in Caxley, and the subject was 'European Birds of Prey', illustrated by slides taken by the speaker.

I was a little surprised by the invitation. The Mawnes are always very kind to me, but we do not meet a great deal, except by chance, in the village. The vicar and Mrs Partridge were also going, and several other people from Fairacre.

All had been invited to lunch with the Mawnes at the Buttery, a restaurant in Caxley, conveniently placed near the hall, and offering a varied menu at modest prices. The Buttery is always busy, and many a local reputation has been shredded beneath its oak beams.

If I had been rather more alert when Mrs Mawne invited me I might have excused myself, for Saturday afternoons are usually taken up with household chores, cooking, mending, or entertaining, which get left undone during the week. But as usual, I was not prepared, and found myself at twelve o'clock on the Saturday in question, trying to decide between a long-sleeved silk frock (too dressy?) or a pink linen suit, rather too tight in the skirt, which Amy had kindly told me made me look like mutton dressed as lamb.

I decided on the latter.

There were four cars going from Fairacre, and I went with Diana and Peter Hale.

'Wonder how long this affair will last?' mused Peter Hale. 'I want to drop in at school to see some of the cricket. Diana will drive you home. I'm getting a lift with the new classics man. He passes the house.'

'I think, you know,' said Diana gently, 'that Henry Mawne is afraid that the Corn Exchange is going to be far too big for this afternoon's lecture. I hear that he suggested that a party from Beech Green might help to swell the ranks.'

Light began to dawn.

'He'll need several hundreds to make a good sprinkling in that barn of a place,' I said. 'Why not find something smaller?'

'Everything was booked up,' said Peter, jamming on his brakes as a pheasant strolled haughtily across the road. 'Half the jumble sales and bazaars seem to take place on Saturdays. I can't think why.'

'Most people have been paid on Friday,' I told him. 'It's as simple as that.'

We had the usual trundling round Caxley to find a place to leave the car, and were lucky enough to snap up the last place in a car park fairly near the restaurant. Secretly, I was glad. It was not the pink skirt alone that was tight. My new shoes were killing me. Could I be growing a corn on my little toe? And if so, would I need to go to a chiropodist? What a terrible thought! Hopelessly ticklish, I should be hysterical if my feet were handled, and what if she – or he, perhaps? – wanted to file my toe-nails? That could not be borne.

A prey to these fears, I hobbled in the wake of the Hales and entered the bustle and heat of the Buttery.

The Mawnes greeted us cheerfully, and we were seated at the Buttery's largest table. It was clear that we should be about a dozen in all, and the manager had done us proud with six pink carnations in a hideous glass vase with coloured knobs on it.

Margaret and Mary Waters, two spinster sisters who share a cottage in Fairacre, arrived, with the vicar and Mrs Partridge, and four more friends of the Mawnes made up the party.

Menus were handed round, and we studied them seriously. For most of us it was a pleasure to have a choice of dishes. After all, I was usually grateful, at this time of day, for a plain school dinner. To be offered such attractions as melon, prawn cocktail, pâté or soup – for first course alone – was wholly delightful, and I began to enjoy myself enormously.

Our host did not appear to be so happy. I remembered that his wife had once told me that he dreaded any sort of public speaking, and was a prey to nerves before these events.

'What is this blanket of veal?' he was asking her crossly.

'You won't like it. It's veal in white sauce.'

'How disgusting! *Blanket*'s just about the right word for it.' He turned to the vicar. 'Don't you hate white gravy, padre? It's like cold soup – dead against nature.'

'I must admit,' replied Gerald Partridge, 'that I rather like things in white sauce. So bland, you know. Take tripe, for instance—'

'No, *you* take tripe,' exclaimed Henry, shuddering, 'I never could face that awfully rubbery flannel look, let alone put it in my mouth.'

'Done with onions,' said Margaret Waters earnestly, 'it can be quite delicious. And so nourishing. My poor father practically lived on it for the last few weeks of his life.'

Peter Hale caught my eye across the table, and I had to concentrate on the carnations to preserve my sobriety.

'I should have the lamb chops, Henry,' said Mrs Mawne

decisively. 'I see there are new potatoes and peas, and you know you always enjoy them.'

Henry brightened a little.

'But what about our guests? Come now, Miss Read, what are you having?'

I said I should like melon, and then, bravely, the *blanquette de veau*.

The waiter, who had been leaning against a nearby dresser looking bored to distraction, now deigned to approach and started to take down orders.

As always, the meal was good. Caxley people are fond of their food, and are quite ready to complain if it is not to their liking. The Buttery knows its customers, and does its best to give satisfaction.

By the time the cheese board was going the rounds we were all in fine spirits, except for poor Henry Mawne who was becoming more agitated as the dreaded hour drew near.

'I've forgotten my reading glasses,' he exclaimed fretfully, slapping each pocket in turn. 'Now what do I do?'

Mrs Mawne remained calm. 'You use your bifocals, as you always do, Henry. Really, *the fuss*!'

'You know I never feel right with bifocals at a lecture,' wailed Henry, for all the world like one of my eight-year-olds.

Gerald Partridge leant forward anxiously. 'Shall I get the car, and go back for them?' he offered. 'I could be back here in half an hour.'

Mrs Mawne took charge. 'Certainly not, Gerald. I won't hear of it! You are the soul of kindness, but there is absolutely *no need* for Henry to have his reading glasses. And well he knows it!'

She looked severely at her husband, who seeing himself beaten, turned his attention to a splendid Stilton cheese clothed in a snowy napkin, and began to look less fractious.

His guests became more relaxed, and the conversation turned to Arthur Coggs and his future.

'A friend of mine,' said Mary Waters, 'was in court when

they carried in that massive piece of lead. Poor Albert Phipps nearly had a rapture!'

'A careless one?' inquired Peter Hale.

'You mean a *rupture*, dear,' said her sister reprovingly. 'You always get that word wrong. A *rapture*, as Mr Hale has reminded us, is what dear Ivor Novello wrote about.'

'I'm sorry,' said Peter, 'I was being flippant.'

'My English teacher once said: "Flippancy gets you nowhere,"' remarked his wife. 'I'd been trying to show off, I remember, about "trembling ears" in Milton. I said that the phrase smacked of the asinine, and was ticked off, quite rightly. Schoolgirls must be very trying to teach.'

'No worse than schoolboys,' commented Henry.

'I agree with that wholeheartedly,' said Peter Hale, schoolmaster.

Someone then looked at the clock and murmured that perhaps we should be moving. Henry Mawne's agitation returned.

'The bill, waiter! Quickly, my dear fellow. We mustn't be late.'

The waiter ambled off at a leisurely pace, while we collected bags and gloves and various other impedimenta, and Henry Mawne started his pocket-slapping again in the frenzy of finding his cheque book.

'Henry,' said his wife, with a look which could have stopped a rogue elephant in its tracks. 'Calm down! You know perfectly well that I have the cheque book in my handbag. Now, if you will make sure that you have your notes and your bifocals, I will take charge of the account and meet you outside.'

We gave our sincere thanks to the Mawnes for the delicious lunch as we made our way to the Corn Exchange. The Caxley market square was gay with stalls, and I should dearly have loved to buy some eggs and cheese from my favourite stallholder, but this was not the time, I realized, to clutch a piece of ripe gorgonzola for an hour and a half.

The hall was half full, which was a creditable number to assemble on a Saturday afternoon. As we were the speaker's party, we were shown to the front row. On the way to our august places, I was delighted to catch sight of a contingent from Beech Green. Among the party I saw George and Isabel Annett and dear Miss Clare, who taught for many years at Fairacre School, sitting with them.

I was seated by Mrs Mawne, who remained completely unmoved by the pathetic sight of her husband trying to arrange his papers with shaking hands.

The chairman was the president of Caxley's Nature Conservancy Trust and was doing his best to put Henry at his ease before starting the meeting. He might just as well have saved his breath, for Henry took not the slightest notice, and brought matters to a climax by dropping all his papers on the floor.

With startled cries the two men bent to retrieve them, cracking their skulls together, thus occasioning further cries from the audience. The papers were collected, Henry shuffled them together with a look of utter despair, and the chairman rose to introduce him.

Once Henry was on his feet, and the clapping had died away,

he became wonderfully calm and happy. He smiled at us all, as though he were truly glad to tell us about the birds which gave such zest and joy to his life. It was difficult to believe that less than half an hour ago, he had been as nervous as a fretful baby.

It was an enthralling talk, and the slides were superb. When he ended, the audience applauded enthusiastically. Clearly, here was a man who was master of his subject and able to transmit his own excitement to others.

As we drove home, Diana Hale summed up the feelings of us all.

'He's a man who can make you forget your own world, and carry you into his.'

With a start, I realized how true this was.

For the first time for weeks, I had forgotten the shadow which hung menacingly over my future, and gratitude mingled with admiration for our old friend Henry Mawne.

9 · MRS PRINGLE GOES TO WAR

Minnie Pringle continued to wreak havoc in my house every Friday afternoon. I did my best to forestall trouble, but was far from successful.

Now that I realized that she could not read, I tried to put out the bottles and tins she would need for any specific job. Sometimes it worked. Sometimes such bottles as that containing window-cleaning liquid would be put in the bathroom cabinet beside witch hazel or gargle. It was all a little unnerving.

My vacuum cleaner was maltreated weekly by having its cord twisted tightly into figures of eight round the handle, and the plug became so cracked with being dropped on the tiled floor of the kitchen, that I was obliged to renew it. Maddening though she was, I did not want to find Minnie electrocuted on my premises.

She also had a peculiar way with dusters. Somewhere along the extensive line of previous employers, she had picked up the wholly admirable habit of washing the dusters before leaving work.

Unfortunately, how to dry them seemed to be beyond her. I had indicated a small line conveniently near to the back door, but this was ignored. Sometimes she hung a wet duster on the newel post at the foot of the stairs, so that anyone mounting clapped her hand upon the clammy object. When remonstrated with, Minnie changed her tactics and draped them along the newly polished dining-room table, or over the padded back of an armchair.

Irritation gave way to incredulity, and I used to return to my home on Friday afternoons wondering what Minnie had got up to this time. There was always something untoward to greet me. If there were not some new places for the dusters to dry, then it might be a few broken shards of a favourite cup, carefully arranged on a half-sheet of newspaper on the draining board. At least, she did not try to cover up her little mishaps with my property. I supposed it was something to be thankful for, but I longed for the day when Minnie's future took her far, far away.

Her own domestic affairs seemed to be shrouded in mystery. I had heard rumours about Mrs Fowler and her new paramour, and some said that she was asserting her authority to such an extent that it was likely that Minnie's husband might return to his wife and children. Others said that Minnie too was finding consolation elsewhere, and that the under-gardener at Springbourne Manor had been seen leaving Minnie's premises at some very odd times.

I rarely saw Minnie, only the results of her labours, and that was quite enough for me. Mrs Pringle, who usually volunteered any village news, was unusually taciturn these days, and I put it down to the debilitating effects of the diet. Not that she seemed any thinner, but she was certainly paler, and her limp seemed to be permanent these days.

I ventured to ask how the dieting was progressing one day.

'You wants to ask Dr Martin,' she said sourly. 'It's him what does the worrying. I told him straight: "Them scales of yourn are wrong," but he never batted an eyelid. He reckons I've only lost another two pound, after all this time. Not my fault, you know, I sticks to what's writ down.'

It did seem odd.

'Of course, I eats what's put afore me if I'm invited out. Stands to reason you can't offend people when they've slaved over a hot stove getting a nice bit of roast pork and potatoes ready, and a good suet pudden to follow.'

'But do you go out often?'

'Twice a week to my sister's. And of course I have her back, and have to do much the same for her.'

'That can't help,' I felt obliged to point out.

Mrs Pringle bridled. 'I've halved my chocolate! I'm used to what we knew as a tuppeny bar in the old days, after my tea. Well, I makes that do for two days now, and I only takes one spoonful of sugar instead of two in my tea. No call for Dr Martin to be so sharp with me, I tell him. After all, I'm still *losing* weight, aren't I?'

I began to feel sorry for Dr Martin.

'Couldn't you use those sweeteners instead of sugar, and perhaps have half an apple instead of the chocolate?'

Mrs Pringle looked at me as if I were an earwig discovered in the bedclothes.

'And start my heart-burn up again? It's plain to see, Miss Read, as you and Dr Martin is hand in glove. If you wants me to go on working here, day in and day out, giving of my best and my heart's blood to this 'ere thankless job, then I must have a bit of nourishing food.'

She made her way towards the door, limping heavily.

I said no more. I know when I am beaten.

The second half of the Summer term brought some of the hottest weather of the century. Day after day dawned clear and cloudless, and by half past ten in the morning, it was beginning to get too hot for comfort outside.

Our ancient schoolroom was one of the coolest places in the village. With its lofty ceiling and high windows, it was remarkably airy, and the gnarled elder trees which tapped against the west-facing windows, cast a green shade which was more than welcome.

The door was propped open permanently to let in any stray breeze. It also let in Tibby, much to the rapture of the children, and an assortment of wild life ranging from wasps – which threw the children into violent demonstrations of assumed fear – to butterflies and, once, a fieldmouse.

The latter threw *me* into a transport of fear, which was certainly not assumed, but which I tried to hide from the children. My efforts were not completely successful.

'Shall I whack it on the 'ead?' inquired Ernest, advancing with his geography reader in hand.

'No, no,' I said hastily. After all my exhortations on kindness to animals, it was disappointing to see Ernest's blood-thirsty reaction to the intruder. 'It will find its way out in a minute.'

Nose twitching, it scampered along by the map cupboard, watched by the class. I observed its movements with inward horror. Suppose it turned in my direction?

As luck would have it, Patrick gave an enormous sneeze, which sent it bolting from the room, and out once again to the field from which it had emerged.

I breathed again.

The afternoons were so hot that it was impossible to expect much in the way of work from the children. The older ones went by school bus to Caxley once a week for a swimming lesson, and were the envy of all those left behind to swelter in the heat of Fairacre.

I did my best to make their lot easier by taking them outside. We have one particularly fine beech tree near the edge of the field which borders the playground; and here the shade was deep and refreshing on those baking afternoons.

I read them folk tales, and let them lie as they pleased, flat on their backs, or lodged on an elbow, their hair lifting in the light wind that stirred the leaves above them. What did it matter if they heard little of the story? On those golden afternoons they absorbed more than any printed page could give them – happy summer memories which would remain with them for a life-time.

Whether it was the heat, or Mrs Pringle's growing touchiness, or a combination of both, which triggered off the great row between that lady and inoffensive Mrs Rose, it is impossible to say.

It began one hot after-dinner session, and the battleground was the lobby at the back of the school where Mrs Pringle does the washing-up.

It is usually a peaceful period, preceding the afternoon session, and occasionally running into the first lesson. I am quite used to giving out handiwork material to the background of clashing cutlery and Mrs Pringle's contralto rendering of the more lugubrious numbers from *Hymns Ancient and Modern*.

The first I heard was the sound of infants on the move next door. They were obviously surging towards the door leading into the lobby. Adult voices were raised, one shrill, one booming. The latter was only too familiar to me, but I could not think who the other shrill-voiced contestant could be.

Daring my children to bat an eyelid, I strode forth to investigate.

'Into your seats this minute!' I bellowed at Mrs Rose's excited children, who were milling round the door. Reluctantly they obeyed, and I posted the largest infant at the front to tell me on my return who had been the quietest. The battle was gaining in volume and speed of action behind me.

It was now plain that Mrs Rose was engaged in combat with Mrs Pringle, and I quaked at the thought of what I might see by – or even under – the lobby sink.

There was something Wagnerian about the sight which met my eyes. Steam from the washing-up bowl wreathed the forms of the two martial bodies. Mrs Pringle held a saucepan aloft as though about to cleave Mrs Rose's skull, some inches below her own. Mrs Rose, her normally pale face suffused with blotchy red patches, clung to Mrs Pringle's flowered overall and screamed her head off.

'*Ladies!*' I shouted. It seemed a singularly inappropriate title to bestow upon the two viragos before me, but was the best I could manage. At least it had the desired effect, and the combatants parted and faced me, bosoms heaving and eyes flashing. They were too winded with warfare to speak.

'What on *earth*,' I said sternly, 'are you two doing? You are frightening the life out of the children.'

This was not strictly true. Even now, some bold bad infants had crept to the doorway and were surveying the scene with every appearance of joy. This little contretemps would soon be common knowledge in Fairacre, I surmised.

'Go back,' I hissed, 'into your seats this instant! The very idea!'

This last phrase, idiotic though it may be, has an uncanny power over the young, if expressed forcibly. It worked yet again, and the faces vanished.

Mrs Rose tidied her hair, and without a word, followed her pupils, leaving Mrs Pringle muttering malevolently to herself.

'I don't know what all that was about, and I don't *want* to know,' I said loftily, 'but if it happens again we shall have to look for another cleaner.'

'And lucky you'll be to get one with that old cat on the premises,' boomed Mrs Pringle, as I departed with as much dignity as I could muster.

Mrs Rose was tying a shoelace with trembling fingers, as I passed through the infants' room on the way to my own.

'Sorry about that,' she whispered. 'I'll tell you all at play-time.'

A rare silence had fallen upon her class. They gazed upon her round-eyed. I left her to face the infants alone. My own children were equally silent, but their eyes were bright with expectation.

'See if you can stay as quiet as that for the next ten minutes,' I said frostily, propping myself on the edge of the table, and trying to regain composure.

Long-suffering looks were exchanged. Obviously not a word of explanation was going to be given them. Was there no justice?

I saw Mrs Pringle departing soon afterwards, her black bag swinging on her arm, her stout back registering martyrdom, and her limp much in evidence.

Mrs Rose, calmer now, told me about the cause of the fuss, as we sipped our tea in the playground.

The real culprits were some new infants who had emptied their dinner scraps into the wrong bucket. It was as simple as that.

From time immemorial, Mrs Pringle has taken home a dank parcel of plate-scrapings for her chickens. This is one of the many uses to which her black oilcloth bag is pressed. One bucket stands beneath the sink for such revolting left-overs as fat-trimmings, tough morsels of cabbage stalk and so on, combined with gobbets of custard, jelly or pastry from the second course.

Sometimes, turning from this receptacle with nausea, I am reminded of the tubs which are reputed to have been left outside the gates of Blenheim Palace, years ago, for the poor of Woodstock. It took an American Duchess to suggest that at least the savoury matter could be put in a separate container from the sweet. Mrs Pringle's chickens are not so fortunate, but appear to thrive on what they get.

The second bucket contains the true rubbish destined for the dustbin, along with the contents of the wastepaper baskets. What had happened was that four or five innocents had scraped their plates into the latter, and such delicacies as half chewed gristle, dear to the hearts of Mrs Pringle's hens, were in danger of being thrown out.

Nagged by pain from her empty stomach, Mrs Pringle reacted furiously to this scandalous filching from her hungry hens, and began berating the poor infants who soon began to weep.

Mrs Rose, as zealous for her children as Mrs Pringle was for her chickens, rushed to their defence, and the ugly scene then ensued.

'She had no business to shout at the children like that,' asserted Mrs Rose, pink at the memory. 'Nor at me. I've never in my life been subjected to such impertinence.'

'I think you could have been a little more tolerant,' I said mildly. 'You know what Mrs Pringle is – and since this confounded dieting she's been twice as touchy.'

'She's not going to yell at my babies and get away with it! I shall expect an apology!'

'You won't get it.'

And of course she didn't. Mrs Pringle wrapped herself in majestic silence, and so did Mrs Rose, so that the atmosphere fairly quivered with taut nerves whenever the two ladies were in the same room.

It was a trying time for us all, and the fact that nothing more had beeen said, one way or the other, about Fairacre School's possible closure, I found particularly unnerving. More measuring had been going on at Beech Green School, according to Mr Annett, but otherwise he too was in the dark.

'I think it will all blow over,' he told me one sunny Friday evening. He had called before choir practice to lend me an

American treatise on educating young children which he thought I might enjoy.

I had not the heart to tell him that any book more than three inches thick, with footnotes and five appendices, killed any desire to read it, from the start. A quick look inside had confirmed my suspicions that this one had been written in the brain-numbing sort of jargon I cannot abide. There was no doubt about it. It was one of those books one keeps safely for a decent interval, dusts, and returns, praying that the lender refrains from asking questions on it.

'After all,' he continued, 'it always has before. Why should they close Fairacre at this particular moment?'

'I don't know, but the numbers are dwindling. We're down to twenty-six this term, and somehow there was a look in Mr Salisbury's eye which I didn't like.'

'He's always got that,' said George cheerfully. 'Comes of working in an office all day.' He put down his glass and sprang nimbly to his feet.

I sighed and rose too.

'You sound uncommonly sad,' he said. 'Old age?'

'Probably. How long notice would I get, do you think, if they do decide to close?'

'Years.'

'Honestly? Really *years*?'

'I believe so. Why, you'd probably be about to retire anyway by the time they get round to it.'

We walked together towards the church. The lime trees buzzed with scores of bees, and the scent from the creamy flowers was delicious – the essence of summer. Fairacre seemed very dear and sweet.

'You've got a good spot here,' said George, as if reading my thoughts.

'None better,' I told him, as bravely as I could.

10. WHO SHALL IT BE?

One afternoon, towards the end of term, four candidates for the post of infants' teacher arrived for interview.

It was a sweltering day. The distant downs shimmered in a haze of heat, and the flowers drooped in the border. Tibby had found a cool spot among some thick grass under the hedge, and lay comatose. Even the sparrows were too exhausted to twitter from the school gutters.

Mrs Rose was taking charge of the school for an hour while I attended the interviewing session in my own dining-room, grudgingly polished by Mrs Pringle.

I had hoped that Mrs Rose might feel like applying for the post. She was not ideal, I know, but better the rogue one knew than the devil one didn't. However, since the row with Mrs Pringle, I was relieved to know that she would be leaving at the end of term, as had first been arranged. The frosty silences and cutting looks, which occurred when they met, may have given them some warped satisfaction, but I found the whole business extremely distasteful and childish.

The vicar, as chairman of the managers, was being supported by Peter Hale. As a retired man, he seemed freer than the other managers, and anyway his experience and wisdom, as a schoolmaster, should prove a help on this occasion.

I had had the job of making a short list from the surprisingly large number of applicants for this modest post. It was a sign of the times, of course, as so many teachers were out of work. Normally, we are lucky, at Fairacre, to get two or three applicants. This time there were over fifty, and it had been difficult to choose four for interview.

They were all young. For too long we have had elderly ladies in charge of our youngest children, and though their motherly qualities were endearing, I felt that we were falling behind in up-to-date methods of teaching. It was time to have a change.

From my own point of view too, I wanted someone who could be trained towards my aims with the children. It is doubly important to have a united team when the staff is small, and I was getting heartily sick of trying to keep the boat up straight with people like Mrs Rose who were set in their ways before they even came to Fairacre, and who had no intention of changing them.

Two of the applicants had been teaching for two or three years. The others had just finished their training and would be in their probationary year if they were appointed. We saw these first.

'Charming girls,' said the vicar enthusiastically, as the second one closed the door behind her.

'They are indeed,' agreed Peter Hale. Both girls were remarkably pretty, and I began to wonder if I were going to get an unbiased assessment of their teaching powers from two males who, although elderly, were clearly still susceptible to female good looks.

The first, a fresh-faced blonde, had answered our questions with intelligence, but was not very forthcoming about methods she would use in teaching reading and number, which I found slightly daunting. She was engaged to be married, but intended to go on teaching for a few years before thinking of starting a family.

The second, Hilary Norman, was a red-head, with the creamy pallor of complexion which so often accompanies auburn hair. Her paper qualifications were very good, and she was thoughtful in her answering. Her judgement, in my opinion, was in advance of her years, and she seemed to have a delightful sense of humour. I warmed to her at once, and said so to my fellow-interviewers.

'She'll have to get digs near by,' observed Peter Hale, studying her address. 'Home is somewhere in Herefordshire. Too far to travel. Know anyone in Caxley who might put her up?'

'Not a soul,' I said.

'And really there's no one now in the village,' lamented the vicar. 'And the bus service gets worse and worse.'

'I think we ought to see the others before going any further,' said Peter Hale. 'Let's have Mrs Cornwall, shall we?'

We turned our papers over, and the vicar ushered in the lady.

To my eyes, she seemed just as attractive as the other two, and I could see that I should easily be out-classed in looks next term – not that that would take much doing, I am the first to admit.

She was very calm and composed, and I could well imagine that the infants would behave angelically in her care. But, as the questioning went on, I began to wonder if she would be able to stimulate them enough. Country children are often inarticulate – not dumb by any means, they often chatter quite as volubly as their town cousins – but they are not as facile in expressing themselves and are basically more reserved.

She had wonderful references, drove her own car, and I felt she would be a loyal aide. But would she stay in Fairacre long enough to be of use?

'If my husband is posted abroad, of course I shall go too, but it might not be for another two years.'

It clinched matters for me, I fear.

The last applicant was amazonian in build, and if anything even better-looking than those who had gone before. She would be jolly useful, I thought, in forcing open the high windows which so often stuck fast at Fairacre School, and her appearance alone would cause respect among her pupils. One sharp slap from that outsize hand would be enough to settle the most belligerent infant.

Again, her qualifications were outstanding, and she excelled in all kinds of sport. This worked both ways, of course, in our tiny school. Would she miss team games? Would there be enough scope for her with small children, and a small class of them at that? I had the feeling that she would be happier in the livelier atmosphere of a large school, and would find Fairacre too confining before long.

It was certainly a problem that faced us, when at last she had returned to await her fate in my sitting-room.

'Fine-looking set of girls,' said Peter Hale. 'Must be something to do with all that National Dried Milk they were brought up on.'

'I thought that finished years ago,' I said.

'I've never even heard of it,' admitted the vicar. 'Is it the same as pasteurized?'

This is the way decisions get made in village life, and only a fool would get impatient with the meandering paths that lead to our end, but Peter Hale brought us back to the point.

'Perhaps it would be sensible to use the eliminating method

here. We've four excellent candidates. Has Miss Read any doubts about any of them?'

'After all,' put in the vicar, 'you have to work with the lady, and at close quarters. You must find her compatible.'

'Well, I feel that the married lady won't stay long. She was quite frank about it, and it seems as though she fully expects her husband to be sent overseas within two or three years. I'd sooner have someone willing to stay longer.'

'Agreed,' said my two colleagues, putting aside one set of papers.

'And in a way, that goes for the engaged girl too, although I'm sure she would be able to give a reasonable length of service.'

'I liked that little red-haired girl,' confessed the vicar. 'She is so lively. I'm sure the children would respond to her.'

'But we haven't gone steadily through our eliminating yet,' protested Peter Hale. 'Let's be methodical.'

'My dear fellow, I do apologize,' said the vicar, flustered. 'How far had we got? Not the married one, wasn't it?'

'Provisionally,' I agreed guardedly.

'Nor the engaged one? Really, it looks as though you disapproved of matrimony, Miss Read! A holy state, we're told, a holy state!'

'My mind is open, I hope. I just think she is less quick than Miss Norman. She was pretty vague about methods she would use, and I suspect the children might find her too easygoing and get out of hand.'

'Right!' said Peter Hale, putting aside another set of papers. The vicar sighed.

'She had a remarkably sweet expression, I thought. Reminded me of the early Italian Madonnas.'

'What about the large lady?' asked Peter, ignoring the vicar's gentle lamentations.

'Useful type,' I said. 'Could do all the jobs Mr Willet can't manage. Why, she could lift Mrs Pringle up with one hand!'

'If that should ever be called for,' agreed Peter gravely. 'But what about working with her? Her qualifications are excellent, and she looks in spanking health.'

'I have a feeling that she would find Fairacre a little constricting. She's obviously cut out for a much more demanding post, a bigger staff, older children and so on. There's not enough scope for her here. I wouldn't mind betting that she'll be a head teacher in a big school within ten years. It's like putting a lion in a rabbit hutch.'

'But why did she apply then?' asked the vicar.

'Not enough jobs going.'

'I'm sure that's it,' I said. 'And we shall find that it's a sidestep for this girl, that she'll regret it herself before long.'

'Then that leaves Miss Norman whom you liked from the first. Still feel the same?'

I closed my eyes and thought again. It really is a staggering decision to make, this choosing someone to share one's life so closely in a remote school. Things can so easily go wrong.

I remembered Miss Jackson who had been with me some years earlier. It had been a disastrous appointment, and yet just as much care had gone into considering her.

The fact is that it is virtually impossible to sum up a person until you have lived and worked with them through good times and bad. Paper qualifications, references, examination successes, can only play a small part, and one interview, with the applicant highly nervous and on her best behaviour, can tell little more. Much must be taken on trust.

'Well?' said the vicar and Peter together.

I opened my eyes.

'Yes,' I said. 'I'd like Hilary Norman, if you feel the same.'

'I think it's the best choice,' said Peter.

'Without doubt,' said the vicar. 'And so pretty.'

He turned to Peter. 'Would you like to ask her in again, and apprise the unsuccessful candidates of the result?'

Peter took it like a man. 'I'll go and break it gently,' he said, and vanished to carry the good – and bad – news to the waiting four.

Amy came over that evening, bearing a beautiful bouquet of roses from her garden, and the news that Vanessa had produced a son and heir, weighing eleven pounds.

'Good grief!' I exclaimed. 'Poor girl! How is she?'

'Absolutely fine amidst all the rejoicing. It all sounds delightfully feudal, I must say. Tarquin rang last night amidst sounds of revelry in the background, and a bonfire to beat all bonfires blazing on the hill, or ben. Is it "*ben*"?'

'Either that or "butt",' I told her. 'I'm not conversant with the lingo. But tell me more.'

'She had what is euphemistically termed "a good time", I gather.'

'Meaning what?'

'Oh, sheer unadulterated misery for twenty-four hours instead of forty-eight or more. But she's remarkably resilient, you know. Takes after Eileen who thought nothing of a twelve-mile walk as a girl. Uphill at that.'

'And what is he going to be called?'

'Donald Andrew Fraser Tarquin. One thing, people will know the land of his birth.'

'But the initials spell DAFT,' I pointed out. 'He'll have hell at school.'

Amy looked shocked. 'How right you are! What a blessing you noticed it! I shall let Vanessa know at once.'

She put her head on one side, and considered me carefully. I waited for her usual derogatory comments on some facet of my appearance.

'You know, you are remarkably astute in some ways.'

I began to preen myself. I so seldom receive a compliment from Amy.

'It's a pity you're so pig-headed with it,' she added.

I rose with dignity. 'Come and help me put these roses in water,' I said. 'I intend to ignore that quite unnecessary last remark.'

'Hoity-toity,' said Amy, following me into the kitchen, and watching me start my flower arranging.

'Are you going to see Vanessa?'

'Yes, quite soon. James has to go to Glasgow on business, and we thought we'd have the weekend with them. There's one thing about being a Scottish laird. It seems that there are hosts of old loyal retainers to help with the cooking and housework. Why, Vanessa even has an under-nurse to help the monthly one! Can you imagine such luxury?'

'Would you take the matinée jacket I've just finished? It's pink, of course, but that's like life.'

'No bother at all,' said Amy. 'By the way, do you really want that red rose just there?'

'Why not?'

'It breaks the line.'

'What line?'

'Aren't you taking the eye down from that dark bud at the top to the base of the receptacle and below?'

'Not as far as I know. I was simply making sure that they were all in the water.'

Amy sighed. 'I do wish I could persuade you to come to the floral classes with me. It seems so dreadful to see you so ignorant of the basic skills of arrangement. You could really benefit with some pedestal work. Those roses call out for a pedestal.'

'At the price pedestals are, according to Mrs Mawne, these roses can go on calling out,' I said flatly. 'What's wrong with this nice white vase?'

'You're quite incorrigible,' said Amy, averting her eyes. 'By the way, how's Minnie Pringle?'

'In smashing form, as the music hall joke has it.'

I told her about some of Minnie's choicer efforts, particularly the extraordinary methods used for the drying of dusters.

'You won't believe this,' I told her, 'but last Friday she had upturned the vegetable colander on the draining board, and had draped a wet duster over that. Honestly, I give up!'

'Perhaps you won't have her much longer. I hear that Mrs Fowler has ejected Minnie's husband. My window cleaner says the rows could be heard at the other side of Caxley.'

My spirits rose, then fell again. 'But it doesn't mean that he'll come back to Springbourne necessarily, and in any case, Minnie will probably still need a job. I don't dare hope that she'll leave me.'

'He'll have to sleep somewhere,' Amy pointed out, 'and obviously his old home is the place.'

'Minnie might demand more money, though, and let him stay on sufferance,' I said, clinging to this straw like a drowning beetle, 'then she wouldn't need to come to me on Fridays.'

'I think you are going too fast,' said Amy, lighting a cigarette and inserting it into a splendid amber holder. 'It's a case of wishful thinking, as far as you are concerned. I imagine that he'll return to Minnie, make sure she's bringing in as much money as possible, and will sit back and pretend he's looking for work. Minnie really isn't strong enough to protest, is she?'

Sadly, I agreed. It looked as though I could look forward to hundreds of home-wrecking Friday afternoons.

'Mrs Coggs,' I said wistfully, 'is doing more cleaning now that Arthur's inside. I gather she's a treasure.'

'You shouldn't have been so precipitate in offering Minnie a job,' reproved Amy. 'Incidentally, Arthur's case comes up at Crown Court this week. It was in the local paper.'

'I missed that. Actually this week's issue was handed by that idiotic Minnie to Mrs Pringle to wrap up the chickens' scraps, before I'd read it.'

'Typical!' commented Amy, blowing a perfect smoke ring, an accomplishment she acquired at college along with many other distinctions, academic and otherwise.

'Well, if you've quite finished ramming those roses into that quite unsuitable vase,' said Amy, 'can I beg a glass of water?'

'I'll do better than that,' I told her, bearing my beautiful bouquet into the sitting-room. 'There's a bottle of sherry somewhere – if Minnie hasn't used it for cleaning the windows.'

11. PROBLEMS

As always, everything seemed to happen within the last two weeks of term.

At the beginning of every school year, I make all sorts of good resolutions about being methodical, in time with returning forms and making out lists, arranging programmes well in advance and so on. I have a wonderful vision of myself, calm and collected, sailing through the school year's work with a serene smile, and accepting graciously the compliments of the school managers and the officials at the local education department, on my efficiency.

This blissful vision remains a mirage. I flounder my way through the multitudinous jobs that surround me, and can always still be far behind, particularly with the objectionable clerical work, when the end of the year looms up.

So it was this July. The village fête, in aid of Church Funds as usual, had to have a contribution from the school, and as Mrs Rose became less and less capable as the end of her time drew nigh, and more and more morose since the tiff with Mrs Pringle, I was obliged to work out something single-handed.

It is difficult to plan a programme which involves children from five to eleven taking part, but with all the parents present at the fête, and keen to see their own offspring in the limelight, it was necessary to evolve something.

After contemplating dancing, a play, a gymnastic display and various other hoary old chestnuts, I decided that each of these activities needed more time and rehearsing than I could possibly manage. In the end I weakly fell back on folk songs, most of which the children knew already.

Mrs Rose gave half-hearted support to this proposal, and the air echoed each afternoon as we practised. Meanwhile, there were the usual end of term chores to do, and the heat continued, welcome to me, but inducing increasing languor in the children.

It was during this period that Arthur Coggs and his partners in crime appeared at Crown Court.

As Mr Willet had forecast, all the accused were given prison sentences. The brothers Bryant were sent down for three years and Arthur Coggs for two.

'Not that he'll be there all that time,' said Mr Willet. 'More's the pity. They takes off the time he's been in custody already, see, and if he behaves himself he'll get another few months cut off his spell inside. I reckons he's been lucky this time. We'll have him back in Fairacre before we've got time to turn round, darn it all!'

Mrs Coggs, it was reported, had gone all to pieces on hearing the sentence.

Mrs Pringle told me the details with much relish. 'As a good neighbour,' she said, 'I lent that poor soul the *Caxley Chronicle* to read the result for herself, and I've never seen a body look so white and whey-faced as what she did! Nearly fell off of her chair with the shock,' said Mrs Pringle with evident satisfaction.

'Wouldn't it have been kinder to have told her yourself, if she'd asked?'

'I didn't trust myself not to break down,' responded the old humbug smugly. 'A woman's heart's a funny thing, you know, and she loves that man of hers despite his little failings.'

'I should think "little failings" hardly covers Arthur's criminal activities,' I said, but Mrs Pringle was in one of her maudlin moods and oblivious to my astringency.

'I was glad to see the tears come,' went on that lady. 'I says to her: "That's right! A good cry will ease that breaking heart"!'

'Mrs Pringle,' I cried, 'for pity's sake spare me all this senti-mental mush! Mrs Coggs knew quite well that Arthur would go to prison, and she knew he deserved it. If I'd been in her shoes, I'd have breathed a sigh of relief.'

Mrs Pringle, cut short in the midst of her dramatic tale, looked at me with loathing.

'There's some,' she said, 'as has no feeling heart for the mis-fortunes of others. It's plain to see it would be useless to come to you in trouble, and I'm glad poor Mrs Coggs had my shoulder to weep on in her time of affliction. One of these fine days, you may be in the same boat,' she added darkly, and limped from the room.

Heaven help me, I thought, if that day should ever come.

As it happened, trouble did come, but I managed to cope with-out weeping on Mrs Pringle's ample bosom.

I received a letter from the Office, couched in guarded terms, about the authority's long-term policy of closing small schools which were no longer economic to run. It pointed out that Fairacre's numbers had dwindled steadily over the years, that the matter had been touched on at the last managers' meeting, and that local comment would be sought. It emphasized the fact that nothing would be done without thorough consultation with all concerned, and that this was simply a preparatory exploration of local feeling. Closure, of course, might never take place should numbers increase, or other circumstances make the school vital to the surroundings. But should it be deemed necessary to close, then the children would probably attend Beech Green School, their nearest neighbour.

A copy of the letter, it added, had been sent to all the managers.

I felt as though I had been pole-axed, and poured out my second cup of coffee in a daze.

The rooks were wheeling over the high trees, calling harshly as they banked and turned against the powder-blue morning sky. The sun glinted on their polished feathers as they enjoyed the Fairacre air. How long should I continue to enjoy it, I wondered?

By the time I had sipped the coffee to the dregs, I was feeling calmer. In a way, it is always better to know the worst, than to await tidings in a state of dithering suspense. Well, now something had happened. The rumours were made tangible. The ostrich on the merry-go-round had come to a stop in full view of all of us. Now we must do something about it.

I washed up the breakfast things, put down Tibby's mid-morning snack, washed my hands, and made my way across to the school.

Now what should I choose for our morning hymn? 'Oft in danger, oft in woe' might fit the case, or 'Fight the good fight' perhaps?

No, let's have something bold and brave that we could roar out together!

I opened the book at:

'Ye holy angels bright
Who wait at God's right hand'
and looked with approval at the lines.

'Take what He gives, and praise Him still.
Through good or ill, whoever lives.'

That was the spirit, I told myself, as the children burst in, breathless and vociferous, to start another day beneath the ancient roof which had looked down upon their parents and their grandparents at their schooling years before.

I guessed that the vicar would pay me a visit, and before playtime he entered, holding his letter, and looking forlorn. The children clattered to their feet, glad, as always, of a diversion.

'Sit down, dear children,' said the vicar, 'I mustn't disturb your work.'

That, I thought, is just what they want disturbed, and watched them settle down again reluctantly to their ploys.

'I take it you have had this letter, too?'

'Yes, indeed.'

'It really is most upsetting. I know it stresses the point of there being no hurry in any of these decisions. Nevertheless, I feel we must call an extra-ordinary meeting of the managers, to which you, naturally, are invited, and after that I suppose we may need to have a public meeting in the village. What do you think?'

'See what the managers decide, but I'm sure that's what they will think the right and proper thing to do. After all, it's not only the parents, though they are the most acutely involved, but everyone in Fairacre.'

'My feelings exactly.'

He sighed heavily, and the letter which he had put on my desk, sailed to the floor. Six children fell upon it, like starving dogs upon a crust, and it was a wonder it was not torn to shreds before the vicar regained his property.

After this invigorating skirmish, they returned to their desks much refreshed. The clock said almost a quarter to eleven, and I decided that early playtime was permissible under the circumstances.

They clattered into the lobby and the clanging of milk bottles, taken from the metal crate there, made a background to our conversation.

'You see there was some foundation for those rumours,' commented Mr Partridge. 'No smoke without fire, as they say.'

'It began to look ominous when the measuring started at Beech Green,' I responded. 'And Mr Salisbury was decidedly cagey, I thought. Oh dear, I hope to goodness nothing happens! In a way, the very fact that it's going to be a long drawn-out affair makes it worse. I keep wondering if I should apply for a post elsewhere, before I'm too old to be considered.'

The vicar looked shocked. 'My dear girl, you mustn't think of it! The very idea! *Of course* you must stay here, and we shall all see that you do. That's why I propose to go back to the vicarage and fix a date for the managers' meeting as soon as possible.'

'I do appreciate your support,' I said sincerely, 'it's just this ghastly hanging about. You know.

"The mills of God grind slowly
But they grind exceeding small." '

The vicar's kind old face took on a look of reproof. 'It isn't God's mill that's doing the grinding,' he pointed out. 'It's the Education Office's machinery. And that,' he added vigorously, 'we must put a spoke in.'

If he had been a Luddite he could not have sounded more militant. I watched him cross the playground, with affection and hope renewed.

They say that troubles never come singly, and while I was still reeling under the blow of that confounded letter, I had an un-nerving encounter with Minnie Pringle.

Usually, she would have departed when I returned to my home after school on Fridays. I would then remove the wet dusters from whatever crack-brained place Minnie had left them in, put any broken shards in the dustbin, and set about brewing a much-needed cup of tea, thanking my stars that my so-called help had gone home.

But on this particular Friday she was still there when I entered the house. A high-pitched wailing greeted me, and going to investigate I found Minnie sitting on the bottom stair with a broken disinfectant bottle at her feet.

She was rocking herself back and forth, occasionally throw-ing her skirt over her mop-head of red hair, and displaying deplorable underwear including a pair of tights more ladders than fabric.

I was reminded suddenly of those Irish plays where the stage is almost too murky to see what is happening, the only light being focused dimly on a coffin with four candles, one at each corner, and a gaggle of keening women, while a harp is being plucked, in lugubrious harmony, by some unseen hand.

'What on earth's the matter, Minnie? Don't cry about a broken bottle. We can clear that up.'

'It ain't the *bottle*!' wailed Minnie, pitching herself forward with renewed energy.

'What is it then?'

She flung herself backward, hitting her head on the fourth stair up. I hoped it might knock some sense into her.

'Ah-ah-ah-ah!' yelled Minnie, and flung her skirt over her head once more.

I took hold of her skinny shoulders and shook her. The screaming stopped abruptly, and the skirt was thrown back over the dreadful tights.

'Now stop all this hanky-panky,' I said severely, 'and tell me what's wrong.'

Snivelling, Minnie took up the hem of her skirt once more, but this time applied it to her weeping eyes and wet nose. I averted my gaze hastily.

'Come on, Minnie,' I said, more gently. 'Come and have a cup of tea with me. You'll feel better.'

She sniffed, and shook her head. 'Gotter clear up this bottle as broke,' she said dimly.

'Well, let's find the dustpan and you do that while I make the tea.'

She accompanied me to the kitchen, still weeping, but in a less hysterical fashion. I found the dustpan – for some reason, best known to Minnie, among the saucepans – and handed it over with a generous length of paper towel to mop up her streaming face. I then propelled her into the hall, and returned to prepare the tea tray.

'At this rate,' I muttered to myself, 'I shall need brandy rather than tea.'

Five minutes later, sitting at the kitchen table, the tale unfolded in spasmodic fashion.

'It's Ern,' said Minnie. 'He's comin' back.'

Ern, I knew, was the husband who had so recently deserted her.

'And you don't want him?'

'Would you?'

'No!' I said, without hesitation. 'But can't you tell him so?'

'What, Ern? He'll hit me if I says that.'

'Well, get the police.'

'He'll hit me worse if I tells them.'

I changed my tactics. 'Are you sure he's going to come back?'

'He wrote to Auntie – she can read, you see – and said his place was at my side.'

'What a nerve!' I exclaimed. 'It hasn't been for the last few months, has it?'

'Well, it's different now. That Mrs Fowler don't want 'im. She's turned 'im out.'

So Amy was right after all, I thought.

'And when's he supposed to be coming?'

Minnie let out another ear-splitting yell, and I feared that we were in for another period of hysteria.

'Tonight, 'e says. And I'm too afeared to go home. And what will Bert say?'

'Bert?' I echoed, in perplexity.

'My boy friend what works up Springbourne Manor.' Minnie looked coy.

I remembered the rumour about the under-gardener who had been consoling Minnie in her loneliness.

'What about Bert?'

'He'll hit him too,' said Minnie.

'Your husband will?'

'Yes. Bound to. And Bert'll 'it 'im back, and there'll be a proper set-to.'

Minnie's fears seemed to be mingled with a certain pleasurable anticipation at the prospect, it seemed to me.

'Well you'd better let Bert know what's happening,' I said, 'and he can keep away. That is, if Ern comes at all. Perhaps he's only making threats.'

Minnie's eyes began to fill again. 'He'll come all right. He ain't got nowhere to sleep, see. And I dursn't face him. He'll knock me about terrible, and the kids. What am I to do?'

'You say Mrs Pringle had the letter?'

'Yes. She read it out to me.'

'She'll be over at the school now,' I said, putting down my cup. 'I'll go and see her while you have some more tea.'

I left her, still sniffing, and sought out her aunt, who was balanced on a desk top dusting the partition between the two classrooms.

'My, what a start you gave me!' she gasped, one hand on her heart.

'Can you come down for a minute?' I said, holding out my hand for support. 'It's about Minnie.'

Mrs Pringle, twisting my hand painfully, descended in a crab-wise fashion, and sat herself on the front desk. I faced her, propped on my table.

'She's in tears about that husband of hers, and seems afraid to go home.'

'I knows that. She's been no better than she should be while he's been away. He's promised her a thundering good 'iding.'

'But he's threatening her just because he wants somewhere to sleep. It all seems most unfair to me. After all, he left her.'

'Maybe. But his place is in his own home, with Minnie.'

'But, he's intimidating her!'

'Natural, ain't it? How else did she get her last baby?'

I felt unequal to explaining the intricacies of the English language to Mrs Pringle, and let it pass.

'The point is, Mrs Pringle, that it really wouldn't be safe to let her go home if he intends to come and knock her about. Should we tell the police?'

Mrs Pringle bridled. 'What, and let the neighbours have a free show? Not likely.'

'But the children—'

Mrs Pringle's face became crimson with wrath. She thrust her head forward until our noses were almost touching.

'Are you trying to tell me what to do with Minnie's children? I'll tell you straight, I'm not having that tribe settling on me with all I've got to do. I'm sick and tired of Minnie and her lot, and the sooner she pushes off and faces up to the trouble she's made the better.'

'So you won't help?'

'I've done nothing but help that silly girl, and I'm wore out with it.'

'I can understand that, and I think you've been remarkably patient. But now what's to be done? I really think the police should be warned that there might be trouble.'

Mrs Pringle's breathing became heavy and menacing.

'You just try it! You dare! I've been thinking about the best way to tackle this ever since I got that Ern's letter. He can talk – going off with that old trollop who's old enough to be his mother!'

I began to feel dizzy. Whose side was Mrs Pringle on?

'What I'm going to do,' said my cleaner, 'is to go back with Minnie and the kids tonight, and to sleep the night at her place, with the rolling pin on one side of me and the poker on the other. I'll soon settle that Ern's hash if he dares put a foot inside the place. We don't need no police, Miss Read, that I can tell you!'

'Splendid!' I cried. 'Can I go and tell Minnie?'

'Yes. And I'll be ready to set off in half an hour sharp, tell her, just as soon as I've got the cobwebs off this partition.'

She heaved herself up on to the desk again, duster in hand, and I returned home, thinking what a wonderfully militant band we were in Fairacre, from the vicar to Mrs Pringle.

12. MILITANT MANAGERS

The extra-ordinary managers' meeting was called during the last week of term, and great difficulty the vicar had encountered before gathering them all together.

The long hot spell had advanced harvest, and Mr Roberts was already in that annual fever which afflicts farmers at this time of year when the vicar rang. However, he nobly put aside his panic and agreed to spend an hour away from his combine harvester, as the matter seemed urgent.

Mrs Lamb was supposed to be at a flower arranging meeting at Caxley where someone, of whom Mrs Lamb spoke with awe in her voice, was going to show her respectful audience how to make Large Displays for Public Places from no more than five bought flowers and the bounty culled from the hedgerows. Mrs Lamb, whose purse was limited but who enjoyed constructing enormous decorations of bulrushes, reeds, branches, honesty and even beetroot and rhubarb leaves, was looking forward to learning more, but gave up the pleasure to do her duty.

Mrs Mawne had a bridge party arranged at her house, but was obliged to do a great deal of telephoning to get it transferred to another player's. As all the ladies vied with each other in preparing exotic snippets of food to have with their tea, this meant even further domestic complications. However, it was done.

Mrs Moffat was busy putting the final touches to a magnificent ball dress which was destined to go to a Masonic Ladies' Night, but set aside her needle to be present, while Peter Hale, recently retired from the local grammar – now comprehensive –

school, cursed roundly at ever being fool enough to agree to being a manager when the grass wanted cutting so urgently.

Resigned to their lot, therefore, they assembled in the vicar's dining-room one blazing afternoon and accepted a cup of tea from Mrs Partridge before she departed to her deckchair under the cedar tree, there to read, or rather to skip through, the final chapters of a very nasty book, strongly recommended by the book critics of the Sunday papers, and dealing with the incestuous relations of a sadistic father and his equally repulsive teenage daughter. The fact, much advertised by the publishers, that it had already sold thirty thousand copies and was now reprinting, gave Mrs Partridge more cause for regret than rejoicing, but she was determined to turn over the pages until the end, so that she could give her trenchant comments on the work, and truthfully say she 'had been through it', in more ways than one.

No one appeared from the Office on this occasion, but I was invited, and enjoyed my cup of tea, and the comments of the managers.

'We've got to be firm about this,' said Mr Roberts. 'Say "No" from the outset. I mean, what's village life coming to?'

'How do you mean?' asked Mrs Moffat.

'Well, we used to have a village bobby. Remember Trumper, padre?'

The vicar said he did, and what a splendid fellow he was.

'Exactly. Used to hear old Trumper puffing round the village every night about two o'clock making sure everything was in order.'

'So sensible,' agreed Mrs Mawne. 'We need more police. That's half the trouble these days.'

'And what's more,' went on Mr Roberts, 'he gave any young scallywag a good clip round the ear-'ole, on the spot, and stopped a peck of wrong-doing. What happens now? Some ruddy Juvenile Court six months later when the kid's forgotten all about it.'

The vicar coughed politely. 'Quite. We take your point, but it is the school closure we are considering.'

'It's the same principle,' said Peter Hale, coming to Mr Roberts' support 'You need direct contact – that's the unique quality of village life. If we lose the village bobby it's a link broken. Far worse to lose our village school.'

'Too little spread too thin,' said Mrs Lamb. 'Same as having to share you, Mr Partridge, with Beech Green and Springbourne. Why, I remember the time, before your day, of course, when the vicar was just for Fairacre, and you could reckon to see him any time you wanted, if you were in trouble. He'd be in his study or the garden, or in the church or visiting in the parish. Now he can be anywhere.'

The vicar nodded and looked unhappy.

'Not that it can be altered,' added Mrs Lamb hastily, 'and a marvellous job you do, but nevertheless, it's not the same.'

'I suppose there's no hope of this school staying open for infants only?' asked Mrs Mawne. 'The biggest objection is hauling the babies to Beech Green, I think.'

'It's too small as it is,' I said. 'Even if the Beech Green infants were brought here, both schools would still be too small according to the authority.'

The arguments went on. I was touched to see how concerned they all were, not only for the children's sake and mine, but for the destruction of a tradition which went back for over a hundred years.

'If we give in,' said Mr Roberts, 'we're betraying the village, as I see it. Our Fairacre children get a jolly sound grounding. You've only got to look at the percentage we used to get through the eleven-plus exam to go on to the grammar school, before it turned into this blighted whatever it's called. I propose we send a reply to the Office saying we're firmly against the idea of closure.'

This proposal was carried unanimously, and the vicar promised to write the letter that evening.

The clock stood at four-thirty. Mr Roberts rushed back to his combine, Mrs Moffat to her ball gown, Mrs Lamb to the telephone to hear all about the flower-arranging from a friend, Mrs Mawne to studying the bridge column in last Sunday's paper in lieu of her game, and Peter Hale to his lawn mower.

I stood in the vicarage garden and looked across at our modest weatherbeaten school across the way.

'Never fear,' said the vicar, clapping me on the shoulder. 'It will be there for another hundred years, believe me.'

'I hope so,' I said soberly.

Amy called in unexpectedly that evening while my head was still humming with the memory of the managers' meeting.

I told her a little about it. To my surprise, she seemed to think that Fairacre School was doomed to close, and that it would be a good thing.

'Well, I'm blowed!' I exclaimed. 'A fine friend you are! I suppose you want to see me queuing up for my dole before long?'

'Well, no,' replied Amy, with what I thought quite unnecessary hesitation. 'Not exactly, but I do think this place is an anachronism.'

'How can it be if it serves a useful purpose in the village?'

'I sometimes wonder if it does. Oh, I know all about fathers and grandfathers doing their pot-hooks and hangers under these very windows, but it's time things changed.'

'My children don't do pot-hooks and hangers.'

'Don't snap, dear. What I'm trying to point out is that things have altered considerably. For one thing, those grandfathers came to Fairacre School when it boasted a hundred children or more, as the log books show. It was a real *school-sized* school then, and enough boys present to play a decent game of football or cricket among themselves if they wanted to.'

'Team games aren't everything.'

'And then this building,' continued Amy, waving a hand. 'It's really had its time, you know. The very fabric is crumbling, as Mrs Pringle points out daily. And those antiquated stoves!

And that ghastly skylight forever letting in rain and a wicked draught! It's really not good enough. I wonder the parents haven't complained before now.'

I was speechless before this onslaught. Perhaps Amy was right. She often was, as I knew to my cost.

I changed the subject.

'You were right about Mrs Fowler by the way. She's pushed out Minnie's husband, and Minnie's afraid he'll come back to her.'

'With that row of children to look after, I should think she might welcome him.'

I told her about Minnie's fears of aggression, and how Mrs Pringle had gone into attack. Amy listened avidly.

'And did he come?'

'No, thank heaven, but they expect him daily and barricade the door with the kitchen table whenever they return home. The children think it is terrific fun.'

'Children are odd,' agreed Amy. 'I remember how Kenneth used to insist on having the more lugubrious parts of *Black Beauty* read to him, while the tears rolled down his cheeks. He was about six then.'

Kenneth was a brother of Amy's who was killed in the last war. I had met him occasionally, and could never take to him, finding him boastful, selfish, and frequently untruthful. He was a confounded nuisance to his parents in his teens, as so many boys are, and they were wonderfully realistic and cheerful about it.

However, no sooner had he died than their attitude to the young man was completely transformed. To hear them talk of Kenneth, after his death, one would have imagined him to be a paragon of all the virtues, kind, noble, a loving son and devoted friend to many. So does death transfigure us. Perhaps it is as well, but personally I think one should cling to the truth – in charitable silence, of course – and not try to deceive oneself, or others, about the rights of the matter.

Even now, so long after, Amy's voice took on a reverent note when Kenneth's name was mentioned. I was glad that she remembered him with love, but wondered if such an outstandingly honest and downright person as dear Amy really conned herself into believing Kenneth the complete hero.

'He was the handsomest of us all,' went on Amy, gazing across the fields outside the window. 'Our Aunt Rose always gave him a better birthday present than the rest of us. We used to resent it dreadfully.'

'Quite natural, I should think.'

'And it's about Aunt Rose I've come tonight,' said Amy, becoming her usual brisk self. 'She died a fortnight ago and I'm clearing out the house for her. When you break up, could you spare a couple of afternoons to help?'

I said I would be glad to.

'It's no joke, I can tell you,' warned Amy. 'She seems to have kept every letter and photograph and Christmas card since about 1910.'

'They'd probably make a fortune at Sotheby's,' I said.

'Make a hefty bonfire,' commented Amy, picking up her handbag. 'Anyway, many thanks for offering. I'll pick you up one afternoon next week, and we'll get down to it. I should bring a large overall and tie up your hair.'

'How's Vanessa?' I said, as Amy slammed the car door.

'Besotted with motherhood,' said Amy. 'I think she's going to be one of those mamas who keep a diary of daily progress. You know the sort of thing:

Thursday: Baby dribbled.
Friday: Baby squinted.
Saturday: Baby burped.'

'It's because it's the first,' I said indulgently.

'Well, her only hope is to have about half a dozen. Surely she would be more reasonable then.'

She drove off, and I returned to prepare a snack for the ever-voracious Tibby.

Village Affairs

*

The last day of term passed off jubilantly, its glory only partly clouded by my secret fears that this might be perhaps the last day of a school year spent under Fairacre School's dilapidated roof.

However, I put such dismal thoughts aside, and fell to tidying cupboards, dismantling the nature table, removing the children's artwork from the walls and ruining my thumb nail as a result, as I do regularly. A broken thumb nail and arthritis in the right shoulder, caused by writing on the blackboard, are just two of a teacher's occupational hazards, I have discovered. Increasing impatience, over the years, seems to be another, certainly in my case.

But today in the golden haze of breaking up, all was well. The children were noisy but busy. The sun blazed down as though it would continue to do so until Christmas. Mr Roberts' combine provided a pleasant humming from some distant field, and a drowsy bumblebee droned up and down one of the school windows.

The afternoon flew by. We stood for grace in the unusually tidy and bare classroom, our voices echoing hollowly, and praised God for mercies received and blessings to come, before the tumultuous rush for home.

Joseph Coggs was the last to leave.

'You want any gardening done this 'oliday?' he asked in his husky voice.

'Why, yes,' I said untruthfully.

It was plain that he needed occupation as well as a little pocket money.

'Can your mother spare you?' I asked. 'Or should you be helping with the baby?'

'The baby goes with 'er,' said Joseph, running a grubby finger along the table edge. 'Anyway the twins does that all right.'

'Well, if you're sure,' I said, making up my mind to have a word with Mrs Coggs before he came, 'then perhaps one morning next week, if it stays fine.'

'Cor!' was all he said, but he raised his dark eyes to mine, and unalloyed delight shone from them.

I patted his shoulder. I have a very soft spot for young Joseph, and life has never treated him well. Despite that, he has a sweetness of disposition which one rarely meets. Things must be pretty grim at home, and pretty tight, too. I should be glad to have him to help, if only to enjoy his obvious pleasure at being of use.

'Off you go then,' I said. 'I'll call at your house soon to fix things up.'

He skipped off, and I followed him.

The sun had beaten down upon the faded paint of the school door all the afternoon, and it was almost too hot to touch. In the distance, the downs trembled through veils of heat haze, and my spirits rose at the thought of weeks of summer holiday stretching before me.

I skipped, almost as blithely as young Joseph, across the playground towards my home.

13. OTHER PEOPLE'S HOMES

As promised, I went to see Mrs Coggs one evening during the first week of the holidays.

I knew better, as a country dweller, than to knock at the front door. In most cases, the knocker is securely fastened by layers of paint and the grime of years, except in the case of those once termed gentry, who still have polished knockers on their front doors, and use them.

The concrete path leading to Mrs Coggs' back door was so narrow and flush with the wall that it was quite a balancing feat to remain on it. The surface was badly cracked, and here and there an iron manhole cover added to the hazards. Fairacre 'went on the mains' a few years ago and we seem to have sprouted more covers than taps in the village.

At the back door three scraggy chickens pecked idly at the concrete, scattering with a squawk when they saw me, and fleeing to cover among some gooseberry bushes almost hidden in long grass. It was apparent that no gardener's hand had been at work here for many a long year, and I wondered if the Council had issued any reprimand about the state of its property.

Mrs Coggs appeared at the door looking like a startled hare. Her eyes bulged and her nose was atwitch.

'I didn't mean to frighten you,' I began.

She wiped her wet hands on the sacking apron which girt her skinny form, and pushed wisps of dank hair from her face.

'You best come in,' she said resignedly, and stepped over the threshold into the kitchen. I followed her.

I nearly stepped straight back again, stunned by the appalling smell. Mrs Coggs was busy wiping the seat of a wooden chair with the useful sacking apron and had her back to me, so that I hoped she had not seen my dismay.

The twins, runny-nosed despite the hot day, now came to the door which led into the other room where most of the living was done. They looked as startled as their mother, and put grimy thumbs into their mouths for comfort.

'Clear off!' said Mrs Coggs. 'Miss Read don't want you lot 'anging around, and no more don't I!'

While I was engaged mentally in correcting the grammar of this last phrase, the two little girls sidled past me nervously, and bolted into the garden. The toddler, who had been hiding behind the back of the sacking apron, now set up a terrible hullabaloo. Mrs Coggs sat down at the kitchen table and hoisted him on to it among towers of dirty saucepans, plates, old newspapers, and a broken colander which seemed to contain a multitude of fish heads. It was this last, I guessed, which contributed the largest and most potent part of the general stench.

'It's gone your bed-time, ain't it, lovey,' she crooned, her face as suffused with tenderness, as she surveyed her youngest, as it had been with exasperation at the sight of the twins only a minute before. I was reminded of mother cats who adore their tiny babies, and cuff them unmercifully as soon as they think they should be off their hands.

'It was about Joe that I've come,' I said. 'I wondered if he could help me in the garden now and again during the holidays.'

She continued to stroke the baby's hair and did not answer. I began to wonder if she were becoming deaf, or if she were still too bemused by her change of fortune to take in anything she was asked. She certainly looked white and pinched, and I wondered if she were getting enough to eat.

'Perhaps one morning a week?' I said. 'He could stop and have his midday dinner with me, if that fits in with your plans.'

The mention of food seemed to rouse her.

'He'd like that. Always likes 'is school dinners, that one. More'n the twins does. They eats next to nothing.'

'What do they like?' I inquired.

'Bread and sauce,' she replied. 'They has that most days. Saves cooking.'

I pointed to the nauseating collection of fish heads. 'Are you going to cook those?' I inquired tentatively.

She surveyed them with some surprise, as though she had only just noticed their presence, although heaven above knew, they made themselves felt quite enough.

'Fishmonger give 'em to me yesterday, and said to boil 'em for soup or summat. But we'd never eat that stuff. I likes tomato out of a tin.'

I could not probe too deeply into Mrs Coggs' culinary arrangements though I was dying to know how she fed the family. Surely they didn't live on bread and sauce exclusively? I returned to Joe's arrangements.

'What about Tuesday mornings?' I suggested.

'Yeh, that's fine. I goes out all day Tuesday charing. I takes the baby, and the twins can come too in the holidays, but I usually leaves 'em 'ere, out of the way.'

'That's settled then,' I said, making my way to the door, and anxious to get a breath of fresh air after the foetid atmosphere inside. Spread over the hedge, I saw some shrunken and torn garments, fit only for polishing rags. Their washing had been sketchy, and they were still stained in many places. The over-powering smell of poverty and neglect saddened me.

'Mrs Coggs,' I said, able to bear it no longer, 'are you being looked after by the Social Security people? I mean, you are getting money regularly?'

Her face lit up. 'I gets over a pound for each kid now and Joe gets a pound too. And there's me own supplementary. I've never 'ad so much in me life. We gotter telly now.'

'But what about food?'

She looked bewildered. 'They has what they likes best. I told you, bread and sauce, and now I buys a few cakes and sweets. We ain't hard up, Miss, if that's what's worrying you. And I've got me work.'

I turned away, sighing. It was quite apparent that Mrs Coggs' home conditions were the result of lack of management rather than lack of money. I guessed that she was brought up in a home as feckless as her own, and marriage to Arthur could not have helped her, but how sad it all seemed! Sad and wasteful!

'Then I'll look forward to seeing Joe next Tuesday,' I said retracing my steps over the manhole covers. 'About ten, shall we say? And I'll send him home about one, after he's had lunch with me.'

She nodded vaguely, and lifted the child from her hip to the ground, where he sat in the dust. His bottom, I noticed, was completely bare. His hand was already reaching for a dollop of dried chicken's mess.

I escaped into the lane, and picked the first sprig of honeysuckle I could find. It mitigated the reek of fish only a little, but it helped.

Amy came to lunch before we both drove over to her late aunt's house, some miles beyond Springbourne, to sort out the old lady's things.

Still worried about the Coggs family, I poured out an account of my visit. Amy remained unperturbed.

'I can't think why you worry yourself so much about other people's affairs,' she said. 'I imagine Mrs Coggs muddles along quite satisfactorily. After all, she's still alive and kicking, and the children too, despite her appalling housekeeping.'

'But it's all so *unnecessary*,' I began.

'It's purely relative,' said Amy, accepting a second helping of gooseberry pie. 'I mean, look at the way I could worry myself stiff about you – but what good would it do?'

'How d'you mean?' I said, bridling.

'Well, the slapdash way you go about things. This pastry for instance. I imagine it's frozen, or something like that?'

'Of course it is. I make ghastly pastry, and the kitchen floor wants a good scrub after I've done it. Why, does it taste horrible? You've had two helpings, so it can't be too bad.'

'I was always brought up,' said Amy, touching her lips delicately with her napkin, 'in the belief that it was excessively rude to comment on the amount eaten by one's guests.'

'Oh, come off it,' I said. 'What I want to know is why you compare me with Mrs Coggs?'

'Simply this. *You* worry about Mrs Coggs because she is so inefficient. I *could* worry about *you* because you, in your way, are just as feckless. Fancy spending all that money on frozen pastry when it would cost you about half to make your own!'

'Don't nag,' I said. 'All right. I take your point, and I'll try not to get too worked up about the bread and sauce menu at the Coggs'. But I shall see Joe gets a decent meal on the days he comes here.'

We washed up amicably, drank a cup of coffee (instant) apiece and drove over the hill towards Aunt Rose's establishment.

There had been a thunderstorm in the night, and the air was fresh and moist. The road ran between thick woods which gave off a delicious scent of wet leaves and moss. A slight mist hung over the little tributary of the Cax at Springbourne, and a flotilla of ducks splashed happily by the humpback bridge.

A magpie flew chattering across the road, just in front of the car.

'*One for sorrow*,' quoted Amy. 'Did you spit?'

'Spit?'

'How ignorant you are! You should always spit if you see a magpie alone. It takes the venom out of the spell.'

'I had no idea you were superstitious.'

'I'm not. But I do spit at one magpie, and I make a cross in spilt salt, of course, and I wouldn't dream of cutting my nails on a Friday, but I wouldn't consider myself superstitious.'

'What about walking under ladders?'

'Common sense not to. Someone might drop a pot of paint over you.'

I pondered on the fact that no matter how long one knows people there still remain depths unplumbed in their make up.

Aunt Rose's house lay some two miles along a narrow and twisted lane. A charm of goldfinches fluttered from the high hedges, bound, I felt sure, for some thistle seeds which were growing near by. A crow was busy pecking at the corpse of a poor squashed hedgehog, victim, no doubt, of a car during its night-time foraging. It was being watched by a pony whose shaggy head hung over a gate. Animals, it seemed, enjoyed each other's company, and were as curious about each other's activities, as any of us village folk at Fairacre.

The house had a forlorn look as we approached it. The curtains were half-drawn and every window tightly shut. It was deathly quiet and still when we went inside, and smelt of dust and old clothes.

'Leave the front door wide open,' directed Amy, 'and let's open a few windows before we go upstairs.'

It had been built in the thirties, when Aunt Rose's father had died, leaving her comfortably off. It was quite a period piece and a very pleasant one too, with its cream walls and paintwork, its fawn tiled hearth, the standard lamp crowned with its beige bell-shaped shade, and the oatmeal-coloured great Knole settee tied at the corners with silk cord.

On the wide window sills stood the sort of flower vases one rarely sees these days – pottery posy rings, a glass bowl containing a heavy glass holder with bored holes, and several fine lustre jugs. On a little table near by lay a half-finished piece of knitting in pale blue wool. It looked like part of a jumper sleeve, and a spider had spun a long gossamer strand across its surface. It brought home to me, with dreadful poignancy, the swift transition from life to death, when our toys are set aside and we have to leave our playing.

We made our way upstairs where a smell of lavender greeted us. A bowl of dried flowers stood on the table on the landing and scented the whole top floor. Amy wanted to go through her aunt's clothes before tackling anything else, and we set to with a will.

Out of the wardrobe came the sort of clothes which a repertory theatre would welcome. There were coats trimmed with silver fox fur, black evening gowns, ablaze with sequins at the neck, and a musquash coat from which flew several moths as we dumped it on the bed.

On the rack at the bottom of the wardrobe we removed beautiful cream kid shoes with Louis heels, and some later ones with stiletto heels and sharply pointed toes. Everything was in apple pie order.

'Now, what I propose to do,' said Amy, 'is to make three piles. One for myself, one for friends and relatives, and one for local jumble sales. Let's make a start.'

It all seemed very well thought out, until we began. Amy's pile was extremely modest. She put aside two almost new tweed skirts and a pretty little fur stole. It was the division of the rest between relatives and jumble which gave us a headache. Amy proved surprisingly dithery over the allotment.

'I think we ought to let the two nieces have a look at these woollies. After all, they're practically new and came from Harrods. Perhaps they're too good for the jumble pile.'

And so they would be transferred, changing places – but only temporarily – with four pairs of elbow-length gloves with rows of pearl buttons.

My head was beginning to buzz by the time Amy called a halt and we went downstairs for a change of occupation.

Aunt Rose, methodical to the last, had left a list of objects which she wanted close friends to have. Our job was to tie on labels bearing the new owner's name.

It was not quite so exhausting as the upstairs sorting, and we duly affixed labels to pieces of beautiful Wedgwood, Venetian glass, a nest of tables, two bronze clocks and a few choice pieces of furniture.

I found the job rather sad. It seemed such a pity that all these lovely things, which had lived together cheek-by-jowl for so many years, should now be parted. But I comforted myself with the thought that no doubt they were going to homes where they would be cherished as dearly as they had been by Aunt Rose.

The sky was overcast as we locked up and drove away.

'More rain tonight,' forecast Amy, dodging a rabbit that sprinted across the narrow lane. 'Bang goes any idea of mowing the lawn tomorrow. Can you come again tomorrow afternoon to finish off upstairs?'

'I've got Joseph Coggs to lunch,' I said, 'but I could be ready by two.'

'You and your gentlemen friends,' commented Amy. 'I only wish this one were more your age and you took him seriously.'

She drew up at the school house, and shook her head when I asked her in.

'No, I must get back. But a thousand thanks for helping. I'll see you tomorrow.'

She let in the clutch, and then shouted over her shoulder as the car moved forward.

'Give Joe a good lunch!'

14. THE SUMMER HOLIDAY

The clock of St Patrick's was striking ten when Joseph Coggs arrived. The sun was beginning to break through the clouds which had brought more rain at dawn, and gilded the wet paths and sparked tiny rainbows from the droplets on the hedge. My temporary gardener looked remarkably happy.

'Wodjer want doin', miss?' he inquired after our greetings. He surveyed the garden appreciatively.

'What about weeding the border?'

'I likes weedin'!' said Joe, accepting a bucket and small fork, 'but if I don't know which is which I'll 'ave to 'oller to you.'

I agreed that that would be wise, and watched him tackle the job. He was quick and neat in his movements, and the groundsel and twitch were soon mounting in the bucket. There is one thing about neglecting a border. By the time you get down to it the results are really spectacular.

Joe began to hum happily to himself and I returned to the kitchen.

I had prepared a chicken casserole, and as the oven was in use I decided to make a treacle tart, for where would you find a small boy who doesn't like treacle tart? With Amy's rebuke still ringing in my head, I resolved to make my own pastry.

I must admit, I found the task quite rewarding, despite the shower of crumbs which managed to leap from the bowl on to the floor. I found myself becoming quite dreamy as I rolled the pastry. It was such a soporific exercise that I was quite startled when Joe appeared at the open window before me. His eyes were bright as he watched me at work.

'Us havin' poy then?'

'Treacle tart.'

'Cor!' breathed Joe. He rested his elbows on the outside window sill and settled down to watch. It was not long before his gaze became as bemused as I guessed my own was. Perhaps it was the rhythmic movement of the rolling pin, I thought.

'I loves pastry,' growled Joe. 'Bein' made, I mean, as well as when I eats it.'

I nodded in reply, and lifted the floppy material on to a shallow dish.

'Like sittin' by the fire, or sleepin' with your back against your mum,' went on Joe, suddenly loquacious. 'You want that bit what's cut off?'

'No,' I said, handing over a strip. 'But should you eat it raw?'

'Gives you worms, my mum says,' said Joe contentedly, retreating rapidly with his booty, 'but I still likes it.'

He returned to the border leaving me to ponder on the primitive needs which still make themselves felt, and which had given Joe such unusual powers of expression.

The chicken stew was relished as keenly as the treacle tart, and while we were demolishing my handiwork we chatted of this and that, his next gardening spell with me, why rabbits have so many babies, what happens to your inside if you eat soap, why Mrs Partridge has summer curtains as well as winter ones, and other interesting topics.

'Is our school truly going to shut?' he said suddenly, spoon arrested halfway to his mouth. A thread of treacle drooped dangerously tableward, and I steered his hand over his plate.

'I don't know. I hope not.'

'Mrs Pringle told me mum it was going to.'

I should like to have said: 'Don't believe anything Mrs Pringle tells you,' but civility and the enforced camaraderie of those in authority forbade.

'No one knows yet.'

Joe's dark eyes looked troubled. 'Well, I don't want to go off in a bus to that 'ol Beech Green.'

'Why not?'

Joe twirled his spoon slowly, winding up the treacle.

'I'm afeared of that Mr Annett. 'E walloped my cousin Fred 'orrible.'

'He probably misbehaved,' I said primly. 'Mr Annett doesn't punish children unless they've been really bad.'

'Well, I'm not going anyways,' said Joe, looking mutinous. 'I 'ates going on buses away from Fairacre.'

'Why? Do you feel ill?'

'No. But I bin to Caxley sometimes, and to Barrisford on the outings, and I don't like it. I don't like being so far away.'

I remembered his look when he described the comfort of sleeping with his back against his mother.

'I likes to be home,' he sighed. 'It's right to be home. It's safe there.'

The vision of that appalling kitchen rose before me, the stinking fish heads in the colander, the dirty rags on the draining board, the grease on the floor, the meals of bread and sauce consumed at that filthy table. But to Joe it meant happiness.

Miss Clare, I remembered, had a sampler hanging on her cottage wall, by the fireplace.

'*Home is where the heart is*' it said in cross-stitch. It certainly seemed to apply in the case of Joseph Coggs.

I told Amy about Joe's disclosure as we continued to sort out Aunt Rose's effects that afternoon.

'It seems to me that everyone in Fairacre is taking it for granted that the school is going to close,' I said, holding up a pair of vicious-looking corsets with yards of pink lacings hanging from them.

Amy took them from me and deposited them on the jumble pile.

'Well, what do you expect? After all, it affects everybody and you know what village life is like, better than most. If there isn't a real drama going on then someone will invent one.'

'But nothing has been decided yet.'

'All the more fun. You can make your own ending, can't you? I suppose you realize that you are the central character?'

'How? I've said nothing.'

'A dispossessed person, you'll be. The evicted innocent cast out into the snow, frail, noble and uncomplaining. The village is dying to rally to your support.'

'That'll be the day!'

'Or maybe you'll be rescued, just in time to save you from complete penury, by some gallant hero who marries you in Fairacre church while the children throw rose petals in your path.'

'Lumps of coke, more likely, knowing them.'

I held up a vest which looked remarkably short. 'What's this?'

'A *spencer*, dear. It's time they came back. You wear it under or over your petticoat in cold weather. A very sensible garment. Put it on my pile. It'll be just the thing for next winter.'

I did as I was bid.

'I hope you're wrong,' I went on, 'about village feelings. Lord knows there's enough to keep all the gossip-mongers busy at the moment, what with Minnie Pringle's affairs, and Mrs Pringle's spasmodic dieting, and talk of Dr Martin retiring at last, and Mr Lamb's brother and his family coming over from America very soon, and the mystery of two dead rats in the rainwater butt outside the vestry door.'

Amy broke into a peal of laughter, and sat down on the side of the bed clutching a black velvet evening cape to her ribs.

'Heavens, how you do go on in Fairacre,' she managed to gasp. 'No wonder you don't want to leave with all that happening around you! But, mark my words, there will still be time left to attend to you and your affairs, even if they do have to compete with two dead rats in the vestry's rainwater butt.'

She shook out the velvet cape and studied it with her head on one side. 'For bridge parties, should you think?'

'For the jumble pile,' I told her.

And, for once, she obeyed.

*

A few days later, I set off for a short holiday in East Anglia, staying with friends and revisiting on my way to Norfolk the little resort of Walton-on-the-Naze where I had stayed as a child with my grandparents. The air was still as bracing as I remembered it from my youth, and I felt no desire to plunge into the chilly waves of the North Sea, despite the sunshine.

I forgot my cares as I travelled. It was a relief to leave all the gossipers to get on with their tongue-wagging and wonderful not to have to guard my own conversation. I returned to Fairacre, after nine days of enjoyment, much refreshed.

It was Mrs Pringle's day for 'doing' me, and she was in the kitchen when I went in, doing something complicated with an old toothbrush at the sink.

'A dirt-trap, these 'ere taps,' was her greeting. 'I'd like to meet the fellow as designed 'em. No room to get behind 'em to scrub out the filth. And filth you can always reckon to find in this kitchen, I can tell you!'

She did, quite often, but I forbore to say so.

'I'm having a cup of tea,' I said. 'Will you have one too?'

'I don't mind if I do,' she said graciously, attacking the crack behind the taps with renewed vigour.

'Well,' I said, when the tray was ready, 'what's the news?'

'Plenty,' she said. 'Our Minnie goes from bad to worse.'

'What now? Is she moving?' I asked, my heart taking a hopeful leap. Would Friday afternoons revert to their former tranquillity again?

'Moving? I wish she was! No, *she's* not moving, but that dratted Bert of hers is. He's moving in.'

'But what about her husband? Ern, isn't it? I thought *he* was going to move in.'

'I settled him,' said Mrs Pringle grimly. I remembered her threat of sleeping with the rolling pin on one side and the poker on the other. Perhaps Ern had met his match.

'After all Ern's hullabaloo Bert said his place was at Minnie's side.'

'But that's just what Ern said!' I expostulated. If all the men who had received Minnie's favours over the years suddenly decided that their place was at her side, she would undoubtedly have to look for larger premises.

Mrs Pringle blew heavily upon her tea, creating a miniature storm in the cup.

'Well, Bert's not a bad chap, although no better than he should be, of course, when it comes to Minnie, and no doubt he could settle Ern's hash if he comes back in a fighting mood. So he's gone to live with our Min. In the spare room, of course,' she added austerely.

'A lodger.'

'A *paying guest*,' corrected Mrs Pringle. 'Five pounds a week. All found.'

I was musing upon the expression 'all found' when Mrs Pringle casually threw in her bombshell.

'So maybe she won't need to do as much cleaning work now. I'll find out if she wants to give you up, for one, shall I?'

'Yes, please,' I said fervently.

I poured Mrs Pringle a second cup. My feelings towards Bert, the philanderer, whose relationship with Minnie I had hitherto deplored, became suddenly much warmer. When it came down to brass tacks – Minnie's moral welfare versus my self-preservation – the latter won hands down.

As always, the holidays rushed by at twice the speed of term-time, reminding me of vague wisps of Einstein's theory of relativity which was once explained to me at Cambridge and involved something to do with Wordsworth's 'Ode on Intimations of Immortality from Recollections of Early Childhood'. I may have taken in one hundredth of the explanation at the time, but now I remember nothing clearly, except the fact that things are not what they seem. Certainly, this time business is purely relative, and I give Einstein points for that.

Hilary Norman was there in the infants' room, looking remarkably fresh and competent on her first morning, in a pale blue denim trouser suit.

The children, round-eyed, and in an unusually quiet mood, studied her with curiosity. I don't think they can ever have had quite such a young teacher before, and they were enchanted. Later I heard that one of them had told his mother that: 'We've got a little girl to teach us now.'

We pushed back the partition between the two classrooms, to the accompaniment of ear-splitting squealings from the steel runners, and embarked on a full assembly, starting with 'We plough the fields and scatter the good seed on the land' which seemed a little premature to me at the end of August, until I looked out of the window to see one of Mr Roberts' tractors busily turning the golden stubble into lovely long ribs of chocolate-coloured earth. Farmers, these days, certainly hurry along with their work, and the gulls were having a splendid time following close behind, mewing and squawking like a trodden cat, as they swooped upon the bounty below them.

As they sang lustily, and not very tunefully – music is not one of our stronger accomplishments – I thought how small the school was just now. Despite the fact that two new infants had joined Hilary Norman's class, we were two down on last term's numbers, as one family had moved into Caxley, taking four children whom we could ill afford to lose at this critical stage.

What would happen to us? I was surprised that nothing further had been heard from the Office, but supposed that the summer holidays had meant a postponement of any decision. No doubt we should hear in good time. It seemed that the general feeling was that closure was inevitable. Far better to know the worst than to hang on like this in horrible suspense.

The matter was further aggravated for me at playtime when, mugs of tea in hand, my assistant and I roamed the playground to keep an eye on would-be fighters and coke-pile climbers.

Things were remarkably tranquil, reflecting the golden summer day about us, and I was beginning to relax into my usual mood of vague well-being when Hilary spoke.

'I heard that the school may have to shut before long? Is there any truth in it?'

I came to earth with a jolt. 'Where did you hear of this?'

'Oh, at my digs. My landlady's old friend was visiting her yesterday evening, and she lives at Beech Green, and there seemed to be a pretty strong rumour that our children will be going there before long.'

So our affairs were already being discussed in Caxley! Not that I was surprised, having lived in a village and knowing how rapidly word is passed from one to another. Nevertheless, it was beginning to look as though something definite must be heard soon from official sources if so many people were assuming that the matter was settled.

'If it's true,' continued Hilary, 'I don't think I should have applied for this post. It's very unsettling to have a short time in one's first school and then have to find somewhere else.'

I could quite see her point of view. She was beginning to wonder if we had kept things from her, and I hastened to explain.

'Truthfully, these are only rumours, and we are no nearer a decision now than we were when you came for interview. If there had been anything known definitely, you would have been told. General policy is to close small schools, but it may be years before Fairacre's turn comes.'

I felt it right that she should know that the managers were resisting any such move, and that if need arose there might well be a village meeting to find out more about local opinion, and I told her so.

'This far from happy position lasted for over ten years at Springbourne,' I told her. 'It's always a long drawn out thing. I feel sure that your post wouldn't have been advertised at all, if there had been any thought of closing in the near future, so I think you can look forward to several years here, if you want to stay.'

The girl looked much relieved. 'I think I *shall* want to, you know. It's a lovely place to teach, and the children seem angelic.'

At that moment, two children fell upon each other with the ferocity of starving tigers upon their prey, and a ring of interested spectators assembled to cheer them on.

'You spoke too soon,' I said, striding into the centre of things.

August slipped into September, and the signs of early autumn were all around us. Already the scarlet berries of the wild roses and crimson hawthorn beaded the hedges, and old man's beard made puffs of smoke-like grey fluff here and there.

In the cottage gardens, the dahlias made a brave show, and the last of the summer annuals, love-in-a-mist, marigolds and verbena added colour in the borders. It was a time to enjoy the last of the summer, for already it was getting chilly in the evenings, and I had lit an occasional fire in my sitting-room, much to Mrs Pringle's disgust.

I had purposely refrained from asking about Minnie's affairs. The lady still flapped about my premises on Friday afternoons, like a demented hen, and wet dusters appeared in the unlikeliest places. By now I was resigned to my lot and had given up hope of ever being free of her attentions.

But one afternoon, Mrs Pringle accosted me when she

appeared to wash up the crockery after school dinner. Her mouth was turned down ominously, and her limp seemed more pronounced to me.

'Got trouble at 'ome,' she said, 'I'll be off as soon as I've done the pots.'

'What is it? Not Minnie again?'

She nodded portentously, like a Chinese mandarin at his most impressive.

'Ah! Minnie it is! That girl and them kids of hers come up my place just now, because Ern's arrived.'

'Where? At Springbourne?'

'That's right. She left him cooking sausages and chips. I must say he'd had the decency to bring the sausages with 'im. Probably knew our Minnie wouldn't 'ave nothing worth eating in the house. Strikes me they lives on cornflakes.'

'Is she staying with you?'

'She'd better not. She knows my feelings on the matter. I've told her to clear off home, but she won't take a hint, that girl.'

Some hint, I thought, but Mrs Pringle was in full spate and I was obliged to listen to the unedifying tale.

'She seems scared stiff of that fellow, and I reckons when Bert turns up after work, there'll be a proper set-to atween 'em. Well, I told her straight: "The house is in your name now. You pays the rent to the Council, so your place is inside it." After all, that Ern – or Bert, for that matter – is no more than paying guests, only they don't pay, and if Minnie would only stand her ground, she could get rid of both of them.'

'But will she?' I managed to slip in, as Mrs Pringle drew breath.

'You may well ask,' said Mrs Pringle, unrolling a flowered overall and donning it ready for her session at the sink. 'Sometimes I wonders,' she went on, 'if our Minnie is quite right in the head, I really do.'

I could have told her, but common civility kept me silent.

PART THREE

Fate Lends a Hand

* * *

15. Two Ladies in Trouble

Autumn is one of the loveliest times at Fairacre. We are not as wooded as Beech Green, but small copses at the foot of the downs turn to bronze and gold as soon as the first frosts come, and the tall elm trees near the school send their lemon-yellow leaves fluttering down. A few sturdy oak trees rise from the neighbouring hedges, and these are the last to turn, but when they do, usually sometime in November, their colour is superb.

Now the children arrive with poisonous-looking toadstools for the nature table, and sprays of blackberries, mostly hard and red fruits remaining, as the juicy black ones have vanished down young throats on the way.

We do well for nuts, too, in this area, and walnuts from cottage gardens, sweet chestnuts and beech nuts from the woods, and hazel nuts from the hedgerows also find their way to school. Horse chestnuts, of course, are put to more vigorous use, and the strings of conkers lie coiled on the long desk at the side of the classroom, awaiting their owners at playtime.

This year we were lucky enough to have a sunny October, with those peculiarly clear skies of autumn which show up the glory of blazing leaves. We took a great many nature walks, watching the flocks of rooks stabbing the newly ploughed furrows for worms and leatherjackets, and noting the starlings, excited and chattering as they wheeled around the sky, the flock getting larger and larger until they decided it was time to set off to their chosen roost.

The swallows had already gone, of course. During September, they had perched upon telegraph wires in the village, preening themselves and twittering noisily, preparing for their flight of thousands of miles to warmer sunshine than Fairacre could provide.

In village gardens, the first bonfires were appearing, and wreaths of blue smoke scented the air with the true essence of autumn. Mr Willet was already planning where to plant his broad beans: 'You can't beat Aqua-Dulce Long-pod for planting in November,' he assured me. 'A good sturdy grower, and it beats that blighted black fly if it gets a fair start.'

The holidaymakers were back from exotic climes, and comparing notes on the beauties of Spain and Italy, and the price of a cup of coffee in Paris and St Mark's Square, Venice. These people, of course, were the more leisured among us. Most of us had taken our breaks, if any, in July or August, ready for the new school year.

I was invited to a cheese and wine party at the Mawnes. Proceeds were to go to the Royal Society for the Protection of Birds, of which both Mawnes were strong supporters. As the house is a lovely Queen Anne specimen, and the furniture is a joy to behold, I walked along the village that evening with more than usual pleasure. The older I get the less I want to leave my own home in the evenings, particularly bleak ones, but it was pleasant to stroll through the gentle darkness, catching sight of the various village cats setting off on their hunting expeditions, and savouring the whiff of bonfires still hanging upon the quiet air.

The house was ablaze with lights, and more than a dozen cars were lined up in the drive. I was glad I had not brought mine to add to the congestion. Far too often I have been the poor wretch penned in behind some glossy monster whose owner always seems to be the last to leave.

The village appeared to have turned out in force, and I was soon going the rounds, glass in hand, meeting Mary and Margaret Waters, two elderly spinsters of whom I am very fond, the Lambs from the Post Office, with Mr Lamb's brother from America and his wife, the Hales from Tyler's Row, a comparative newcomer, Miss Quinn, with her landlady Joan Benson, and a host of other friends.

Mrs Mawne, resplendent in black and gold, introduced me to a middle-aged man called Cecil Richards.

'A fellow ornithologist of Henry's,' explained Mrs Mawne. 'Well more than that really. Sissle here has just had a book published. About fishing, isn't it?'

'Yes, indeed. *With Rod in Rutland* is the title.'

I said I must look out for it.

'And Sissle has had others published,' said Mrs Mawne proudly. 'Wasn't *Beagling in Bucks* the last one?'

'No. *Hunting in Hereford*,' replied Cecil reprovingly.

I felt tempted to ask when *Winkling in Wilts* was coming out, but restrained my flippancy. Obviously, this particular writer took his work seriously, unlike Basil Bradley, our local novelist, who turns out a well-written book a year with a Regency buck as hero and a score of gorgeous girls with ringlets and fans. He aims to entertain, and makes no secret of it.

'You must find writing very hard work,' I said politely.

'Not at all. I find it pleasantly relaxing.'

I remembered reading that: 'Anyone who claims to write

easily must be either a terrible writer or a terrible liar,' but naturally did not quote this to Cecil Richards.

'Ah,' said Mrs Mawne, 'here comes Diana Hale. I know she wants to meet Sissle.'

I bowed away gratefully, only to find that I was in the midst of a three-cornered discussion on holidays.

'You really need a couple of years in Florence to see it properly,' Henry Mawne was saying to Mrs Partridge. 'Did you see Michelangelo's house?'

'We saw his "David",' replied Mrs Partridge.

'Well, naturally,' said Henry. 'But *everyone* sees his "David". The house brings it all to life. You went to Siena, of course?'

'Well, no. We didn't have time.'

'Siena is a *must*,' said Joan Benson. 'I think I really enjoyed Siena more than Florence itself. Those beautiful Duccios in the museum by the Duomo! You really should have gone to Siena.'

'I found the leather school at the Santa Croce one of the most interesting things,' continued Henry. 'I bought this wallet there.' He fished in a back pocket, juggling dangerously with his wine glass, and produced a wallet worn with age.

'Lovely,' agreed Mrs Partridge. 'I bought a handbag on the Ponte Vecchio.'

'On the Ponte Vecchio?' echoed Henry, with horror. 'My dear lady, you must have been mad to buy anything there! You can get the same thing much cheaper in those nice shops near the Bargello!'

I was beginning to feel very sorry for poor Mrs Partridge being batted between the two Florence snobs.

Henry suddenly became conscious of my presence.

'And where did you go this year?' he asked.

'Clacton,' I said, and was rewarded with Mrs Partridge's smile.

Half-term came and went, and a long spell of dark weather, with pouring rain and high winds, set in.

School playtimes became an endurance test for all. Deprived

of their usual exercise in the playground, the children became cross at their enforced incarceration. The tattered comics re-appeared, the jigsaw puzzles, the second-best sets of crayons, and the balls of plasticine, multi-hued by careless hands which had rolled various colours together, were brought out of the cupboard to try to assuage their frustration.

It was uphill work to keep them happily occupied. The first colds of winter swept the classroom, and sneezes, sniffs and coughs rent the air. A large box of tissues seemed to be ex-hausted in two days, and my pleas for them to bring their own, or to bring a handkerchief, fell on deaf ears. The tortoise stoves took to smoking, as they do when the wind gets into a certain quarter, and the skylight, as always, dripped steadily, as the rain swept viciously across the playground.

It was during this bleak period that I received another missive from the Office. It informed me that due note had been taken of the findings at the managers' meeting held some time earlier, and that my own comments were being considered. It was only right to point out, it went on to say, that reorganization of schools in the area was now advancing steadily, and that the possible closure of Fairacre School could not be ruled out.

'Back to square one,' I observed to Tibby, who was trifling with a portion of expensive cat food, much appreciated by the cat in the television advertisement, but not by my fastidious friend.

'Now what?' I wondered.

My problems were further complicated on the next Friday by Minnie Pringle's.

My heart sank when I opened the door and heard the crash of the hand brush against the sitting-room skirting board. Since Minnie's advent, all the skirting boards have been severely dented, and now resemble hammered pewter. I think she feels that the edge of the carpet has not been properly cleaned without a hefty swipe at the skirting board with each movement. My remonstrances have made not the slightest impression, and I doubt if Minnie realizes the damage she is doing. At one stage, I forbade her to touch the hand brush, but that too was ignored.

'You're working overtime, Minnie,' I said.

She looked up from her demolition work, with a mad grin. 'It don't matter. I ain't got nowhere to go.'

I took the brush from her hand and put it on the table.

'You'd better sit down and tell me,' I said resignedly. At least the skirting board was spared for a time, but I had no doubt that my nerves would take a similar pounding.

Minnie sat on the extreme edge of a Victorian buttoned armchair, which, I knew from experience, was liable to tip forward abruptly if so used.

'Sit back, Minnie,' I advised her.

She wriggled forward another two inches, and I gave up. With any luck, her light weight would not affect the chair's balance.

'What's the matter now?'

'It's Bert. Him and Ern has been fighting.'

'Can't you tell them to go? I gather it's your house now, or so your aunt says.'

Minnie's eyes grew round with horror. 'Tell 'em to go?' she echoed. 'They don't take no notice of what I says. Anyway, Ern's gone.'

'Then what's the trouble? I thought Bert was a lodger – paying guest, I mean – so surely you can give him notice, if you want to?'

'He don't pay.'

'All the more reason for pushing him out!'

Minnie twisted her dirty fingers together unhappily. 'It's not that. It's 'is 'itting me I don't like.'

'I thought you said it was Ern and Bert that were fighting.'

'Well, it was, first off. Then when Ern went back to Caxley to give old Mrs Fowler a piece of 'is mind, Bert turned sort of nasty and took a strap to me.'

I thought that 'turned sort of nasty' was the understatement of the year if it involved attacking the minute Minnie with a strap.

'Look here,' I said, 'I think you had better have a word with Bert's employers at Springbourne Manor. Let them speak to him.'

Minnie looked more horrified than ever. 'They'd give 'im the sack, most like, and then 'e'd take it out on me. He's 'orrible strong, is Bert. I'd almost sooner have Ern. 'E never used the strap.'

'Well, you seem in a pretty pickle, I must say,' I said severely. 'Why has Ern gone back to Caxley? I thought he had left Mrs Fowler.'

'She gave him the push, and now he's hollering for the furniture what he pinched from our house. 'E reckons Mrs Fowler's flogged it.'

Despair began to overtake me. Heaven knows, I do my best to simplify my own life, and even so I am beset by irksome complications. To confront someone like Minnie, whose relationships with others are a hopeless tangle, makes my rational mind boggle. Where can one begin to help?

'Well, Minnie, what do you propose to do? I take it Mrs Pringle can't put you up, and you certainly can't stay here. You really must try and get Bert to go away if he's becoming violent.'

Minnie looked vaguely surprised, and wriggled nearer the edge of the chair. As expected, it tipped forward and pitched her on to the carpet, where she remained seated, looking perfectly at ease.

'Oh, I don't want Bert to go. 'E's a good chap apart from the strap. I daresay 'e'll be all right if I gets 'im a good bit of steak for his tea.'

I began to feel somewhat dizzy. This frequently happens during a conversation with Minnie. She veers from one point to another like a storm-battered weathercock.

'Surely, that will cost a mint of money? I shouldn't feel inclined to cook an expensive steak for someone who hit me.'

'Only with a strap,' said Minnie earnestly. 'Could have been 'is belt. Buckle end.'

I gave up, and rose to end the interview. 'Your money's on the mantel shelf,' I said wearily.

She gave me a radiant smile. 'Do just right for Bert's steak,' she said, reaching for the hand brush.

But I got there first.

Not long after this encounter, the village was staggered to hear that Mrs Coggs had been caught shop-lifting in Caxley, and was due to appear in Court.

I could not believe it when Mrs Pringle informed me of the fact. 'But it seems so absurd,' I protested, 'when she's better off now than ever she was! She told me herself that she had never had so much money to manage on.'

'That's why she went to Caxley,' said Mrs Pringle, with a trace of smugness which riled me. 'When she didn't have no money to spend she stayed home. Come she got to the shops in Caxley she was Tempted and Fell.'

It all seemed very odd, and very sad, to me. What had she bought, I asked?

Mrs Pringle bridled. 'She never *bought*. That was the trouble. She *thieved*. As far as I can gather, it was things like rashers and sausages and a great bag of them frozen chips.'

At least a change from bread and sauce, I thought, though no doubt the poor children were still having that ghastly fare.

'Perhaps she just forgot to pay,' I said. 'It happens.'

Mrs Pringle snorted. 'Likely, ain't it! Anyway, she said straight out she'd nicked 'em.' Her dour countenance showed a rare streak of pleasure. 'D'you reckon she'll get put inside? Fancy them both being in prison, at the same time!'

'I shouldn't think so for a moment,' I said shortly. 'And isn't it about time the stoves were filled?'

If looks could have killed, I should have been a writhing corpse by the fireguard, but I was only vouchsafed the back view of my cleaner retreating from the fray with a heavy limp.

Most people, it transpired, felt as bewildered as I did at Mrs Coggs' behaviour, and the general feeling in the village was one of sympathy. The vicar had promised to appear in Court to speak on her behalf, and one of Mr Lovejoy's juniors was to appear for her. Mrs Coggs herself, I heard, hardly seemed to realize what was happening. She made no attempt to excuse her actions, not in any mood of defiance, but simply in her usual mood of apathy. It was all very puzzling.

Our butcher's comments seemed to echo Mrs Pringle's way of thinking.

'She's a poor tool as we all know, Miss Read. Let's face it, she wasn't born over-bright, and any wits she had have been knocked out of her by Arthur. I reckon she got carried away when she saw all the things in Caxley.'

'But she is better off now than ever,' I repeated.

'Yes, but not all that much better off. I mean, she's had a taste of spending a bit extra, and it's gone to her head. When she lives as she usually does, it's hand-to-mouth. She comes in here for a chop for Arthur, never anything for herself and the children. To tell you the truth, I've often given her meat scraps and told her to make a stew or a pudding, but it's my belief she doesn't know how to cook at all. How they manage I can't think.'

Another customer arrived, and we were forced to terminate our conversation, but it gave me food for thought.

We all agreed that as this was a first offence, imprisonment surely was out of the question, although Mr Roberts with unusual severity, said it might be an example to other light-fingered neighbours. However, as we heard later, twenty or so sheep belonging to him had that night been stolen from the downs, within two miles of his home, and naturally his judgement was coloured by his loss.

'And if she's fined, then who is to pay it?' asked another. 'The Social Security people? Meaning us?'

'She might just get a ticking-off,' said one hopeful. 'That

Colonel Austin's got a sharp tongue they tells me, specially with poachers.'

'She might get a conditional discharge,' said Mr Lamb, with such authority that his few customers awaiting their pensions or postage stamps began to wonder if he had first-hand knowledge of Courts and their procedure.

It was thus that we anticipated the Court's decision. Meanwhile, we had to wait and hope that, when the time came, Mrs Coggs' case would evoke mercy as well as justice from the Bench.

16. SNOW

The end of the Christmas term came suddenly upon us, and we were caught up in a whirl of parties, concerts, and carol services. Added to these school and village activities were the personal ones of shopping for Christmas presents, trying to find out the correct time to post parcels to friends overseas, and stocking the larder for what looked like being the longest public holiday on record.

'You wouldn't think the country was dead broke,' commented Peter Hale acidly, when I met him in the village street, 'when you hear that the local factories are closing until January 4th or roundabout.'

I found myself buying mounds of food against the siege, and having considerable difficulty in packing it away. Does everyone, I wondered, as I stacked away tins of this and that, imagine that starving families are going to arrive after all the shops have shut, and will be obliged to stay for days because of sudden blizzards? I always over-estimate my own – and my imaginary visitors' – needs, at these times, and never learn my lesson.

Because of this unwanted bustle, the question of the closure of Fairacre School seemed to be in a state of suspended animation, and I was relieved to have something else to worry over.

But, all too soon, the festivities were over, the Christmas decorations were taken down, I continued to eat left-overs and term started.

It was quite apparent that we were in for a bleak spell of weather. The wind had whipped round to the north-east, and every night brought us frost. The ground was sodden after the heavy rains of autumn, and long puddles in the furrows froze into hard ice. At the sides of the lanes of Fairacre more ice lay in the gutters, and the children had a wonderful time making slides on their way to school.

'Cruel weather,' said Mr Willet. 'My greens look fair shrammed. What with the weather, and the pigeons, and all them other birds, I sometimes wonder why I bothers to grow them. If I had my way I'd stick to root crops, but my old woman says we must have a bit of winter greens, so I doos my best. 'Tis a thankless task though, when the winter's like this.'

'As long as we don't get snow,' I said.

Mr Willet looked surprised. 'Snow?' he echoed. 'You'll get that aplenty, my dear, and afore the week's out too.'

As usual, he was right.

It began during the dinner hour, while the children were tearing about digesting, I hoped, steak and kidney pie and pink blancmange. Hilary was on playground duty, and I was cutting up painting paper for the afternoon session, when the class-room door burst open to reveal a knot of panting children, proudly displaying the spatters of snow on their clothes.

'Snowing, miss! Ennit lovely? It's snowing! And it's laying too.'

They were much too excited to have understood the different uses of the verbs 'to lie' and 'to lay', and anyway I have almost given up hope of any success in that direction.

I contented myself with telling them to let Miss Norman know that they must all come in to school. They clanged over the door scraper with enough noise for a mechanized army, and I went to the window to see the worst.

The snowflakes were coming down in great flurries, whirling and turning until the eyes of the beholder were dazzled. The icy playground was white already, and the branches of the elm trees would soon carry an edging of snow several inches deep. Across the playground, sitting inside the window of my dining-room, I could see Tibby watching the twirling flakes as interestedly as I was doing.

The snow hissed against the glass, but that sibilant sound was soon drowned in the stamping of feet in the lobby and the excited voices of the children. I could see we were in for a boisterous afternoon. Wind is bad enough for raising children's spirits to manic level. Snow is even more potent a force.

I judged it best to give out the paints and paper as soon as the register had been called, for it was quite apparent that my voice could never compete with the drama that was going on outside the windows.

'You can paint a snow scene,' I said, working on the principle that if you can't beat your rival you join him.

'What like?' said Ernest.

Our Fairacre children are chary of anything involving the imagination. If I had told them to paint the tasteful arrangement of dried flowers and leaves, concocted by Amy and kept on my desk, they would have set to without a word. But to be asked to create a picture from nothing, as it were, filled them with dismay.

I used to be rather hard on them, refusing to suggest themes, and urging them to use their imaginations. But they are genuinely perturbed by these forays into the unknown, and advancing age has made me somewhat kinder.

'Well, now, you could make a picture of yourselves running about in a snowy playground. Or making a slide.'

'Or a snowman?' suggested Patrick, in a burst of inspiration.

'Quite. Or a picture of men clearing the snow away from the roads. Perhaps digging a car out of a snow drift.'

'Or a bus,' said Ernest, 'Only I ain't got much red for a bus. Might do a tractor.'

They seemed to be fairly launched now, and they began their attempts without too much hesitation. A fierce argument broke out, at one point, about the best way of depicting snow flakes which looked black as they came down, but which one knew were white really, and anyway *turned white* when they reached the ground. Linda Moffat said she was going to leave spots of paper showing through her sky, to look like snow. Joseph Coggs said they'd look like stars then, and anyway the sky wasn't blue like that, it was 'grey sort of'.

Altogether, it was a distracting art session, considerably enlivened by the constant uprising of children looking to see how deep the snow was in the playground. Certainly, by the time their afternoon break arrived, the snow was thick enough for Hilary to consult me about sending the infants home early.

'I think the whole school had better go early,' I replied. The sky was low and heavy with snow to come, and there was no respite from the blizzard around us.

The news was greeted with even greater excitement. One or two were apprehensive because their mothers were still at work.

'I knows where our key is,' said one. 'It's in the secret place in the coal hole. I can easy get in.'

'Old Bert can come in my house till his mum gets back,' offered another, and gradually we were able to account for all the children's safety from the storm.

Except, as it happened, for the Coggs children. No one seemed to offer to have them. Mrs Coggs was out at work and would not be home until after three-thirty. I was not very surprised that there were no invitations from the other children. For one thing, the Coggs had no near neighbours with children at the school. For another, the Coggs family has always been a little ostracized by the more respectable villagers, and I had a suspicion that since Mrs Coggs' shop-lifting escapade, the family was even less popular. So far, her case had not been heard, but as she herself admitted her guilt, there were quite a few who censored her, and her innocent children.

'You'd better come home with me,' I said to the three, 'and I'll run you home when your mother is back.'

They waited patiently by the tortoise stove, warming their

grubby hands, while Hilary and I buttoned and tied the others into their outdoor clothes and threatened them with all manner of retribution if they forbore to go straight home.

They vanished with whoops of joy into the veils of snow which swept the outside world, and I ushered my three visitors across the playground to my warm sitting-room.

I had had the foresight to light the fire at dinner time, and by now it was a clear red glow, ideal for making toast, which no doubt would be welcomed before taking the children home.

Joseph was inclined to be unusually self-confident in front of his little sisters. After all, his attitude seemed to say, I know this place. You don't.

They watched me cut some substantial slices of bread. The toasting fork intrigued them, and I set them to make toast while I brewed a pot of tea which I really did not need, but it made an excuse to pass the time before Mrs Coggs returned.

Their faces were flushed with heat and excitement. They handled the toast reverently.

'Never cooked toast,' announced Joseph. 'Never knew a fire done cooking like this.'

I remembered that the Council houses had a closed stove for cooking and heating the water. But surely, there was an open fire in the living room?

'We never lights that,' said Joseph, slightly shocked. 'Us has the electric if it's cold.'

And pretty cheerless too, I thought. No wonder that the children enjoyed my fire, and their first attempts at toast-making.

They demolished several slices of their handiwork, plentifully spread with butter and honey. Outside, the snow drifted along the window ledges, and settled on the roofs and hedges. It was time we made a move before the snow became too deep to open the garage door.

Mrs Coggs had just arrived home when we reached their house. I saw them indoors with a sinking heart. It looked as sordid, and was certainly as smelly, as ever.

Driving back through the driving snow, I pondered on the differences between neighbours and their surroundings in such a tiny place as Fairacre. I was not comparing the fairly well-to-do such as the Mawnes and Hales, with those who had very little, but people like the Willets, for instance, or my sparring partner Mrs Pringle, who really had no more money coming into their homes than Mrs Coggs had at the moment. In most of the homes in Fairacre, one could be sure of finding a welcome. There would be a fire in winter, a cup of tea or coffee offered, biscuits or a slice of home-made cake, or a glass of home-made wine (deceptively innocuous, incidentally) put into one's hand. The house would be as welcoming as the householder. There would be the smell of furniture polish, the gleam of burnished brass and copper, and a bunch of flowers from the garden standing on the window sill.

It was lucky that Mrs Coggs was in the minority in our little community, I thought, as I put away the car and shuffled through the snow to my own home.

But hard luck on those children!

It snowed, off and on, for over three weeks, and a very trying time was had by all. Mrs Pringle seemed to take the snow as a personal insult directed towards her by a malevolent weather-god, and loud were her daily lamentations about the state of the school floors, and the wicked way the children brought the snow inside on their boots.

It was useless to try and placate her, and useless too to bully the children into greater care. The snow was everywhere and, after a time, I decided that the only thing to do was to be philosophical about it.

'It can't last for ever,' I said, trying to comfort my surly cleaner. 'Look, the catkins are showing on the hedge!'

'Sure sign the spring-cleaning will want doing,' replied Mrs Pringle, enjoying her misery.

Irritated though I was by her dogged determination to see the gloomy side of things, I was not blind to the fact that she was not looking at all well. One day I ventured to comment on it. Was she still dieting?

She gave a grunt. 'I lost two pounds last month, and even that never pleased Dr Martin. He's a hard taskmaster that one. I wouldn't care to be under the knife when he's holding the handle. "Got no feelings," I told him straight, I get the stummer-cake something awful some nights, but he only laughs when I tell him.'

'Perhaps you are doing too much,' I said, in an unguarded moment.

Mrs Pringle rose to the bait beautifully. 'Of course, I'm doing too much! It's me nature. "You're a giver, not a taker, my girl," my old mother used to say, and I fair gets wore out. What with this 'ere school to keep clean – well, *try* to keep clean would be truer – and our Minnie driving me mad and the worry over this place closing next year—'

'Closing next year?' I echoed in astonishment. 'Who told you that?'

Mrs Pringle looked surprised in her turn. 'Why, it's general knowledge in the village! And at Beech Green, and at Caxley, come to that. Why else are they havin' new buildings at Mr Annett's? And what about that managers' meeting? I tell you, Miss Read, you must be the last person to know. It's the talk of the parish, and a fine old rumpus there's going to be before long!'

I gazed at her, speechless with dismay. All my old worries, suspended for some weeks, and ignored because of more pressing claims on my time, now flocked back to haunt me, like so many evil birds.

'So it's no wonder I'm not meself,' continued Mrs Pringle, with some satisfaction. 'I can feel meself growing old afore my time. It's as much as I can do to get round my own housework these days, let alone this lot. You'll see my place looking like Mrs Coggs' before long, I shouldn't wonder.'

'Never!' I said, finding my voice.

'Which reminds me,' said my cleaner, picking a piece of squashed clay from the front desk, 'that silly woman's been in Court, and got to go again in three weeks.'

'Why?'

'Them magistrates want reports on her before passing sentence. At least that's what the *Caxley Chronicle* said.' She snorted with disgust. 'Reports! I ask you! I could have given 'em a report on Mrs Coggs, on the spot. It wouldn't have needed three weeks, if I'd been consulted!'

She straightened up and went, limping pathetically, to the lobby.

'Bring any more of that dratted snow in here,' I heard her shout threateningly, 'and I'll larrup the lot of you!'

'Can't help it,' Patrick shouted back impudently. 'And anyway, it's started again, so there'll be lots more, for days and days and days!'

He sounded exceedingly happy about it, Mrs Pringle's

rumblings could be heard in answer, but I could not catch the exact words.

Above the turmoil Patrick's clear treble rang out triumphantly. 'And anyway, I likes it!'

17. Renewed Fears

The Court at Caxley meets twice a week, and Mrs Coggs duly appeared three weeks after her first attendance.

The vicar had promised to escort her, and to make himself available to speak on her behalf, should the magistrates so allow, but on the very day of the hearing Mr Partridge was stricken with gastric influenza, and was obliged to keep to his bed.

Mrs Partridge, having left various drinks and some very unpleasant medicine on the bedside table, left the patient and collected Mrs Coggs herself. The vicar, ill as he was, nevertheless struggled into an upright position for long enough to write a letter to the Court expressing his view on Mrs Coggs' hitherto blameless character, and his apologies for absence.

Armed with this, Mrs Partridge entered the annexe to the Court and prepared to wait indefinitely with her luckless companion.

When the case was called, Mrs Coggs faced the Bench with apathetic bewilderment, and Mrs Partridge sat at the back, feeling over-awed by the general solemnity.

Reports were handed up to the magistrates by the probation officer, and silence reigned as they perused them. Every now and again old Miss Dewbury gave a snort of disgust. Her fellow-magistrates were quite used to this. It did not express shock at the facts presented by the probation officer, but simply impatience with such dreadful phrases as 'peer group', 'siblings' and 'meaningful relationship' with which such reports are invariably sprinkled, and which drove Miss Dewbury, as a lover of plain English, near to despair.

Mrs Partridge gave the vicar's letter to the usher, who duly gave it to the clerk, who gave it to the magistrates, to add to their papers.

At length, Colonel Austin rose saying gruffly: 'The Bench will retire to consider this case,' and the three magistrates, papers in hand, made their way to the fastness of the retiring room. The clerk to the justices, the usher, the solicitors and general public were just wondering if there would be time for a quick cup of hot liquid, from a machine in the lobby labelled TEA or COFFEE but bearing no resemblance to either, or better still a hasty smoke, when the magistrates returned and hope was deferred.

'We propose,' said Colonel Austin to the trembling Mrs Coggs, 'to make a probation order for a period of two years. Just listen carefully.'

He turned over a dozen or so pages of a booklet before him. His fellow-magistrates were used to this delay, and their chairman's growing impatience as he stumbled through 'Taking the Oath on the Koran', 'Conditional Discharge' and other irrelevant matters, and were relieved when their ever-ready clerk leapt to his feet and found the place for him, with the sort of fatherly smile fond papas give their offspring when they have tracked down the collect for the day at matins.

Colonel Austin read out the order in a military fashion, and on being asked if she would comply with the requirements, Mrs Coggs said: 'Yes, please, sir. Yes, sir, thank you.'

'You may stand down,' said Colond Austin, and Mrs Coggs, still quaking, was led by the usher to Mrs Partridge who accompanied her from the Court, closely pursued by the probation officer.

'She got off lightly,' said Mrs Pringle later to me. 'Wouldn't have got probation in my mother's day. I wonder they didn't let her off altogether.'

'It means that someone will have access to the household,' I said mildly, 'and surely that's a good idea. Arthur will be out before her probation order ends, and I think it is a very good thing that she'll be having some guidance then.'

'But what about them things she took? Never paid for 'em!'

'They were returned at the time,' I said.

'Well, I wouldn't want to eat anything Mrs Coggs had been handling,' said Mrs Pringle, determined to have the last word and making sure by leaving me rapidly.

The rumours of closure still rumbled about the village, but I did my best to ignore them, despite inner qualms.

George Annett, however, brought all my fears to the fore again by calling in on choir practice night to acquaint me with a new problem.

'I heard today,' he said, 'that Mrs Allen is leaving at the end of this term. She's only got a couple of years to do, but her husband has had a stroke, and she's decided to give up now. What about it?'

I felt a little nettled. I like plenty of time to consider things. Too much, Amy tells me. Some things are better decided at once.

'What about what?' I said, to gain time.

'Putting in for the post, of course,' said George impatiently. 'It's one of the largest junior schools in Caxley, and very well thought of. Suit you well.'

'I don't think I really want it,' I said, slowly, 'and anyway, after such a small school as this one, I doubt if I stand a chance.'

'Rubbish!' exclaimed George. 'You're damn well qualified, and you know the county want to appoint from their own people at the moment, before advertising. You stand as good a chance, or better, than the rest. You think about it, my girl.'

He vanished churchwards, and left me in turmoil.

How I hate having to make a decision! I have the reputation, I heard once with amazement, of making up my mind very swiftly. The answer is that I find suspense so exhausting that I decide quickly in order to cut short the agony.

Now, here I was again, faced with 'Shall I?' or 'Shan't I?' and very unpleasant I found it. Mrs Allen's school was on one of the new estates on the edge of Caxley, and had earned a shining reputation for solid schooling with fun thrown in. It would be a post which would attract a great many applicants, and I spoke truly when I told Mr Annett that my chances would be slight.

On the whole, I felt that I should be wasting my time to apply. Then too, there was the problem of a house. No doubt, I should be allowed to stay on at Fairacre for a time, but if the school closed, then presumably the school house would be sold when the rest of the property came on the market.

I certainly had no money to buy a house in Caxley, and anyway, would I want one? Oh dear, why did George have to unsettle me like this?

I pottered about distractedly in the kitchen, wet dishcloth in hand, wiping the top of the cooker. The stains seemed worse than usual and I squeezed a large dollop of liquid cleaner on to the top and rubbed bemusedly.

If only I could hear something definite from the Office! It would be disastrous if I applied for that post and got it – some hope, I thought – and then found that Fairacre School was to stay as it was. What a problem!

The stains seemed to be a problem too, and on investigation, I found that I had squeezed a dollop of hand lotion instead of cleaner on to the surface. The stove was not improved.

I chucked the dishcloth into the sink and went to get a glass of sherry. At times, drink is a great solace.

The snow lingered on into February, lying under the hedges and along the sides of the lanes.

'Waiting for more to come,' Mr Willet told me, with morose satisfaction. 'I fair 'ates to see it laying this time of year! Still plenty of weeks to get another lot.'

'Cheer up,' I said. 'There are some snowdrops in bud at the end of the garden, and some lovely yellow aconites showing. And the children brought catkins for the nature table – a bit stubby yet, but cheering all the same.'

'Well, you was always one for looking on the bright side,' said Mr Willet 'Heard any more about this 'ere school closing? Someone told me Mrs Allen's leaving. That'd suit you a treat, that school of hers. Should think about it, if I was you.'

As I had done exactly that for a considerable time, with no firm result, I found Mr Willet's remarks a little trying.

'No, I haven't heard any more,' I said, 'and I don't think I should get that job, even if I wanted it.'

'Well, there's plenty in the village thinks you would, when this place shuts up—'

'What do you mean? "When this place shuts up?" We don't know that it will!' I broke in crossly.

'No need to fly off the handle,' said Mr Willet. 'I'm only saying what's going the rounds in Fairacre. If you ask me, it's time the village had a say in this business. It's fair upsetting for us all, and we don't want to see you go. You knows that.'

I began to feel ashamed of my rudeness, and apologized.

'Oh, don't you let that trouble you,' replied Mr Willet easily. 'It's a worrying time, especially for you, and at a funny age.'

And on this unsatisfactory note he left me.

The vicar appeared at playtime, and I took him across the playground, dodging boisterous children in full flight, to have a cup of coffee while Hilary coped with playground duty.

The gastric influenza, which had prostrated him at the time of Mrs Coggs' Court appearance, had left him looking remarkably pale and shaky, and he seemed glad to put his moulting leopard skin gloves on the table beside the chair, and sip hot coffee. Tibby, unused to mid-morning visitors, graciously climbed on to his lap and purred a welcome.

'You really have the gift of making a proper home,' smiled Mr Partridge. 'And, of course, a cat is absolutely essential to that. I hope you'll be here for many, many years.'

'It rather depends on the county,' I told him. 'If only we knew!'

'It's about that that I've come,' said the vicar. My heart sank. Had he, as chairman of the managers, heard at last?

'I've no further news from the Office,' he said, and my heart started beating again, 'but there are so many rumours and conjectures going round the village that I've had a word with the other managers, and we feel we should call a public meeting to air our views.'

'An excellent idea!'

'I'm glad you agree. I feel we should put everything possible before that fellow Rochester—'

'*Salisbury*,' I broke in. 'Rochester was in *Jane Eyre*.'

'Of course. Salisbury then – so that the authority has some idea of the strong reaction to this proposal of closing the school. You'll be there, naturally.'

'When?'

'Now you're asking! It will need to be in the village hall, and what with the cubs and brownies, and square dancing, and Women's Institute and the muscular dystrophy jumble sale and three wedding receptions, it's quite a problem to find a date. However, something will turn up, and meanwhile we must put up posters, and perhaps the children could write a note to take home?'

'Willingly, but we shall have to know the date.'

The vicar picked up his gloves, deposited Tibby tenderly on another chair, from which the animal got down immediately with umbrage, and made for the door.

'So you will! What a wonderful grasp of affairs you have, Miss Read! I wish I were as practical. I think I'd better spend the rest of the morning working out a few dates with the managers, and then I'll call again with the result.'

He ploughed his way to the gate through the screaming mob, and smiled kindly upon one bullet-headed urchin who butted him heavily in the stomach as he fled from a pursuing playmate.

'A thoroughly good man!' I told Tibby as I collected the coffee cups.

Amy called a few evenings later with an invitation to drinks at her house in Bent.

'And stay on to eat with us,' said Amy. 'The rest of them should have gone by eight, and we'll have a nice little cold collation ready, and a good natter.'

'Suppose they don't go?' I queried. 'I've been to lots of these dos – particularly before Sunday lunch, where the joint is getting more and more charred as the visitors all wait for other people to make a move, not realizing that the luckier ones are staying on.'

'That's why it will be cold,' said Amy. 'Please allow me to run my own parties as I wish. Sometimes you are a trifle bossy.'

'*Well!*' I said, flabbergasted. 'Talk about the pot calling the kettle black! You're the bossy one, as well you know!'

Amy laughed. 'I didn't come here to have a vulgar brawl, darling, but I should love a cigarette if you have such a thing in this non-smoking Paradise.'

'Of course, of course!' I said, reminded of my duties as a hostess. 'They're donkey's years old, as I only buy them when I go abroad and get them duty free, as you know. Still they should be a good vintage by now.'

Amy puffed elegantly, and seemed quite content.

'Are you trying for Mrs Allen's job when she goes?'

Not again, I thought despairingly.

'No, I don't think I am. I've been turning it over, and I really feel I can't be bothered until I know more definitely about the plans for this school.'

'I believe Lucy Colgate is trying for it,' said Amy, naming a contemporary of ours at college, whom I always detested.

'She's welcome,' I said shortly.

'She'll be at the party, incidentally,' said Amy, tapping ash from her cigarette with a rose-tipped finger.

'Well, it's your party, as you've already pointed out. I can be as civil as the next, I hope.'

'I can't think why you dislike her.'

'I don't actively dislike her. I just find her affected and a liar to boot.'

'She's very well connected. Her uncle's the Bishop of Some-where.'

'So what! It doesn't alter Lucy Colgate for me. However, I promise to behave beautifully when we meet.'

'She would have loved this place, you know. She always hoped you would apply for another job, so that she could come here.'

I began to feel decidedly more cheerful.

'Well, she won't have the opportunity now, will she? If Fairacre stays, then I do. If it closes, no headmistress will be necessary – not even horrible Lucy Colgate!'

Amy began to laugh, and I followed suit.

'Tell me the latest about Vanessa,' I said, changing the subject. 'How's that baby?'

'My dear, she's having another.'

'She can't be! She's only just had this one!'

'It can happen,' said Amy. 'It's not due for another seven months. She told me on the phone last night. I must say that in my young days one waited until one was quite five months gone, as the vulgar expression is, before admitting coyly to one's hopes. But there. I gather from a doctor friend, that you have to book your nursing home bed quite twelve months in advance, so I suppose there's no encouragement to be over-modest about the proceedings.'

'I'd better look out my knitting patterns for baby clothes again,' I said. 'I suppose she wouldn't like a tea-cosy this time? I'm halfway through one.'

'Try her,' advised Amy, looking at the clock. 'I suppose there's no chance of a cup of coffee?'

'I do apologize,' I said, making for the kitchen. 'I seem to have forgotten my manners.'

'You must take a lesson from dear Lucy,' said Amy wickedly, following me. 'Her manners are quite perfect, and what's more, she makes delicious coffee.'

'So do I,' I told her, putting on the kettle. 'When I think of it.'

A few days later the vicar appeared, waving a slip of paper in triumph.

'At last, my dear Miss Read! We have fixed a date, though at what cost of time and telephone calls I shudder to think. Here we are! It is for March 1st, a Friday. That seems to be the only free day for most of the managers. Henry Mawne has a lecture on sea birds to give in Caxley, but Mrs Mawne says she has heard it dozens of times and there will be no need for her to attend.'

I remembered how competently she looked after her dithering husband on these occasions, and asked if he would be able to manage without her support.

'Oh yes, indeed. George Annett is going and says he will see that Henry has his papers in order, and his spectacles and so on.'

As George Annett can be just as scatter-brained as Henry Mawne under pressure, I felt that it would be a case of the blind leading the blind, but forbore to comment.

'We'll copy this out today,' I assured the vicar, securing the slip of paper under the massive brass inkstand which has adorned the head teacher's desk here since the time of Queen Victoria.

'Splendid, splendid!' said Mr Partridge making for the door. 'It will be a good thing to see how the wind blows in the village. Nothing but good can come of airing our feelings, I feel sure.'

'Help me up with the blackboard, Ernest,' I said, as the door closed behind the vicar. 'We'll start straightaway on these notices.'

'Good,' said Ernest with approval. 'Save us doin' them 'orrible ol' fractions.'

'They'll come later,' I told him.

18. A Battle in Caxley

Spring came suddenly. We had grown so accustomed to the miserable dark days, and to the flecks of snow still dappling the higher ground, that to awake one morning to a blue sky and the chorus of birds seemed a miracle.

The wind had veered to the south-west at last, and moist warm air refreshed us all. The elms were beginning to show the rosy glow of early budding. The crocuses were piercing the wet ground, the birds were looking about for nesting sites and the world seemed decidedly more hopeful.

Even Mrs Pringle seemed a little less morose as she went about her duties and was heard singing 'Who Is Sylvia?' instead of 'Lead Kindly Light Amidst the Encircling Gloom'.

I complimented her, and was told that she 'learnt it up the Glee Club as a girl'.

It was good to have the schoolroom windows open, although I had to call upon Mr Willet to leave his usual coke-sweeping in the playground to give me a hand.

'They's stuck with the damp,' puffed Mr Willet, smiting the wooden frames with a horny hand. 'Needs to be planed really, but then, come the summer you'd get a proper draught. Bad as that there skylight.'

He looked at it gloomily.

'Useless to waste time and money on it. Been like that since I sat here as a boy, and will be the same when I'm dead and gone, I shouldn't wonder.'

'You're down in the dumps today,' I teased. 'Not like you.'

Mr Willet sighed. 'Had bad news. My brother's gone home.'

'I'm sorry,' I said, and was doubly so – for his unhappiness and for my own misplaced levity. The old country phrase for dying, 'gone home', has a melancholy charm about it, a finality, a rounding off.

'Well, he'd been bad some time, but you know how it is, you don't ever think of anyone younger than you going home, do you?'

'It's a horrible shock,' I agreed.

'That's the third death this year,' mused Mr Willet, his eyes on the rooks wheeling against the sky. The fresh air blew through the window, stirring the scant hair on his head.

'Like a stab wound, every time,' he said. 'Leaves a hole, and a little of your life-blood drains away.'

I could say nothing. I was too moved by the spontaneous poetry. Mr Willet's utterances are usually of practical matters, a broken hinge, a tree needing pruning or a vegetable plot to be dug. To hear such rich imagery, worthy of an Elizabethan poet, fall from this old countryman's lips, was intensely touching.

Mrs Pringle's entry with a bucket of coke disturbed our reverie.

'Well,' said Mr Willet, shaking himself back to reality. 'This won't do. Life's got to go on, ain't it?'

And he stumped away to meet it.

Minnie Pringle was still about her ministrations when I returned home on Friday afternoon. She was flicking a feather brush dangerously close to some Limoges china dishes which I cherish.

'Lawks!' she cried, arrested in her toil, 'I never knew it was that late! I never heard the kids come out to play, and the oil man ain't been by yet.'

'Well, it's quarter to four by the clock,' I pointed out.

Minnie gazed blearily about the room.

'On the mantelpiece,' I said. 'And there's another in the kitchen.'

'Oh, the *clock*!' said Minnie wonderingly. 'I never looks at the *clock*. I don't read the time that well. It's them two hands muddles me.'

I never cease to be amazed at the unplumbed depths of Minnie's ignorance. How she has survived so long unscathed is astounding.

'How do you know what time to set out from Springbourne to get here?' I asked.

'The bus comes,' replied Minnie simply.

I should like to have asked what happened if there were a bus strike, but there is a limit to one's time.

'I'd best be going then,' announced Minnie, collecting an array of dusters from an armchair.

'Don't bother to wash them, Minnie,' I said hastily. 'I'll do them later on. I have to wash some tea towels and odds and ends.'

It would be a treat, I thought, to see the dusters hanging on a line for a change. Their last Friday's resting place had been over a once shining copper kettle which stands in the sitting-room.

Minnie shrugged herself into a fur fabric coat which pretended to be leopard skin, and would have deceived no one – certainly not a leopard.

'Had a bust-up down home,' said Minnie, her face radiant at the memory.

'Not Ern!'

'Ah! It was too. 'E turned up when I was abed. Gone twelve it was 'cos the telly'd finished.'

'Good heavens! I hope you didn't let him in.'

'No, I done what auntie said, and put the kitchen table up agin the door, and I 'ollered down to him from the bedroom window.'

'And he went?'

Minnie sniffed, grinning with delight.

'Well, after a bit he went. He kep' all on about 'aving no place to sleep, and I said: "What about that ol' Mrs Fowler then?" and what he says back I wouldn't repeat to a lady like you.'

'I thought he'd left her long ago.'

'He went back for the furniture, and she wouldn't let 'im in, so he chucked a milk bottle at her, and there was a real set-to until the neighbours broke it up.'

'Who told you all this?'

'Jim next door. He took Ern into Caxley when 'e went in for the night shift. Said it was either that, or 'e'd tell the police 'e was molesting me.'

'He sounds a sensible sort of neighbour.'

'Oh, Jim's all right when he's not on the beer.'

'So what happened to Ern?'

'Jim dropped 'im at the end of the town. Ern's got a sorter cousin there would give 'im a doss down probably.'

'Well, I only hope he doesn't come again,' I said. 'You seem to have managed very well.'

'It's auntie really,' said Minnie. 'She's told me what to do, and I done it. Auntie nearly always wins when she has an up-and-a-downer with anybody.'

I could endorse that, I thought, seeing Minnie to the door.

I heard more about Ern's belligerence from Mrs Pringle, and later from Amy, whose window cleaner had the misfortune to live next door to Mrs Fowler in Caxley.

Town dwellers who complain of loneliness and having no one to talk to, should perhaps be thankful that they do not live in a village. Here we go to the other extreme. I never cease to be astonished at the speed with which news gets about. In this instance I heard from the three sources, Minnie, Mrs Pringle and Amy, of the Caxley and Springbourne rows, and all within three or four days. It is hopeless to try to keep anything secret in a small community, and long ago I gave up trying.

'Heard about that Ern?' asked Mrs Pringle.

I said I had.

'I must say our Minnie settled him nicely.'

'Thanks to you, I gather.'

Mrs Pringle permitted herself a gratified smirk. 'Well, you

knows Min. She's no idea how to tackle anyone, and that Ern's been a sore trial to us all. She gets in a panic for nothing.'

'I don't call midnight yelling "for nothing",' I objected.

'Well, they're married, aren't they?' said Mrs Pringle, as though that explained matters. 'Mind you,' she went on, lodging a full dustpan on one hip, 'we ain't heard the last of him. Now Mrs Fowler's done with him, I reckon he'll badger Min to take him back.'

'Where is he now?'

'Staying with that cousin of his, but she don't want him. He's got the sofa of nights, and the springs won't stand 'is weight. She told me herself when I saw her at the bus stop market day.'

'Is he working?'

Mrs Pringle snorted in reply. 'He don't know the meaning of the word! Gets the dole, I suppose. I told our Minnie: "Don't you have him back on no account, and certainly if he's out of a job! You'll be keeping 'im all 'is days, if you don't watch out." But there, I doubt if she really took it in. She's a funny girl.'

Amy's account, at second or third hand, covered the Caxley incident. According to her window cleaner, the rumpus started sometime after nine, when Ern, a little the worse for drink, arrived at Mrs Fowler's front door and demanded admittance.

Mrs Fowler's reply was to shoot the bolts on front and back doors, and to go upstairs to continue the argument from a bedroom window.

Ern called her many things, among them 'a vinegar-faced besom', 'a common thief' and 'a right swindling skinflint'. He accused her of trapping him into living there, and then taking possession of his rightful property, to wit, chairs, a table, pots and pans and a brass bird-cage of his Aunt Florence's.

Mrs Fowler, giving as good as she got, refuted the charges. He had given her the chattels of his own free will, and a poor lot they were anyway, not worth house room, and if he continued to molest a defenceless and respectable widow, whose husband had always been a paid-up member of the Buffaloes she would have him know, she would call for help.

After a few further exchanges, Ern, incensed, picked up the first handy missile, which happened to be an empty milk bottle standing in the porch, and flung it at his adversary's head. Mrs Fowler's screams of abuse, and the crash of glass, roused her neighbours, who until then had been hidden but fascinated observers of the scene, to open protest.

The window cleaner threatened to send for the police if they didn't pipe down and let honest people sleep and, amazingly enough, he was obeyed.

Ern, still muttering threats, slouched off, and presumably walked out to Springbourne in the darkness, and Mrs Fowler slammed the window and presumably went to bed.

'Obviously,' commented Amy, 'neither wanted the police brought in. I suspect that Mrs Fowler knows jolly well that she's hanging on to property that isn't hers, and Ern doesn't want to be run in for causing an affray, or whatever the legal term is.'

'I thought it was something to do with "behaviour occasioning a breach of the peace"!'

'Comes to the same thing,' said Amy carelessly. 'I feel very sorry for our window cleaner.'

'I reckon Ern is going to have a job to get his stuff back,' I said. 'Mrs Fowler was always avaricious. The Hales had trouble with her when she was their neighbour at Tyler's Row.'

'The best thing he can do,' replied Amy, 'is to cut his losses, find a job, and get Minnie to take him back.'

'Some hope,' I said. 'I can't see Mrs Pringle allowing that, even if Minnie would.'

'We must wait and see,' said Amy, quoting Mr Asquith.

The first day of March arrived, and came in like a lamb rather than the proverbial lion. Balmy winds had blown gently now for a week or more, a bunch of early primroses adorned my desk, and the blackbirds chattered and scowled as they trailed lengths of dried grass to their chosen nesting places.

With all these signs of spring to cheer one, it was impossible to worry about such things as schools closing, and I made my way to the village hall that evening in a mood of fatalistic calm. What would be, would be! I had got past caring one way or the other, after all the weeks of suspense.

There were a surprising number of villagers present, and all the managers, with the vicar in the chair. Mr Salisbury had been invited and sat in the front, with an underling from the Office holding a pad for taking notes.

The meeting was scheduled to start at seven-thirty, but it was a quarter to eight by the time the last stragglers arrived, puffing and blowing and excusing their lateness with such remarks as: 'Clock must've been slow' or 'Caxley bus was late again'.

'Well, dear people,' said the vicar at last, 'I think we must make a start. You know why this meeting has been called. So many people have been concerned about the possible closure of our school that it seemed right and proper for us to hear what is really happening, and to put our own views forward.

'We are lucky to have Mr Win – Mr Salisbury, I should say – here with us, to give us the official position, and I know you will all speak frankly about our feelings. He will, of course, answer any questions.'

He smiled at Mr Salisbury, who looked solemnly back at him.

'Perhaps you would care to outline official educational policy before we go further?' suggested the vicar.

Mr Salisbury rose, looking rather unhappy, and cleared his throat.

'I am very pleased to have been invited to meet you all this evening but I must confess that I am not at all sure that I can help a great deal.'

'Must know if the school's closing or not, surely to goodness,' grumbled old Mr Potts, who is somewhat deaf, and speaks as though everyone else is too.

'Our general policy,' continued Mr Salisbury, ignoring the interruption, 'is to provide the best service possible with the money available. Now you don't need me to tell you that times are hard, and we are all looking for the best way to stretch our money.'

'But what about the children?' called someone at the back of the hall.

'Exactly. As I was saying, we want to do our best for the children, and we have been looking very carefully at ways and means.

'A small school, say under thirty pupils, still needs two teachers and sometimes perhaps a third, for extra work. It needs cleaning, heating and supplying with all the hundred and one pieces of equipment found in a school.

'Now, it does seem sensible to put some of these smaller schools together, to make a more workable unit.'

'When's he coming to the point?' asked old Mr Potts of his neighbour.

'And so, for some time past, we have been going into this question very carefully. There are several small schools, such as Fairacre, in the area, and we think the children would benefit from being in larger ones. Let me add that nothing definite has been decided about closing this particular school. There would be consultations all the time with the managers, and parents too. That is why I am so glad to be here tonight, to answer your questions.'

'I've got one,' said Patrick's mother, leaping to her feet and addressing Mr Salisbury directly. The vicar, as chairman, made an ineffectual attempt to regularize the situation, but is so used to having the chair ignored that he becomes philosophical on these occasions, and really only intervenes when matters become heated.

'Do you think it's right that little children should have to get carted off in a bus, ever so early, and back again, ever so late – in the dark come winter-time, when they've always been used to walking round the corner to school?'

'I think "walking round the corner to school", as you put it, is the *ideal* way. But we don't live in an ideal world, I fear, and we have to make changes.'

'Then if it's ideal,' said Patrick's mother, 'why change it?' She sat down, pink with triumph.

Mr Salisbury looked a little weary. 'As I have explained, we have to do the best with the money available. Now, if we can put these small schools together to make one of viable size—'

'Now there's a word I *loathe*!' commented Mrs Mawne, in what she fondly imagined was a discreet whisper.

'It would seem the best solution,' continued Mr Salisbury, diplomatically deaf.

'Mr Chairman,' said Mr Roberts, who tries to keep to the rules at our meetings, 'I should like to ask Mr Salisbury about something different from the financial side. What about losing a valuable part of our village life?'

'Hear, hear!' came a general murmur.

'We've lost enough as it is. Lost our dear old bobby, lost half our parson, in a manner of speaking, lost our own bakery, and now it looks as though we might lose our school.'

'He's right, you know,' said old Mr Potts. 'And I mind other things we've lost. We used to have two lovely duck ponds in Fairacre. Dozens of ducks used 'em, and the horses drank from 'em too. And where are they now? Gorn! Both gorn! And the smithy. We used to have a fine smithy. Where's that? Gorn! I tell you, it's proper upsetting.'

There were murmurs of agreement, and the vicar broke in to suggest that perhaps questions could now be directed to the chair, and had anyone anything else to add?

'Yes,' said someone at the side of the hall. 'What happens to Miss Read?'

'I understand,' said the vicar 'that Miss Read would be well looked after. Am I right?' he added, turning to Mr Salisbury.

He struggled to his feet again and assured the assembly that I should suffer no loss of salary, and that a post would most certainly be found for me in the area.

'But suppose she don't want to go?' said Ernest's father. 'What about her house and that? Besides, we want her to go on teaching our children.'

I was feeling slightly embarrassed by all this publicity, but was also very touched by their obvious concern.

Mr Salisbury elaborated on the theme of my being looked after, but it was plain that few were satisfied. There was a return to the subject of doing away with a school which practically all those present had attended in their youth, and their fathers before them.

I felt very sorry for Mr Salisbury, who was really fighting a losing battle very gallantly and politely. His assistant was busy scribbling down notes, and there certainly seemed an amazing amount to be recorded.

Countrymen do not talk much, but when their hearts are touched they can become as voluble as their town cousins. The meeting went on for over two hours, and Mr Salisbury, at the end of that time, remained as calm, if not quite as collected, as when he arrived.

His final words were to assure all present that no definite plan had been made to close Fairacre School, that should that situation arise there would be consultation at every step, there would be nothing done in secrecy, and that all the arguments put forward so lucidly tonight would be considered most carefully.

The vicar thanked everyone for attending, and brought the meeting to a close.

'Wonder if it did any good?' I overheard someone say, as we stepped outside into the gentle spring night.

'Of course it did,' replied his neighbour stoutly. 'Showed that chap you can't push Fairacre folk around. That's something, surely.'

19. Dr Martin Meets his Match

Whatever the long-term results of the village meeting might be, the immediate effect was of general relief.

We had made our protest, aired our feelings, and those in authority had been told clearly that Fairacre wished to keep its village school, and why. We could do no more at the moment.

We all relaxed a little. The weather continued to be seductively mild, and all the gardeners were busy making seed beds and sorting through their packets of vegetable and flower seeds, with hope in their hearts.

I was busy at the farthest point of my own plot when the telephone bell began to ring one sunny evening. My hands and feet were plastered with farmyard manure, but I raced the length of the garden to get to the instrument before my caller rang off. Too rushed to bother to take off my shoes, I grabbed the receiver, dropped breathless upon the hall chair, and gazed with dismay upon the new hall carpet.

'What a long time you've been answering,' said Amy's voice. 'Were you in the bath, or something?'

I told her I had been in the garden.

'Picking flowers?'

'Spreading muck.'

'Muck?'

'Manure to you townees. Muck to us.'

'Lucky you! Where did you get it?'

I told her that Mr Roberts usually dumped a load once a year.

'I suppose you couldn't spare a bucketful for my rhubarb?' said Amy wistfully.

'Of course I can. I'll shove some in a plastic sack, but I warn you, it'll make a devil of a mess in the boot of your car. You should see my hall carpet at the moment.'

'You haven't clumped in, straight from muck spreading, all over that new runner?'

'Well, I had to answer this call.'

'I despair of you. I really do.'

'You didn't ring me up to tell me that old chestnut, surely?'

Amy's voice became animated. 'No. I've just heard some terrific news. Guess what!'

'Vanessa's baby's arrived.'

'Don't be silly, dear. That's not for months yet. Try again.'

'I can't. Come on, tell me quickly, so that I can get down on my haunches to clean up this mess.'

'Lucy Colgate's engaged to be married!'

'Well, she's been trying long enough.'

'Now, don't be waspish. I thought you'd be interested.'

'Do you think it will come to anything this time? I mean, she's always been man-mad. Remember how she used to frighten all those poor young men at Cambridge? And I could name four fellows, this minute, who rushed to jobs abroad simply to evade Lucy's clutches.'

'You exaggerate! Yes, I'm sure this marriage will take place.'

'Well, my heart bleeds for the poor chap. Who is he anyway?'

'He's called Hector Avory, and he's in insurance or the Baltic Exchange, or one of those things in the City. This will be his fourth marriage.'

'Good heavens! What happened to the other three?'

'The first wife died in childbirth, poor thing. The second was run over, and the third just faded away.'

'He doesn't sound to me the sort of man who looks after his wives very well. I hope Lucy knows about them.'

'Of course she does. She told me herself!'

'Ah well! Rather her than me. I take it she'll stop teaching?'

'Yes, indeed. He's got a whacking great house at Chislehurst which she'll be looking after.'

'I bet she won't have muck on her hall carpet,' I observed.

'I'm going to ring off,' said Amy, 'and let you start clearing up the mess you've made. Don't forget the contribution to my rhubarb, will you?'

'Come and collect it tomorrow,' I said, 'and have a cup of tea. We never seem to have time for a gossip.'

'What was this then?' queried Amy, and rang off.

Spring in Fairacre takes some beating, and we took rather more nature walks in the exhilarating days of March and early April than the timetable showed on the wall.

At this time of year, it is far better to catch the best of the day sometime between ten in the morning and three in the afternoon, so Fairacre saw a ragged crocodile of pupils quite often during that time of day, while the weather lasted.

The birds were flashing to and fro, with feverish activity, building their nests or feeding their young. Mr Roberts had a score or so of lambs cavorting in the shelter of the downs, and in the next field was a splendid lying-in ward, for expectant ewes, made of bales of straw. Sometimes, when the wind was keen, the children suggested that we sheltered in there, and it was certainly snug enough to tempt us, but I pointed out that the ewes, and Mr Roberts, would not welcome us.

Polyanthuses, yellow, pink and red, lifted their velvety faces to the sun, and the beech leaves were beginning to show their silky green. Friends and parents would straighten up from their seed planting to have a word as we passed, and this brought home to me, very poignantly, the strong bond between the villagers and their school.

Joseph Coggs attached himself to me on one of these outings. He was obliged to walk at a slower pace than the others for the sole of his shabby shoe was flapping, and he had secured it with a piece of stout binder twine tied round his foot.

'Do you think you ought to go back, Joe?' I asked, when I saw his predicament.

'It'll hold out,' he said cheerfully, as he hobbled along beside me. He seemed so happy that it seemed better to let him take part with the other children, and if the worst happened we could leave him sitting on the bank, and collect him on our way back to school.

'That lady come again last night,' he volunteered.

'Which lady?'

'The office one. Comes to see Mum.'

I realized that he meant the Probation Officer. Naturally I had heard from several sources – including Mrs Pringle – that the officer in question was doing her duty diligently.

'She brung us—'

'Brought us,' I said automatically.

'She *brought* us,' echoed Joe, 'some little biscuit men. Ginger-bread, she said. They was good. The leg come off of mine, but it tasted all right. His eyes was currants, and so was his buttons.'

Joe's eyes were alight at the happy memory. My opinion of this particular officer soared higher than ever. It looked as though the Coggs family had found a friend.

'We've got a tin now,' went on Joe, 'to put money in. When we've got enough, my mum's going to buy me some more shoes.'

Looking down at his awkward progress, I observed that he would be pleased when that happened. His eyes met mine with some puzzlement.

'It don't *hurt* me to walk like this,' he explained. He was obviously troubled to know that I was concerned on his behalf, and anxious to put me at ease.

I realized suddenly, and with rare humility, how much I could learn from Joseph Coggs. Here was a complete lack of self-pity, uncomplaining acceptance of misfortune, delight in the Probation Officer's generosity and thoughtfulness for me.

I wished I had as fine a character as young Joe's.

Mrs Pringle arrived one sunny morning, bearing a big bunch of daffodils lodged in the black oilcloth bag which accompanies her everywhere.

'Thought you'd like some of our early ones,' she said, thrusting the bunch at me. I was most grateful, I told her. They were splendid specimens.

'Well, yours are always much later, and a bit undersized,' said Mrs Pringle. 'It always pays to buy the best with bulbs.'

'What sort are these?' I inquired, ignoring the slight to my own poor blossoms still in bud.

'King Alfred's. Can't beat 'em. I likes to have King Alfred's, not only for size, but I likes his story. Burning the cakes and that, and fighting them Danes round here. Some time ago, mind you,' she added, in case I imagined the conflict taking place within living memory.

I was still puzzling over the reason for this unexpected present when Mrs Pringle enlightened me.

'And talking of battles, I've just had one with Dr Martin, and feels all the better for it!'

'About the dieting?'

'That's right. Half-starved I've been all these months, as well you know, Miss Read, and fair fainting at times with weakness. And yet, to hear doctor talk, you'd think I'd done nothing but guzzle down grub.'

'I know you've been trying very hard,' I said diplomatically, admiring my daffodils.

'Well, it all come to a head last night, as you might say. Got me on that great iron weighing machine of his, up the surgery, like some prize porker I always feels balancing on that contraption, when he gives a sort of shriek and yells: "Woman, you've gone up"! *Woman*, he calls me! *Woman*, the cheek of it!'

Mrs Pringle's face was flushed, and her pendulous cheeks wobbled, at the memory of this outrage.

'So I gets off his old weighing machine, pretty smartly, and I says: "Don't you come calling me *Woman* in that tone of voice. You takes my money regular out of the National Health, and I'll have a bit of common courtesy, if you don't mind"! And then I told him flat, he was no good as a doctor, or I'd have been a stone lighter by now, according to his reckoning. He didn't like it, I can tell you.'

My heart went out to poor Dr Martin. I remembered Minnie's remark about Auntie always winning when it came to a battle.

'What did he say?'

Mrs Pringle snorted. 'He said I'd never kep' to my diet. He said I was the most cantankerous patient on his list, and the best thing I could do was to forget about the diet, and go my own way. What's more, he had the cheek to say that for two pins he'd advise me to go to another doctor—'

She stopped suddenly, bosom heaving beneath her purple cardigan.

'Yes? What else?'

'Go to another doctor,' repeated Mrs Pringle, quivering at the memory, 'but that he wouldn't wish any such *trouble maker* on any of his colleagues. Those was his very words. Burnt into my brain, they is! Like being branded! *A trouble maker!* Me!'

'I shouldn't let it worry you too much,' I said soothingly. 'You were both rather heated, I expect, and after all, Dr Martin's only human.'

'That I doubt!'

'Well, getting old, anyway, and rather over-worked. He's probably quite sorry about it this morning.'

'That I can't believe!' She sniffed belligerently. 'Anyway,' she went on more cheerfully, 'I felt a sight better after I'd had my say, and I went home and cooked a lovely plate of pig's liver, bacon and chips. It really set me up after all that orange juice and greens I've been living on. Had a good night's rest too, with something in my stomach instead of wind. I woke up a different woman, and went to pick some daffodils afore coming along to work. Sort of celebration, see? Thrown off my chains at last!'

'It was kind of you to include me in the celebrations.'

'Well, you've looked a bit peaky off and on, these last few months. Thought they might cheer you up.'

There was no trace of a limp as she made her way to the door. Discarding the diet had obviously had a good effect on all aspects of Mrs Pringle's health, and we at Fairacre School might benefit from this unusual bout of cheerfulness.

George Annett was buying a sweater in Marks & Spencer's in Caxley when I saw him next. He seemed to be in a fine state of bewilderment.

'Which would you choose?' he asked me.

'What about Shetland wool?'

'Too itchy round my neck.'

'Botany wool then. That washes very well.'

'Not thick enough. What's the difference between wool and nylon?'

'How? In expense, do you mean?'

'No. The stuff itself.'

I looked at George in surprise. Surely, he knew the difference.

'Well,' I began patiently, 'wool is a natural fibre, from the sheep's back, and nylon—'

'I know all that!' he said testily.

He really is the most impatient fellow at times.

'Say what you mean then!' I answered.

'Which wears better? Which stands up to washing better? Is one warmer than the other? Will one go out of shape quicker? Which, in fact, is the better investment?'

I began to get as cross as he was. 'All Marks & Spencer's stuff is good,' I began.

'Have you got shares in them?' he demanded suspiciously.

'No. I wish I had. Honestly, I think I'd choose a woollen one, but some people like a bit of nylon in with it.'

George flung down a rather fetching oatmeal-coloured confection he had been fingering. 'Oh, I don't know. I'll let Isobel choose for me. It's all too exhausting, this shopping! Come and have a cup of coffee.'

Over it, he asked if I had heard anything recently from the Office.

'The usual flood of letters exhorting us not to waste anything,' I replied. 'Not that I get much chance at Fairacre, with Mrs Pringle keeping her hawk-eye on me. She handed me an inch stub of pencil she'd found in the wastepaper basket only yesterday, and she certainly sees that we don't waste fuel.'

'We're going to need more drastic cuts than that,' said George. 'Since these government announcements about making-do and cutting-back and so on, in education, I've seen nothing more of the chaps who were measuring the playground for those proposed new classrooms.'

'You mean we shall all stay as we are?' I asked, the world suddenly becoming rosier.

'Well, nothing definite's been said yet, but I've had no reply to a whole heap of numbers I was requested to send to the Office, "without delay" a term or two ago.'

'What sort of numbers?'

'Oh, footling stuff like estimated numbers on roll if the Fairacre children came along. How many were leaving? How many desks were available, and what sizes were they? How many children could be seated at school dinner? How many trestle tables were in use? You know, the usual maddening questions involving us crawling about with a yard stick, and counting dozens of pieces of furniture.'

'I've heard nothing,' I said cautiously.

'That's the point. It's all delightfully negative at the moment. I think we shall have to hear one way or the other pretty quickly. After all, if the county is going to go ahead with re-organization as planned, it will need to give plenty of notice. If not, we should be told very soon. Either way we ought to know where we are before next term, I should think.'

'Mr Salisbury said we should be consulted at every stage,' I agreed. I suddenly felt extremely happy.

'Have a chocolate biscuit,' I said, offering the plate to George, the dear fellow. Any passing irritation with him was now forgotten, for was he not the harbinger of hope?

When Amy came to collect a second sack of manure for her garden, I told her of my encounter with George Annett.

She looked thoughtful. 'As you've heard nothing definite, I imagine that some committee or other is going into which would be cheaper – to take yours to Beech Green, or to hang on as you are.'

'That shouldn't take long to find out.'

'Well, you know what committees are,' said Amy. 'Sometimes vital decisions get lost in transit between the steering committee, and the pilot committee, and the finance committee, and the general policy committee and Uncle-Tom-Cobley-and-all's committee. James talks about these things sometimes, and what with all the complications, and the Post Office thrown in, I wonder if it wouldn't be simpler to be completely self-supporting in a comfortable peasant-like way with just a potato from the garden to eat, and a goat skin to wear.'

'Smelly,' I said.

'Unless your children can be squeezed into Beech Green without any building being done, I can't see Fairacre School closing,' said Amy. 'And surely, the building programme will simply cease to be, with the country's finances in the state they are.'

'Well, it's an ill wind that blows nobody any good,' I said. 'I certainly shan't bother to apply for any other jobs. I'm glad I didn't do anything about Mrs Allen's. Things look so much more hopeful now.'

Amy rose to go. 'Your trouble is that you are too idle to arrange your own life,' she said severely. 'You simply let things drift and when they appear to be going as you want them to, then you start congratulating yourself on doing nothing. I warn you, my girl, the fact that you haven't heard anything yet, one way or the other, doesn't automatically mean that you are out of the wood.'

'No, Amy,' I said meekly.

'One swallow doesn't make a summer,' she went on, opening the car door.

'You sound as though you'd swallowed *The Oxford Dictionary of Quotations*,' I shouted after her, as she drove off.

It was good to have the last word for a change.

20. RELIEF ON TWO FRONTS

The end of term came, without hearing any more definite news from the Office. The Easter holidays were an agreeable mixture of work in the house and garden, and occasional outings with Amy and other friends.

Earlier in the year, I had been pressed to go with the Caxley Ornithological Society on a lecture tour in Turkey. It all sounded very exotic but, apart from the expense, which struck me as too much for my modest means, I was too unsettled about the fate of Fairacre School to make plans so far ahead, and I had turned down the invitation to accompany the Mawnes, and several other friends, when they set off in April.

I did not regret my decision. My few trips abroad I have enjoyed, and one with Amy to Crete some years earlier was perhaps the most memorable of all. But Easter in Fairacre, when fine, is very beautiful and there were a number of things I wanted to do and see which were impossible to fit in during term time.

Mrs Pringle offered to come an extra day to give me a hand with spring cleaning upstairs. I received this kindness with mixed feelings. Left alone I could have endured the condition of the upper floor of my house with the greatest equanimity. Mrs Pringle however confessed herself appalled by the squalor in which I seemed content to live.

'When did you last dust them bed springs?' she demanded one day.

'I didn't know that bed had springs,' I confessed.

Mrs Pringle swelled with triumph. 'There you are! When I does out that room, I expects to strip the bed, pull off the mattress, and get a lightly oiled rag into them cup springs. That's what should be done weekly, but as it is there's always some excuse from you about "leaving them". Now, Mrs Hope when she lived here—'

'Don't tell me,' I begged. When Mrs Hope, wife of an earlier head teacher at Fairacre School, is brought into the conversation, I just give in to Mrs Pringle. According to that lady, Mrs Hope was the epitome of perfect housewifery. The furniture had a light wash with vinegar and warm water before polishing. Everything that was scrubbable was done twice a week. Sheets were never sent to a laundry, but every inch of linen used in the house was washed, boiled, clear-starched and ironed exquisitely.

My own slap-dash methods scandalize Mrs Pringle, and I sometimes wonder if the spirit of Mrs Hope ever returns to her former home. If so, no doubt I shall see her one day wringing her ghostly hands over the condition of the house under my casual care.

We were washing down the paintwork together one sunny morning when I inquired after Minnie's affairs. I had not seen her on the previous Friday, having spent the day with Amy, and returned just in time to lift the wet dusters from a row of upturned saucepans on the dresser before going to bed.

'Ern's back,' said Mrs Pringle.

I looked at her with dismay. 'Oh no! Poor Minnie!'

'There's no "poor Minnie" about it,' replied Mrs Pringle, wringing out her wet cloth with a firm hand. 'She's a lucky girl to have him back at Springbourne. You can't expect her to bring up that gaggle of children on her own. She needs a man about the place.'

I was bewildered, and said so.

'Yes, I know Ern left her, to go to that Mrs Fowler who's no better than she should be, as we all know. But it's no good blaming Ern.'

'Why not? I think he behaved very badly towards Minnie. Dash it all, half those children he left with her are his own!'

'Maybe. But he's a man, ain't he? Men do go off now and then. It's their nature.'

'I'm sure Mr Pringle doesn't,' I dared to say, attacking a particularly grubby patch of paint by the door.

'I should think not!' boomed Mrs Pringle. 'He's nothing to go off for, living peaceable with me!'

'But is Ern behaving properly?' I said, changing the subject. We seemed to be skating near very thin ice.

'As nice as pie. He'd better, too. He knows he's got a bed to sleep in at Minnie's. That cousin of his give him the push after a few days. The springs of the sofa give way, and she's trying to make Ern pay for the repairs.'

'And is he in work?'

'That's not for me to say,' said Mrs Pringle, buttoning up her mouth. 'There's a lot going on at the moment, I'm not to speak about it. No doubt you'll hear, all in good time.'

'I didn't mean to pry,' I said apologetically. 'I beg your pardon.'

'Granted, I'm sure,' said Mrs Pringle graciously. 'And if you'll give me a hand with these 'ere pelmets, I'll take them outside for a good brushing. They can do with it.'

Term began in a blaze of sunshine, and I returned reluctantly to school.

The children appeared to be in the highest spirits, and attacked their work with even more gossiping than usual. I do not expect dead silence in my classroom when work is in progress, as did my predecessors at the school, but I object to the sort of hubbub which hinders other people and gives me a headache.

It took a week or more to settle them down again to a reasonable level of noise, and a reasonable rhythm of work, so that I did not think about Minnie's affairs until I discovered that she was in the house when I returned one Friday afternoon. She was scouring the sink with considerable vigour when I approached.

'You're working overtime, Minnie,' I told her. 'It's nearly ten to four.'

'Don't matter. Ern don't finish till five, and we don't have our tea till then.'

I remembered Mrs Pringle's secrecy about Ern's employment. Presumably, all was now known.

'Is he working at Caxley?' I asked.

Minnie put down the dishcloth and sat herself on the kitchen chair, ready for a gossip.

'No. He don't go into Caxley no more. That Mrs Fowler and his cousin are after him. He's best off at home.'

'Where is he working then?'

'Working?' queried Minnie, looking dazed, as though the word were foreign to her. Then her face cleared. 'Oh, *working*! Oh, yes, he's *working*! Up the manor.'

'At Springbourne Manor?' I said. It seemed odd to me that Ern should go to work at the same place as his erstwhile rival Bert.

'That's right,' agreed Minnie. She found a hole in her tights at knee level, and gently eased a ladder down towards her ankle. She concentrated on its movement for some minutes, while I wondered whether to pursue the conversation or simply let it lapse.

Curiosity won.

'But doesn't it make things rather awkward' I said, 'with Bert still there? After all, they are both – er – fond of you, Minnie.'

She smiled coyly, and removed her finger from the ladder. 'Oh, Bert's been and gone! The boss sent him packing.'

'Mr Hurley did?'

Minnie looked at me in amazement. 'There's no Hurleys now at Springbourne. Mr David was the last, and he sold up to these new people. Name of Potter.'

I remembered then that I had heard that the last of the old family had been obliged to part with the house because of death duties, and had gone abroad to live.

'Of course! And why was Bert dismissed?'

'Pinching things. He had a regular job selling the vegetables and fruit and that to a chap in Caxley. Made quite a bit that way.'

Minnie spoke as though it were to Bert's credit to be so free with his master's property.

'I'm glad he was found out.'

'Oh, he wouldn't have been, but for Mrs Potter goin' into this 'ere greengrocer's for some lettuces, because Bert told her that morning there wasn't none ready for the table yet.'

'What happened?'

'She said what lovely lettuces, and where'd they come from and the man said he got a lot of stuff from Springbourne Manor, and it was always fresh, and everyone liked it. So, of course, she come home and faced Bert with it.'

'I should think so!'

'A shame, really,' commented Minnie. 'He was doin' very nicely till then. Anyway, Mr Potter packed 'im off pronto, with a week's wages and no reference. Still, he done him a good turn really, seeing as Bert's got a job laying the gas pipes across the country, and they makes a mint of money.'

'So Ern has got Bert's job?'

'That's right! Mr Potter come down to me one evening and talked about Ern coming back and settling down to be a good husband and father, and what did I think?'

'What did you say?'

'I said I wanted him back. He never hit me nor nothing, and as long as he behaved proper to me, he was lovely.'

'So you've forgiven him?'

'Well, yes. And Mr Potter said he could have this job, and free fruit and veg as long as he behaved hisself. And if he didn't, I was to go and tell him, and he'd speak sharp to him.'

'Well, it all seems to have turned out very satisfactorily,' I said. 'But look at the time! You must hurry back.'

Minnie began to twist her fingers together. 'I waited to tell you. Now Ern's back, I don't need to come out so much, and I wondered if you could manage without me.'

'Manage without you?' I echoed, trying to keep the jubilation from my voice. 'Why, of course, I can, Minnie! I'm just grateful to you for helping me out these last few months, but of course you need more time at home now.'

'That's good,' said Minnie, getting swiftly from the chair and collecting her dues from the mantelpiece. 'I've really enjoyed coming 'ere. You just say if you ever wants me again.'

She looked around the kitchen, her brow furrowed.

'I've never done the dusters,' she said at last.

'Don't worry about those, Minnie,' I said hastily. 'You hurry along now.'

I watched her untidy figure lope down the path, her tousled red hair gleaming in the sunshine.

Relief flooded me, as I gently closed the door. Long may Ern behave himself, I thought!

One morning, soon after the happy day of Minnie's departure, a letter arrived from the Office in the usual buff envelope.

I put it aside in order to read more important missives such as my bank statement, as depressing as ever, a circular exhorting me to save with a local building society, pointless in the circumstances, and two letters from friends, which made ideal breakfast reading.

After washing up and dusting in a sketchy fashion, I took the letter from the Office over to the school. No doubt another tiresome directive to save equipment, or else measure it, I thought, remembering George Annett's remark.

It remained unopened until after prayers and register-marking. It was almost ten o'clock, and the children were tackling some English exercises, when I slit the envelope and began to read.

It was momentous news. The gist was that because of the devastating cuts in government spending, all local authorities must make do with the present buildings, apparatus and so on. There would be cuts in staff, both teaching and domestic. Reorganization plans were shelved until the country's finances improved.

There were two more pages after this first staggering one. This circular had obviously been sent to every head teacher. But

in my envelope there was a covering letter signed by Mr Salisbury, making it clear that there was now no need to have any
fears for the closure of Fairacre School, in the light of the
accompanying directive, and that the status quo both at Fairacre and Beech Green would remain until such time, in the far
future, when the matter of combining the two schools could be
reviewed again.

I put down the letter on the desk, securing it under the brass
inkstand, and wondered why my legs were trembling. It would
have been more rational, surely, to have capered up and down
the aisles between the desks, but here I was feeling as though
I had been hit on the head with Mr Willet's heavy wooden
mallet. I began to realize just how desperately I had been
worrying all these months. This, presumably, was what medical
men called 'delayed shock'.

My teeth began to chatter, and I held my jaw rigid in case the
children heard. Perhaps I ought to make a pot of tea, and have
lots of cups with lots of sugar? Vague memories of First Aid
procedure floated through my mind, but before I had time to
dwell any longer on my symptoms, a diversion arose.

The door was open, letting in the scents of a June morning,
and at this particular moment Tibby entered, bearing a squeak-
ing mouse dangling from her mouth.

As one man, the class rose and rushed towards her. Tibby
vanished, followed by half the class, and by the time I had
restored order my weakness had passed.

Ernest was the last to return, looking triumphant. 'Got it off
of 'er!' he announced. 'It run off into your shed. Old Tib's
waiting for it, but I reckon it's got 'ome all right.'

'Thank you, Ernest,' I said with genuine gratitude. People I can
cope with – even Minnie Pringle, in a limited way – but not mice.

'I think we'll have early playtime today. Put away your books
and fetch your milk.'

When they were at last in the playground, I told Hilary the
good news, and then went indoors to see if I could get George

Annett on the telephone. He has an instrument in his staff room, a rather more convenient arrangement than my own.

'Isn't it splendid?' roared George, nearly deafening me in his enthusiasm. 'I bet you're pleased. And so am I. The thought of building going on in term time was beginning to get me down. Frankly, I think we're all a damn sight better off as we are. I shall have to lose one teacher, I think – perhaps two – but the main thing is I shan't be cluttered up with your lot.'

I felt it could have been put more delicately, but was far too happy to voice objections. All my shakiness had gone, and I returned to the classroom in tearing high spirits.

It seemed a good idea, bursting as I was with unaccustomed energy, to tackle one or two untidy cupboards, and I set some of the children to work on this task.

The map cupboard is always the worst. Patrick grew grubbier and grubbier as he delved among the piles of furled maps, bundles of raffia, odd tennis shoes, a set of croquet mallets bequeathed us by the vicar, innumerable large biscuit tins 'which might come in useful' and, right at the back, a Union Jack.

Patrick shook it out with rapture. 'Look! Can us put it up?'

It seemed to me, in my state of euphoria, to have been sent straight from heaven to be put to its proper use of rejoicing.

'Why not?' I said. 'You and Joe can stick it up over the porch.'

They vanished outside, and could be heard dragging an old desk to the porch. By standing on it, I knew they could reach comfortably a metal slot which Mr Willet had devised some years ago, for holding the flag stick.

The flag met with general approval when the children had finished their tidying inside and went to admire Joe and Patrick's handiwork. I managed at last to get them in again, and we spent the rest of the morning wrestling with decimals of money.

The children worked well, glowing with the virtuous feeling of having tidied cupboards and desks.

And I glowed too, with the relief which that plain buff envelope had brought me.

That afternoon, when the children had gone home and I was alone in the quiet schoolroom, I opened the bottom drawer of my desk, and took out the weighty log book which holds the record of the school.

I heaved it up on to the desk and turned to the last entry. It had been made a few weeks earlier, and recorded the visit of the school doctor.

I took out my pen, and put the date. Then I wrote:

'Today I received official notice that Fairacre School will not be closing.'

As I gazed at that marvellous sentence, the door-scraper clanged, and Mrs Pringle appeared, oilcloth bag on her arm, and an expression of extreme surprise on her face.

'What's Fairacre School flying the flag for?' she asked.

'For mercies received,' I told her, shutting the log book with a resounding bang.

Village Centenary

To
Mary and Victor
with love

CONTENTS

* * *

1 · JANUARY

It was Miss Clare who first pointed out that Fairacre School was one hundred years old.

It was a bleak Saturday afternoon, and we were enjoying hot buttered toast by the schoolhouse fire. Outside, the playground, and beyond that the fields and distant downs, gleamed dully white in the fading light. It had snowed every day since term started over a week ago, and from the look of the leaden skies, more was to come.

The leafless trees stood stark and black in the still air. Distant hedges smudged the whiteness, and a flock of homing rooks fluttered by like flakes of blackened paper.

It looked like a sketch in charcoal from the schoolhouse window. The only spot of colour in this black and white world came from the crimson glow of a bonfire in Mr Roberts' field next to the school. During the day, the flames had leapt and danced while a haze of blue smoke wavered about them, but now that the men were homeward bound the fire was dying down – the one warm, glowing thing to be seen.

Indoors, we were snug enough. Between us, in front of the log fire, stood the tea tray, the cups steaming fragrantly with China tea. The lamp glowed from the table behind Miss Clare's white head, making a halo of her silver hair. Miss Clare knows Fairacre School well, for she was both pupil and teacher there for many years, and was serving as infants' teacher when I was first appointed as headmistress, until ill health caused her retirement.

Since she was six years of age she has lived in a small cottage

in the next village of Beech Green – a cottage thatched by her father, and later by the young man who inherited her father's thatching tools. She lives alone in her old age. Her childhood friend, Emily Davis, shared the cottage with her until she died some time ago, and although Dolly Clare has adapted herself to solitary living with the courage and sweetness of disposition which has characterized all her life, nevertheless, I know that at times she is lonely and appreciates a few hours in someone else's company.

I suspect that the winter is a particularly lonely time for her. In the summer, she busies herself in the cottage garden, or makes the jams and jellies for which she is renowned. Friends from neighbouring villages or from the market town of Caxley drive out to visit her, enjoying a country outing. There are more calls around Christmas, with visitors bearing gifts and good wishes. But after Christmas, with excitement past and dark evenings, icy roads, and the blight of winter ailments all taking their toll, the long dark nights hang heavily and I try to fetch Dolly occasionally to share my hearth and modest repast, and to give me the inestimable pleasure of her quiet and wise companionship.

'My mother used to say,' said Miss Clare, stirring her tea, 'that once January was over you could look forward to having a walk after tea in daylight.'

'That really is something to look forward to,' I agreed. 'Let's hope we get an early spring. The children haven't had one playtime outside yet, and they are all suffering from the January blues – a horrid disease.'

'It was always so. I expect the first headmistress said much the same thing a hundred years ago. By the way, are you proposing to celebrate the centenary?'

'To be honest, I hadn't realized we were a hundred until you pointed out the date over the door just now. I suppose we'll have to do something to mark such an occasion.'

'We had quite a bustle, I remember, when we were fifty years old in the thirties,' said Miss Clare. 'Mind you, it made a lot of

3

talk. Some people wanted to take the children to London for the day. The Wembley Exhibition some years before had been a great success with the village people, all bowling up in chara-bancs, and having a marvellous time.'

'Did you go?'

'Indeed I did, and I think the statue of the dear Prince of Wales in butter was the thing that impressed me most!'

'Were there any other suggestions?'

'Oh, plenty! You know what village decisions are as well as I do. There were weeks of discussion – I was going to say *wrangling* – and dozens of ideas, but in the end we just celebrated with a marvellous tea party, and really everyone was happy.'

'I can see I shall have to start thinking about it. You'll have to let me know what some of those ideas were. One thing sparks off another when it comes to sharing suggestions.'

'No doubt you'll find some help in the log book,' said Miss Clare. 'There were lots of meetings held in the school, and I expect some of the decisions were recorded. And I'll certainly rack my brains for possible ideas. It will be fun to have something to look forward to.'

Her eyes sparkled at the thought, and I could not help feeling that my old friend was more enthusiastic about the village centenary than I was at the moment. No doubt though, I told myself bracingly, once I got down to it I should feel quite as excited about the celebration of our historic century as did my companion.

Later that evening I drove Miss Clare through white lanes to Beech Green. The roof of her cottage was topped with snow. The moon was rising and the sky was pricked with stars. Already the frost had formed, and we crunched our way up to the front door.

We made our farewells and before I returned to the car I turned to her. 'Let's make another date for the first of February,' I said. 'I'll fetch you after school, and we'll have that walk in daylight after tea, as your mother said.'

'That would be lovely,' agreed Miss Clare, and I left her at her door, the light from the cottage streaming out upon the winter garden, and our breath making little clouds before us as we waved farewell.

As so often happens when one's attention is drawn to something, references to the coming centenary came thick and fast.

Mr Willet, who is our school caretaker, church sexton, general odd job man for the village, producer of hundreds of plants for cottage gardens, as well as chief organizer of our village functions, raised the matter one slippery morning when I was approaching the school across the treacherous playground with considerable caution.

'What you needs,' said Mr Willet, holding out a horny hand to steady me, 'is a stout pair of socks over your shoes. No need to teeter along like a cat on hot bricks if you've got summat to foil the ice. Socks is the answer. It's a good tip, miss.'

I promised to remember.

'We doin' anything about us bein' a hundred this year?' he asked.

'I expect so.'

'Well, it ought to be done proper. Stands to reason, us should have a fitting sort of celebration. A hundred's a hundred. Fairacre'll expect summat good.'

I said that I would start thinking about it, and passed through the school door, almost colliding with Mrs Pringle who was advancing with a large wastepaper basket clutched to her cardigan.

Mrs Pringle is our school cleaner, a martyr to unspecified ailments in her leg, particularly severe when asked to undertake extra work, and a thorn in my flesh. While it is always a pleasure to encounter Mr Willet, to come face to face with Mrs Pringle calls for courage, patience and a bridling of one's tongue. Quite often, when my patience is exhausted, as Herr Hitler was wont to say, we have a sharp argument. Mrs Pringle is invariably the victor in these combats as she is quicker-witted, better-prepared and, I like to think, more intrinsically malevolent than I am.

However, she is an excellent worker, and if one can turn a deaf ear to the accompanying grumbles the results of her labours are splendid. I doubt if any other school in the county has such jet-black tortoise stoves, burnished to a satin finish with blacklead and elbow grease. Woe betide any child who is foolhardy enough to sully their perfection, particularly when they have been 'done up for the summer'. In that term, no matter how low the mercury in the thermometer drops, the stoves remain inviolate, and instead we don our cardigans philosophically.

Once a week she switches her attention to my house across the playground. I can't think that I am really much more slatternly than the majority of working women, but Mrs Pringle soon makes me think so. The odd crumb on the carpet, the splash of grease on the kitchen stove, or a day's dust on the mantelpiece, are seen instantly by Mrs Pringle's eagle eye and magnified tenfold. The day that she discovered a small crust of mouldy bread '*behind*, not even *in* the bread bin' was a red-letter day for the lady, and I have never been allowed to forget it.

When Mrs Pringle tells me that she intends 'to bottom the sitting room', I make hasty plans to be away from home for the allotted time. I prefer to be absent when she finds the assorted objects which have hidden themselves at the sides of the arm-chair cushions. Life is quite complicated enough for a village schoolmistress without seeking further confrontations.

On this particular occasion, Mrs Pringle put the waste-paper basket on the floor and supported herself on her upturned broom. She looked a little like Britannia with her trident, but less elegant.

'Mr Willet tells me there's a lot of talk about us getting to the century. What, if anything, are we doing about it?'

'Oh, something, I hope,' I said airily. 'But of course it will need some thought. I shall have to have a word with the vicar, and the managers. And Miss Briggs,' I added, as an afterthought.

'Humph!' grunted Mrs Pringle. 'A fat lot of use *she'll* be!'

I was inclined to agree, but could not countenance our school cleaner criticizing my new infants' teacher, straight from college and trailing clouds of educational theories which were enough to curdle one's blood. She had only been with me since the beginning of term, and I sincerely hoped that she would soon settle down and do a little plain teaching instead of what she was pleased to call 'pastoral counselling'.

I decided to ignore Mrs Pringle's interjection, and changed the subject.

'There doesn't seem to be much soap in the wash basins, Mrs Pringle.'

'And whose fault's that?' demanded the lady. 'There was four pieces put out by my own hands when school started, and if them children is allowed to leave it wasting in the water, that's not my affair.'

She picked up the wastepaper basket and made towards the door, where she turned to face me, her three chins wobbling fiercely.

'I'm not made of soap!' she declared, having the last word as usual, and vanished.

The weather continued to be abominable, with icy roads, fresh snowfalls and great difficulty in getting about.

Nevertheless, on my few visits within sliding distance in the village, I had been questioned by Mr Lamb of Fairacre Post Office, our vicar Gerald Partridge, Henry Mawne our local ornithologist, and a number of parents about the possibility of celebrating the school's centenary.

I took evasive action on all occasions. With the weather as it was, there was quite enough to do keeping warm oneself and seeing that the children, the school building and one's own house were protected as much as possible from the devastating cold. Time enough to think about the centenary when the temperature rose, I decided. However, I did consider one or two ideas as I sat close to my fire in the evenings, my feet on the fender courting chilblains.

What about a concert? With songs, or music from each of the ten decades? The fact that the Fairacre children are not particularly musical, and that I am the only one who can attempt to play the piano – preferably compositions cast in the key of C – and that the audience was equally limited in musical knowledge, seemed to make that idea a non-starter.

Or a pageant? It could be based on the log book, with various scenes. But then there were costumes to devise, and we had no stage, and the thought of putting it on in the playground made me realize the many hazards to be faced. Or a display in the school of its hundred years of history? I suppose one could collect photographs, and even a few old exercise and text books, and the children could have theirs on show, as on open days at the school.

I began to think that Miss Clare's recollection of the fifty years' celebration had much to commend it. A mammoth tea party sounded much more festive than my own doubt-ridden ideas. But surely we could do better than that?

Certainly, Miss Clare had fairly sparkled with enthusiasm when she remembered the trip to Wembley and the sight of the Prince of Wales, unforgettable in butter. What about an outing? One of the historic houses within fifty miles of Fairacre, perhaps? But we could do that at any time, and outings were no great treat these days when most parents owned a car. Besides, it seemed silly to go away for a centenary celebration. The whole point of celebrating a hundred years of Fairacre School's progress was surely to have the occasion at the school, by the school, and for the pupils of that school, both past and present.

At that point in my mental meanderings I noticed that the fire needed more fuel, the coal scuttle was empty, and the log basket in the same sad condition. The clock said twenty to ten. Quite late enough for Fairacre folk to be up!

I put up the fireguard, looked out of the front door at the frosty world, and went thankfully to bed.

Miss Briggs, as Mrs Pringle had forecast, was not much help. Since Miss Clare's departure some years ago, I have had a number of infants' teachers, most of them young and very good company.

In a tiny school like ours, with only two teachers, it is essential that the staff is compatible. In most cases we have enjoyed each other's company, although a certain Miss Jackson, some years ago, was a sore trial, not only as a member of staff, but by being so silly as to fall headlong in love with the local gamekeeper, in the best tradition of D.H. Lawrence, and so worrying us all to death.

Miss Briggs had left college in the summer before, had been unable to obtain a post at the beginning of the school year in

September, but arrived at Fairacre to take up her appointment in January. Her predecessor, a cheerful young married woman who had driven from Caxley each day, was starting a family, and I could only be grateful for the year of hard work and good company the school and I had enjoyed during that time.

For the first few days Miss Briggs had little to say to me but quite a lot, and in a loud hectoring tone, to her charges. The result was a noisy class, but I decided to bide my time before I interfered. The girl must find her feet, and I knew that a certain amount of noise – 'a busy hum', as college lecturers like to call it – was looked upon as downright beneficial these days. I am all for 'a busy hum' if it can be halted whenever the teacher so desires, but too often, I notice, that is not possible.

Then she was unduly anxious to leave school at three-thirty, when the infants were sent home. Those with older brothers and sisters usually waited the extra fifteen minutes until my class was free, and in the normal way, the infants' teacher was clearing up her classroom, or buttoning children into garments, in that quarter of an hour.

On several occasions I had seen her car drive away smartly at 3.31, and found a little knot of restless infants at large in their classroom awaiting the release of their kinsfolk in my room. Twice parents had risked the icy roads to speak to her about some particular problem after school, but the lady had vanished, and I had to pass on their messages.

Clearly, I should have to speak to the girl before many days passed, and I did not relish it. I was fast coming to the conclusion that she was quite without humour, taciturn – perhaps a sulker when crossed – and decidedly lazy. On the whole, I like young people, and had been lucky with many vivacious and enthusiastic teachers in their first job with me. It seemed sad that I could strike no answering spark from Miss Briggs. 'A fair old lump of a girl,' Mr Willet had opined, three days after her arrival.

I was beginning to think that it just about summed her up.

*

Towards the end of the month, I began to wonder if a new skylight might be the best way of celebrating Fairacre School's hundredth birthday. For all that time, it seems, the skylight, strategically placed over the obvious site for the headteacher's desk, has let in rain, snow, wind, and the rays of the sun.

Throughout the pages of the log books mention of the skylight crops up:

'A torrential storm this afternoon delayed the pupils' departure from school, and precipitated a deluge through the skylight, damaging some of the children's copybooks and the Holy Bible.' So runs one entry in 1894.

Four years later we read the following somewhat querulous entry:

'Was obliged to shift my desk, as a severe draught from the skylight had resulted in a stiff neck and earache, both occasioning great pain.'

Hardly a year goes by without reference to new glazing or new woodwork needed by this wretched window. Nothing seems to improve it, and I can vouch for the beastly draught which had dogged all the headteachers, and the diabolical way it lets in water.

Mr Willet takes it all very philosophically and quotes irritatingly 'that what can't be cured must be endured'. The wind had been in the north-east, and I was in a more militant mood. If I have complained once about the skylight, during my term of office, I must have complained twenty times. The result has been some sympathy, a little tinkering, and not a jot of difference in improvement.

After three days of howling draught and wearing a silk scarf round my neck, I sat down to write to the Office even more forthrightly than usual about my afflictions. On reading it through I was quite impressed with my firmness of tone, which was tempered with a little pathetic martyrdom, and which surely should bring results. I added a postscript about our hundred years at the mercy of this malevolence overhead, and hoped that something could be done permanently. Cunningly, I pointed out what a drain on the county's economy this must have been over the past century. Every little helps when pleading one's cause.

I posted my letter, wondering if it was a waste of a stamp. Time would tell. On the way back, picking my steps through the slushy snow which was taking its time to disappear, I met Henry Mawne, our eminent ornithologist, who has been a good friend to all in the village.

'How's Simon?' was my first question. His young godson had attended my school for a short time, but his brief stay was ended when a rare albino robin, the pride of the village, came to a sudden death at the boy's hands.

'Settling down well at his prep school,' said Henry, 'and I may as well tell you now, before you hear it on the grapevine, that his father and Irene Umbleditch are getting married.'

'I am delighted to hear it,' I said warmly. 'He's had so much unhappiness, and he couldn't have anyone nicer than Irene, What's more, Simon is so fond of her too.'

'Well, we're all mightily pleased about it,' said Henry. 'No doubt they'll be visiting us before long, and I hope you will come and see them. They've never forgotten how much you did for Simon. And for us,' he added.

We parted, and I returned home much cheered by this good news. David's first wife had been afflicted by mental illness and eventually had taken her own life. It was time that he and poor young Simon had some sunshine, after the shades of misery which they had suffered.

When I entered my house I found a fat mouse corpse on the hearth rug, and Tibby sitting beside it looking particularly smug. Far from being praised, she was roundly cursed as I put on my Wellingtons again, collected the corpse by the tail, and ploughed my way, shuddering, to the boundary hedge and flung the poor thing into Mr Roberts' field.

I often wonder if he notices a particularly fertile patch within a stone's throw of the schoolhouse garden. It is nourished by a steady flow of Tibby's victims, and must have made a substantial difference to his crops over the years.

Like most people in Fairacre, my pupils enjoyed feeding the birds during the winter, and our school bird-table was always well supplied with bread, peanuts and fat.

As well as these more usual offerings, Mrs Pringle supplied mealworms which the robins adored. She had first undertaken this chore when our famous albino robin appeared on the scene. After his death, in the grievous state of mourning which followed, the supply of mealworms ceased, but to our delight a second albino, probably a grandchild of the first, was seen, and the mealworms were hastily added to the menu.

Not that we saw a great deal of the second white robin. It was obviously less bold than its predecessor, and more cautious in its approach to the food we put out. As Henry Mawne had warned us, the robins and other birds of normal colouring would tend to harass the albino. It certainly seemed timid, but was all the more adored by the children on that account. The first robin had frequently come to the jar of mealworms during the day. The second one only came occasionally, and there were many days when it did not appear at all.

One afternoon the children were busy making what they term 'bird pudden', which consists of melted dripping mixed with porridge oats, chopped peanuts and some currants. We had melted the fat in an old saucepan on the tortoise stove, and I kept a weather eye on the door in case Mrs Pringle should walk in unexpectedly and catch us violating her beloved stove.

There was a comfortable smell of cooking in the classroom as Patrick stirred the ingredients with my wooden jam-making spoon. The saucepan by now was on the floor. Nevertheless, when the door opened, I nearly jumped out of my skin with guilt.

Luckily it was only the vicar.

'I seem to have startled you,' said the Reverend Gerald Partridge. 'I suppose I should have knocked.'

'Not at all. I just thought you were Mrs Pringle.'

'*Mrs Pringle*?' echoed the vicar. A look of the utmost perplexity distorted his chubby face. 'Now why on earth should you think that?'

'I'll tell you later,' I said hastily. 'Can I help you?'

The vicar put the plastic bag he had been carrying on my desk.

'A friend of mine who is in the publishing business has most kindly given me some children's books. I think he said he was *remaindering* them – a term I had not heard before, I must confess. Anyway, I thought they might go on the library shelf here.'

'Oh, splendid! We can always do with more books.'

He began to haul them out of the bag which bore the interesting slogan: *Come to Clarissa's For Countless Cosmetics*. It seemed an odd receptacle for a vicar to have acquired.

'I have looked them through,' he said earnestly, 'and they seem quite suitable. Really, these days, one can find the most unnecessarily explicit descriptions of deeds of violence, or of biological matters too advanced for our young children here.'

'I am sure your friend wouldn't give you anything like that,' I said reassuringly, 'but I will read them first if you like.'

'It might be as well,' said the vicar. He suddenly became aware of Patrick's activities.

'Whatever is the boy making?'

I explained, the children joining in with considerable gusto.

'Well, I heartily approve,' he said, when he could make himself heard. 'We must do all we can to keep the birds healthy and strong during this bitter weather.'

He began to walk to the door and I accompanied him. He

spoke in a low voice. 'Are you sure that mixture is all right? It looks most indigestible to me.'

'The birds lap it up,' I told him. 'They've been doing so for months now so don't worry.'

He smiled and departed. I had barely returned to the stove preparatory to clearing away any mess before Mrs Pringle caught us, when the vicar reappeared again.

'I forgot to give you a message from my wife. Could you come to the vicarage for a drink on Friday at six-thirty? A few people are coming to discuss the arrangements for the Caxley Spring Festival.'

'Thank you. Yes, please, I should love to come,' I said.

He said goodbye for the second time and we set about the stove with guilty speed. Mrs Pringle's name had not been mentioned by anyone in the classroom, but we all knew what lent energy to our efforts.

That evening my old friend Amy rang me. We first met at college many years ago, and the friendship has survived separation, a war, Amy's marriage and the considerable differences in our views and temperaments.

Amy is all the things I should like to be – elegant, charming, good-looking, intelligent, rich and much travelled. I can truthfully say that I do not envy her married state, for I am perfectly content with my single one, and in any case James, although a witty and attractive man, is hopelessly susceptible and seems to fall in love at the drop of a hat, which Amy must find tiresome, to say the least of it.

'Come and have some supper,' I invited when she proposed to visit me one evening in the near future.

'Love to, but I must warn you that I'm slimming.'

'Not *again*!' I exclaimed.

'That would have been better left unsaid.'

'Sorry! But honestly, Amy, you are as thin as a rail now. Why bother?'

'My scales which, like the camera, never lie, tell me that I have put on three-quarters of a stone since November.'

'I can't believe it.'

'It's true though. So don't offer me all those lovely things on toast that you usually do. Bread is *out*.'

'What else?'

'Oh, the usual, you know. Starch, sugar, fat, alcohol, and the rest.'

'Is there anything left?'

Amy giggled.

'Well, lettuce is a real treat, and occasionally a *small* orange, and I can have eggs and fish and lean meat, in moderation.'

'The whole thing sounds too damn moderate for me. What would you say to pork chops, roast potatoes and cauliflower with white sauce, followed by chocolate mousse and cream?'

'Don't be disgusting!' said Amy. 'I'm drooling already, but a nice slice of Ryvita and half an apple would be just the thing.'

'I'll join you in the pauper's repast,' I promised nobly, and rang off.

2. February

I remembered my promise to Miss Clare and brought her over to tea on the first of the month.

A gentle thaw had set in and the snow had almost vanished. It tended to turn foggy at night and the roads were still filthy, with little rivulets running at the sides, but it was good to have milder weather during the daytime, and a great relief to let the children run in the playground at break. Under the garden hedge a few brave snowdrops showed. I had picked a bunch for the tea table, the purity of the white flowers contrasting with the dark mottled leaves of the ivy with which I had encircled them.

I was glad that I was not slimming like poor Amy, as we munched our way through anchovy toast and sponge cake. After school I am always ravenous, and how people can bear to go without afternoon tea, and all the delightful ingredients which make it so pleasant, I do not understand.

When we had cleared away, we set out on the first after-tea walk of the year. A few early celandines showed their shield-shaped leaves on the banks at the side of the lane, and it was wonderful to see the green grass again after weeks of depressing whiteness.

A lark sang bravely above, and blackbirds and thrushes fluttered among the bare hedges, scattering the pollen from the hazel catkins that nodded in the light breeze. In the paddock near Mr Roberts' farmhouse, sixty or seventy ewes, heavily in lamb, grazed ponderously upon the newly disclosed grass. There was a wonderful feeling of new life in the air despite the

naked trees, the bare ploughed fields and the miry lane we walked.

'I know most people dislike the month of February,' said Miss Clare, as we returned, 'but I always welcome it. With the shortest day well behind us, and the first whiff of spring about, I begin to feel hopeful again.'

'Your mother was quite right,' I told her. 'Everyone should have an after-tea walk on February the first. It's the finest antidote to the January blues I've come across.'

Dolly Clare laughed, and slipped her frail arm through mine. It was sharply borne in upon me how light and thin she had become during the last few years. Her bones must be as brittle as a bird's. Would my old friend survive to see the next spring? Would we share another first-of-February celebratory walk?

I hoped with all my heart that we might.

On the following Friday, I dutifully made my way to the vicarage. I had not heard any more about the Caxley Spring Festival which the vicar had mentioned, and wondered exactly how our small downland village, some miles from the market town, would become involved.

There were about twenty people in the Partridges' drawing room, and only two were strangers to me. Diana Hale, wife of a retired schoolmaster, was there. Their house, Tyler's Row, once four shabby cottages, is one of the show places of our village, and she and her husband are tireless in their good works.

I was pleasantly surprised, too, to see Miriam Quinn who came to live in Fairacre a few years ago. She is a most efficient secretary to a businessman in Caxley, likes a quiet life, and is somewhat reserved.

Like most newcomers to a village, I know that Miss Quinn was approached by most of the village organizations when she first took up residence at Holly Lodge on the outskirts of Fairacre, for her qualities of hard work and intelligence had gone before her and everyone said, as I find to my cost as a spinster, that a single woman must have time on her hands and enjoy a nice bit of company. Holly Lodge is the home of Joan Benson, a sprightly widow, and she and her lodger seem very happy together. Joan was not at the meeting, and I wondered how it was that Miriam Quinn had been coralled with the rest of us.

It was soon made clear. The vicar, who was acting as chairman, introduced the two strangers as the organizers of the Festival in Caxley, and Miss Quinn as Fairacre's representative. We all sat back, sherry in hand, to listen obediently.

The Arts in Caxley, one of the strangers told us with some severity, were sadly neglected, and the proposed Festival was to bring them to the notice of Caxley's citizens and those who lived nearby. Let him add, he said (and who were we to stop him?), that he was not accusing Caxley people of *Philistinism* or *Cruelty to Creative Artists*, but merely of *Ignorance* and *Apathy*.

There was a great fund of natural talent in Caxley – and its surrounds, he put in hastily – and there would be two plays by local playwrights put on at the Corn Exchange, several concerts at the parish church, and exhibitions of painting, embroidery and other crafts at various large buildings in the town, and outside.

'What happens to the money?' Mr Roberts, our local farmer, asked bluntly. Farmers are noted for their realistic approach to life, and ours is no exception.

The speaker looked a little surprised by the interjection of such a materialistic inquiry in the midst of his eulogy about Caxley's artistic aspirations, but rallied bravely.

'I was just coming to that. Any profits will go to three local charities so that a great many people will benefit. They are named in the leaflets which we are distributing at this meeting.'

Mr Roberts grunted in acknowledgement, and the speaker resumed his talk. Miriam Quinn's involvement was then revealed, and she gave a sensible description of her part in the Festival.

'I'm really here to get suggestions,' she said. 'One way of

helping, particularly for us in the country, is by opening our gardens. The vicar has already offered to have his open, and so has Mr Mawne. We can arrange a date to suit us all, and in May, when the Festival takes place, our gardens here are at their best.'

'What about the schoolchildren having a maypole? Dancing and singing and all that,' called out someone, well hidden from me.

Miriam Quinn looked at me hopefully.

'I'll think about it,' I said circumspectly. What with the centenary, and the skylight waiting to be repaired, I had some reservations about a May Day celebration as well.

'Beech Green had a street fair once,' said somebody.

'And only once,' said her neighbour. 'The traffic was something awful when Mr Miller's tractor broke down where the road narrows.'

The vicar, adept at handling situations like this, suggested that any ideas might be given to Miss Quinn at the end of the meeting. He was quite sure, he added, that she would receive every possible support from Fairacre in the part that the village would play in this excellent enterprise.

Were there any more questions?

At this, as always, silence fell upon the gathering. Sherry glasses were refilled, the guests circulated again, and we all knew, as we chattered of everything under the sun bar the matter in hand, that the Caxley Spring Festival would get plenty of attention once the meeting had dispersed.

Amy paid her visit to me one evening when the wind was scouring the downs, whistling through keyholes and making the schoolhouse shudder beneath its onslaughts.

Out in the garden the bare branches tossed up and down, and dead leaves flurried hither and thither across the grass. Overhead the rooks had battled their way home at dusk, finding it difficult to keep on course.

But my fire burned brightly in the roaring draught and Tibby, on her back, presented her stomach to the warmth, paws above her head. We were pretty snug within, whatever the weather did outside.

Amy arrived in a new suede coat of dark brown and some elegant shoes that I had not seen before. She held a bowl of pink hyacinths in her hands.

'Coals to Newcastle, I expect. I know you do well with bulbs.'

'Not a bit of it! Mine are over, and you couldn't have brought anything more welcome, Amy dear. Come in, out of this vile wind.'

She divested herself of the beautiful coat, and exclaimed with pleasure at the fire.

'I've been trying to do without one. After all, the central heating should really be enough – heaven knows it costs a small fortune to run – but there's something rather *soulless* about the electric fire which I'm forced to put on for an hour or two, now and then.'

'Well, you know me, Amy. I light a fire at the drop of a hat. I can always console myself with the thought that I have no central heating to make me feel guilty.'

'I've felt the cold far more this winter,' said Amy, stroking Tibby's stomach. 'Whether it's *anno domini* or just this slimming business, I can't tell. A bit of each, I expect.'

'How's the poundage going?'

'Much too slowly. If only I habitually drank gallons of beer, or ate pounds of chocolate, I should find it quite easy to cut down the calories, but I eat like a bird.'

'Not worms, I hope.'

'Don't be facetious, dear. You know what I mean. I'm heartily sick of salad and cold meat.'

'Well, that's what you've got tonight. Unless you'd rather have a boiled egg.'

'Either would be delicious,' said Amy, lying bravely. 'Do you know, as a child, I refused to eat salad, particularly tomatoes.'

'My *bête noire* was beetroot,' I recalled. 'Now I love it, and coffee. I didn't touch it until we went to college. I'm sure tastes change as one goes through life.'

'They certainly do. But perhaps it's simply our aging digestive systems, do you think? I used to adore potted shrimps, but these days they go down like greased nails, and I have terrible indigestion.'

'We could have a nice bowl of thin gruel on our laps here,' I remarked, 'if you feel in such an advanced state of decay.'

'Not likely!' said Amy. 'Besides, gruel is fattening.'

'Who was it said that anything one enjoys turns out to be fattening or immoral?'

'No idea, but he knew what he was talking about,' said Amy with feeling.

Over our frugal repast, the conversation turned to Caxley's Festival. I told Amy about Miss Quinn's part in it and our dearth of suggestions in Fairacre.

'Well, in an expansive moment I agreed to have a poetry reading in my house,' she said. 'Do you think anyone will come?'

'The poets will, presumably.'

'That's what I'm afraid of. I mean, shall I be stuck with half a dozen sensitive types, possibly all jealous of each other and with no audience to listen to them? How can I be sure we get a nice, kind, attentive crowd?'

'They'll come,' I assured her. 'Lots of people will simply come to see your house and garden, poets or no poets. Others will be culture-vultures, and game to listen to anything in the cause of Art, and others will feel they can't waste the ticket.'

'And there are bound to be the poets' relations,' agreed Amy, looking more hopeful. 'I wonder if we could organize a group from the evening classes in Caxley? You know the sort doing English Literature? The Beowulf bunch, for instance.'

'"Weave we the warp. The woof is wub" sort of thing, you mean? I don't see why not. English Literature classes should swell the audience nicely, and if you're short, I'll come and sit in the front row.'

'I'm counting on you, anyway,' said Amy, selecting a large stick of celery, 'to pass round the sausage rolls.'

'You'll need something far more spiritual than sausage rolls,' I told her. 'You'll have to have nectar and ambrosia, and lots of "beaded bubbles winking at the brim" for a poetry evening.'

'We'll have lashings of the latter,' promised Amy, and crunched into the celery.

It was still blowing a gale when Amy left me at about nine-thirty. I saw by the light of her headlamps that a sizable branch had been torn from the horse chestnut tree in the garden, and the path was strewn with twigs and dead leaves. It was going to be pretty draughty sitting under that skylight tomorrow, I thought, if this weather continued.

I sat down by the fire again, and had a belated look at the daily papers. It was the usual conglomeration of strike threats, travel delays, violence, war and sudden death, and the most peaceful reading was the crossword and the obituaries.

The wind howled like a banshee and I found it distinctly unnerving. With Amy for company I had not noticed the vicious elements outside. Now, alone and responsible for any damage done, I became unusually jittery.

A cupboard door by the fireplace creaked slowly open, and I felt my blood pressure rising. Would a yellow claw-like hand with immensely long nails, Chinese fashion, appear round it? Or a black hand perhaps, holding a dagger? Or a white one dangling a knuckle duster?

'You've been reading too many thrillers,' I thought, and steeled myself to shut the door firmly. At the same moment, Tibby rose, fur bristling, and advanced towards the kitchen door, growling horribly. I watched her, mesmerized. Could someone have broken in? Had I locked the back door earlier? Probably not, we are a trusting lot in Fairacre, and, under cover of the appalling racket outside, it would be quite easy for someone to gain entry.

What should I do? Should I ring Caxley police? Should I arm

myself with the poker and fight it out? Reason told me that any burglar, no matter how puny, could easily twist a weapon out of my grasp and use it to belabour me.

Surely I had read somewhere that it was best to offer no resistance. After all, hospitals are severely overcrowded without unnecessary casualties awaiting admission. If it were money that the intruder wanted, he was going to be unlucky. I might rustle up three pounds or so, but that would be the most I could find in the schoolhouse at short notice. True, Aunt Clara's seed pearls might be acceptable, but that would constitute the bulk of my jewellery.

I took a deep breath, and flung open the door. The kitchen was as quiet as the grave. Tibby sat down and began to wash her face in the most maddeningly unconcerned fashion.

'Time I was in bed,' I told her, and went.

To my surprise, I had a letter from the Office about the skylight. Obviously my pleas had touched some compassionate heart, and the gist of the reply was that this particular item, under 'minor works', would be treated as an emergency, and that Mr Reginald Thorn, of the Nook, Beech Green, had been instructed to call and examine the offending structure.

'Should have thought the Office could've found someone with a bit more up top than old Reg,' commented Mr Willet, when I imparted the good news. 'Proper dog's dinner he'll make of it. I reckon I'd make a better job of it meself.'

I too had no doubts on that score, for Mr Willet's handiwork, whether with seedlings, paintbrush or bolts and screws, is always beautifully done. But the Office had appointed Reg Thorn and that was that.

'When do you think he'll come?'

Mr Willet pushed back his cap to scratch his head. 'Now that's asking! I know for a fac' he's making a dresser for that new chap at Beech Green post office, and Mrs Mawne is going up the wall about some shelving he promised her last autumn and hasn't never done yet.'

'He's like that, is he?'

Mr Willett pursed his mouth judicially. 'Well, he's not a bad sort of chap, old Reg, but he's no flier. I mean, he *says* he'll do summat, and he means it too, but his trouble is he can't say "No" to no one, so the work sort of piles up.'

'So you reckon it'll be the summer before he gets round to our skylight?'

'Now, I'm not saying that. This bein' an Office job like, and with forms and that to fill in, well, it might make old Reg get a move on. On the other hand, if all the other people get a bit whacky, and bully him, maybe he'll do their jobs to keep 'em happy. There's no telling.'

He raised his voice to a bull-like roar.

'Get off that there coke, you young devils, or I'll tan the skin off of your backsides, and you can tell your mums and dads why I done it!'

Mr Willet's method of dealing with the young might not find favour with modern psychologists, but it clears the coke pile in record time.

Whether Reg Thorn was awed by the county's official letter, or simply wished for a change of job, thus evading his earlier customers who were breathing fire, no one will ever know. But the outcome was decidedly cheering for me. Reg Thorn arrived within the week just as we were dishing out minced lamb (alleged – I suspected some man-made fibre) and mashed swede.

He was a tall lantern-jawed fellow, and said very little. He gazed up at the skylight with an expression of gloom. I had served all the children, and dispatched the containers to the lobby to await Mrs Pringle's ministrations, before he spoke.

'Rotted,' he said.

I agreed.

He sighed heavily. 'Still leaks?'

'It's been doing it for nearly a hundred years.'

'Ah! Looks like it.'

He remained rooted to the spot, very much in the way of the children returning their plates, but I did not like to say so. At length, he spoke again. 'Best see outside. All right?'

'Yes indeed. Mr Willet's ladder is by the wall if you want it.'

'Got me own. Insurance, see.'

To my relief he vanished, only to reappear framed in the skylight some minutes later. He appeared to be gouging pieces of wood from the window frame, and I only hoped that this operation would not add to the draught trouble.

I served helpings of crimson jelly decorated with blobs of rather nasty artificial cream. It is the children's favourite sweet and I was kept so busy scraping the tin for second helpings that I was quite startled to see Reg again at my elbow.

'Needs a dormer,' he shouted above the clatter.

'Won't that be expensive?'

'Yes.'

'Well, it's up to the people at the Office,' I shouted back. 'You can only tell them what you think.'

'Ah!' agreed Reg, and plodded off towards the door.

'My mum,' said Patrick conversationally, 'says old Reg don't get nothin' done in a month of Sundays.'

'That will do,' I replied witheringly. Privately, I feared that Patrick's mum was probably dead right.

Time alone would tell.

There is a widespread belief among town dwellers that remarkably little happens in the country. As any villager will tell you, the amount of activity that goes on is quite exhausting.

I am not thinking of the agricultural pursuits by which most of us get our living, but of the social side of life. What with the Women's Institute, amateur dramatics, various regular church activities such as choir practice and arranging the flowers, Cubs and Brownies for the younger people, fêtes, jumble sales and whist drives, one could be out every night of the week if one so wished.

As village schoolmistress I try not to take on too much during term time, although I do my best to make amends in the holidays, but nevertheless one has to face pressing requests for such things as two dozen sausage rolls for the Fur and Feather Whist Drive, or a raffle prize for the Cubs' Social.

It was no surprise then, when Mrs Pringle approached me one morning and asked if I would do her a favour. This polite phrase, accompanied by a slight lessening of malevolence in her expression, was the prelude to my whipping up a sponge for some cause dear to her stony heart, I guessed.

I was right, or nearly so.

'I'm helping Mrs Benson with Cruelty to Children,' she announced. 'Could you give us a bottle of something? It's a good cause, this Cruelty to Children.'

I wondered if a bottle of arsenic, or even castor oil, would be fitting in the circumstances.

'Anything, Mrs Benson says, from whisky to shampoo. Or even home-made wine,' she added.

At that moment the children surged in in a state of wild excitement.

'It's snowing, miss,' they yelled fortissimo.

In the stampede, Ernest stood heavily and painfully upon my foot.

'I'll find you something,' I promised Mrs Pringle, as I retired, wincing.

And if ever anyone needs support for the Prevention of Cruelty to Teachers, I thought, nursing my wounds, I shall be in the forefront.

Fortunately the snow was not severe. One or two flurries during the afternoon soon died out, leaving the playground wet but not white, for which I was thankful. It was good to get home again by the fire on such a cheerless day. I was relishing a cup of tea and Tibby's welcoming purrs, when Mrs Willet arrived.

She is a neat quiet little person and renowned in Fairacre for her domestic efficiency. Mrs Willet's sponge cakes and home-made jam invariably take first prizes at our Flower Show, and if there were awards for laundry work and exquisite mending she would doubtless take those too.

She accepted a cup of tea after some demurring and sat rather primly on the edge of her chair. Tibby rubbed round her lisle-clad legs affectionately, and soon Mrs Willet began to look more relaxed.

'Has Mrs Pringle asked for a bottle?' she said at last.

'Yes. I can find her one quite easily.'

This sounded as though I had a cellar stuffed with strong drink, and as I knew that Mrs Willet and her husband were staunch teetotallers I wondered if she would disapprove.

'Then I hardly like to ask you for anything more, Miss Read, but the truth is I've taken on a book stall at this bazaar of Mrs Benson's, and I wondered if you could spare one.

'You can have a dozen,' I cried. 'Probably two dozen. I'll bring them down during the week.'

'Bob'll do that,' Mrs Willet assured me. 'You put 'em in a sack, and he'll hump 'em home all right.'

I was not too happy about my books – even rejected ones – ending up in a sack, but said I would have a word with Mr Willet when they were ready.

'And what's happening about the centenary?' asked Mrs Willet. 'Any plans?'

'Not *firm* ones,' I prevaricated. 'Do you remember much about the school when you were here?'

'Quite a bit, though I started school in Caxley. We didn't move out to Fairacre until the end of the Great War, sometime in 1918. I had an auntie that lived in one of those cottages near the post office.'

'What brought you from Caxley?'

'Lack of money,' said Mrs Willet sadly. 'My dad was killed in the January in France, and Mum had three of us at home with her. Mum got a good job helping at the Manor here, so we up-sticks and came to Fairacre.'

'A big change for you.'

'We liked it. Mr Hope was the headmaster here then, and a good kind chap he was although he was on the bottle then, poor soul, and that was the ruin of him. Fairacre was a lot different then – more shops and that. There was a smithy and two bakers, as well as a butcher and the stores. I used to have my dinner at the baker's sometimes.'

'Why was that?'

'Well, once a week my mum and auntie had to stay all day at the Manor. I believe Auntie did a bit of dressmaking there, and Mum had to do the windows. Something extra anyway. Most of the children took sandwiches to school, but there was a lot of horseplay among the big boys and Mr Hope didn't come over to stop 'em, as by rights he should've done. I was fair scared, so Mum made an arrangement that I had two boiled eggs and bread and butter and a cake at Webster's, on the day she was up the Manor.'

'What happened to the other two children?'

'Oh, they were younger, not school age, and went with Mum and Auntie. So they had their dinner in the Manor kitchen. Best meal of the week, Mum said. Always a cut off the joint and vegetables from the kitchen garden, and a great fruit pie to follow, but I wasn't envious. I felt like a queen having my boiled eggs at the shop.'

'With the baker's family?'

'Oh no! Much better than that! There were two or three marble-topped tables for customers. Not that anyone ever came in to eat when I was there, but the Websters did teas for these cyclists that were all about, and ramblers, as they were called before they turned into hikers. Sometimes someone from the village would pop in for a loaf or a pennorth of yeast, and then I'd feel very superior being waited on. My meal cost sixpence, I remember, and I could choose any cake I liked from the window, after the eggs and bread and butter.'

'And what did you choose?'

'Always a doughnut. It was either that, or a currant bun or a queen cake. I reckoned a doughnut was the best value. I had that with a glass of milk. Not bad for sixpence.'

I agreed. Mrs Willet's eyes became dreamy as she looked back almost sixty years.

'There was a lovely picture pinned up on the wall. I think it was an advertisement for Mazawattee tea. There was this lady in a long skirt and a fur stole, with a beautiful hat on top with her Queen Alexandra fluffy fringe just showing. She was sitting on a park bench, and dangling a little parcel, with "Mazawattee" written on it, from one finger. She had on the most beautiful long suede gloves. I often wondered why she was sitting on a park bench in such gorgeous clothes. It might have dirtied them.'

'Probably collapsed exhausted after carrying a quarter of tea,' I suggested.

'She had a lovely face,' went on Mrs Willet. 'I thought I should like to look like that when I was grown up. But there, it never happened.'

She put down her cup, and began to get up.

'How I do run on! But it's nice to talk of old times. Bob thinks it's a waste of time to hark back, but I enjoy it. That's why I hope you'll be able to think of something for the centenary. We've got a lot to be thankful for in this village, and the school's the real centre of it.'

'It's good to hear you say so,' I told her. 'Never fear! We'll do the thing in style. And I won't forget the books.'

I showed her out into the murky winter dusk, and returned to my fire with much to think about. One day soon, I told myself, I must look through the school log books for some inspiration.

But before I had a chance to do this, Miss Briggs put forward an idea of her own.

'What about dressing the children in the costume of the 1880s, and making the schoolroom much as it was then? We could have copybooks, with pot hooks and hangers, and let them chant their tables, and even have a cane on the teacher's desk.'

I agreed that such a *tableau vivant* would no doubt appeal to the parents, but wondered if it might be rather ambitious.

'Why?' demanded Miss Briggs.

'Rigging out the children, for one thing. Plenty of parents could make the clothes for one, say, but I can't see big families like the Coggses even beginning.'

Miss Briggs began to look mutinous, and I hastily made amends.

'But I do like the idea, and we'll keep it in mind. After all, any brainwaves we have will probably need to be modified. We must remember, though, that space is limited, and if all the children are present there won't be a lot of room for grown-ups.'

My assistant looked slightly less aggressive, and I began to wonder if this would be a good opportunity to discuss her too-prompt departure after school, but decided to postpone the task, as a bevy of infants swarmed in bearing one of their number with a bleeding knee, all bawling as fiercely as the wounded one. It was not the time for a delicate matter of school discipline, but I determined to broach it before the week was out.

Later that day, Miss Briggs approached me, starry-eyed.

'I've had another idea. Perhaps the vicar would dress up as the Reverend Stephen Anderson-Williams. I see from the log book that he was here for the first ten years of the school's existence, and seemed to pop in daily.'

I hardly liked to tell her, after throwing cold water on her earlier idea, that the reverend gentleman she had named was still remembered by the older generation, as the man who had left a perfectly good wife and six young children at his vicarage to run off with a sloe-eyed beauty from Beech Green. He was never seen again, but it was believed that he and his inamorata made a home together in Belgium.

Somehow, I doubted if the present vicar would wish to portray him in our revels. The Reverend Stephen Anderson-Williams would be better forgotten in my opinion, especially as some of his descendants still lived in the Caxley area.

'It's quite a thought,' I said guardedly, and we left it at that.

There was a sudden lull in the bleak weather, and for the best part of a week the sky was a pellucid blue, and the wind from the downs was warm and balmy. The catkins fluttered in the hedge. Bulbs thrust their stubby noses through the soil, and the birds, bright in their courting finery, began looking for nesting places.

We all felt ten years younger, and the children were as happy as sandboys now that they could play outside. Even Mrs Pringle looked a little less dour and sported a new flowered overall.

'Minnie give it to me for Christmas,' she said, when I

admired it. 'I was keeping it for best, but what with the sun and this nice bit of spring, I thought why not wear it?'

'Why not indeed,' I agreed.

'Besides,' she added, 'what's the good of hoarding things? I mean, for all we know we may be knocked down by a bus before we have a chance to use our good stuff.'

This sounded more like Mrs Pringle to me. 'Always merry and bright,' as someone sang lugubriously in *The Arcadians*, but at least she had shown herself momentarily in tune with the spring sunshine around her. One must be thankful for small mercies.

I took advantage of this blessing of early warmth and ushered the children out for an afternoon walk. The rooks were wheeling about the high trees, and one or two little birds flew across our path, trailing dry grass and moss in their beaks, intent upon their nest building. There was even a bold bumble bee investigating the ivy on the churchyard wall, and someone said the frogspawn might be starting in the pond. Of course we had to go and see, but there was none there.

I looked at my watch. It said almost three-thirty, and we set off for school at a brisk pace. There were several things to put away before Mrs Pringle appeared, and grace to be sung before the end of school at a quarter to four.

As we approached the school gate, Miss Briggs's little car appeared. The children scattered to left and right, but I stood my ground. The church clock said three-thirty exactly, and so did my watch.

Miss Briggs peered from the side window.

'Can you spare a minute?' I said. She looked a little annoyed, but duly reversed into the playground.

The children and I entered the school, tidied up, sang *Now the day is over* and wished each other good afternoon.

Miss Briggs came into the room as the last of the footsteps died away. It was not quite ten to four. No time like the present, I thought, and invited her to sit down.

'I oughtn't to stop,' she said. 'I'm picking up a friend at four o'clock.'

'This won't take a minute,' I promised her, and began to point out the necessity of staying until all her children were accounted for at the end of the day.

'But the hours are nine till three-thirty,' she protested.

'Not in teaching, they aren't,' I assured her. 'The children are in your care. What would have happened if one had injured himself before I got back? There were seven or eight infants under seven left to their own devices.'

She did not appear particularly contrite, or even fully aware of having been at fault, but I made it clear that she must not leave until my children had collected their younger brothers and sisters, and she went off looking more irritated than chastened.

Well, I had said my piece, I told myself, locking my desk drawers. Now it was up to my assistant to profit from it.

3. MARCH

The 'soft weather', as the Irish say, remained with us, and March came in like the lamb rather than the lion. I was pottering about in the garden after tea, admiring the swelling buds on the lilac bushes, when a car stopped at the gate, and out stepped Miss Quinn.

The little I know of Miriam Quinn I like. She is an extremely hard-working and efficient secretary to an eminant industrialist whose offices are in Caxley. So far, she has managed to stay fairly clear of the multitudinous activities in the village, and one rarely sees her.

She and Joan Benson, her landlady at Holly Lodge, are good friends despite their difference in temperament. Joan, since her husband died recently, has taken on all kinds of public work in Fairacre, and her good humour has endeared her to us all.

This visit from Miriam, I surmised, was something to do with the Caxley Festival. I took her indoors with pleasure and offered her a drink, but she shook her head.

'We've just had a farewell party for one of our staff at the office,' she told me, 'and I've had quite enough for one evening, I think.' She went on to explain her visit which, as I had guessed, was about the festival.

'I hope you aren't going to ask me to open my garden,' I said. 'Not that people might not be delighted to see more weeds than in their own, but I can't compete with real gardeners.'

She laughed, and I thought how attractive she was when her usually serious expression was lit by laughter.

'Don't worry! It's something far less arduous. We're going to have teas in the village hall, and I'm trying to find out who would be willing to help. Joan's in charge, but would need about a dozen people to make a rota.'

'Oh, I'll willingly help,' I cried, much relieved. 'And if you want a cake, I am rather a dab hand at an almond one.'

'Splendid!' she said, producing a notebook and pencil. I noticed how neat the list was, and how quickly she made her notes. Obviously a treasure in the office at Caxley. No wonder she had been importuned by all the local clubs for help.

'Joan will be so grateful. We've got four names so far, including Mrs Willet who is marvellous, I hear.'

'You couldn't do better,' I assured her.

'What a pretty house this is,' said Miriam.

'I love it,' I said, 'but the snag is, of course, that it's a tied house and I really ought to look for somewhere else for my old age. I keep putting it off, which is quite mad, as house prices get more impossible each week.'

'It's not easy to find a place,' she agreed.

'Would you like to see the rest of it?'

'I'd love to. Houses are a great interest of mine. I was so lucky to find the annexe at Holly Lodge. Nothing in Caxley could compare with it.'

She followed me through the few rooms of the schoolhouse and seemed enchanted with all she saw, pausing at the bedroom windows to exclaim at the superb views which I am lucky enough to enjoy.

'I find this downland country marvellously exhilarating,' she said. 'When I get back from Caxley I feel pretty jaded, but ten minutes in this air, and with these views, and I'm a new woman. The thought of leaving it fills me with despair.'

'But you don't have to leave it, do you?' I asked, puzzled.

She made a grimace. 'I don't know. It will soon be common knowledge, I expect, so that I don't think I'm betraying confidences. Joan is probably moving nearer her daughter whenever anything suitable turns up. She will sell Holly Lodge then, of course. I suppose I could stay on, but I shouldn't care to

live at such close quarters with strangers, and in any case Joan would get a much better price without a tenant in the place.'

'She'll be missed,' I said. 'Let's hope she won't have to go for some time. Isn't she happy here?'

'Very happy. But she's about seventy, and getting less and less fond of driving, and I think her daughter feels she should be at hand if her mother were ill. It's all very sensible and understandable, but I dread her going, and dread house-hunting all over again even more.'

'Well, it was nice of you to tell me, and I won't say anything until I hear from other people that it's known in the village. Not that that will take long, knowing Fairacre,' I added.

Miriam laughed and made for the door.

'No secrets in a village!' she agreed, and departed down the path to the car.

One morning, soon after Miriam Quinn's visit, Reg Thorn appeared again with two men from the Education Office. They wanted to inspect the skylight again, and to see if the roof would stand a more solid structure built upon it.

This sounded hopeful to me. Could Fairacre School really be getting a proper dormer window to replace our temperamental skylight after a hundred years? I readily gave my permission for them to clamber about on the roof, and they departed.

Luckily, the weather was still fine, and apart from a good deal of thumping overhead which produced a light shower of flaked paint, dead leaves and an assortment of defunct wasps, spiders and earwigs upon my desk, we managed to continue our lessons in comparative peace.

The three vanished just before playtime, and I listened to the children's comments as they imbibed their morning milk.

'I bet them two men was telling ol' Reg the best way to do it.'

'What's a dormer anyway?'

'Do it have curtains like a proper window?'

'My auntie up Caxley says dormers lets in the draught something cruel.'

'D'you reckon we'll get it by the summer?'

'You'll be lucky! What with ol' Reg doin' it?'

It was like hearing their parents talking. Fairacre loves a new topic. The replacement of our skylight was going to keep everyone happy for a long time to come.

But not too long, I fervently hoped. I had a feeling that the fine weather would break the minute the glass was removed.

Mr Willet was of the same opinion. He was surveying the school roof when I went across to my house during the dinner hour.

'That'll never stand nothin' stronger than a skylight, that roof,' he asserted. 'Stands to reason, all that was gone into when this place was built. If it wouldn't bear the weight then, when them beams was new, what chance will it have now?'

'Perhaps it was too expensive to have a proper window put in then,' I hazarded.

'What, with all the money the Hurleys put up to help pay for it? They'd not grudge a few more quid to make the school shipshape and Bristol fashion. Always had to be the best for the Hurleys.'

'Come and look at my broad beans,' I urged, anxious to change the subject, and to collect a book of Greek myths to read to the children in the afternoon.

He followed me obediently as I led the way.

He studied my two rows of beans with a serious expression. 'You got blackfly comin' on,' he said. 'And them weeds is doing all right too. I better come up for an hour this evening.'

'Thank you,' I said. 'I'd be glad of your help. Have a look round while I nip in to fetch a book.'

He was still plodding morosely round the vegetable patch when I returned. It was unlike him to look so depressed. Could it be the state of my garden? I had been thinking that it looked unusually tidy. Not that it could hold a candle to Mr Willet's own plot, which was always a miracle of neatness and fertility, but not at all bad by my lowly standards.

'See you this evening then,' I said to the pacing figure. 'Any time suits me.'

'Ah!' answered Mr Willet absently, kicking a stone from the grass on to the garden bed. 'I tell you, Miss Read, that skylight was *right* for that roof. The Hurleys would've known, and I'll wager old Reg don't. It's not going to be as simple as they makes out.'

So it was the skylight that was casting this unaccustomed gloom upon Mr Willet! I felt mightily relieved.

'Well, cheer up,' I said, making my way towards the playground. 'That's Reg's look-out, isn't it?'

'It'll be mine before the pesky thing's been up a month or two,' forecast my caretaker. 'I'm the mug as always has to clear up other folk's mess!'

As he was still eyeing my weeds, I forebore to comment, but carried my Greek myths across to school in prudent silence.

News of Joan Benson's departure from Holly Lodge was very soon common gossip in the village, as Miriam had forecast.

The first to tell me was the vicar. 'A grievous loss!' he said. 'We were all so delighted when she and her husband and mother arrived, but now we must lose the last of the three. I wonder when she is moving?'

I was unable to tell him, but Mrs Pringle told me an hour or two later.

'Getting down to her daughter's as soon as she can,' she informed me. 'Going to look out for a little place down there. A bungalow, I don't doubt. Stairs get somethin' cruel as you get on, and she's got a touch of arthritis already.'

I said, somewhat shortly, that it was the first I had heard of it.

Mrs Pringle continued undismayed: 'Holly Lodge ought to fetch a good price on the market. Nice garden and that, and you can call your soul your own with that holly hedge all round. Don't get no busybodies peering in like I do at home.'

This was a side swipe at her immediate neighbour, and I was careful to make no comment. It would soon have got back in Fairacre, and I do my best to steer a steady course.

'I wonder what Miss Quinn will do?' was her next surmise. 'She won't find it easy to find as quiet a place as that little flat of hers, and I don't suppose she earns enough to buy anything outright, do you?'

'I have no knowledge of Miss Quinn's income nor of her future plans,' I said stiffly. Was there no way of stopping this gossip? Evidently not, for the lady continued.

'That little hovel near Miss Waters is in the *Caxley Chronicle* this week for thirty thousand pounds. I ask you! Who'd buy that shack anyway? I can remember when old Perce Tilling bought it for three hundred pounds, and then we told him a fool and his money was soon parted. Not that Perce cared. He'd just won a packet at Caxley races, and his old auntie who kept the shop at Beech Green had just died, and they found over four hundred under the mattress when they lifted her into her coffin, so Perce got that as well. Not fair really, as that daughter of hers, although no better than she should be when it came to American soldiers, did do her best by her mum, and kept her lovely and clean, right to the end.'

'You got a minute?' shouted Mr Willet from the door. Once again he was my saviour, and I escaped thankfully from Mrs Pringle's reminiscences.

Within the week I had been told by Mr Lamb at the post office that it was a great shame Mrs Benson had got to give up. The place was too big for her, no doubt, now her husband and mother were dead. Still, it should fetch a tidy sum these days. He reckoned anything between thirty and forty thousand.

The butcher, cleaving lamb chops, told me between hacks that it was a pity Mrs Benson's daughter was in trouble of some sort, and such a nice old lady had got to sell up and go to help. On the other hand, this was the right time to sell, and she would probably clear forty or fifty thousand.

Mr Roberts, the farmer, said that we should miss Joan Benson. She'd been a nice body to have in the village, and he was sorry to hear her health was obliging her to leave Holly Lodge. Nevertheless, that was a tidy little property and on a nice bit of rich soil, as his father had always said, a fair treat for root crops. To his mind it should fetch somewhere round fifty thousand.

The price of property in our village has always occasioned the greatest interest. It was obvious that the amount finally given for Holly Lodge would provide Fairacre with an enthralling topic in the future.

It so happened that I met Joan Benson returning from the grocer's shop about this time. She was hurrying along, as round and cheerful as a robin, and put down her basket to talk to me.

'I've just been told,' she said, looking amused, 'that my house should fetch between fifty and sixty thousand pounds. As it isn't even on the market yet, I'm rather tickled. Does Fairacre always rush ahead like this with conjectures?'

'Always,' I told her. 'It's all part of the fun!'

Amy rang up one evening to invite me to dinner to meet the poets who were to take part in the Caxley Festival in May.

'I thought it would be a good idea for them to see where it would be held, and perhaps to meet each other.'

'How many are there?'

'Well, I'm sorry to say I can only rustle up a couple. There were going to be four, but one is having a nervous breakdown, poor thing, and the other is touring the United States with his poetry programme. What stamina!'

'Americans are noted for their strength and energy,' I told her.

'Not the *Americans*! The poet, I meant. He looks such a weed too, as though walking up the steps of Caxley Town Hall would finish him off, but there he is – all eight stone of him – bouncing about all over America. I can't get over it. Not that Tim Ferdinand, who will be coming, is much sturdier.'

'How's your weight going?' I asked, reminded of Amy's slimming efforts by these poets' obvious fragility.

'Don't speak of it. I seem to have put on three pounds in the last week.'

'The scales have gone wrong.'

'Do you really think so?' Amy sounded wonderfully cheered. 'I hadn't thought of that. I'll try yours when I come over.'

'Please do, but I warn you that mine are almost half a stone too much, and friends come tottering downstairs looking demented until I explain it to them.'

'I'll remember. By the way, as the poets are so thin on the ground I've found a nice pianist as makeweight, and I'm just wondering if I could ask that marvellous singer Jean Cole who sang at the Fairacre festival some years ago.'

'It's flying rather high,' I said doubtfully. 'I think she only came because she was a relation of Major Gunning's, and he left some time ago.'

'Do you know where he went?'

'I could find out. I've an idea he's in a nursing home or private hotel somewhere not too far away. The vicar might know.'

'Be a lamb and see what you can do. Two poets, a pianist and Jean Cole should fill the bill beautifully.'

I promised to do my best.

'See you on Thursday week then. Long skirt to do honour to my four-course dinner, and make yourself as smart as possible.'

I blew a raspberry down the line to my bossy old friend.

I spent the rest or the evening looking out bottles and books for Joan Benson's bazaar. The bottles presented no problem. I had three bottles of tomato ketchup, a comestible of which I partake sparingly, so two of those went into the basket, and a bottle of home-made lemon essence.

The upstairs cupboard yielded a bottle of shampoo, and another of pungent scent, called *Dusky Allure* which had been given me by one of the children. As the said child had now moved from the district, I felt I could safely donate it. One has to be careful in a village; reputations have been ruined over just such little matters. Not a bad haul, I thought, surveying my five bottles. I only hoped I did not win any of them back again.

But the books occupied me for the rest of the evening. I began in a fine crusading spirit, ruthlessly putting aside half a dozen novels which I told myself I should never read again. It seemed prudent, though, to cast a cursory glance over them, and in no time I was deep in one which I had completely forgotten and found enthralling. I put it back on the shelf to finish later.

Meanwhile, crouched as I was on the floor, I became horribly stiff, and decided to look through the rest in my armchair. At a quarter to ten I realized that I had galloped through most of them, and five were put aside as absolutely essential to my needs. One book alone remained at hand for Mrs Willet's stall. I decided that I had done enough sorting for one evening. Tomorrow I would be firm and start again. It would be a good thing to clear out the bookshelves, but now bed called.

I took a final look at the rows of books. Would anyone read that life of Marlborough? Or that terrible edition of *Lorna Doone* with illustrations presumably executed in weak cocoa? And what about *Whitaker's Almanack* for 1953, and that glossy American cookery book full of recipes about squash and scallions and clams, and every one of them in cupfuls? Any takers, I wondered?

Who would have thought that giving away books would prove so tiring? It would have to wait until tomorrow.

I went to bed carrying my first rejected book with me.

The next morning I determined to find out when Fairacre School had first opened its doors to the children of the village. The forthcoming celebration, once we had decided on its nature, should take place approximately around the same time of year, I felt.

The earliest log book is a battered affair, leather covered and with beautifully mottled endpapers. It weighs several pounds, and the ink has now faded to fawn. The entries make fascinating reading.

I was mightily relieved to discover that the school opened at the beginning of December in 1880. If we were to celebrate the occasion then at least we knew that it must be an indoor affair. No playground nonsense, wondering if the heavens would open in a summer shower. The longer I live in a village, the more I marvel at the touching faith with which folk organize outside affairs in our climate. June can be cruelly chilly, and I well remember that on Coronation Day on 2 June the most joyful moment was when we lit the bonfire and could huddle round the welcome blaze.

No one would expect anything outdoors at the beginning of December, so that cleared the ground nicely in my opinion. Something in the school must be arranged and, if need be, repeated to accommodate all the parents and friends.

The first headmistress was a Miss Richards, and her sister looked after the infants. Judging by the first entry, the opening of the school had been awaited for some time. The builders had not finished their work in the time allotted. Could some of Reg Thorn's forebears have been employed, I wondered?

The two ladies obviously had difficulty with discipline. There are a good many entries describing canings, and one John Pratt who seems to have been a sore trial and quite unmoved by frequent chastisement. What became of him, I wondered? He was evidently a resourceful boy, for he was discovered 'putting on the Hands of the Clock with the greatest Audacity' in July 1882, and a little later released a frog during the vicar's lesson on the Good Samaritan.

The two sisters resigned in 1885, giving their reason as ill health, but the boisterous spirits of their country pupils must have had something to do with it.

A widow and her daughter came next, and this pattern of a headmistress and woman assistant continued for some years. It was interesting to note that for all its hundred years Fairacre School had remained a two-teacher establishment. There must have been some odd pairings, I guessed, but probably no more difficult than my present companion-in-harness, Miss Briggs. Two women, thus yoken, must learn to pull together to their mutual advantage and that of the school.

I closed the log book and replaced it in the desk drawer with a feeling of relief. There would be plenty of time to work out something to celebrate our centenary, and at least it would not clash with the Caxley Festival in May, which was showing signs of impinging on our rural tranquillity.

I was slamming back the drawer when the vicar entered. He came to the point at once, after greeting the children and admiring the progress of our hyacinth grown over water.

'As a child I used to grow acorns over medicine bottles,' he told me. 'I had a splendid collection one year.' His eyes grew misty at the recollection, but he returned to the reason for his visit. 'Have you any idea when the school first opened? I confess I can find no reference to it anywhere.'

I told him, with some pride, and his face cleared.

'Ah! That is good news! It gives me plenty of time to arrange a suitable service. Do you think the first Sunday in December, in the afternoon, would be a good idea, or perhaps an evening one during the week?'

I wondered privately whether his parishioners would prefer to forego their Sunday-afternoon nap, or to turn out on a dark December evening, leaving their cosy firesides for the chill of St Patrick's church. It was difficult to offer advice, and I said so.

Luckily the vicar appeared to make up his own mind. 'On the whole, I think an afternoon service would be best. We want the children to attend, after all, and it would be a great pity if they were deprived just because it was their bedtime.'

I did not like to point out to our innocent pastor that the majority of the children would be glued to their television sets until about ten o'clock or later, imbibing all sorts of dubious knowledge, no doubt.

'There's a lot to be said for a service during the hours of daylight,' I replied diplomatically.

And we left it at that.

'By the way,' I said, as I accompanied him to the door. 'Do you happen to know Major Gunning's address?'

I told him about Amy's hope of inviting Jean Cole to dinner. He looked doubtful. 'She's so much in demand,' he said.

'I know.'

'But I can give you the major's address. He's at a private hotel in Caxley. It's either Ash Tree Hotel, or Elm Court or possibly Hawthorn House. Something arboreal, I know. I will look it up and let you have it, Miss Read.' He gave a sigh. 'This Caxley Festival is, no doubt, an excellent project, but it does seem to make an inordinate amount of *planning*.'

I agreed, and returning to my class, thought that centenary celebrations shared the same problems.

4. April

Amy's party took place on the second day of the month.

After a boisterous morning which toppled the crocuses and blew the rooks off course, the sun came out, and by the time I set off all was tranquil. The western sky was dappled with little pink clouds as the sun went down, and the air was so clear and still that I could see a range of hills some twenty miles away to the south.

Obedient to Amy's request, I had donned a long black skirt bought at Caxley's most favoured outfitters, and identical to quite half a dozen I had observed on various local friends during the past winter. The blouse that topped it was of black and white silk which I thought looked rather fetching, but as it had a back zip I was resigned to undertaking violent contortions to do it up every time I wore it, and was beginning to wonder how long it would be before such exercises were beyond me.

As usual, I was the first to arrive. Amy greeted me with unusual affection.

'You look splendid! Truly elegant! Come and see the table. I'm rather proud of the flowers.'

She led the way into the dining room, and it certainly was a vision of delight. Daffodils and narcissi scented the room, and in the centre of the table was a magnificent arrangement of freesias and miniature daffodils in shades of cream and gold.

Amy stood surveying it, a look of supreme satisfaction on her face.

'It's perfect,' I told her.

'And that damask tablecloth was my grandmother's. It's a devil to launder, and so it doesn't get used very often, but those Victorians had some good ideas about dressing a table.'

'Do you remember Mrs Beeton's illustration for a simple supper party? Three epergnes of red roses down the centre, and smilax trailing everywhere?'

'Our old edition had a picture of a tray for an invalid,' recalled Amy. 'There were two silver trumpet-shaped flower vases with carnations, as well as two or three dishes complete with silver covers, a coffee pot, milk jug and sugar bowl. I don't think you could lift the thing, let alone stagger upstairs with it. But I must say it looked superb.'

'I pity anyone being taken ill in my house. A plate of toast and a mug of tea would be about my limit.'

'James has occasionally brought me my breakfast in bed when I've been too ill with flu, or something equally horrid, to get up. He can manage very thick bread and butter, with the crusts rather touchingly cut off, and the marmalade pot, and a cup of tea with most of it in the saucer by the time he's negotiated the stairs. But I certainly don't get carnations, and to be honest, I don't think I should appreciate them in the state I'm in when I have to stay in bed.'

'Now, tell me who's coming,' I said when we returned to the sitting room.

'The two poets I told you about, and Betty Mason the pianist. Jean Cole is on tour in Belgium. I managed to get in touch with Major Gunning, thanks to you, and he says she'll be back next week and he'll find out her plans.'

'He won't forget,' I assured her. 'He was the mainstay of dozens of our village committees.'

'I invited him tonight, but he says he's become rather too old for parties. A shame really, he sounds a dear.'

'And James?'

'No James, I'm afraid. At a company dinner in South shields. But I've invited Horace Umbleditch to make up the six. He's giving an organ recital in the church as part of the Caxley

Festival, so he'll enjoy meeting some of the others, I hope. And anyway, he's devoted to you.'

'He's nothing of the sort!' I protested. 'I hardly know the fellow!'

'Well, I know better. And he's moved into such a charming house in the school grounds now, and could well do with a wife.'

'Amy, you are incorrigible! You know I have no wish to marry, nor presumably has Horace Umbleditch, and if he had, I'm sure he could find someone younger and keener than I am. Do leave us happy old spinsters and bachelors in peace!'

'Hoity-toity!' cried Amy, as the front-door bell rang. I watched her as she hurried to answer it, admiring the back view of her elegant cream silk caftan. Had she chosen it for tonight's occasion as the perfect complement to her flower arrangements? Knowing Amy, I guessed that she had.

She returned with Betty Mason in tow, a short rather dumpy person wearing black with a sparkling necklace. She had beautifully waved silver hair and a soft, powdery pink and white complexion which reminded me of marshmallows. During the evening I was to discover that she was as sweet and gentle as her looks.

We had scarcely greeted each other when Amy was called to the door again, and Horace Umbleditch arrived. There was no need for introductions as Betty and Horace knew each other. Horace teaches at a prep school not far from Bent, and he is organist at Bent Church. He and Betty were soon deep in discussion about the best choice of music for a country festival.

Then, turning to me, Horace asked if I had heard the good news about his sister Irene.

'Henry Mawne told me,' I said, and then wondered if the good news he spoke of was about the proposed marriage to David Mawne after all. Perhaps it was something quite different – a new post, maybe, or a fantastic win on the pools, always supposing that Irene went in for such things.

However, I did not have to endure suspense for long, as

Horace said that the wedding was to be in early June, at a registry office, and no doubt I should see them before then as they proposed to stay for a few days with Henry during the Caxley Festival.

'It is marvellous news,' I agreed, glad to be right for once. 'And where will they live?'

'For the moment in David's flat, but I expect they will move further out sometime. It's not much fun there for Simon in the holidays, and I'm sure Irene will look forward to making a home elsewhere.'

Away from the haunting horrors which that flat must hold for David, I thought privately, and for young Simon who had seen his mother at her most terrifying in those surroundings.

Amy came in and glanced at the clock, which said a quarter to eight. 'I do hope the others haven't lost their way. They are coming together.'

'Tim Ferdinand's usually pretty punctual,' said Horace.

'Oh, you know him! I hadn't realized that.'

'Very slightly. He came to the school one evening to read poetry to the boys. They were remarkably well-behaved.'

No one knew quite how to react to the last remark, and Amy said she must go and check that the crab was all right, conjuring up visions of a sickly crustacean with a bottle of medicine alongside.

'Something smells delicious,' commented Betty kindly.

'I just hope it won't be overdone,' said Amy, setting off for the kitchen. 'It's in a light cheese sauce, and you know how easily that can dry up.'

'Amy is the best cook I know,' said Horace with enthusiasm. 'After school meals, all cabbage and custard, the food here is sheer ambrosia.'

'It's so nice,' said Betty, 'to find people interested in food. I can't bear those who profess to have a mind above it, particularly when you have spent all day and a great deal of money in preparing something you think they will enjoy.'

The bell rang again, and we heard voices in the hall.

'I can't *think*,' we heard a despairing voice say, 'where I went wrong, but we took a short cut and ended up on the downs. It really is too bad the way some of these roads simply peter out into sheep tracks. A hundred apologies, Amy dear.'

'All is forgiven,' said Amy, 'and you really aren't late at all. Come and meet the others.'

She ushered in a short tubby man with a florid complexion set off by a neat white moustache. He could have been taken for a retired colonel or a particularly kindly bank manager. Perhaps he was, I thought, and simply wrote poems in his spare time on the back of Queen's Regulations or the bank's blotting-paper.

'John Chandler,' said Amy. 'He has just published his third book of poems.'

We all gave cries of admiration and welcomed our fellow guest.

'And Timothy Ferdinand. You know Horace, I believe, and this is Betty Mason the pianist, and Miss Read.'

We made more polite noises and I thought how much more like a poet he looked. For one thing, he was painfully thin and pale, as Amy had told me, with a wobbly Adam's apple which showed to advantage as he wore an open-necked shirt above blue jeans carefully fringed at the ankle. I was glad to see he had socks on under the inevitable sandals, and his hands were clean.

He looked a pleasant, if vague, young man, and still seemed to be brooding about the way he became lost on his journey.

'It happens to us all,' I assured him. 'It's those crossroads at Springbourne. Someone said once that it seems to be moved overnight. As a matter of fact, some young people did turn the signpost round one night, and confusion was worse confounded.'

He looked a little happier. 'You're quite right. It was at the crossroads we went wrong. But why not say "No thoroughfare", or "Downs only"?'

'I suppose the reasoning is that there is a road for about a mile before it dwindles into a track.'

'Possibly,' said Timothy doubtfully. He took out a rather grubby red and white spotted handkerchief and polished his sherry glass in a preoccupied way. I was glad that Amy was out of the room at the time.

Before long she returned, and we talked about the Caxley Festival while the most delicious smells wreathed around us.

The attitude of the two poets towards this event varied considerably, although both agreed, somewhat vehemently, that Caxley needed 'to be awakened'. John Chandler looked upon it as a useful way of becoming known to a larger number of readers than before.

'Good publicity,' he said briskly. 'Might even sell a dozen or so extra books. Though one can't help feeling that at these affairs one is preaching to the converted. Still, it all helps.'

Timothy Ferdinand's attitude was less commercial. 'Oh surely,' he cried, 'it is the artist and his work that really matters! He needs an audience to stimulate him, and I think that the festival will do that very well.'

'Let's carry on this discussion while we eat,' said Amy.

We followed our hostess into the pretty dining room and confronted our sizzling ramekins.

'If you don't like crab,' said Amy, 'there is melon ready on the sideboard.'

Only Betty asked if she might change. 'I adore crab, but can't digest it,' she said apologetically, and John rose swiftly to make the replacement.

I thought how sensible Amy was to offer an alternative to one's first course. So often the hostess has gone to no end of trouble to produce something rather exotic, often with shellfish or avocado pear which many people cannot take. I myself have several times been faced with taramasalata which, with the best will in the world, I cannot get down. If only I had been offered a slice of melon or a nice little tot of orange or tomato juice waiting on the sideboard, how much happier I should have been!

Horace Umbleditch sat beside me and John Chandler

opposite. They were both exuberant talkers and Amy and I had little to do in the way of keeping the conversation going. Timothy Ferdinand still seemed slightly distraught, at the foot of the table, facing Amy, but gulped down his crab as though he had not seen food for weeks, and nodded abstractedly at Betty's gentle remarks.

Cold turkey and ham with a handsome salad followed the crab, and a dish of mammoth baked potatoes with butter melting in their floury tops. As Amy served us, I was amused to notice that Timothy was engrossed in cleaning between the prongs of his perfectly spotless fork by inserting them busily in the edge of Amy's beautiful damask tablecloth. He seemed quite unaware of anything amiss. His periodic nods at Betty's gallant monologue continued as before, as with eyes on his work he polished assiduously.

Whether Amy saw him or not, I could not say, but she continued serving with her usual charm, whilst commenting on the possibility of getting Jean Cole to attend the poetry reading during the festival week.

Fortunately, the arrival of his main course saw the cessation of Timothy's cleansing operations, and he fell to with a will and did not seem to feel the need to polish anything else during the sweet and cheese courses.

At last he leant back and gave a sigh of contentment. 'What a perfect dinner! I hardly ever sit down to a meal when I'm alone, and certainly never to one as splendid as this.'

'But don't you get hungry?' enquired Amy.

'I suppose I do,' replied Timothy, looking about him vaguely. 'I eat an apple or a biscuit sometimes. Anything that's lying about, you know.'

No wonder he looked so emaciated, I thought.

Conversation then became concentrated upon the form of Amy's proposed evening, and later she took us all into the drawing room to see the best way of arranging things for the great night.

John Chandler appeared outstandingly practical about this,

pointing out the best place for the piano with relation to the lighting and the french windows which, with any luck, might be open to admit the warm evening air, scented with roses and stocks. He also suggested seating arrangements which would ensure the greatest number of people being at ease, and reminded me yet again of a military commander deploying his resources to the best advantage.

Timothy did not contribute much to the plans, but sipped his coffee thoughtfully, only surfacing once to remark that it was a blessing no microphone would be needed in a room this size as he had a horror of the things, and had been hurt by falling over one once, and hurt even more by the BBC mechanic's remarks about the accident.

This led to a general discussion about whether it was a good thing to understand machinery, or whether it was better to disclaim all knowledge at the outset of how to deal with the objects, and to let someone else tackle the problem.

Eventually the delicate task of allotting time for each artist's performance was undertaken, and it was agreed that roughly half an hour, give or take five minutes, for each, should ensure a full evening's pleasure, and that it was up to each performer to rehearse his own contribution to fix the time it would take.

By eleven o'clock the company had dispersed, looking happy and well fed. Amy turned down my offer to help with the washing up. Evidently, unheard by me and probably by everyone else in Amy's beautifully soundproof house, her daily help had been hard at it and the kitchen awaited the morrow as spotless as ever.

'Do you think it went well?' asked Amy, on the doorstep.

'Everything – but *everything*,' I assured her, as I let in the clutch, 'was absolutely perfect.'

I was delighted to have a letter from the Office, a day or two later, to inform me that work on the new window to replace the present skylight would begin at the end of term and should be completed before the beginning of the summer term.

This was good news indeed, although I should have preferred to read '*will* be completed' rather than that cautious '*should* be completed'. However, it was better perhaps to face the probability of a half-finished job than to be disappointed later.

Mrs Pringle shared Mr Willet's doubts about Reg Thorn's ability to do the job at all, let alone to a deadline even as vague as this one.

'What he done to my poor sister-in-law in Caxley you'd never believe,' she assured me. 'You'd think he'd feel downright sorry for a widow woman as suffers something so cruel with arthritis in her hands that she hasn't done her back hair for years now. She told me herself as Reg promised faithful to have her straightened up by last Easter. He'd only got the porch to put to rights. Bob Willet would have done it in two days flat, but Reg hung it out, just when the wind was in the east, fairly scouring out Peg's hall with the front door off, and the bill – which came pretty smartish, I can tell you – was twice the estimate, and give poor old Peg indigestion for a week.'

'Let's hope he's improved since then,' I replied.

Mr Willet, who had joined us, snorted with disgust. 'We'll be lucky to get that dratted dormer by next winter, and then I don't reckon it'll work. If there ain't trouble with the roof I'll eat my hat.'

I refused to be depressed by my two Job's comforters. Nothing could be worse, I felt, than the present ancient skylight. I acknowledged the Office's letter in enthusiastic terms, and looked forward to seeing the workmen on the job before the Easter holidays.

I felt less enthusiastic about Miss Briggs's progress in the infants' room. To be sure, she did not rush away at three-thirty as she had done previously, but I rarely saw her smile, she shouted at the babies who, naturally, became noisier than ever, and she made no response to any of my overtures. Mr Willet's early summing up of the young lady as 'a fair old lump of a girl' was true.

It was difficult to know how to improve matters. Over the

years, I had worked with dozens of infants' teachers with just the screen between us. Some had been shy, some bold, some flighty, but all had been fairly cheerful, and some outstandingly gifted. A two-teacher school must be harmonious. There is no getting away from each other, which is possible in a large establishment, and I was at a loss to know how to overcome the girl's sulkiness.

Was she ill perhaps, I wondered? Was she in love? Was she homesick? Or had she realized that she was in a job she disliked, and worried about how to get out of it?

As far as I could find out, she had few friends in Caxley and had not joined any clubs or societies. She must be lonely, I felt, and her digs, though adequate, were not particularly comfortable, I gathered.

I should have to have a word with her sometime, I supposed

gloomily. Only a week of the present term remained, and she was having a holiday in France at Easter. With any luck she would return with more zest to Fairacre School.

I did not need much persuading to put off this problem until her return, telling myself – not for the first time – that things might sort themselves out. My faith in the power of destiny to resolve my problems is touching, but usually misplaced.

The April weather, which had been kindly, now switched to the other extreme and became violently windy, with sudden vicious storms which scoured the countryside, dowsing newborn lambs and tossing the daffodils to the ground.

The skylight dripped steadily during these onslaughts, and the worst of the storms always seemed to coincide with playtime, so that the children were obliged to spend their break indoors, much to everyone's annoyance.

Several new puddles appeared in the playground, and on the rare occasions when the children spent a few minutes outside a new game had been devised, called, I gathered, 'Splashem'. This involved jumping in the deepest part of a puddle just as someone passed, preferably an infant too small to retaliate and likely to get more of him drenched, and then to enjoy not only the victim's discomfiture, but also the hilarious glee of the onlookers.

It was a game I did my best to stamp out promptly, but not before several cross mothers had called to complain about sopping clothes and squelchy shoes.

On one of the stormiest days, the dinner lady slipped over in the playground, all the gravy was spilled, her knee was badly grazed and her tights ruined. Miss Briggs took care of the school while I rendered first-aid in the schoolhouse. She seemed more agitated about the loss of the gravy than her own injuries.

'I could easily pour some of Beech Green's into a jug for you,' she offered, as I dabbed at her knee with TCP.

'Don't worry, it won't hurt us to go short for once. This skirt is soaked. Would you like to borrow one?'

The offer was accepted, and she went off dry if not particularly elegant, and full of apologies.

Mr Annett, the headmaster at Beech Green, and also choir-master at Fairacre, called that evening on the way to choir practice, to tell me that Miss Clare was staying with them.

'She's not too bad,' he began, shaking a wet umbrella energetically, 'but Isobel found her with a heavy cold yesterday when she called, and persuaded her to have a day or two in our spare bed.'

'You are good Samaritans,' I said.

'Not a bit. But come and see her if you can.'

'I'll come tomorrow if it suits you.'

'Fine. We'll look forward to it.'

He sprinted churchwards, and I went indoors out of the beastly wind. This was no weather for poor frail Dolly Clare, I felt, but was comforted to think of her in such safe hands at Beech Green.

If anything, the weather was wilder still when I drove the few miles from Fairacre to Beech Green. The windscreen wipers could scarcely keep pace with the torrent of rain which lashed the car. Young leaves and scraps of early blossom littered the leafy road as though it were an autumn evening. A fast-running rivulet ran each side of the lane, and every puddle sent up a shower of drops, reminding me of 'Splashem' and my naughty boys.

The few people I passed on the road were well wrapped up in waterproof garments ranging from sou'westers to Wellingtons. I only saw one umbrella, and that was causing its owner considerable trouble. In rough weather, our downland winds can soon rip such a thing to pieces, and it is wiser to have one's hands free to tighten a headscarf or to turn up a raincoat collar against the onslaught.

I found Miss Clare sitting by a cheerful fire. She was dressed, and had a pretty lacy shawl round her shoulders.

'Isobel had to go out,' she told me. 'She is giving a talk over at Springbourne and I wouldn't let her put it off. Really, I'm quite rested now after two nights and one whole day in bed.'

She certainly looked very well, though as thin as ever, but her eyes were bright and I think she was enjoying the company of the Annetts.

'They are so kind,' she went on. 'And the more I know of them the more I am reminded of my early teaching days when Mr and Mrs Hope looked after me so well.'

'Was that the headmaster who had to leave Fairacre?'

Miss Clare nodded sadly. 'He was a gentle soul, and very musical like the Annetts, but they lost their only child when she was twelve or so, and he never got over it. He took to the bottle, you know, and left soon after the Great War in 1919, if I remember rightly.'

'You remember the war well enough,' I said.

'Too well,' she said. 'Not only because I lost my dear Arnold in France, but because of the appalling number of young men from here who never came back. One of the saddest sights in Fairacre School was the black armbands worn by so many of the children. And the tears! You would see some little mite busy writing, and then the pen would stop, and the head would go down and the crying begin. It was dreadful to feel so helpless in the face of such sorrow. Mr Hope felt it all terribly. Sometimes I wonder if that was another reason for his taking to drink.'

'He didn't drink in school?'

'No, thank goodness! He made up for it at home, and was simply morose and befuddled in school towards the end. He still worked hard though, and did a great deal to help the war effort, and saw that the children helped too. Why, I remember that even the youngest babies were set to fraying pieces of white cotton and linen with a darning needle to make field dressings. And of course we all put as much as we could spare – which wasn't much, in those days – into War Savings stamps.'

'But at least you were spared bombings and rushing into air-raid shelters in that war.'

'We saw practically nothing of the war in Fairacre,' agreed Miss Clare, 'and I think, despite the horror stories in the newspapers, that there was less real hatred towards the Germans. We prayed every morning for the war to end, and I daresay we realized that German children were doing the same. We *disliked* them, of course, and *intensely* and I remember Mr Hope taking a grammar lesson at the other end of the classroom. He was trying to get the children to stop using the word "got" – with small success, as you might imagine. He wrote it on the blackboard, and crossed it through. "Got, got, got," he cried. "A horrible word! It must be German! Simply leave it out, and say: 'I *have* a pen! I *have* a new nib!' Understand?" And one of the Bryant boys, a real little gipsy said: "I ain't got neither, sir!" and everyone broke into laughter, including Mr Hope.'

'He sounds a good chap,' I said. 'A pity he had to leave.'

'A tragedy,' agreed Dolly. 'He was as much a casualty of war as my dear Arnold.'

She fingered the gold locket which hung under the lacy shawl. She wore it constantly, and I knew that it contained a photograph of the red-haired young man who had shared the fate of thousands of others whose names were written upon country memorials, and in the hearts of those who loved them.

'Heard the latest?' enquired Mr Willet the next morning. 'About the vicar?'

Elevated to rural dean? Broken a leg? Off on holiday? All these dramatic possibilities leapt to mind before Mr Willet spoke again.

'He's going to keep *bees*. I only hope he knows what he's letting himself in for. My old gran had three of those straw skep hives on an old table by her bottom hedge, and by gum, you didn't dare go near 'em to scythe the grass or pick a few runner beans nearby. Fair vicious they was.'

'I expect he's gone into all that.'

'I doubt it. Mr Mawne's been eggin' him on, and got him a couple of hives from some chap over at Bent who's giving up. Seen the light, I reckon. Why, I remember getting some of my gran's bees up my jersey as a kid, and havin' swellings like pudden basins.'

'They tell me that's good for rheumatism.'

Mr Willet snorted. 'Them old wives' tales! My gran had rheumatics something terrible and I bet she was stung often enough. She still told them old bees all that went on, like you hear about. She told 'em about Grandad dying in Caxley Hospital of the dropsy, and about the grandchildren being born. Funny really. People says bees are wise, but the more I hear about 'em the more I wonder. Did you know they goes for people dressed in blue?'

'Never heard of it.'

'No, nor I bet you haven't heard as they don't like compost heaps or bonfires or mowing the grass and a lot of other things you finds in a garden. Pesky little objects! I don't envy the vicar, that I don't!'

'But think of all the lovely honey,' I said.

'Bet you a dollar they'll be getting rape honey. Mr Roberts usually has a good field of that – you know, that blazin' yellow stuff.'

I said I knew what rape looked like. I had not lived in the country all these years without—

Mr Willet interrupted me. 'All right, all right! All I'm saying is that the vicar will have to take his honey off smartish if it's rape, or it'll gum up the whole works. Terrible stuff to extract, as my old gran could tell him, if she'd been spared. No, he don't know what he's letting himself in for, and I only hope he's got a blue bag for banging on the stings.'

'Can you still get a blue bag?'

'I doubt it,' said Mr Willet. He sighed and moved off. After a few steps he stopped and called across the playground: 'Hope

64

you aren't thinkin' of startin' bees,' he shouted. 'That's one thing I'm not helping you with, I can tell you.'

During the last day or two of term, I turned over in my mind the snippets of history that I had heard from Dolly Clare. Somewhere here there was the theme for our centenary celebrations, I felt sure.

To give Miss Briggs her due, the idea of dressing the children in the costume of 1880 had some merit. Perhaps we could have just two children in costume telling Fairacre School's story in each decade? Or, more practically, a boy and girl of each of the five reigns – six, if you included Edward VIII – through which the school had passed, suitably apparelled for their particular narrations.

It would be best if we could let the whole school take part, and perhaps a song or poem typical of each period could intersperse the narration. I discussed my nebulous ideas with Miss Briggs, who seemed remarkably cooperative for once. Perhaps her impending holiday in France was having a stimulating effect.

'Have you fixed a date?' she enquired sensibly.

'Sometime in the first week in December,' I told her. 'And for two performances definitely, otherwise we shan't have room for everyone. I thought parents of infants one afternoon, and the others next.'

'What a good idea! And perhaps we could combine it with the tea party the children usually give at Christmas.'

'That's a thought,' I agreed.

The Christmas party for parents, with the children acting as hosts, is a long-standing tradition in the school. Sometimes we are hopelessly overcrowded; dividing the party into a two-day event might help considerably. I looked at my assistant with new respect. At times she was quite bright, I thought.

'Of course, there's heaps of time for making arrangements,' she said.

'We'll have to start pretty early,' I assured her. 'We must

know what we propose to do next term so that the mothers can think about costumes, and it looks to me as though the whole of the autumn term will be devoted to rehearsing, whatever we decide upon.'

'Let's hope the dormer window will be done by then,' said Miss Briggs, watching a steady drip dropping into a bucket by my desk.

'It had better be!' I said grimly.

Mercifully, the rough weather subsided as suddenly as it had arrived, and the last day of term ended in a clear, serene evening.

Its blissful tranquillity matched my own feelings. The empty school basked in the golden rays of the setting sun. The rooks' cawing was the only sound above the tidy playground, and Tibby and I sauntered in the garden relishing our solitude. The narcissi wafted heady draughts of fragrance towards us. The grape hyacinths were a sea of blue in the shrubbery, and some fine scarlet tulips, straight as guardsmen, towered above them. What if the groundsel and dandelions and chickweed were making steady progress? With the holidays ahead I could soon root them out.

The hooting of a car horn brought me back to earth, and I found Amy at the door.

'I've been shopping in Oxford,' she said, 'and thought I'd call on my way home. Is it convenient, or are you having a cocktail party or anything?'

'Don't be funny,' I begged her. 'Whenever have you caught me preparing for a cocktail party?'

'You never know,' replied Amy vaguely. 'How pretty your garden looks.'

We strolled happily around my small plot, enjoying the unusual calm and warmth.

'Do you want to see my new purchases?' enquired Amy, as we made our way back to the house.

She dived into the car and emerged with two exotic-looking

dress boxes which she carried into the house. There seemed to be half a hundredweight of tissue paper in each one, but at last the garments were revealed. One was a set of glossy underwear, petticoat, knickers and brassiere in what was called, in my youth, oyster satin. The other was a stunning three-piece in silk jersey, cream in colour with delicate gold decorations at hem and neck.

'Well!' I exclaimed. 'They are all truly gorgeous!'

'So they should be at the ghastly price I had to pay for them. Now I'm beginning to wonder if they are a trifle young for me.'

'Rubbish!' I told her. 'You're a very good-looking woman, as well you know, and can wear anything. You always could.'

'So could you, my dear,' said Amy kindly. 'You were really quite pretty at eighteen when we first met.'

'Everyone is quite pretty at eighteen,' I retorted. 'A few decades later it is really quite enough to be clean and respectable, and I only hope I'm that. Anyway, I have no doubt that you would soon tell me if I weren't.'

Amy laughed, and began putting the clothes back among the tissue paper.

'Are you going away?' she asked.

'Not these holidays. At least, I haven't booked anything. I might slope off to Devon for a few days and hope to find bed and breakfast somewhere.'

'You'll be lucky! You really should organize yourself better. I'm always scolding you about it.'

'You are indeed,' I agreed, pouring her a glass of sherry.

'You know, even the *simplest* holiday needs to be arranged well in advance. James and I are having a few days in the Scillies at the end of next month, and we booked the hotel and the helicopter flight across from Penzance, way back in January.'

'Well, you're well-organized people, and I'm not.'

'With James so terribly busy we simply have to plan things, or we'd never get a break together. We propose to sleep, sunbathe, birdwatch and eat.'

'Sounds heavenly,' I said. 'I'll do it myself one day, when I can get round to arranging a holiday six months ahead.'

'I hope to live to see the day,' said Amy, putting down her empty glass. 'Well, I must be off. I'm glad you approve of my purchases.'

She looked rather sadly at my cardigan. 'How long have you had that shapeless garment?'

'About six years. And don't suggest that I give it to a jumble sale. It's pure wool, and hand-knitted by dear Mrs Willet. What's more, it's got *pockets*, which mighty few garments have these days, and I shall wear it till it drops into rags.'

'That won't be long!' Amy assured me, and drove off.

5. MAY

This is easily my favourite month and I greeted its arrival by remembering to say 'White Rabbits' aloud before uttering another syllable.

This childish superstition, told me first by a fellow six-year-old, is supposed to bring you luck for the rest of the month. When discussing such matters now, I tend to pooh-pooh the whole field of folklore, astrology, horoscopes and the rest of it, but I find myself hastily throwing spilt salt over my shoulder, dodging ladders and, if not in polite company, spitting in a ladylike way if I see one magpie.

Fortified by my 'White Rabbits' incantation, I got up and hung out of the bedroom window to relish the perfection of a May morning. The copper beech was in tiny leaf, which spread a rosy gauze over the tracery of bare branches. Dew shimmered on the grass, and drops of moisture on the hawthorn hedge sparked a hundred miniature rainbows.

Out in Mr Roberts' clover field a pheasant squawked. It was probably an anxious mother warning her chicks of the dangers that lurked around. Somewhere, high above, a lark was vying with another in the distance, the song pouring down from the blue in drops of pure music.

The air was cool, and deliciously scented with hyacinths and narcissi from the garden bed below. Later, it would be hot, and with luck I should be able to take my tea tray into the garden after my day's work, and relish the joy of growing things. I remembered, with immense pleasure, that there was nothing in the diary for the evening of May the first. What bliss!

As I dressed, I pondered the problem of loneliness. I receive a great deal of unnecessary sympathy for my single state, and am touched by kind people's concern for the fact that I live alone. If they only knew! I find it much more exhausting to share my home with friends who come to stay, much as I love them, and the places I visit I remember much more clearly, and with keener affection, when I have visited them alone. I suppose that this is because one wanders around, looking at objects which are of particular personal interest, and absorbing their aspect and history without the distraction of a friend diverting one's attention to something which she has discovered.

No doubt it tends to make one extremely selfish, but such solitude has its compensations. For one thing, it is possible to pursue a train of thought, or to carry out a piece of work unmolested. I heartily sympathize with widows and widowers who are used to a shared life, and suffer horribly when that is shattered. The fact that so many of them adjust relatively quickly to the situation is indicative of their bravery; the fact that others never really recover is understandable. But, as a spinster, I have never been called upon to try to mend a broken life, and I am deeply grateful for that mercy. Amy's many attempts to marry me off have failed, I like to think, largely because of my contentment with my lot. It would be insupportable, of course, to think that the men were lukewarm!

The postman arrived as my egg was boiling. He brought a six-page document from the Office about the necessity for Stringent Economies in Schools, and a glossy circular exhorting me to invest in a gold pendant which could be mine for rather more than two months' salary.

The latter went into the wastepaper basket, and the former I resigned myself to reading when I felt stronger. But not today, I told myself, taking a refreshing look at the shimmering glory outside.

The first of May was going to be devoted to savouring its hope and beauty.

*

The Caxley Festival began to loom large. An enormous amount of organization had gone into its arrangements and the *Caxley Chronicle* carried copious advance notices of the pleasures in store and the absolute necessity of sending early for tickets, not forgetting the stamped addressed envelope for their return.

Although Fairacre was only on the edge of these stirring events and was spared the feverish activity in the market town itself, yet even so we had our small part in the excitement. The gardens, which were to be open on the first Saturday and Sunday of the month, were being tended with unnatural fervour. Mr Willet, whose garden is always in a state of perfection, was somewhat scathing about these unseemly efforts.

'There's no call for panic,' he told me, 'if you keeps the hoe going regular. Some of these people is going fair demented! Why, I heard as that new couple up the other end of the street, is planting out their geraniums, pots and all, from the greenhouse! Just to make a show! It's a scandal, I reckon, and if there's a sharp frost, as can often happen in May, they've lost the lot.' He puffed out his moustache in disgust, and moved off about his business.

Mrs Pringle was equally censorious when she arrived. 'Never saw so much fuss in all me borns,' she said, chins quivering. 'Did you know as Mr Mawne borrowed Mr Hales' electric shears to tidy up his yew hedge, and nearly killed hisself by cutting through the cable?'

I expressed my concern.

'Oh, he's come to no harm,' shrugged Mrs Pringle. 'But if he hadn't got into this fever it would never have happened. And they say the vicar's now worrying about people disturbing his new bees, and wishing he hadn't offered to open the garden at all. These 'ere festivals can cause a mint of trouble it seems.'

'They sometimes raise a mint of money,' I pointed out, and waited for the expected answer.

'As my dear mother used to say: "Money isn't—"'

Linda Moffat burst in upon Mrs Pringle's mother's well-known maxim to tell us that the youngest Coggs had locked himself in the lavatory and was yelling for help.

I went to supply it.

So often was my attention drawn to the Caxley Festival that I was not in the least surprised to hear Amy's voice on the telephone, and confidently awaited the news about some festival plans. I was surprised to find that it was something entirely different that she had in mind.

'Am I right in thinking that in these decadent days you get a whole week's holiday around what, in our youth, was known as Whitsun?'

'That's right. Spring Bank Holiday is its official name, Amy, and it starts some time at the end of the month, and I believe we go back to school on Monday the third – maybe it's the fourth. I've mislaid my diary.'

'*Mislaid your diary?*' squeaked Amy, profoundly shocked. 'What on earth will you do?'

'It'll turn up,' I said vaguely. 'I may have chucked it into the wastepaper basket with some other rubbish, or I may have left it in the post office. I shall have a look today some time.'

'I have never met such a wholly lackadaisical person in my life,' scolded Amy. 'Why, if I were so careless as to lose my diary, I should be absolutely *daunted*! Life would have to stop until I'd found it again.'

'My life will tick over quite well without it for a day or two,' I assured her. 'What's the news?'

'Not very good, I'm afraid. James has muddled his dates, and now finds it is impossible for him to come to the Scillies at the end of the month. He has some engagement in Canada then, and we both wondered if you would like to come with me instead. What do you think? We were to go on the Sunday, stay overnight at Penzance, then fly across on the Monday morning. Do say you can come!'

'It sounds blissful! How long for?'

'We had planned to come back on the Thursday or Friday, so you'd have time to do any chores before school started again, if that's in your mind.'

I thought rapidly. I could not think of any particularly pressing engagement during that week, but without my diary it was difficult to be sure. I said as much to Amy, thanked her sincerely for an exciting invitation and promised to set about searching for my missing diary immediately.

'I'll ring you the minute it's found,' I assured her.

'And make the answer Yes,' said Amy, and rang off.

The first two or three days of May had been deliciously balmy, and we all told each other how lovely it would be if it lasted over the weekend.

Visions of suntanned visitors in summer frocks sauntering about the newly spruced Fairacre gardens kept most of us happy, but one or two pessimists shook their heads sadly. To my alarm, Mr Willet was one of them. He is such an accurate weather prophet that I viewed his forebodings seriously. The sky was cloudless on Friday afternoon and I only hoped that this time he might be wrong in his weather forecast.

But, sure enough, when I watched the weather man on television that evening, some ominous whirligigs, like well-spun spiders' webs, hovered unpleasantly near the west coast, and would bring rain and strong winds to the entire country. It was small comfort to learn that the weather would be more severe in the north than the south. The hardy types up there can take it, I thought callously, turning to our own dispiriting outlook which affected my feelings much more sharply.

I woke very early on Saturday morning. It was about five o'clock, and sure enough, a steady rain splashed along the gutters, and dripped from the trees. From the look of the garden, it had been pouring for several hours. Half a dozen sparrows splashed energetically in a large puddle by the box edging. The bird bath was full to the brim, though not being used for its right purpose by any of my bird friends.

The trees glistened, the roof tiles dropped miniature cascades on to those below, and some of the roses already drooped their heads, heavy with moisture. I decided to make myself a cup of tea and take it back to bed. Delicious Saturday morning, despite the rain, when I could call my time my own!

Tibby burst through the cat flap on the kitchen door, as I poured my tea, and rubbed her sopping-wet bedraggled body round my bare legs, ignoring my vituperation in an ecstasy of love. To salve my conscience, and to give myself time to get safely upstairs with my precious cup, I hastily put down some Pussi-luv, and hoped that she might mistake it for liver.

Hunched comfortably against the pillows I surveyed the streaming window over my cup. Would this rain stop? If not, would it be possible to postpone the opening of the gardens? And if so, how could it be advertised? I knew that a lot of people had planned to come from some distance to support the project. It was too bad.

I remembered that Irene Umbleditch and David Mawne were to be among our visitors, and looked forward to hearing their news. My mind went back to the time when David's unhappy little boy, Simon, spent a short time at Fairacre School. He would be away at boarding school now, and I wondered if we should ever meet again.

The rain continued all the morning, and by noon a nasty little wind had got up and was blowing the rain diagonally across the countryside. The sky was of uniform greyness. It was like being in a canvas tent, and the chances of a break in the clouds seemed non-existent.

The gardens were to be open from two o'clock until eight on both Saturday and Sunday, and I knew that several coachloads of people were expected from Caxley. At two o'clock, I donned Wellingtons, my stoutest mackintosh and a rain hat which made me look like a witch, and set off bravely to do the rounds, or until exposure sent me home again.

It was heartening to see how many other people were doing

the same. We met under umbrellas, in porches, under trees, anywhere to escape the relentless rain, and admired the dripping and battered beauty before us. A wonderful sense of camaraderie united us, as we sloshed our way around, and I was delighted to meet the Mawnes, their nephew and his bride-to-be, Irene, acting as hosts to the brave visitors in their garden.

They gave me good news of Simon.

'He's settled down very well now, and may move up next term. He's made friends with a pair of twins, two solid matter-of-fact youngsters who are marvellous ballast for our volatile Simon,' said David. 'We hope to take all three away in the summer, if their parents agree.'

Henry Mawne espied Miriam Quinn alone in the distance, and hurried to bring her over to meet his nephew. Once they were in conversation over a rare shrub of Henry's, I excused myself and splashed my way homeward.

To my surprise, the clock said four-thirty. It was no wonder I was wet. My expensive mackintosh had let water through the shoulders. My hair was plastered to my head by pressure from the ugly rain hat. My feet were soaked, as the rain had run down my legs into my Wellingtons, but I was aglow with a sense of duty well done.

In this complacent and self-congratulatory state I decided to treat myself to a small fire on such a cheerless day. Whether the chimney was damp, which was understandable, or whether the wind was in the wrong direction, no one could say, but the result was unpleasant.

Clouds of acrid smoke blew into the room. My vision of 'the small but bright wood fire' beloved by novelists vanished in three minutes flat, as I set about opening windows, holding up newspapers over the fireplace to assist in the right sort of draught, and cursing generally whilst my smug feeling of virture rapidly evaporated.

Trust Fate to deflate one's ego!

*

The rain continued throughout the night. By morning, sheets of water covered the roads and some of Mr Roberts' fields. But slowly it improved, and by early afternoon a watery sun was visible fleetingly between the scudding clouds. It looked more hopeful for visitors to Fairacre's gardens, I thought.

Having done my duty the day before, I decided to do my ironing, polish my few pieces of silver, write some letters, and generally catch up with some long-neglected household jobs. But as I was about to switch on the iron, I saw that a bird was fluttering madly at one of the schoolroom windows.

I put down the iron, took the school key from its hook, and went to the rescue. As anyone who has been engaged on such an errand of mercy will know, the fact that every available window and door is open seems to make no difference to the demented captive, which dashes itself wildly against all the closed apertures. After ten minutes' pandemonium the wretched sparrow darted out of the door, and I sank thankfully into my chair.

It was suddenly and blissfully peaceful. A shaft of watery sunshine illumined the classroom, a few dusty motes disturbed by the bird's and my agitation floating in its beam of light. A little breeze stirred one of the children's pictures pinned to the partition, but otherwise nothing ruffled the tranquillity of this ancient room.

It must be full of ghosts, I thought, or at least of memories. I found the idea comforting. How many children had sat in this place, imbibing knowledge both good and bad, observing the quirks of their neighbours, forming their own judgements, growing into the adult people they would be in a few years?

These same walls had seen the gamut of emotions from hilarity to despair. I remembered Miss Clare's remark about the celebratory tea party in the thirties, and the grief of children left fatherless in the First World War. This building had weathered sunshine and storm, peace and war. It had sheltered many who grew to be good men and women, and a few felons too. How far, I wondered, did the influence of this ancient school spread? All over the world there must be men and women who remembered something of the things taught them here, or were told of them by their forebears who knew the old school.

It came to me, with a poignancy I had not felt before, that I was an insignificant part of a worthy and long heritage. It was a humbling thought. Here was the heart of the matter, the spirit of the place, the unifying thread which ran through a hundred years. If only something of that spirit could be transmitted during our centenary celebrations!

I rose to return to my neglected kitchen tasks. As I locked the school door, holding that same ancient key which had chilled the palms of so many of my predecessors, I thought with keener appreciation of the centenary story which was to be told. Would it be possible, I wondered, to express that feeling of continuity which had enveloped me in my silent schoolroom?

I had been busy with thoughts of Amy's kind invitation, and decided that I should love to go with her to Tresco in the week's holiday ahead. My diary turned up within ten minutes of our earlier conversation, but I had been unable to reach her on the telephone.

'I can only have been in the garden,' she assured me, when at last we made contact, 'and I can't tell you how glad I am you can come.'

'Not as glad as I am to have been invited. I've always wanted to see the Scillies, and never got round to it.'

'You won't be disappointed. Now, I think our best plan is for me to pick you up about eleven on the Sunday. We'll stop for a pub lunch, and then take our time getting to Penzance. We should be there in good time for a nice dinner. We're booked in at the Queen's, and the food is always good.'

'Perfect,' I said.

'Have you found that diary?'

'Of course I have!'

'No "of course!" about it,' said Amy severely. 'But put down these arrangements while you remember them.'

'I'm not *quite* senile,' I protested.

'And don't forget my poetry reading on Wednesday. I'm counting on you to lead the clapping.'

'I'll be there,' I promised her, and we rang off.

But Fate decreed otherwise.

A week or so earlier, a sizeable chunk of stopping had dropped out of a back tooth. As it had not hurt, and I already had an appointment with the dentist within a month, I had ignored the gaping hole, except for wiggling at it with my tongue now and again.

Wednesday's school dinner consisted of rissoles, mashed potato and peas, followed by a sticky treacle tart which was welcomed rapturously by the children. Without thinking, I tackled my slice, only to be smitten with the most piercing pain in my damaged tooth.

I was obliged to leave the children to Miss Briggs' care and rush to the schoolhouse for first aid. The oil of cloves bottle, well hidden behind cough mixture, alka seltzer, aspirin tablets, and a particularly sinister bottle labelled 'The Mixture' – for what malady I had completely forgotten – was found to have about two drops of thickened syrup at the bottom which I did my best to apply with a wooden cherry stick wrapped in cotton wool.

If anything, this treatment seemed to aggravate the pain, and I hastily mixed a solution of my old mend TCP with warm water and tried again. But this time the pain was throbbing in my ear as well. By dint of holding warm TCP solution in my mouth, a slight diminution of pain resulted, but it was obvious that I could not take a class with my mouth bulging with water.

I tottered back just in time to see Mrs Pringle arriving for the washing up.

'Why, you do look bad!' she greeted me, with much satisfaction. 'You mark my words, that face'll be up like a plum

79

pudden in an hour or two. You wants to tie a stocking round your jaw, and my auntie in Caxley always swore by some mustard in the tooth to keep it warm.'

I felt unequal to replying, and watched Mrs Pringle make for the lobby with a heavy limp. This was a sure sign that she was affronted, had taken umbrage, and was in her martyred mood. By this time, my tooth hurt so much that I was beyond caring if Mrs Pringle slit her throat with one of the school knives, although she would have had to be pretty determined in the face of such uncooperative bluntness.

I stuck it out until playtime when I confessed my plight to Miss Briggs, who proved sympathetic and willing to cope with the school for the rest of the afternoon. I returned to the schoolhouse and rang the dentist.

'Aren't you lucky?' said his receptionist, and while I was recovering from this remark, she added, 'We've just had a cancellation. If you can get here by a quarter to five, Mr Bennett will see you then.'

Kind Mr Bennett! Dear Mr Bennett, I thought gratefully! I was positively longing to see him. Usually the thought of going to the dentist – even one as humane as Mr Bennett – casts a gloom over my life for days ahead. Now, crazed with pain, even with a mouthful of hot TCP, I viewed my trip to Caxley as a drowning man must view a lifeboat.

I went across the playground to apprise Miss Briggs of events and to lock up my cupboards and desk. The children were blissfully quiet, as they usually are in a crisis. The dividing door was propped open, so that the infants' teacher could keep an eye on them, and I returned to get wrapped up when I remembered Amy's party.

There was nothing for it but to cry off. In my present state, I could not have sat through a commercial television jingle, let alone two or three hours of Caxley culture. Amy was wholeheartedly sympathetic, and magnanimous about my defection.

'You poor old darling! Take as many painkillers as you can, and a warm bath, and crawl into bed as soon as you get back.

I'll ring tomorrow to see how you are, and tell you how it went tonight. Now, tie something round your face before you venture out, or you'll have earache as well.'

'I have already. And Mrs Pringle suggests a stocking.'

'Mrs Pringle is a fool!' said Amy forcefully. 'Nylon's useless. You want a silk scarf.'

Wonderfully cheered by hearing Mrs Pringle denounced in such a forthright manner, I rang off, and went upstairs to swathe myself as directed.

I fairly galloped into Mr Bennett's presence when summoned. He looked astounded at the speed with which I clambered into the dreaded chair and displayed my raging tooth. Usually he is obliged to lead me to the seat murmuring soothing noises as grooms do to nervous horses.

'We'll soon settle that,' he said. 'Just temporarily, of course. I'll give you a shot, and a temporary filling, and we'll make an appointment to do the job properly when the inflammation has gone.'

I surrendered myself to his ministrations with only an occasional yelp and whimper, and was home again within half an hour.

I took Amy's advice and went to bed. Tibby followed me, and we snuggled down together, the cat on top, pinning the bed clothes down uncomfortably, but I was past worrying.

It was bliss to be in bed before six o'clock, and comparatively free from pain. My final thought was of Amy's concert, and all the hard work she had put into providing a successful evening. What a broken reed I was!

Nevertheless, despite my guilt, I fell asleep within minutes, and only surfaced when the alarm clock called me to face another day.

Amy was as good as her word and rang me after school the next day. After kind enquiries about my temporarily quiescent tooth, she told me that the evening had been a huge success.

'And you were *much* missed,' she added. 'Everyone enquiring after you and desolated to hear about the toothache. Do you know, we made nearly sixty pounds?'

'Marvellous,' I said, suitably impressed.

'Including the raffle, of course, and some records Jean Cole sent as she couldn't come herself. And the food seemed to suit everybody.'

'I bet it did, knowing your usual efforts.'

'Do you know, there were some veal patties left and Tim Ferdinand asked if he could have them to take home! What a strange man he is! Not that I minded. He's so emaciated I was glad to provide tonight's supper as well as yesterday's, but I must say I felt that I was making up a doggie bag as I packed the remnants.'

'It's probably because he's a poet. His standards of behaviour are quite different from normal, no doubt.'

'Yes, well, there it is. The veal patties have found a kind home evidently. For two pins I believe he would have taken the dregs of wine too. He was looking rather keenly at the bottles as he left.'

Amy reminded me about our holiday plans. I promised to be ready in good time, and we exchanged farewells.

The few days before that longed-for holiday were spent in reading tests, a school medical inspection, patching up my tooth, and in writing a letter to the Office pointing out that work on the skylight had still not begun, and why not?

But on Friday we broke up, and Sunday morning dawned clear and bright. Here was May at its best, and I carried my case downstairs with a glad heart.

Amy was punctual, refused coffee, complimented me upon my neat appearance, and we set off westward. After ten minutes' secret anxiety about whether I had switched off everything switchable, whether I had left out the tin-opener for Tibby's Pussi-luv which Mrs Pringle was kindly giving her, and whether I had shut the pantry window which usually gets forgotten, I gave myself up to the enjoyment of the drive. Time enough to worry if I returned to a smoking ruin, I told myself, looking resolutely through the side window.

There was comparatively little traffic, and in any case Amy is an excellent driver. The green hedges streamed past, sprinkled here and there with curds of white May blossom. Cows stood knee deep in lush meadows, the sunshine gleaming on their glossy coats. The heat shimmered on Salisbury Plain. The distant hills were smudges of blue in the clear atmosphere, and the sun grew hotter as we sped on.

We stopped for lunch, and again later in the afternoon to have a walk. The lane where we drew off ran deep between steep banks. Primroses were still out on the shady side, and young bracken and hart's tongue fern delighted us both. Through a gateway we saw a little stream far below us, and on a tree stump a humped bird.

'Look!' whispered Amy, and even as she grabbed my arm, the bird spread its wings and dived towards the water – a vivid flash of pink and blue.

'A kingfisher!' we cried together.

'That means good luck,' Amy told me, as we set off to the car to resume our trip.

We reached Penzance soon after tea, wandered round the town, ate an admirable dinner, and slept like tops.

The helicopter journey across to St Mary's the next morning was exciting. Below us the farms and trees looked like the models which my children so enjoy setting out, and between the islands the sea glinted in the sunshine, green and blue, with creamy surf lashing the rocks. I wished the journey could have lasted longer. One saw so much, at just the right height it seemed to me, and I looked forward to the return journey.

We took a boat from St Mary's to Tresco, and were soon settled in our hotel. Hanging out of the bedroom window, I surveyed the scene.

The light was wonderful, pellucid and luminous. It reminded me of the light Amy and I had rejoiced in when we spent a holiday in Crete together some years earlier. Perhaps all islands have this peculiar quality, a reflection, maybe, of the water around them.

The sea was as vivid a blue as the kingfisher's flashing wings, and toppled lazily upon white sandy beaches which I had only seen before in holiday brochures. Gorse blazed yellow near by, and the accumulation of dazzling colours was heady stuff indeed.

Amy entered the room as I gazed, entranced.

'I think I could settle here for ever,' I told her.

'It can be pretty windy,' she warned me. 'You've only seen its fair-weather face.'

'It can be pretty windy at Fairacre,' I retorted, 'and not half as beautiful.'

'Wait until you've seen the rest,' said Amy. 'There's plenty to fall in love with.'

As usual, she was right. Everyone told us how lucky we were with the weather, for the sun shone for every day of our short stay, and we were able to quarter the island of Tresco on foot and visit the miraculous Abbey Gardens. Sometimes we took a boat to one of the neighbouring islands, and Amy, who is almost as knowledgeable about birds as Henry Mawne, was thrilled to study all sorts of rare varieties at St Agnes through her field glasses.

I was far less energetic, being quite content to soak up the wonderful sunshine and sea air, and to give admiring grunts when Amy told me about such wonders as rock thrushes and buntings and kittiwakes and divers she was observing with rapture.

The days passed all too swiftly. As our boat chugged away from Tresco and its white sands, I promised myself another visit before I was too old and decrepit to enjoy tramping round its beautiful bays.

On our long drive back I tried to tell Amy how much I had appreciated the holiday, and how perfect she was as a companion and guide.

She patted my knee.

'You do me good,' she said, and then went on to say the most surprising things.

'I envy you, you know, teaching away at Fairacre, always busy, knowing where you are going, seeing progress with those lucky children of yours. I seem to lead such a *useless* sort of life.'

'I've never heard such rubbish,' I protested. 'Why, you run that house perfectly, and look after James, and still find time for all sorts of good works, like that poetry evening, for instance. What's more, you look a dream always and are a delight to everyone's eye.'

'Well, thank you, my dear. I'm grateful, but the truth is, it's not enough. I can do all those things quite easily, I suppose, and so do thousands of other ordinary women like me, but I should like to do something which is especially *me*! I used to paint passably, but I know I shall never be much good at it. I wondered – don't laugh at me – but do you think I could *possibly* write my autobiography?'

'I know you could. And very well too. When are you starting?'

Amy laughed, and the tension was broken. 'Lord knows! I expect I shall be one of those people who is constantly saying she is going to write a book "when she can find the time". Lucy Clayton is one of them.'

Lucy Clayton was at college when we were, and I found her insufferable. Amy sees her occasionally, while I try to avoid her.

'Lucy Clayton,' I said, 'is incapable of *speaking* the Queen's English let alone *writing* it. But you carry on, Amy. I'll see you keep at it, and I promise to buy the first copy.'

'You are very encouraging,' said Amy. 'As good as a tonic.'

'Or a holiday in the Scillies, maybe? Do you know, Amy, we shall be home in less than an hour, and for once in my life I shall have mixed feelings about being in Fairacre again.'

6. June

Of course, when it came to it, I slipped back into my usual routine within hours, and the glories of the Scillies seemed just a happy dream. A surprising number of people commented on my improved appearance.

'You was looking a bit peaky,' Mr Willet told me. 'I said to the missus a way back, "Miss Read looks proper poorly," but now, well, you looks as hearty as my old porker in his sty!'

Mrs Pringle's description was even more impressive.

'They've fattened you up a treat. You looked like a ghost before you had that holiday – real white and spiteful, if you know what I mean.'

I replied civilly that I was glad to know that I looked better. Privately I wondered what on earth I must have looked like to have been described as 'proper poorly', 'white and spiteful' and even now – after my metamorphosis – as 'a porker'. Ah well! At least vanity would not be added to my array of sins.

'See the *Caxley* since you've been back?' asked Mrs Pringle. I translated this as meaning the *Caxley Chronicle*. The phrase the *Caxley* can cover one or two objects, such as the local bus to the market town. I have heard people say, 'You'll have to catch the *Caxley* and then change.'

I admitted that I had not yet looked at the paper.

'It's got Mrs Benson's house in it this week. Nice place it looks – bigger than it is really. Something to do with the way they tilts the camera no doubt.'

'We shall all miss her,' I said.

'The worst of it is, it don't give no price,' said Mrs Pringle gloomily. 'I do like to see how much people has the nerve to ask these days. Looks as though it's going to be auctioned. I suppose these 'ere estate agents hopes people will be carried away and offer more than it's worth. I remember my brother-in-law going crazy at one sale and buying a piece of stair carpet for three pounds.'

'That sounds quite a bargain to me.'

'Not when you had to lug away a broken fireguard, one of them exercising bicycles, a zinc bath and four chamber pots, if you'll excuse my mentioning them.'

'Not at all,' I said graciously.

'My sister fairly gave him a taste of her tongue, for all she belongs to the Plymouth Brethren. They had to pay Percy Potter another pound for bringing the stuff home on his carrier's van, and of course all the neighbours fell about laughing and making coarse remarks when the stuff came up the front path. No, my brother-in-law never heard the last of that, I can tell you!'

Mrs Pringle heaved herself from the front desk where she had been resting, and made for the stove. A dead leaf was sullying its summer perfection, and Mrs Pringle removed it with as much venom as she would have displayed if it had been a tarantula spider.

Later that day I looked up the advertisement. Holly Lodge certainly made an attractive picture, and the accommodation sounded ideal.

'Too big for us,' I told Tibby, 'and too expensive. But I hope some nice family comes to enjoy it.'

'The property includes a self-contained flat comprising a large sitting room, bedroom, bath and kitchen, on the ground floor, all in immaculate condition.'

Poor Miss Quinn, I thought! How she will hate leaving her flat, all in immaculate condition! I knew how happy she had been in Joan Benson's company. As Fairacre folk had said truly, it would not be easy for her to find such a home elsewhere.

And although I only knew Miriam Quinn slightly, I should be sorry to see her go from Fairacre. I liked her quiet contentment, the tranquil exterior which hid, I suspected, a power house of energy. She obviously loved Fairacre, her solitude and her un-interrupted thoughts.

We had a lot in common.

During our stay in Tresco I had tried to tell Amy something of the feelings which had stirred me that afternoon alone in the schoolroom. Was it possible, I asked her, to put across such a theme in our centenary celebrations?

Amy was thoughtful for a time, and then said that she doubted if it would be possible.

'It's something purely evocative,' she said. 'I'm quite sure that lots of people in Fairacre feel the same way about their old school, but to express it, especially through the children who are the agents in this case, is well-nigh impossible, I think.

'You'll have to be content with coming down to a more earthy approach. Your idea of various happenings during the hundred years seems far more practical, and incidentally will show the continuity you are aiming at. Play for simplicity is my advice.'

I was sure Amy was right, the more I thought about it. Anything verging on the high-falutin' could prove boring or sentimental.

I asked Miss Briggs to stay to tea one afternoon, and we set about tackling the programme. Not that our surroundings were conducive to heavy thought. The pinks in my border were beginning to shake out their shaggy heads, and the crimson feathers of peony petals fluttered to the baked earth beneath.

We sat in the shade of my old plum tree, tea cups in hand, and relished the peace of a June afternoon. In the distance we could hear the steady thumping of a baler. Someone had cut an early crop of hay, it seemed. A blackbird scurried among the plants in the dry border, searching for titbits for its young family, and overhead our ever-present downland larks kept up their fervent outpouring.

'Well, I suppose we'd better make a start,' I said at last. I

could easily have drifted into sleep in these soporific surroundings, but it was hardly a good example to my assistant.

'Are you thinking of ten scenes, one for each decade,' asked
Miss Briggs with unusual briskness, 'or a scene for each reign?'

'I hadn't really decided that point,' I admitted.

'And we shall have to have a narrator, of course. You'd
better do that.'

I began to feel some awe for Miss Briggs. Who would have
imagined she would be quite so efficient?

'I had dallied with the idea of one of the children doing that,'
I replied.

'Oh, I think the thing needs to be held together by someone
with authority,' said Miss Briggs. 'Besides, none of the children
really reads well enough, and all of them are bound to be
nervous in front of an audience.'

I did not like to say that I should be nervous myself, but
agreed meekly that it might be a good idea for me to do the
linking. 'But not much of it,' I added. 'Just a few sentences to
show what is happening in the world outside, and then a true
scene straight from the log book.'

'And what about music?'

'Oh, heavens above,' I groaned. My piano playing is mini-
mal, and Miss Briggs's non-existent. We could have records, I
supposed?

'Well, we'll think about that,' said my assistant, now busily
making notes on a pad. 'But some singing might go down well,
if we can get an accompanist. After all, that piano of ours has
been here since the school started. It ought to have a part in the
performance.'

We worked for an hour or more as the teapot cooled in the
grass at our feet, and a few early gnats hovered around. By that
time, we had decided that the next step was to ransack the
log book for suitable scenes, with not too many players in them,
and to use the whole school as a chorus whenever it could be
incorporated.

'Must let the mums see their offspring in the limelight,' remarked Miss Briggs sagaciously. 'It's half the battle.'

With that, we carried in our tea things and I saw the lady off, feeling more respect for my partner than ever before.

As all Fairacre had foreseen, work began on the skylight some two months later than planned, and it was quite clear that the rest of the summer term would pass to the accompaniment of loud noises above, and showers of a century's rubbish falling about us.

To give Reg Thorn his due, he certainly apologized very prettily. No doubt he got plenty of practice, was my private tart comment. He also rigged up a tarpaulin just under the skylight which was intended to catch the bits, but also blocked a great deal of light. I had not realized how much we relied on this ancient window for illumination until the tarpaulin flapped above my desk.

It was all very annoying, and of course the children's attention was more distracted than ever. Reg Thorn appeared himself for the first hour or so each day, and then left his two younger assistants to carry on.

'Got quite a lot of other jobs on hand,' he explained. 'Got some shelving for the Mawnes, and a little job at Beech Green. If I keep an eye on them it keeps you all happy.'

I should like to have pointed out that finishing one job satisfactorily and then proceeding to the next on the date given originally and staying there till *that* job was done, would make us all a great deal happier. But before I could voice these sentiments Reg Thorn had departed. Such expert slipping away could also be the result of years of experience, I thought to myself.

Later in the morning, when we were about to clear the desks ready for school dinner, Eileen Burton rushed in from the lobby in a state of panic.

'There's a funny man in the playground,' she gasped.

At once there was a rush to the door. The mob checked there and turned to me in some dismay.

'He's all dressed up in white, miss.'

'Got one of them sun 'ats on, miss.'

'He's blowing smoke, miss.'

'Looks like a man from Mars to me, miss,' said the school wag.

'Well, let me come through and then I can see,' I said. A narrow passage was made through the milling mass.

Sure enough, a white-clad figure, crowned with a topee from which white veiling fell to the shoulders, roamed apparently aimlessly round the playground. In its hand was a contraption with a nozzle which occasionally belched blue smoke. Memories of a recent television programme, which I had been too idle to switch off, came back to me.

'It's the vicar,' I told them.

'He'd never dress up all funny,' Ernest rebuked me.

'Looking for bees,' I continued. 'Now go inside, and I'll have a word with him.'

Reluctantly they moved back a few feet. I did not imagine for a moment that they would return to their desks. Curiosity was too strong for them, but at least they stayed in the safety of the lobby and watched the proceedings.

I was within touching distance of our vicar before he became aware of me, so engrossed was he in surveying the hedges and trees which border the playground.

'Oh, my dear Miss Read,' he exclaimed. 'How you startled me!'

I expressed my regret.

'I should have let you know that I was coming, but time pressed. Mr Lamb rang to say a swarm of bees was passing over – he thought they might be mine – so of course I got my things together, and ventured out.'

He compressed the bellows of the gadget in his hand and smoke issued forth.

'My smoker,' he said, with pride. 'It's still working, thank heaven. It calms the bees so that you can drop them into the skep easily.'

He nodded towards the school wall where a fine straw skep awaited the elusive swarm.

'But surely, they might be miles away,' I said. At that moment, Mrs Partridge's face peered over the wall which divides the school playground from the vicar's garden.

'Gerald! Gerald! Margaret Waters has just rung to say the bees are in her damson tree, and could you come quickly before they get into the chimney.'

'Into the chimney?' echoed the vicar in amazement. 'Why on earth should they wish to go into a *chimney* when they can enjoy the sunshine and fresh air on a damson tree?'

'I don't know the *reason*, Gerald,' said Mrs Partridge, sounding justifiably exasperated, 'I am simply repeating her message – so *hurry*!'

The vicar obediently collected his skep, threw back the veil from his perspiring countenance, and set off on his errand of mercy.

Later, Mr Willet spoke of the episode.

'D'you see the vicar in his moonship gear this morning? My word, he fair set all the village dogs barking their heads off as he went by! And young Mrs Smith's baby was outside in his pram, and hasn't stopped bawling since.'

'But did he take the swarm?' I asked.

'Oh, he took 'em all right,' said Mr Willet off-handedly. 'They're in the skep in the shade. Miss Waters said the vicar's coming to get them at dusk. But just to be on the safe side she told Mr Mawne, and he's promised to help collect 'em. He's a better man than I am, Gunga Din,' said Mr Willet, misquoting Kipling. 'I wouldn't go near a swarm of bees for all the tea in China. Did I ever tell you about my old gran's?'

'Yes,' I said, and went to pick up an infant who had fallen painfully and deservedly from the coke pile.

There was an agreeable literary sequel to this adventure.

When the vicar called to bring in the hymn list at the end of the week, I naturally enquired after the bees.

'It was an extraordinary thing,' said the vicar. 'Henry and I collected the skep during the evening, and he helped me to transfer it to an old hive he lent me. But do you know, they simply would not stay in it! Luckily, I had a new hive not in use, so later we transferred them to that one, and since then we've had no trouble.'

'What was wrong with Henry's hive, do you think?'

'I think dear old Parson Woodforde put his finger on it some two hundred years ago. You know his diary, I have no doubt?'

I very nearly said it was my Bible, but remembering to whom I was speaking, hastily said it was a great favourite of mine.

'I looked up the passage, and he says something to the effect that he too had to hive a swarm twice. The first hive had evidently been kept in a barn and he suspected that mice or other small animals had used it. I liked his final comment that: "Bees are particularly Nice and Cleanly." He must have been a singularly kind and observant man, and obviously loved his bees.'

Such a warm smile illumined the cherubic countenance of our own parson, that I thought he shared many of Parson Woodforde's virtues.

The Caxley Spring Festival had netted over a thousand pounds, the local paper informed us, and more was expected as one or two extra efforts were still to be held. One of these was a flower festival involving half a dozen beautifully decked churches, St Patrick's being one of them.

I wandered in one evening to admire the exquisite arrangements. To my mind every one was perfect, a miracle of form and fragrance. It astonished me to hear the comments of two women who were following me round the display. They were evidently keen flower arrangers and knew all the things one should be looking for.

'My dear,' said one, 'just *look* at that pedestal! One can positively see the Oasis!'

'Dreadful,' agreed her friend, with a shudder, 'and she has obviously *never heard* of the Hogarth line!'

I only hoped that the 'arranger was not within earshot.

When I emerged from the church into the golden evening, a woman hailed me. Her name, luckily, I remembered. She was a Mrs Austen, and once belonged to our Women's Institute. We had not seen each other for months, and we greeted each other enthusiastically. As she had seen the flowers and had time to spare, she came back to the schoolhouse with me.

'We're at Springbourne now,' she told me. 'My husband had the chance of a job in London, but we wouldn't take it although the money was better. We've been countrymen ever since we were evacuated.'

'Tell me more,' I begged her. 'Were you at Fairacre School? You know it's our centenary this year?'

'Yes, I was, and no, I didn't know,' she replied. 'I came down right at the beginning of the war. We lived in Camberwell in south London, and pretty crowded we were in our flat. There were three of us children. I was the youngest, just six when war broke out. We'd all been to the big LCC school round the corner, and a very good grounding we got there.

'Mind you, the classes were big – over fifty of us altogether, and the teachers had to keep order pretty well or nothing would have been learnt. Looking back, we did a lot of class work the children today wouldn't like. Chanting tables, and reading round the class out of the same reader, that sort of thing. And no end of spelling tests and mental arithmetic, all done very fast, and devil take the hindmost.'

'But you got on, obviously.'

'Oh, we all got on. In those days the teachers were the best in the country, we were told. They got the highest salaries, so the committee could take the pick of the training colleges when they appointed staff. They certainly made us work. I think that's partly why I liked Fairacre so much. The pace was slower and the teachers were quieter.'

'Was that all you liked? It must have been an upheaval to be evacuated.'

She shook her head. 'I told you we were crowded at home, and at school. Mine was a very respectable family. Mother kept us all spotless, and the house was polished to the nines. But we only had one room really to live in comfortably – the front room – and that was turned into a bedroom at night for my two brothers.

'Behind that was the kitchen, and it was always so dark that we had to have the gas burning. And behind that was the only bedroom, where I slept on a little truckle-bed next to my parents.'

'Any garden?'

'Just a tiny paved yard where Mother hung her washing. If we wanted to see grass we had to be taken to the park. We weren't allowed to go on our own, because the roads were too busy.'

'So all these fields seemed wonderful?'

'Do you know, when we got out at Caxley Station and stood in lines with our little cardboard boxes holding our gas masks, some of the children were crying. But not me! There were lovely grassy banks, and roses in flower, and the air was just beautiful. I felt I had come home.'

'And that feeling stayed?'

'It's never gone away! As we drove to Fairacre with our new foster parents I grew happier and happier. Of course, I missed my father and mother, and at night-time, if I woke, I sometimes wept a bit for them. But Fairacre was bliss to me, and the children were kind to us as well as the teachers.'

'I'm glad to hear it.'

'We all squashed up together in the desks. Two of our teachers had come with us, nice lively girls they were. It couldn't have been easy for anyone, because every scrap of space was used, and we even had a couple of classes in the village hall. But after a bit, a lot of the children drifted back to London as there weren't any raids, so things settled down very comfortably. Mr Fortescue was the headmaster, and Miss Clare was teaching here then. How is she?'

I gave her news of our old friend.

'If ever there was a saint, she's one,' said Mrs Austen. 'I suppose she's coming to the celebrations?'

'I hope she'll tell us some of her memories,' I replied. 'She knows more about Fairacre School than anyone living.'

'She helped us all to settle in,' remembered Mrs Austen. 'You know there were a lot of things that shook us about the country. Cows for one, and earth closets for another. And I was scared stiff of real darkness in a winter's lane, after lamp posts along the pavements. I think our hostesses had plenty to put up with. On the whole I like to think that we three didn't give too much trouble. We'd been brought up quite strictly, and my parents came down at least twice a month, and made sure we behaved properly. But there were some pretty rough families, as you can guess, and all that talk about bed-wetting and head lice and impetigo and scabies and so on – well, a lot of it was true.'

'We get the odd case now,' I told her. 'Fairacre isn't unadulterated Arcady, you know.'

'I realize that, but to me as a six-year-old Fairacre *was* Arcady, and this part of England has stayed that way, to my mind, ever since.'

'I'm inclined to agree,' I said.

Mrs Pringle arrived the next morning looking full of importance, and with no trace of a limp. She had the appearance of one with a message to deliver.

It was sad news.

'Bob Willet says he won't be in today until later. His poor brother Sid has passed on, and Bob's gone over there to see his sister-in-law and fix up the funeral.'

I murmured condolences.

'Well, he's been bad for months, poor soul. Something to do

with his digestion – the *lower* end of it, if you know what I mean. I never liked to ask Bob too much about it, as it was rather a *personal* complaint.'

'Aren't they all?'

'Some,' said Mrs Pringle frostily, 'is more personal than others.' And she swept away.

Mr Willet looked rather subdued when he appeared in the late afternoon, and shook his head sadly when I expressed my sorrow.

'Thank God I didn't have to see him dead,' he said. 'Never let anyone show you a corpse, specially if you've been fond of the person. My mum made me kiss my grandma in her coffin, and I've never got over it. What's more, I can never remember my gran as she was when she was alive. The look of her dead face is the only one I can see. A pity! She was a lively old party and I loved her a lot.'

I said I'd heard about her from several of her Fairacre friends.

'She was good to us kids. There was five of us, and not much money, of course. We lived in a cottage at Springbourne and my gran lived near by. We always called in going to and from school, and she used to put an apple or some plums in our dinner basket.

'Sid was the eldest. He was quite a scholar, used to sit there when old Hope was headmaster,' Mr Willet nodded towards a corner desk at the back. 'He could have gone to the grammar school, but with all of us to keep, Dad said he'd best get out working. Old Sid never complained and he made a durn fine cabinet maker in the end, but I reckon he minded a bit about not going to Caxley Grammar.'

Mr Willet sighed, and began to make for the door. 'It's a funny thing, when someone dies, you never remember them as they were then, but always as children. I saw poor old Sid in hospital last week, but all I can see now is Sid about ten, lugging the rush basket with our school dinners up the hill here to Fairacre School. Or swinging our little sister round and round by her hands, or feeding his pet rabbit.'

He opened the schoolroom door. 'Old Sid will always be about ten for me. Funny really!'

'Perhaps that's as it should be,' I told him.

When I saw Amy next I repeated Mr Willet's remarks about viewing the dead.

'It's perfectly true,' she agreed. 'I can't say I've seen many dead people, but the two aunts whose bodies I saw simply will not come to life for me now. I always do my best *not* to see corpses for that reason. I like to remember my relatives as they were.'

'I'm remarkably short of close relatives,' I said, 'though I'm told I look more and more like my Aunt Bessie the older I grow. I'm sorry to say she was remarkably plain, but very determined.'

'I often wonder if we only see the *good* points of relatives in ourselves. You say your Aunt Bessie was *determined*. Maybe she was just pig-headed. I know I like to think I have my Aunt Maud's efficiency, but really I know she was plain *bossy*, and nearly drove poor Uncle Edward demented. She would tidy away his jigsaw puzzle and put it back in the box when he was only halfway through.'

'Strong grounds for divorce,' I said. 'Have some coffee?'

And we went into the kitchen together to make it.

7 · JULY

Speculation about Holly Lodge grew keener as the weeks passed. The preliminary announcement of its sale by auction, 'unless sold privately beforehand', whetted all appetites.

Mrs Pringle had heard from an unspecified source, but she told me it was as true as she stood there, that nothing under fifty thousand pounds would be considered. Mr Willet observed that people must need their heads examined when it came to buying houses these days, and Reg Thorn said he could remember when Holly Lodge belonged to that miserable old faggot that drove a Liverpool phaeton. His name was on the tip of his tongue, but he reckoned it had gone for the moment. Anyway, when he had died – and no one mourned his going, that was a fact – Holly Lodge went for six hundred to a nice old party from the other side of Caxley. Six hundred, mark you!

Later in the morning, he drew aside the tarpaulin, sending a shower of dried paint and wood splinters upon us, poked his face through the gap, and said:

'Potter! That was the name! Josiah Potter, and a nasty bit of work he was too.'

He then withdrew, allowing me to send Ernest out to the lobby for the dustpan and brush, whilst I continued my interrupted discourse on medieval farming methods.

The sale of Holly Lodge occupied the inhabitants of Fairacre very pleasurably. The history of the house, the quirks of its various owners and, of course, the scandalous amount of money being asked for it at the moment, were all mulled over with the greatest enjoyment.

Whether any would-be purchasers had inspected the house was difficult to say. Holly Lodge was a little distance from the centre of the village and well hidden from prying eyes by the high hedge which gave the house its name. It was one of Fairacre's more retired establishments, and as Mrs Pringle remarked wistfully: 'It's difficult to find out what goes on in there.'

It so happened that I met Miriam Quinn and Joan Benson on separate occasions within a week. I had gone into Caxley on one sunny Saturday morning to buy a pair of summer shoes, and was still reeling from the shock of the amount I had just handed over, when I bumped into Miriam Quinn.

She commiserated with me. 'I can sympathize. I've just come from inspecting cotton frocks, and have decided that my present shabby collection can do another year – if not two or three.'

I asked after Joan.

'Run off her feet at the moment, with people coming to view. She won't have any difficulty in disposing of it, I'm sure, but she does so want to see it in good hands. Half the viewers have appalling plans for turning it into flats, or a home for delinquent boys or some such.'

I said that it must be a trying time for them both.

'Well, there it is. I haven't found anything remotely suitable for myself, and I'm now at the limbo stage, telling myself I may as well wait and see, and perhaps something will turn up. Somehow one gets numb after a bit.'

'Maybe that's nature's protection,' I said, as we parted.

I met Joan Benson in the village a day or two later. She was struggling with an overloaded carrier bag which had collapsed under the strain, and only had one handle intact.

'I really should have brought the car, but I thought it would do me good to walk on such a heavenly day. In any case, I only intended to buy about four things, and now look at me!'

'Here, put some in my basket, and come back with me and

I'll let you have a good tough bag. I'm going to have a cup of tea anyway, so do join me.'

The children had gone home, and I had been to the post office to send off a couple of urgent missives to the Office, which would probably not be opened for days, if I knew anything about it.

Over tea, Joan told me more about the horrors of selling a home. 'I don't know which is worse – trying to find a home, or trying to get rid of one. For two pins, I'd call the whole thing off and just stay at Holly Lodge until I'm carried out feet first.'

'There would be general rejoicing if you did decide to stay,' I told her.

'Well, that's nice to hear, but I really must be sensible and look ahead. This wretched arthritis gets steadily more troublesome, and sometimes I find it quite difficult to get upstairs. And the house is far too big now that I'm alone, and costs the earth to heat. And much as I love gardening, I simply cannot cope with that great one at Holly Lodge, and help gets more and more impossible to find, and more and more expensive.'

She sighed, and shook her head at the proffered biscuit tin.

'What a misery I sound! I'm not really unhappy, I've been so kindly looked after in Fairacre I shall miss the life here horribly. But my daughter is quite right. If I can't drive, I shall be absolutely done for in Fairacre, and I'm finding it quite painful sometimes. And I'm sorry to say that I am now refusing to drive at night, or if it's foggy or icy.'

'That cuts it down quite considerably,' I agreed, and she laughed.

'But it's selling the house which is the real problem. I don't want Miriam to have to go. She's been quite wonderful to me, and is so happily ensconced in that little annexe. If only we could find a nice quiet family that would be glad to have her there, and people that Miriam could get on with, it would be perfect. But that means selling to someone we know, and so far no one in that category has emerged. And some of the viewers have fairly curdled my blood with their plans for the house!'

'They probably wouldn't get them passed anyway when it came to the point.'

'But I *love* that house,' cried Joan. 'I simply hate the idea of it being torn about. If only some nice couple who like it as it is would appear, I should sell cheerfully. As it is, I still have to find myself somewhere near Barbara. She is quite marvellous about vetting places, but with young children she is very tied, and I feel I must go and stay with her before long to have a good scout round myself.'

She began to collect her shopping.

'I've run on far too long, but you are so sympathetic. And thank you for the delicious tea, and the bag, and best of all for *listening*.'

On the doorstep she paused. 'You won't mention my concern about Miriam, will you? I should hate her to think I was turning buyers away because of her. It's not *quite* like that, as I'm sure you understand, but she is so independent . . .'

Her voice trailed away.

'Never fear,' I assured her. 'I've lived in a village long enough to know how to be discreet. Though even then, it's sometimes difficult to keep the boat up straight.'

She waved, and departed with her burden.

Mr Lamb at the post office unearthed a handful of ancient postcards from the back of a little-used drawer. He came across one of Fairacre School which he kindly gave me, and I pored over it with a magnifying glass.

This photograph must have been taken in the first decade of this century, judging by the dress of the children. They are all gathered in the lane outside the school and there is not a single piece of traffic in sight.

How instantly that picture carried me into a vanished world! The boys are grouped together on one side of the lane, and every one of them wears a cap. Some are in Norfolk breeches, some in short and some in long trousers. Quite a few have jackets too big for them, some too small, with their bony wrists

hanging from tight sleeves, but almost all sport Eton collars and stout boots.

The girls, carefully separated from the boys by the width of the lane, wear black stockings and boots, white starched pinafores over their frocks, and some have hats as well. Altogether there must be around seventy children in this photograph. The staff seems to be hidden by the throng, with the exception of one stolid-looking young man who towers above the girls.

I looked in vain for Miss Clare who must have been there at that time, but either she was absent that day or was engulfed by her charges somewhere at the rear of the party.

The school building looked exactly the same, and I recognized several trees as old friends, although considerably shorter. But a magnificent barn, end on to the road, has now gone. The rough grass still grows as thickly at the edge of the lane, and one small child holds a flower to his face, enjoying its scent forever.

With so many memories crowding upon me during this centenary year, I found this scene particularly moving, and shall always be grateful to Mr Lamb for presenting me with such an irreplaceable treasure.

With the end of term in sight I conferred with Miss Briggs about our plans. It seemed wise to let parents know in good time about our centenary affairs, especially those who might have costumes to prepare.

'After all, it is *next term*,' I pointed out, 'and Fairacre folk don't like to be hurried into things.'

'I should think that seldom happens,' replied my assistant. 'I've never met such a slow lot of parents. It's about time Fairacre moved with the times, and woke up.'

I was too taken aback by this attack to answer for a moment. Talk about the pot calling the kettle black, was my first reaction!

'And I'm beginning to wonder,' she went on, 'if I don't owe it to myself to change to a livelier job.'

I hardly liked to point out that she had had some months of unemployment before she landed the Fairacre post. Also that she would need a glowing reference from me, which in all honesty I could not supply, to take her to another job, and in any case her probationary year had at least another term to run.

'If you do decide to try your luck,' I said at last, 'you know how much notice you must give. But if you'll take my advice I should get all the experience you can here before you think of changing.'

'Nothing seems to *happen* here!' cried my discontented assistant. 'I should think Fairacre School was exactly like this a hundred years ago! And, as far as I can see, it will be exactly the same a hundred years hence!'

Privately I hoped it would be, but I know full well that the wind of change buffets us daily, and that a school which has shrunk from that thriving community in Mr Lamb's photograph to the twenty-odd children who now comprise the school cannot hope to survive long.

'I think you must make an effort to join some activity or other which you'll enjoy in Caxley,' I said. 'What about the Operatic Society, or Caxley Dramatic Club? You like tennis, I know, and there are two good clubs in Caxley which you might enjoy. At least you would meet other young people. I know it must be pretty lonely for you here with no other young staff.'

'No one's asked me to join anything,' muttered Miss Briggs sulkily.

I began to feel my small stock of patience becoming as exhausted as Herr Hitler's.

'Well of course they haven't! They don't know you are *there*! Go along to a meeting, or find out the name of the secretary, and say you want to join. It's up to you. You can't expect these organizations to search the highways and byways.'

'I don't know if I shall have time, with all this centenary fuss to arrange,' said Miss Briggs, as though the entire burden of our celebrations rested on her dandruff-sprinkled shoulders.

I took a deep breath. 'Which brings us to the point. You'd better come to tea tomorrow and we'll draft out our plan.'

'I wash my hair tomorrow after school,' she said.

Far be it from me to stop that, was my unworthy thought.

'Make it Friday,' I said shortly, and got out the register.

Amy called the following evening, and I was glad that Miss Briggs was elsewhere attending to her hair. I enquired after the progress of the autobiography.

'Well, it's uphill work, I can tell you! As you know, I always think one's childhood is the most interesting part of an auto-biography. But then, where does one begin?'

'I should think: "I was born on May the Whatever in Nether Wallop or Somesuch."'

'I feel that's too bald. I think people are glad to be told something about one's parents, but I dread going back too far and having sixteen, if not thirty-two, dubious portraits of fore-bears on each side.'

'I rather agree.'

'On the other hand, there were some very colourful ancestors on my mother's side. Two brothers were transported to Australia for stealing sheep and cattle.' Amy spoke with considerable pride.

'Well, put 'em in,' I advised.

'It would certainly swell the volume a little. You've no idea how much writing is needed to make a page of print. It's really quite daunting. I'm thinking of throwing in a distant great-uncle too. He was defrocked sometime in the last century for conduct not befitting the clergy. Something to do with the choir boys, I gather, but it's so difficult to find any clear evidence after all this time.'

'I'd no idea you had such a disreputable background, Amy.'

'My immediate background is blameless,' she assured me. 'And very dull too. My grandparents and parents seem to have worked hard, kept out of debt, looked after their small families, and generally been worthy and respectable. The consequence is that they make pretty dull reading matter, and I wonder if it might be a good idea to start farther back. I could have a family tree in the front.'

'Does anyone ever look at them? All I find is that having pulled the thing out, it is impossible to fold it correctly again, and you have a yard of tissue paper in your lap all the time you are reading.'

'That's true,' agreed Amy. 'But going back to your first idea of plunging straight in with one's birth – do you think readers are *really gripped* by hearing about your being bottle fed and having your adenoids out, and the way you had hysterics at the age of four when Father Christmas kissed you, reeking of whisky?'

'All those things might create a sympathetic bond,' I said. 'As these confounded educationists tell us *ad nauseam*, children should be able to identify themselves with the characters they are reading about. Though how you can identify with Sinbad the Sailor or Tom Thumb beats me.'

'Well, all I can say is that I have spent a good hour after tea every day for the past fortnight, pushing along my reluctant ball point, and I don't suppose I have written enough to fill four pages of a real book. It's very disheartening.'

'Cheer up!' I said. 'Think how splendid it will look piled up in the book shops with queues outside fighting to get in to buy it. And you on television. Possibly on *This Is Your Life*. Just think of that!'

'I refuse to consider it,' said Amy firmly.

Mrs Partridge, the vicar's wife, called at the school the next morning, and the children sat up with smiles wreathing their faces.

They like Mrs Partridge. I like to think it is for herself alone, for she is a kind, warm-hearted person and devoted to the young, but I have the feeling that she is welcomed more for the bag of boiled sweets which she so often brings with her.

Today was no exception, except that the sweets were toffees and not fruit drops. The children's response to this largesse was ecstatic, as Patrick handed round the bag.

'Now, my dear,' said Mrs Partridge when all were busy sucking, 'I wonder if you can do me a favour.'

What answer is there to that after such generosity?

'Of course,' I said rashly.

'I'm short of collectors for my Save The Children flag day next week, and I wondered it you could help.'

'Where would you want me to go?' I asked, resigned to my lot.

'Well, I'm doing from The Beetle and Wedge to the cross-roads, and Margaret Waters is doing the other side of the road, and Joan Benson was to have done that outlying part from her house to Tyler's Row, but she has had to hare off to look at a couple of houses her daughter has found. It is that stretch that I hoped you might find time to do.'

I agreed to take over Joan's territory, and Mrs Partridge whipped a piece of paper from the top of the basket she was carrying, and placed a collecting tin on my desk with incredible speed.

'That's *most* kind of you, dear,' she said briskly. 'Could you let me have it back by next Thursday? And here is your official badge, and the flags.'

The piece of paper had successfully hidden all these things in the basket, and I noticed yet another collecting tin and more flags, still to be allotted presumably.

'I'll do that,' I promised. Bang go the two evenings I had earmarked for making strawberry jam and bottling cherries, I thought!

She wished the children goodbye, and they replied with their diction somewhat impeded by toffee, but true love shining in their eyes.

The door had hardly closed before Eileen Burton was sick on

the floor, and one of the Coggs twins began to choke on a large piece of sweet which had gone down the wrong way.

I hastily put the collecting box on the window sill before going to the rescue.

Save The Children indeed! What about the teachers?

Miss Briggs duly stayed late on Friday, and accompanied me to the schoolhouse for tea. She appeared somewhat monosyllabic and sulky, but whether she was feeling resentful at staying after school, or whether she was simply being natural – Mr Willet's 'a fair old lump of a girl' came to mind – I could not say.

However, she cheered up a little after three cups of tea, brown bread and honey followed by a large slice of Dundee cake, and we settled down with pencils and notebooks to our task.

'I think six scenes will be ample,' I said, 'which means something from the reigns of Victoria, Edward the Seventh, George the Fifth, Edward the Eighth – unless we leave him out – George the Sixth, and our present Queen.'

'Good idea,' agreed Miss Briggs, sucking a sticky finger. 'If we had a scene for every decade that would make . . . how many?'

'Ten,' I told her. 'You ought to know that – child of the metric system as you are.'

'Yes, well – if we had the scenes lasting ten minutes each that would be far too long, wouldn't it?'

'My feeling entirely. We can't expect people to sit on the school seats for more than an hour altogether, and if we have a few songs, and then tea afterwards it is as much as the human frame can take.'

'Have you found some likely stories from the log book?'

'One or two. I thought for the first scene we could use the boy Pratt putting on the school clock, and being caught by the headmistress.'

'Lovely! But how will he climb up? Would he pile up the desks?'

I repressed a shudder. 'No. We'll have Mr Willet's step ladder to hand. After all, it just *may* have been left in the schoolroom. And through all the scenes we'll use the old side desk, and the actors will be in period costume, of course. When we get to Elizabeth the Second we can push on a modern desk. The old style were in use when I first came here. I must say, they were pretty sturdy.'

'Then what?' asked my assistant, bringing me back to the work in hand.

'Well, for Edward the Seventh, I thought it would be marvellous if I could say something like: "It was in this reign that a new pupil teacher took up her duties", and in walks Miss Clare!'

'Perfect!'

'Then she could tell us about her experiences of that time. I have sounded her, and she's game to do it. Frankly, I think it will be the high spot of the whole proceedings.'

'What about George the Fifth?'

'I think it will have to have something to do with the Great War.'

I told her about Miss Clare's memories of the babies fraying pieces of cotton material to make field dressings. We could enlarge on the helping-the-war-effort theme, without dwelling unduly on the horrors which many of the older people in the audience would remember all too well. I wondered if one of the parents who went as a child from Fairacre School to the Wembley Exhibition might give an enthusiastic first-hand account of a country child's memories of that memorable charabanc ride to London in the twenties. Mr Lamb perhaps? Or Mrs Willet? I promised to follow up the idea.

The more we thought about Edward the Eighth's brief reign the stronger became our resolve to leave out a scene, and simply let the narrator comment on that passage of time. Apart from the Abdication, which really had very little impact on the children of the school, there was little to mark the reign's fleeting impression on the village.

The 1939–45 war, which followed within three years, had much more effect, of course, and we resolved to show the crowded desks, with the gas mask boxes lodged thereupon, and one or two wartime posters pinned up – as evidently there had been in Mr Fortescue's session as headmaster at that time. Luckily, Mr Willet still had two precious relics, one showing the results of careless talk and the other of wasting food. There were one or two incidents in the log book which could form the basis of a scene, and perhaps Mrs Austen of Springbourne might be prevailed upon to give her impression of Fairacre School from an evacuee's point of view.

As for our last, and present-day, scene, what could be better than drawing the audience's attention to the children's exhibition of work in both rooms, singing by the whole school, and the narrator pointing out such facts as the vanishing of those over eleven to the local comprehensive school and cutting down the numbers of Fairacre School drastically after the 1944 Act?

Finally, I had asked the vicar if he would appear at the end and remind us all that the church had always played an important part in the hundred years of Fairacre School. He was willing to do this, and to end our proceedings with a prayer for blessings received in the past, and our hopes for the future.

'That should take us up to tea very nicely,' said Miss Briggs kindly.

'We'll all need it by then,' I assured her. 'And now let's rough out which children would be best as the actors.'

It took us until nearly seven o'clock, but we felt it had been worth it. Certainly, Miss Briggs departed looking very much more cheerful than when she arrived, and had been surprisingly helpful.

The weather had been perfect, at least in my eyes, for the last few weeks of term. The sun had shone from a cloudless sky, every playtime had found the schoolroom deserted and the playground crowded with good-tempered children playing with unusual placidity. But I was surprised, nevertheless, to hear that an official drought had been declared, and we were all being exhorted to save water.

It always beats me how, in the temperate climate we are supposed to enjoy, panic sets in as soon as any mild and foreseen variations from the normal weather conditions prevail. If three inches of snow fall in January, the headlines scream about disrupted rail services, motorway chaos, children marooned in school buses and lambs dying in drifts. The country, they say dramatically, has been brought to a standstill. They seem to cope pretty well in Canada, or America and Switzerland, it seems to me, with about thirty times the amount of precipitation.

And why, as in the present circumstances, have we to watch each precious drop of water? Way back in February, we were sloshing about knee-deep in the stuff, as the swollen rivers overflowed, and Mr Roberts was out rescuing lambs at Springbourne.

In any event, we were all blissfully happy in the scorching sun, and I scuffed through the dust at the edge of the road on my way to the grocer's after school, glorying in the heat. It was beginning to look like the end of summer, with the grass drying prematurely and even some yellow leaves appearing on the fruit trees. Miss Waters' privet hedge was in flower, the small white pyramids of blossom giving out that faint sickly smell which is the essence of summer.

White convolvulus plants scrambled along the wire fence which borders the post office garden, the purity of their trumpets sadly tarnished with dust and heat. Below them, a root of scarlet poppies flamed, giving out their hot peppery fragrance as the dry wind shook them.

I met the vicar as I returned. He greeted me cheerfully and told me that his bees were extremely active.

'No more swarms?'

'Not yet, but this is the sort of weather that might set them off,' he told me. 'The swarm I collected from Margaret Waters has settled in beautifully. Very attractive bees – rather paler than my first, and so busy! Really they are an example to one in this heat. I must confess I find it most trying, and shall welcome the rain when it comes.'

Mr Willet hailed me from the churchyard when I was nearly home, and I walked across to see him. It was cool in the shade of the massive yew tree where I stood. Mr Willet was busy cutting long grass from some of the ancient burial mounds with a bill-hook.

'Hot work,' I commented.

'Suits me,' said my caretaker, mopping his glistening face. He came and stood beside me, and together we surveyed the sleeping place of the Fairacre dead. It was all very peaceful. Some midges drifted in clouds near the hedge, and a peacock butterfly opened and shut its beautiful wings upon the warm stone slab commemorating some village worthy.

With the centenary always to the front of my mind these days, I wondered how many of those resting here had attended the little school hard by, and what they had thought of it. As if reading my thoughts, Mr Willet said that there was a mort of folk these days as preferred to go up in smoke, and he wondered if it was right.

'We certainly miss all those lovely inscriptions,' I said. 'Personally, I enjoy a potter round this churchyard reading about virtuous wives and devoted mothers mourned by their fourteen sorrowing children. I've even got a soft spot for that terrible marble angel in memory of Mr Parr who died in 1870, "Benefactor and Brother To All".'

'Nice bit of work,' agreed Mr Willet. 'I likes a bit of white marble myself. Can't take to that polished pink granite. Might just as well have a bit of cold brawn on top of you, from the looks of it.'

'Well, I must go home,' I said reluctantly. 'Tibby expects a meal.'

'You spoils that cat. It'll get fatty heart the way you feeds it.'

'She's got a large frame,' I protested.

'Not surprising, the amount she packs away,' replied Mr

Willet. 'I'd better get on too. There's plenty of old Fairacre pupils wants tidying up by the south wall. You ever thought of that? You'll maybe get some ghosts at them celebrations of yours.'

'I rather hope we shall,' I said, stepping round the gravestone of one Sally Gray who died in 1890 in her 63rd year. She would have been fifty-three when Fairacre School was newly built, I thought, making my way home through the heat.

How the history of this little village pressed around one!

Obedient to Mrs Partridge's behest, I set off on my collecting stint one hot evening.

For once, clouds covered the sky. They were ominously dark, but made no appreciable difference to the heat. It was about to break, and I only hoped that I should get my job done before that happened.

People were generous with their donations, and my tin was soon quite heavy, and chiefly with silver, not copper coins. I had left Joan Benson's house until last, as it was the furthest from home, and I could then have an uninterrupted walk back to feed my overweight cat at the right time.

A few drops of rain began to patter against the holly hedge round the garden as I opened the gate. All the windows were shut, including those in Miriam Quinn's annexe at the side, and there was that indefinable feeling of blankness that always seems to emanate from a deserted house. However, I decided to try my luck. I remembered that Joan had been going to look at a house near her daughter's, but hoped that she would have returned.

I was unlucky. No one answered the bell, and the rain began to fall in torrents. I was well sheltered in the deep porch, and sat down on a sturdy bench which ran along one side to watch the downpour.

It was wonderful to see the plants reviving in the heavy shower. The dusty drive was soon pock-marked with large raindrops, and then with tiny rivulets that snaked their way downhill to the gate. The holly hedge began to glisten with drops, and the thirsty flowers in the parched border seemed to lift their heads in response to this benison of refreshing rain.

Drops began to stream from the porch and I began to feel that I was surveying the garden through a curtain of glass beads. The smell of water on hot stone rose all around me, and I began to realize how desperately the earth had been waiting for the rain.

It was obvious that Miriam Quinn had not returned yet from the office in Caxley. It was quite likely that there would be flooding there, I surmised, for the river Cax overflows very readily, and the low-lying parts of the town, particularly the area known as 'The Marsh' floods with depressing regularity, despite the efforts of drainage experts to control this nuisance.

But my spirits rose when I heard a car scrunching up the back drive on the wet gravel. Here, no doubt, was Miriam returning. But I was wrong. The car did not stop at the annexe, but swept up to the porch where I was sitting, and pulled up with a squealing of brakes.

Out of the car leapt Henry Mawne, head down through the blinding rain, and met me face to face.

'Good Lord! Have you rung?'

'Yes, but there's no one at home. I was waiting for the worst of the rain to go.'

Henry looked agitated. He jingled some coins in his pocket, and bounced up and down on his toes, gazing at the watery scene.

'Oh dear! Oh dear! Now I wonder when she will be back. Any idea?'

'None at all, I'm afraid.' I told him about Joan's departure for her house hunting.

'Well, let me give you a lift back. You might be stuck here for hours. It looks as though it has set in for the night.'

I was very grateful, and we drove back through the glistening lanes, with the rain drumming on the roof of the car, and the windscreen wipers working away like maniacs.

'Come in,' I said, when we drew up at my front door, but he refused.

'It's about Joan's house,' he began, rather explosively. 'Is it still on the market, do you know?'

I said I thought it was.

'We've been in Ireland for the past three weeks, looking up relatives there, and I missed the *Caxley Chronicle*'s advertisement. You see, I was wondering if it would suit David and Irene.'

'Do they know about it?'

'No, that's the point. I thought Joan might let me have a look, and if I thought it a possibility I would tell them on the telephone, and they could come down at once to view. It seems to me that you have to work at the speed of light these days if you want to buy a house. What's she asking for it?'

Again I had to confess ignorance. I really wanted to get into my own abode, but Henry seemed to want to unburden himself.

'I do wish you'd come in,' I urged him, but he was adamant. He sat staring straight ahead through the rain-beaded windscreen, his fingers drumming on the wheel, and a little nerve twitching in his cheek.

'It's all very difficult. I know they hope to move from the London house, and get further out. Better for Simon too, in the holidays. Better for all of them when you think of what David and the boy went through there when poor Teresa lost her sanity.'

I murmured sympathetically. I knew only too well how strung up that young boy had been when he had been one of my pupils for a few summer weeks.

'On the other hand, I don't want to interfere. A second marriage can always be a bit dicey, I think, and they may loathe the idea of being near us, or any relatives, for that matter. But this place looks about the right size for them. Three bedrooms, I believe?'

'And the annexe,' I said.

'But surely Miriam Quinn's in that?'

'She is at the moment.'

'Nice woman. I shouldn't think Irene and David would want her to go.'

There was silence for a time. The rain continued to throb relentlessly above and around us. A few blackbirds scrabbled joyfully under the bushes, enjoying the softened soil after the hard surface of the past weeks.

'He has regular trips these days to Holland, Belgium and Norway, so Irene would be glad of Miriam next door, I should imagine. And it's only an hour's drive to Heathrow. It took him pretty well that time to get across London.'

I could see that he was thinking aloud, putting the pros and cons to himself, and really attempting to make a decision.

'I should simply ring David and let him think it over,' I said, stating the obvious.

To my surprise, he seized my hands in his and shook them warmly. 'An excellent notion!' he exclaimed. 'After all, it's his decision, isn't it?'

He leant across to open the door for me, beaming the while.

'Yes, I'll do that immediately. What a help you've been!'

He sped off, cutting short my thanks, and I entered to be greeted by my starving Tibby.

While she wolfed down raw liver I sipped a drink and thought, for the umpteenth time, about this business of buying a house.

For years I have meant to do it. After all, the time flies by, and when I reached retirement age I should have to have somewhere to live. Now that Fairacre School's numbers had sunk perilously low, I might well find myself homeless if the school were closed.

I felt reasonably sure that I would not be turned out into the snow like some Victorian heroine. I might even be offered the house first, if it were to be sold, as no doubt it would be eventually. In any case, I should get plenty of notice to quit, if it came to that. But the thing was, where should I go? Somewhere nearby would be ideal.

And secondly, what should I use for money? My meagre savings might rise to a deposit on the house, but would a building society give me a mortgage at my age?

I had been a fool not to buy when prices were less astronomic, as Amy pointed out when she called one afternoon.

'I've told you time and time again,' she said severely, 'and you've done nothing all these years.'

'I know,' I said meekly. 'Well, I've just lived from day to day. And jolly nice it's been,' I added defiantly.

Amy laughed. 'Well, my dear old silly, you know you can always have a bed at Bent, if the worse comes to the worst.' She looked at me speculatively. 'How much could you raise if you saw something you liked?'

I told her.

'It would hardly buy the bathroom,' she said. 'Would you let me lend you some money?'

'No, indeed!' I said.

'I've got quite a nice little nest egg, and you might just as well have some of it. Think it over, anyway.'

'You are sweet to think of it, but honestly I couldn't possibly accept.'

'Well, the offer will stand, darling,' said Amy, getting up to go.

'Besides, if I bought now, I should have to let it while I'm still teaching, and you know how impossible it is to get tenants out if they dig in their heels. No, I think I must just soldier on as I am. Lord knows I'm happy enough this way.'

'Bless you, so you are! And as the old song says: "You die if you worry, You die if you don't, So why worry at all?"'

And on this cheering note Amy departed.

'Nice drop of rain,' commented Mrs Pringle, with unwonted affability the next morning. 'My lettuces have picked up wonderful, and the water butt's full again.'

I said it seemed to have done a lot of good everywhere except for the aperture where the skylight once had pride of place. A fine puddle had cascaded on to the tarpaulin and thence to the floor. Luckily, I had been prudent enough to shift my desk during these protracted building operations, or we should have had more serious damage.

Mrs Pringle's countenance assumed its usual gloom as she surveyed the mess. 'I'll have a straight word with Reg Thorn when I see him,' she boomed.

I felt a pang of sympathy for the poor wretch, maddening though he was. He would meet his match in Mrs Pringle.

The delays and confusion which had accompanied the removal of the skylight and the replacement by a simple dormer window had to be seen to be believed. It seemed to me that Reg Thorn was constantly driving to the builder's merchant, or the timber yard, in Caxley, to acquire or replace new pieces of window equipment which surely should have been bought at the beginning and assembled in his own workshop. What he spent in petrol alone must have made a hole in the taxpayers' pockets, but I suppose none of his fuming customers could get at him whilst in transit, so that from his point of view he was leading a comparatively peaceful life.

Mrs Pringle began to mop up, muttering to herself the while and clanging the bucket. I looked up a hymn for morning prayers before getting Ernest to ring the school bell to alert any stragglers still in the lanes or fields of Fairacre.

These last few days of term are always busy. This time, the last week seemed fuller than ever, for I wanted to visit the parents of the principal actors to see their reaction to making costumes for the favoured few.

Linda Moffat was to be one of the stars as Miss Richards, the first headmistress of Fairacre School. It was she who caned John Pratt in July 1882, and we had cast Patrick, who is small but with a good loud voice, as the youthful sinner. Mrs Moffat is a skilful dressmaker, and I felt sure that she would not only make Linda's costume superbly, but would be generous enough to lend a hand with the others if need be.

I also rang Mrs Austen to sound her out about her

contribution of an evacuee's memories to our performance. To my joy, she was most enthusiastic and promised to prepare a script which we could discuss.

Altogether it was a satisfactory ending to the school year. There was a chance of another family coming to live in the village, as Mr Roberts had engaged a new shepherd who had three children. This was encouraging as it would mean an increase next term in my dangerously low numbers. The sun appeared again after the storm and, apart from the annoyance of the skylight non-activity, all appeared hopeful in my little world.

The vicar called to wish the children a happy holiday, and added his usual rider about helping their mothers. This was followed by the ritual: 'The same to you, sir!' which is always considered the height of humour by my pupils.

They dispersed boisterously into the summer sunshine, and as their voices died away down the lane, I wandered across to the schoolhouse, rejoicing in the long weeks of blissful freedom ahead.

8. August

My holiday plans were simple. The first few days had been spent in coping with neglected jobs such as weeding the border and washing the kitchen paintwork.

I had made arrangements to spend a fortnight in Norfolk with an old friend, and meanwhile Miss Clare had accepted an invitation from me to spend a few days at Fairacre at the beginning of the month.

The spare room lay in an unusual state of pristine splendour. The furniture gleamed from Mrs Pringle's ministrations. The feather bed was beautifully puffed up beneath a fresh chintz bedspread. On the table at the bedside was a posy of all the sweetest-smelling flowers I had been able to pick in the garden. Lavender, roses, pinks and a sprig or two of night-scented stock made a handsome nosegay in a little lustre jug which had once been my mother's.

I had been invited to tea at Miss Clare's, and went over to fetch her with a buoyant heart. I always enjoy visiting that neat cottage. It had two downstairs rooms, both of good size, and two bedrooms above. A little bathroom had been added when mains water had come, at long last, to Beech Green some years ago.

The garden was large for a cottage. Miss Clare still kept the front one tidy and gay with flowers, but the larger part at the back was used as a vegetable plot by a young man in the village who was glad to have the produce for his large family. He kept Dolly supplied with all that she needed, so that it was an ideal arrangement.

The best white cloth had been spread in my honour, and the thin ancient teaspoons of silver gleamed brightly. The best tea set, with a pretty pattern of pansies, was in evidence, and the usual plate of wafer-thin bread and butter and a splendid sponge cake, which I knew would be as light as a feather, showed that the mistress of the house had been busy.

Beyond the lattice windowpane the downs shimmered in a blue heat haze. It was a tranquil spot and Dolly Clare had lived there from the age of six, first with her family, and then alone for a number of years. To her great joy, her lifelong friend Emily Davis had joined her for several years, and the two old ladies had lived in perfect harmony until Emily's death a few years earlier.

Much had happened under this old thatched roof. The joys and griefs of a family, the sharing of a nation's wars, and always the relentless pressure of poverty. But it was a happy house; one felt it as soon as one crossed the threshold. Here was a haven, a quiet backwater where one could rest tranquilly away from the turbulent mainstream of life. This blessed peace, I well knew, stemmed mainly from the quiet spirit who lived there, but even without her presence one was conscious of a home which had been loved by many generations.

'I have been given some nerine bulbs,' said Miss Clare, entering with the teapot. 'Do you know anything about them?'

'They say that if they like you they grow like weeds. If not, you'll never be able to rear them.'

'We'll live in hope then. George Annett says they need lots of manure, but Bob Willet says the exact opposite! Lots of sandy soil at the foot of a south-facing wall was his advice.'

'Why not do that, and bung on lots of manure in the autumn? That way you are hedging your bets, I should think.'

'I remember seeing them years ago in Devon, when a friend took me away for a few days at the October half-term. So many of the gardens had great clumps of these beautiful rose-pink heads. I've never felt I could afford to buy them, but now I've been given some I should grieve if I mistreated them.'

I promised that we would look up the care of nerines in my new gardening book the minute we were home, and our conversation turned to her contribution to the centenary celebrations.

'I am quite looking forward to it,' said Dolly, carefully folding a thin slice of bread and butter. 'I suppose I ought to feel nervous, but I'm not, you know. After all, most of those present will be old pupils of mine. And that particular period, in King Edward's time, was a very happy one for me. I was a pupil teacher for several years then at Fairacre School, and dear Emily was my constant companion. We were so lucky to have Mr Wardle as our headmaster. He was a cheerful soul, and always out to help us both.'

'And you and Emily stayed together?'

'Well, no. She found a post south of Caxley, and I can't tell you how I missed her. We met when we could and caught up with our news, and exchanged our views on teaching. And if we met in Caxley, we went window shopping. That's all we could afford.'

Miss Clare laughed. 'We were very short of money. Everybody was. I don't suppose there was a single child at Fairacre School in those days who wasn't dressed in secondhand clothes. They were handed down from one child to the next, and gratefully received from any of the more well-to-do families. As for jumble sales, they were serious shopping expeditions then, not just an afternoon's spree in the village. I had a tweed cape cut down from a full-sized one of poor Miss Lilian's, which I wore for years.'

Poor Miss Lilian, I remembered, had been the feeble-minded daughter of one of the leading families in Beech Green. It was a never-to-be-forgotten tragedy that she and her mother perished on the *Titanic* in 1912 as they crossed the Atlantic to consult an eminent American brain surgeon in the hope of effecting Lilian's recovery.

'I think shortage of money was the chief worry then. There wasn't so much concern with health. As long as you could keep going and earn a bit, you tended to ignore minor aches and pains, and perhaps it was a good thing, although people often struggled on when really they should have gone to the doctor. But he needed paying, you see. It was all an uphill struggle, and I know many of the children came hungry to school. The older people could remember the rebellion of some of the agricultural workers when they smashed machinery, and shouted for bread. When I see the bonny children of today, and remember some of those in my early classes, I feel thankful that times have changed.'

'You'll talk about this, I hope, when you give us your memories?'

'Indeed I will,' said Miss Clare with spirit, 'for now I think too much is taken for granted, and thankfulness is becoming as dead as perseverance and truthfulness and a great many other fine old-fashioned virtues.'

She sat back from the table and looked through the window at the tall hollyhocks outside. From her pensive expression I knew that her thoughts were years away.

She took a deep breath, and gave me her sweet smile. 'Well, shall we be going?'

We cleared away, and Dolly went slowly round the house, closing windows and locking doors.

Within half an hour we were travelling along the familiar lane which Dolly had traversed daily for many years, in fair weather and foul, until St Patrick's church spire pierced the skyline, and we were back in Fairacre again and looking up 'Nerines' in my latest gardening book.

Mr Willet turned up the next morning, balancing a pair of shears on the bars of his bicycle.

'Promised I'd do that box edging,' he shouted through the kitchen window. 'All right to tackle it now? Got a wedding this afternoon.'

'Hello, Bob,' said Miss Clare, appearing in the doorway.

'Well, I'm blowed!' said Mr Willet beaming. 'And how be

you keeping, Dolly? You looks younger than ever. Got some magic secret, have you?'

Dolly Clare laughed. 'I don't say much about my aches and pains, Bob. Doesn't do any good, and bores people stiff.'

'I tells everyone if I've got a finger ache,' replied Mr Willet robustly. 'Makes me feel a durn sight better when I've unloaded all my woes on to someone else.'

She followed her old friend into the sunshine, and I watched them talking animatedly as Bob Willet surveyed the job to be tackled. They would have plenty of gossip to exchange, I guessed.

Reg Thorn's business was closed for a fortnight's holiday, so that we were spared the racket of banging tools, the boys' transistor and their vigorous exchange of opinions over football and cricket matters.

When I carried out the coffee cups some time later, the sun was so hot that we dragged my ancient deckchairs into the shade of the apple tree.

'Funny how you can drink hot coffee winter and summer,' commented Mr Willet, drying his moustache on the back of his hand, 'and still it do you a power of good.'

'They're a fine pair of shears,' observed Dolly, eyeing the shining blades resting on the grass by Bob's feet.

'Yes, well, I likes my own tools. Miss Read here do have a pair of shears – so-called – but they does more harm than good, twizzling up the sappy bits and wrenching away at the twiggy bits like a host of rats 'ad been at work.'

'Thanks,' I said.

'No need to be sarky,' said Mr Willet amiably. 'Some knows how to look after tools, and some don't, that's all I'm saying.' He struggled from the deck chair. 'I suppose I'd best get on. You women would keep me here all morning with your gossiping.'

'Well – !' I began.

'By the way, I see that young Simon in the village as I come up here. He staying with the Mawnes, d'you know?'

'I hadn't heard. How does he look?'

'Much the same as ever – a long streak of nothin', and lookin' as though butter wouldn't melt in his mouth, the young varmint. When I think of our Snowy as he did in, I could give that boy a leathering and enjoy it!'

Mr Willet's face grew puce at the remembrance of Simon's part in the death of Fairacre's albino robin not so long ago. I decided to change the subject.

'Any chance of seeing you here tomorrow?'

'Ah! I might manage that if I'm spared. This edging of yours will need a few hours on it, the state it's got into.'

I picked up the tray, and left Dolly to watch her old friend at work.

In the kitchen, putting the cups to soak, I wondered if Simon's parents had come to Fairacre to have a look at Joan Benson's house. I did not propose to mention this possibility to anyone, as I did not want to spread any rumours. However, no matter how prudently I held my tongue, there was no doubt in my mind that whatever was decided under the Mawnes' or the Bensons' roofs would very soon be common knowledge in our little community.

Miss Clare was with me for a week, and the weather stayed sunny for all that time. We took picnic lunches up on the downs, or down by the little brook at Springbourne, as it purled along beneath drooping willows on its way to join the Cax before the river flowed through Caxley. Everywhere we went held memories for Dolly and, like all old people, her early years were clearer in her mind than more recent ones.

I found her recollections fascinating, and only wished I had a recording machine with me all the time. It certainly made me decide to get one ready for the centenary day when I could record her talk for future generations. Dolly's lifetime spanned the age-old rural life of hard work geared to the pace of man and horse, and modern life geared to the pace of cars, lorries and aircraft. Children of Dolly's generation were lucky to have

travelled twenty miles from home. Many of them had never seen the sea, some sixty or seventy miles distant, nor travelled in a train, nor visited a town any larger than Caxley.

Their grandchildren thought nothing of flying anywhere across the globe, of talking to relatives in New Zealand as they sat by their own firesides, and of buying the produce of the world set out temptingly at the village shop. Once Dolly and her contemporaries had gone, the way of life which had been known and expressed in poetry, prose and pictures for centuries would vanish. It was a sobering thought.

But it was the small personal memories that I cherished as we took our drives around the countryside which Dolly knew so well.

'That was where old Mrs Johns lived,' she said as we passed a tumbledown cottage with a collapsed roof of thatch. 'She wore a bustle, you know, till the end of her life. A funny little soul, who kept that place spotless.'

'Ernie White was killed in that field,' she commented. 'A tractor tipped over and pinned the poor soul there for hours. People said it was a judgement for doing away with the horses.'

She sighed.

'And that's where Emily's Edgar lived. She should have been there by rights, but he married his nurse, you know, and my dear Emily never got over it, brave face though she showed to the world.'

She showed me where she and Emily tobogganed as children, where she took her pupils to collect hazel nuts and frogspawn, and then holly to decorate St Patrick's church at Christmas time. It was borne in upon me how closely the seasons were woven into the fabric of the country child's life in those days. They were out so much more than today's children. They walked everywhere. No school buses whisked them past beds of violets, wild strawberries, sprays of luscious blackberries, all known and treasured by their grandparents.

One afternoon, I invited Mrs Austen to tea and it was a rare treat for me to listen to the war-time reminiscences of evacuee and teacher at Fairacre School in the early forties.

'Everything was so different from our home and school at New Cross in south London,' said Mrs Austen. 'For one thing, I was used to an enormous three-storey building with infants on the ground floor, big girls on the next, and boys at the top. It was lovely to be mixed up together, such a *few* of us it seemed, in a dear little school like Fairacre's.'

'You certainly settled down wonderfully,' commented Miss Clare.

'I think I found the biggest differences, though, at Mrs Pratt's, where we were billeted. She couldn't have been kinder, and I kept in touch with her until she died, but there were some things which shook me as a child. No flush lavatory for one. And lighting lamps and candles, instead of switching on the electric light. I dreaded having to go down the garden to the privy in the dark. Mrs Pratt used to light a hurricane lamp for me, but it cast such shadows I was even more terrified.'

'Was there no commode in your bedroom?' enquired Miss Clare with concern.

'Well, yes – but I hated using It. It seemed so *wrong* to me. I'd never met such a thing, you see. And another thing that appalled me was the number of flies everywhere, and all taken for granted. At home, in London, my mother bustled a stray fly away as if it were poisonous – which it was, I always thought – but Mrs Pratt even had a paper ball hung up near the ceiling and called it the flies' playground.'

'We had one too, I remember,' said Miss Clare.

'There was another ball on the mantelpiece made of silver paper. We all collected every scrap of tin foil and it was carefully wrapped round the ball. It was an enormous weight. I can't think what happened to it eventually.'

'It went to the hospital in Caxley,' Miss Clare told her. 'Still does, I believe, but now they like it flat.'

'I was very fond of Mrs Pratt,' said Mrs Austen, 'but

frightened of her old mother who lived down the road. Do you remember that little boy – I forget his name – who lived with her?'

'I do indeed,' said Dolly. 'He was called Stephen, a foster-child, and really old Mrs Hall had no business to have him. She was far too frail and suffered from tuberculosis, and in any case much too ancient to take care of a young child. But it was difficult to find homes for those orphans, and I suppose the local authority thought it was suitable. In any case, the Halls needed the maintenance money, but I was glad when that child was moved elsewhere.'

'So was I! I used to collect him to bring him along to school, and the smell in that house was ghastly. And the poor old thing was always coughing. She used to crouch on the rag rug in front of the fire with the ash pan pulled out, and spit horribly into the hot ashes. Sometimes she had no breath to speak to me, but just gazed at me with those watery blue eyes and motioned me to take Stephen out of the way. I did too, as quickly as I could.'

'He went into the army eventually,' Dolly told her, 'and did very well. I still hear from him at Christmas, dear boy.'

Her voice was warm with affection. Were there any of her pupils, I wondered, who failed to kindle a spark of remembered happiness in their old teacher? Even the malefactors, dealt with sternly in their youth, were now seen through the rosy haze of time. And why not?

I took Dolly back to her cottage with the greatest reluctance, I had enjoyed her serene company so much. But she insisted that she had a number of little household jobs to do, and some bottles of fruit to prepare for the store cupboard, so that I left her looking happy in her shining kitchen with the cat for company.

I went on to Bent to lunch with Amy. I found her house as welcoming and beautiful as Dolly Clare's, although three times the size, of course.

'How do you manage to keep it so immaculate?' I cried. 'I've never seen a speck of dust or one dead flower in this place, all the years I've visited here.'

'Elementary organization,' said Amy. 'You too could have an immaculate house if you planned your routine.'

'You remind me of those advertisements, Amy. "You too can have a beautiful bust".'

'I liked the one about piano-playing in our youth. "You too can be a concert pianist", or something like that.'

'Better than that! "My friends used to laugh when I sat down at the piano." Remember?'

'Mine still do,' said Amy. 'It must be lovely to have a talent of some sort.'

'How's the autobiography?'

'Oh dear, oh dear! I was afraid you'd ask! I'm stuck at myself aged eight, and all I can remember are idiotic things like tying reef knots as a Brownie, and my father cranking up our first family car, and having to help him fix canvas and mica side curtains to it when it rained. I don't think it's very stirring stuff, not a bit like some of these successful memoirs where the authors remember all sorts of psychological hook-ups and traumatic experiences when they found the cat having kittens in the laundry basket. I wonder why they can do it, and I can't?'

'Probably because you have a much more normal mind,' I assured her. 'And anyway, who's to know they didn't make it all up?'

'I never thought of that!'

'Frankly, I should shelve it for a week or two, and go back to it when you feel like it. Anyway, the weather's too good to stick about indoors pushing the pen.'

'I believe you're right. I've hardly been into Caxley at all since starting the book. Incidentally, I saw your young teacher there the last time I was shopping.'

'Our Miss Briggs? I wonder what she was doing in Caxley? I thought she was at home, in one of those spas – Droitwich or Buxton or somewhere up north. Malvern perhaps.'

'Malvern's *west*, dear. She was with a young man, and they appeared to be very affectionate.'

'Well, I'm blowed! Perhaps she came back to collect something, and brought her young man with her from Harrogate or whatever. It was during the holidays, I take it, that you saw her?'

'Yes, the beginning of last week.'

'Well, I'm glad to hear she's found an interest at last. It may liven her up. Mr Willet calls her "a fair old lump of a girl", and I don't think one can better that description.'

'Poor thing!' said Amy. 'Anyway, she looked quite animated and pretty in the High Street.'

'Ah! The transformation wrought by love! I must try it some time.'

'I wish you would,' said Amy forcefully, returning to a well-worn theme, 'but aren't you leaving it rather late?'

Trust old friends to tell you the unpalatable truth!

Mrs Pringle arrived 'to bottom' me as she elegantly terms performing the house cleaning. Sometimes she only has time 'to put me to rights', and that is bad enough. 'To be bottomed' involves taking down curtains and pictures, pulling out a heavy Welsh dresser and generally creating mayhem. I try and make myself scarce when threatened with bottoming, but on this occasion there was no escape as I was expecting the lawn-mower to be returned from the repairer's and wanted to pay him.

Halfway through the dire proceedings I was allowed to pick my way through displaced furniture piled in the kitchen to put on the kettle for a restorative cup of tea.

Mrs Pringle, militant in a flowered overall with the sleeves rolled up to expose wrestler's forearms, had a fanatical look in her eyes.

'You seen the top of that dresser of yours?' she asked.

'No. What's wrong with it?'

'*Wrong with it?*' echoed Mrs Pringle triumphantly. 'It's got two inches of dust on it as you could grow potatoes in.'

'Oh, come . . .' I began weakly.

'And what's more, down the back, was a letter unopened and dated months ago.'

'Good heavens! Where is it?'

Mrs Pringle handed me an envelope. The address was handwritten, and I recognized it as Lucy Clayton's writing. I had cordially detested her when we'd been at college together.

'No one that matters,' I said with some relief, and made the tea.

We took it into the garden. The sight of my house I found upsetting.

'Well, I must say it's a treat to breathe a bit of clean air after all that dust and filth,' announced Mrs Pringle, stirring her tea. 'You heard about Mrs Partridge?'

'No. What's happened?'

'She had to go to hospital, poor soul.'

I was genuinely shocked. I am devoted to our vicar's wife, and the thought of her in hospital was even more upsetting than the chaos in my house.

'When did she go?'

'Last Saturday.'

'And it's Wednesday today! I am sorry. What is it, do you know?'

'Bees. The vicar's bees.'

'But she wouldn't need to be three, I mean four, days in hospital with a bee sting, surely?'

'Who said she was?'

'What?'

'In hospital for four days. All I said was that she went in Saturday. She come out Saturday too.'

Mrs Pringle took a long draught of tea and looked complacent. She has brought irritating her listeners to a fine art, I'll give her that.

'Well, go on. Tell me it all from the beginning.'

'Mrs Partridge told me herself as she was simply up the garden picking some nice sprigs of parsley to make parsley sauce for a nice bit of fresh haddock she'd got from that nice fishmonger in Caxley . . .'

Who probably had a nice shop, I thought impatiently.

'*Miles* away from the hive, she said, when one of the nasty things came and bit her by the eye, and she swelled up awful. Couldn't see out of that eye in a quarter of an hour, and the other not much better, and the vicar looking everywhere for his glasses to read how big a dose of some bee medicine you had to take if bitten – as she had been, of course – and worried to death all the time, in case it was fatal. It can be, you know. My old uncle was never right after being set on by bees, and he died soon after.'

'Really? How dreadful!'

'Mind you, he was ninety-four,' Mrs Pringle admitted, 'but we all said as it was the bee stings as hastened his end. I told the vicar about it.'

Job's comforter, as ever, was my private comment.

'Anyway, she took these tablets, and the vicar got out the car and took her into Caxley Cottage Hospital, and her head was fair swimming by the time she got there. She reckoned it was the medicine. The doctor said it could have been, and give her something to help, and some ointment. She come straight back and went to bed, poor thing, and you can still see where its fangs went into her.' She heaved herself to her feet. 'Well, I'd best get on. No rest for the wicked, my mother used to say.'

She surveyed my reclining form with a sour expression.

'Though that don't always seem to fit the case, come to think of it.'

After she had returned to the fray, I opened Lucy's letter. It was dated 12 February, which showed how long it had been collecting dust at the back of the dresser.

In it Lucy informed me that Mr and Mrs Ambrose B. Edelstein and their two grown-up children were to be in England for three months. They came from – here an illegible place

name, possibly Minnesota, Minever or even Minnehaha –
where they took a keen interest in Education, and the Professor
had several degrees in the subject. They were such a nice family
– I thought of Mrs Pringle – and would be fascinated by a
glimpse of Fairacre School, so she had taken the liberty of
giving them my telephone number, and they would be ringing
me to arrange a convenient day to visit. No need to put them
up, or get them meals, as they were planning to stop in Caxley,
but she was sure I would enjoy having them in school for a day
just letting them have a free rein talking to the children and
looking through their work.

She was ever my affectionate Lucy, and added a postscript
saying that there was absolutely no need for me to feel that I
must reply. I breathed a sigh of relief for mercies received,
calculated that the Edelsteins had now been safely back in
Minniewhatsit for several months, and fell into a blissful sleep.

Mrs Pringle and the lawn-mower man brought me back to
earth, half an hour later, and life began anew.

My Norfolk holiday was a great success. There is something
about the bracing salty air of that magnificent county, with its
massive skies and pellucid light, which is wonderfully restorative. In the summer, that is. I have only once experienced really
wintry weather in that area, and hope never to again. Such
piercing cold, straight from the steppes of Russia, it seemed,
had an intensity never met with in Fairacre, even though we are
always telling each other that we live in a cold spot.

On the way to stay with my old friend, and on my return
journey, I spent a few hours in Cambridge, so dear to me, and
renewed my delight with walks along the Backs, Parker's Piece
and Midsummer Common. August is not the best month to see
Cambridge, or any other place for that matter, for the trees and
grass begin to look worn and shabby, the first glory of summer
has gone, and the true fire and radiance of autumn has not
begun. But to my devoted eye, there was beauty enough and to
spare, and I hung over Clare Bridge and watched the scattered

yellow willow leaves floating gently beneath me with the same rapture which I felt in my youth.

There is so little water in Fairacre, and I do not realize how much I miss it until I come across a river, or a lake, or even a modest garden fountain, and experience that surge of joy for this most beautiful of the elements.

But, as always, it was good to get back to my own home. Tibby greeted me with some hauteur. She looked upon my absence as dereliction of duty, and was not going to put herself out with a lot of fulsome welcoming. Later, if I did the right thing with offerings of rabbit or finely chopped pig's liver, she might condescend to accept me again.

Mrs Pringle had obviously been bottoming me in my absence, and the house shone. She had even put some sweet peas in a vase on the mantelpiece, a gesture which, from one of her morose mood, I much appreciated.

Later, I wrote to my Norfolk friend and decided that it would do me good to walk to the post office. Looking out of the kitchen window, I noted that the evening was overcast, and it was sad to see how much shorter the days were growing. Already there were yellow leaves fluttering down from the old plum tree in the garden, and dahlias and Michaelmas daisies were opening in the border. Far too soon, autumn would be upon us and lovely though it always was at Fairacre, with its flaming beech trees and bronzed hedges, yet there was sadness too at the passing of summer and all its outdoor pleasures.

Letter in hand, I opened the front door to find Joan Benson about to thread the Parish Magazine through the letter box.

'Come in,' I cried.

'But you're just going out.'

'Not really. The post's gone anyway, and this will keep till tomorrow.'

'Then I will. I've a stone or something in my shoe, and perhaps I can sit down and investigate.'

It turned out to be a nail, and we had a few minutes of amateurish hammering to try and remedy the matter. We found the activity extremely frustrating, as there was not room enough inside the shoe to manoeuvre the hammer. However, by dint of banging energetically we effected a partial cure.

'We ought to have one of those little anvil things,' said Joan 'with three feet on them. Is it called a cobbler's last?'

I confessed ignorance. 'All I know about a cobbler's last is that he should stick to it,' I said, 'but I never really knew what it meant.'

'Like so many sayings,' agreed Joan, standing up to test her shoe. 'All my eye and Betty Martin, for instance.'

'Or right as a trivet.'

'Or being on tenterhooks. This shoe's fine now, thank you. You could set up as a cobbler, as a side line to teaching, you know.'

'I'll consider it. I might need something to do when I retire.'

'You're not thinking of that yet, surely? Incidentally, will you stay here?'

'I doubt it. By that time I rather think this house and school will be on the market. Any sensible woman would have bought a little place of her own before now, but I'm afraid I've left it a bit late.'

Joan Benson nodded understandingly. 'Well, I can sympathize. This house hunting is so *wearing*. I've had another week with my daughter searching for a suitable home, but the more I look the less I like.'

'What exactly are you looking for?'

'You may well ask! Something with no stairs – a ground-floor flat or a bungalow. But I *must* have a little bit of garden, and ideally it should have some trees, and be the sort of private place where one can sit and ruminate without too many people around. The snag is, of course, that it's virtually impossible to find such a place. Barbara is very anxious for me to have an apartment in an old people's home near her, and lovely though it is – it's an old vicarage with a cedar tree on the lawn and even an old nuttery with Kentish cob nuts – one would be among a score or so of other old people, all individually quite charming I have no doubt, but never *alone*.'

'I can understand how you feel.'

'Do you like your solitude too?'

'It's the breath of life to me,' I confessed, 'Perhaps it's because I am with a crowd all day. All I know is, that to come into this little house and to hear the clock ticking and the cat purring, is sheer bliss to me. I can truthfully say I've never felt lonely in my life.'

'Well, I can't say that,' admitted Joan. 'When you've had a husband and children, and latterly my darling mother, always about the place, then to be alone is – not exactly *frightening*, but definitely *disconcerting*. I suppose the ideal thing would be to find a flat near Barbara so that she could see me frequently, but not have me under her feet. She presses me sometimes to make my home with them, and sometimes when I get back exhausted from house hunting I almost give in. But it would never do. It wouldn't be fair to her, or to the children, or to me, to be honest. Grandchildren are adorable for a time, but it's asking too much to have them with you constantly when you are getting on, and I'm quite sure the same thing applies in reverse.'

She picked up the basket containing the few remaining copies of the parish magazine. 'I must finish my little job. Mrs Partridge usually does it, noble soul, but she's away for a few days. You've heard, I expect, about Holly Lodge?'

'No, indeed. I only came back from Norfolk a couple of hours ago, so I haven't caught up with the Fairacre news.'

'I think I've sold it. Henry Mawne asked me if his nephew David and his wife could come and have a look at it. A very nice couple. Do you know them?'

I told her the little about them that I knew.

'Well, they are now trying to sell their own place, which shouldn't be too difficult. Miriam knows them rather better than I do, and the marvellous thing is that they hope Miriam will continue to live in the annexe.'

'She must be very pleased.'

A little frown of worry puckered Joan's brow. 'It is *exactly* what I'd hoped for, and I'm sure it will work out beautifully, but at the moment Miriam is now wondering if they are only being kind, and would really want the annexe for themselves. We've all done our best to persuade her that she need not have such qualms, and as she's such a sensible person I'm sure she will realize that is the truth very soon.'

She began to make her way towards the door.

'Do you sometimes find even the most straightforward people horribly *complicated*?' she asked.

'Frequently,' I replied. 'Perhaps that's why we relish our solitude.'

Reg Thorn and his two young men were at last back on the school roof. The dormer window was now recognizable, but still seemed to be giving the three of them a certain amount of trouble. In my innocence, I had imagined that the job might take about three weeks, with perhaps a few more days allowed for bad weather, or difficulty in obtaining parts for it. But here we were, months later, and still no sign of completion.

I never seemed to be able to catch Reg himself. I would see him in the distance from my kitchen window, but by the time I had walked across to speak to him he had leapt into his van and driven off in a cloud of dust. Dodging irate employers, I guessed, was second nature to him by now.

The young men were fast becoming as evasive, at least in making excuses. One was fair, with receding hair; this seemed sad, as he could not have been much more than twenty-five. The other seemed to be covered in thick black hair: head, beard and chest were one luxuriant growth. Only his dark eyes seemed to be visible among this lushness, and it was he who usually answered my questions. His name was Wayne.

'Well, it's like this, miss. The timber merchant's been closed for the holidays, and when he opened last week he couldn't let us have what we wanted because he'd had a sudden order in from that new estate.'

It all sounded pretty weak to me, but there were any number of excuses, equally futile, that were trotted out in answer to my queries, and I began to give up.

Wayne was a nice young man, anyway, and I half respected his loyalty to Reg Thorn. He told me that he had been with him for four years, and had learnt a lot.

'My dad's in the same trade,' he told me, 'and when he gives up I'll probably take over there.'

'Didn't he want you to work with him?'

'Not my dad! Said he didn't want me under his feet while he could still do a day's work, and got me fixed up with Reg. Better for us both, he said. And anyway, I've promised to carry on when he retires.'

'And will he?'

'Not before he's ninety, I don't suppose. I'll be drawing me pension, I reckon, before he gives up.'

Wayne's father, I thought, seemed worthy of respect.

*

Term began again in the last week of the month. The children, as always, appeared to have forgotten in six weeks everything they had ever learnt under my tuition, but looked brown and cheerful and ready for the new school year.

Miss Briggs looked equally healthy and almost vivacious. She gave me a large smile when I met her in the playground, and included the two young men on the roof in her affability. The infants welcomed her with affection when we went into school, and one of the smallest presented her with a stick of peppermint rock.

'I got it at Berrisford,' he told her. 'My dad took us there on his day off, and we've kep' it safe on the dresser ever since.'

Miss Briggs thanked him with such obvious gratitude that I thought it would be churlish to point out that it had obviously been sucked at one end.

After all, I told myself, it was the thought that counted, and what were a few germs between friends?

9. September

I always enjoy the early part of the autumn term. The new entrants soon settle down, and it is good to have fresh faces in the infants' room. This year there were four new babies and luckily all were good-natured youngsters who refrained from bawling when their mothers left them, but looked about them, bright-eyed and as inquisitve as squirrels at all these fresh interests.

For the last few years we have tried to let the newcomers visit us for a half-day a week in the preceding term, so that they become familiar with their surroundings.

This has helped enormously when they finally make a start at the beginning of the school year. It is a great strain on a young child to be thrust, not only among large numbers of bigger children, but also into a strange building where each has to find his own clothes peg, his desk, the wash basins and, most important of all, the lavatory.

Miss Briggs seemed much more settled, I thought, and certainly better tempered. No one could call her enthusiastic or charming, but her general demeanour was much more cheerful. This had a good effect on her class, and I supposed that the change in attitude resulted from the mellowing influence of the unknown young man, and also the fact that she now felt more confident in her work after two terms of teaching. She was far readier too, I was relieved to see, to remain after school when needed. Quite often she did not go until Reg Thorn's workmen finished at four-thirty, and seemed glad to take on extra little jobs connected with the coming celebrations.

Things were going well in that direction. Mrs Moffat invited me to see Linda's Victorian dress, and I accompanied her from the butcher's where we had met one Saturday morning.

In the room set aside for her sewing, there hung her latest masterpiece. It was a perfect replica of Miss Richards' frock of the early 1880s, as dimly seen in a faded photograph I had found among the school records.

It was made of black woollen crêpe, complete with bustle, and draped over a pleated underskirt of black satin. At the neck was a ruffle of white lace, and embedded in the snowy froth was a beautiful jet brooch.

I exclaimed with admiration.

'Well, it's mostly bits and pieces,' she said modestly, though obviously pleased at my reaction.

'The black material is from an evening frock of mine. The satin was a skirt lining, and the lace I had by me. The bustle is made of foam rubber – much more comfortable than the original horse hair, I should think.'

'And that lovely brooch?'

'My grandmother's. It was the mourning brooch she bought when her father died. She also had a pretty little mourning ring made from his signet ring, but it was lost not long afterwards.'

'Well, Linda's going to be the belle of the ball on this occasion,' I said, stroking the costume.

'Don't be too sure! I think young Patrick will run her pretty close. I've been helping his mother make a serge suit with knee breeches – Norfolk style, you know – and with an Eton collar and bow tie he's going to look absolutely splendid. The only difficulty is persuading Patrick that he won't look what he terms "a proper sissy" in it.'

'I'll work on that problem,' I promised her as I took my leave.

Mrs Pringle arrived at school one morning looking unusually militant. I soon learnt the cause.

'That niece of mine, that Minnie, that *awful* Minnie!' She gulped with fury, slapping viciously at a desk with her duster.

My heart sank. Minnie Pringle, still known by that name although she is a married woman, is the mother of several children, most of them illegitimate. In a weak moment I once engaged her as a second cleaner, and the havoc she managed to wreak in my house had to be seen to be believed. Whatever had happened to Minnie, I decided now, nothing would persuade me to have her in my home again.

'What has she done?' I ventured to ask her irate aunt.

'She's been and left her Ern, that's what. Had some sort of tiff last night, and up and left him with all those kids.'

'You mean she left the children with Ern?'

'No, no, no! I wish she had! She's brought 'em all up to our place, and I've left her grizzling over the cornflakes. I've told her straight she's to go back to Ern as soon as she's got breakfast down 'em.'

'What went wrong, do you think?'

'Well, you know our Min as well as I do. She's come across that chap Bert again, as she was sweet on once.'

I remembered that Bert was the man who had taken up his abode in their house at Springbourne. Rather naturally Ern had resented it, and there had been ructions.

'But surely Bert got a job elsewhere?'

'Only laying gas pipes. He soon got done with that and made a pretty penny too at it. Now he's having a rest on the Social Security, and you know what they says about Satan finding work for idle hands to do? Well, he's found some with our Min, and Era's cutting up rough.'

At this moment Eileen Burton rushed in to ask if she could pull the school bell 'as it wasn't fair the boys always done it'.

I was too surprised by this passionate plea on behalf of equality for women to correct her grammar, and agreed to her request.

Meanwhile Mrs Pringle, limping heavily, had taken herself

into the infants' room to continue her onslaught on the furniture, and I shelved Minnie Pringle's problems to face my own.

We were having a spell of unsettled weather. Two days would be calm and golden and the farmers would be wreathed in smiles as they fetched home the last of the harvest, or busily baled the golden straw. Then two or three days of rain would follow, drenching the straw awaiting collection, and filling our playground with extensive puddles which positively challenged the naughtier children to play 'Splashem' in defiance of my veto on the game.

I had just dashed across the playground through a shower at the end of afternoon school, when the telephone rang. Elizabeth Mawne was calling.

'I'm begging a favour,' she began.

'Fire away.'

'Well, I know you often go to Caxley on a Saturday morning, and I wondered if you could give me a lift. I'm going to Jenner's to pick up a christening mug – the christening is the next day and Jenner's have kept me in suspense all this time. Our car's out of order, or I wouldn't bother you.'

I said that I should be delighted, particularly as I had a clock which had been waiting to be mended for quite six months, and I too would visit Jenner's with her.

By half-past ten on Saturday we were on our way, driving through the streaming lanes on one of the wettest days of our changeable spell.

'It really is annoying,' said Mrs Mawne. 'All my roses are turning brown with the rain, and I am doing the church flowers this Sunday and need the roses for my arrangements. The most reliable flowers in the garden at the moment are marigolds. Perhaps not quite right for church decoration.'

'Why not? Everyone likes them, and they always look so cheerful. I'd plump for the marigolds every time.'

'Perhaps I will,' agreed Mrs Mawne, but she sounded doubtful. There is no gainsaying, I thought, that the ladies who take their flower-arranging seriously store up a mint of trouble for themselves one way or another.

'You've heard that David hopes to move into Holly Lodge?' I said that I had.

'Henry was so grateful to you for advising him. He gets into rather a tizzy over things like that.'

'But I did nothing,' I protested.

'You let him *bumble on* to you,' said his wife. 'It helped. He rang David straightaway, and he and Irene think it is exactly what they want. David can go to town by train quite easily, or on the motorway. He'll have to get a second car, but there we are. It will be good to have them at hand, and it will be so much healthier for them all, particularly for Simon. He's a frail child.'

I thought of the strength which had gone into the hurling of that quoit which had killed our dear albino robin, but said nothing.

'Of course, Joan Benson has to find somewhere, and David is still advertising his place, but we hope the move can be made well before Christmas. At a pinch, they can move in with us temporarily, but we hope it won't come to that. It wouldn't please *any* of us, and between ourselves, I think poor Henry would go mad.'

I jammed on the brakes to avoid a suicidal pheasant who strutted with great dignity and deliberation across the road in front of us.

'Of course,' continued Elizabeth, when we drove on, 'you are so lucky having a place of your own. I imagine you will stay on there when you retire?'

I explained my position.

'So what will you do? I hadn't realized that the schoolhouse was virtually a tied cottage.'

'Oh, something will turn up,' I said with a cheerfulness I did not feel. 'Well, here we are, and miracles will never cease! There's actually a parking place.'

Jenner's is an old-fashioned shop, run in earlier times by the widow of the original jeweller, Edward Jenner. Although she is now bedridden, her two sons who run the business consult her over every transaction in the shop, which is somewhat trying if you are in a hurry.

Sometimes a good bellow up the stairs suffices. A faint reply is vaguely heard by the customer, and one of the sons returns to cope with the matter, fortified by mother's help. But today, Mrs Mawne and I had to wait while John Jenner pounded up the stairs holding two christening mugs.

Time passed. We shifted from one foot to the other, and studied barometers, clocks, wrist watches, dress rings, engagement rings, babies' spoons and pushers, rose bowls, and innumerable candlesticks.

It was obvious that Elizabeth was growing even more impatient than I was. She has not had to put up with waiting for others, and is extremely forthright in her speech when crossed. I wondered what sort of welcome John Jenner would get on his return. Elizabeth's foot was tapping dangerously when he appeared at last.

'Your mother, Mr Jenner,' she said severely, 'reminds me of the Almighty. Invisible and omnipotent.'

'She's all of that,' agreed John Jenner.

Determined though I was not to get mixed up in Minnie Pringle's matrimonial squalls, yet nevertheless I found myself unwillingly involved.

She arrived one day in the following week with three of her brood to see if they could attend Fairacre School while she was 'with auntie'. There was not much I could do about it, and so I agreed with as much grace as I could muster.

I handed the three into the charge of Linda Moffat, who is a kind motherly child with plenty of sense. She undertook to show them where to hang their coats, and so on.

Meanwhile, Minnie showed no desire to leave my presence. The children were still out in the playground as it was only twenty to nine. Miss Briggs had not yet arrived, and so had no inkling of two new infants to be added – temporarily, I trusted – to her roll. The eldest child would be with me.

Minnie looked as much like a scarecrow as she had always done. Her ankle-length frock must once have been an evening dress. Over it she wore a thick ribbed pullover which had half a dozen grimy badges tacked on to it. Her bare feet were thrust into broken peep-toe sandals of scarlet plastic material, and her red hair was as unkempt as a well-used floor mop.

A young baby was asleep under the hood of the battered pram in the lobby, and a toddler with a repellently runny nose sat at the other end. With five children under nine one could not help but feel sorry for poor silly Minnie, but I steeled myself to withstand any offers of renewed housework. I had suffered enough in the past.

'You heard about my Ern?' she enquired.

I said guardedly that Mrs Pringle had said that he had left home.

'Ah! But did she tell you where he'd gone?'

'No.'

'Back to that Mrs Fowler in Caxley!'

Minnie spoke triumphantly, as though she had scored a point. Frankly, I was flummoxed. An earlier union between the renowned Mrs Fowler and Minnie's Ern had ended in such acrimony that I should have thought that they would never see each other again.

'She's been at him for months to go back as a lodger. Misses the money, see? Well, now he's gone.'

'Just like that? He must have had a reason.'

Minnie hesitated, running her dirty fingernails through her equally dirty locks. She seemed to be struggling with a desire to tell me all.

It won.

'I don't mind you knowing, but Ern got a bit nasty about Bert popping in, and he took his belt to me. Then Bert got wild and clocked him one, so Ern cleared off, and the language what he used I wouldn't tell a lady like you. Real *rude*, it was! Animals and that!'

'But where will you live? I believe the house is in your name, isn't it?'

'That's right. But I'm feared of sleeping there alone in case Ern comes back.'

'I should certainly move back as soon as you can,' I advised her, thinking of myself as much as Minnie, I don't mind admitting. 'The council won't want the place empty, and I gather your aunt can't have you there.'

'She don't seem very pleased about it,' agreed Minnie, taking a grubby handkerchief to the toddler's nose, and not before time. 'I'll be all right. I'm going to get Bert to sleep in until Ern comes back.'

She gave me her wide demented smile and pushed the pram out of the lobby.

'I'll be all right,' echoed in my brain for most of the day. Inconsistent, crazy, immoral, come to think of it, there was no doubt that Minnie would emerge from this little battle quite unscathed. It would be the non-belligerents, encountered on the way, who would be scarred.

Amy called to see me one blustery afternoon. She had brought me the latest collection of Flora Thompson's writings as a present, and as a lover of *Lark Rise to Candleford* I could hardly wait to begin *A Country Calendar*.

'You spoil me,' I told her.

'I know. You can give me a cup of tea in exchange.'

'And where have you been?' I asked, as I warmed the teapot.

'Oxford. Bumbling round Blackwell's in a happy daze, and spending far too much money. I tell myself I am getting Christmas presents, but I know damn well I shan't be able to part with any of them.'

'Never mind. Think how it boosts trade.'

'Mind you, I did get a splendid eiderdown for the spare room, but can you guess what it's called?'

'Not a clue.'

'Well, wait for it. On the label it says: *Morsnugga!*'

'I don't believe it.'

'I'd show you if I could be bothered to unwrap it, you doubting Thomas! For two pins, I would have given it back, but it was the only one which was the right colour, and I only hope my visitors will sleep too soundly to want to read eiderdown labels. But I ask you – *Morsnugga!* It really is the end, isn't it?'

'It could have been something with "cosy" in it, spelt with a "K".'

'That's true. This is a first-class cup of tea. I can well do with it. Shopping creases me these days, and I used to enjoy it.'

'How's the book getting on?'

'It isn't. I'm still aged eight, and I honestly don't think I can go on. It seems a pity. I've done about eight thousand words, and the thought of doing another fifty or sixty, which is what is needed, I gather, for a book's length, is too daunting for words.'

'Can't you do something with the bit you've done? Make a magazine article, say, or a talk for the radio?'

Amy looked thoughtful. 'That's an idea. I could make something of being a Brownie half a century ago, and there's quite a nice episode about my mother opening a flower show when the marquee collapsed.'

'It all sounds good clean fun to me,' I told her, refilling her tea cup. 'You have a bash. You can't waste all that effort.'

'I agree. Do you know, I sometimes think you are more intelligent than you look.'

'Thank you, Amy,' I said. 'I shall treasure that remark.'

The wind was more violent than ever when Amy departed. Branches clashed overhead, plants shuddered in the onslaught, and a weird hooting came from the television aerial as the wind whistled around it.

Tibby rushed in through the front door as I waved farewell to Amy. She looked startled and affronted. I had little sympathy for her as she can get into shelter through the cat flap on the back door, but this is beneath her dignity if anyone is about to open a proper door for the lady.

It was good to get indoors again. I cleared away our tea things, put aside a pile of exercise books due to be corrected, and settled down gleefully with my lovely new book. After twenty minutes' bliss, a strange sound became evident. It was difficult to pin-point just what and just where it was in the confusion of noises outside, but to my horror it sounded remarkably like heavy breathing.

A burglar with bronchitis? But he would hardly be at his

work in such a condition. An escaped lunatic? But our nearest asylum was some twenty miles away. Some poor traveller taken ill and needing my assistance? If my conjecture was correct, he would need a doctor and oxygen tent immediately.

It was all very unnerving. The longer I listened, the more sure I became that it really was breathing that I could hear. What on earth should I do? It is on occasions like this that I realize how useful a husband could be. How lovely to be able to say: 'I think someone is breaking in, dear,' and to settle back while a masculine hand raises the poker.

However, spinsters learn to cope alone, and I decided that I must go and investigate. Tibby remained quite unmoved by the noise, which was unusual. Anything strange often causes her to growl, and to bristle with fright or fury, which only adds to one's misgivings.

I took the poker in hand, and went to the front door, switching on lights as I went. Outside, grazing peacefully among my herbaceous plants was a fine Guernsey cow, one of Mr Roberts' herd, I guessed. By the light from the hall I caught sight of my lawn, heavily indented by hoofs, and wondered what Mr Willet would have to say about his newly mown grass when he turned up next morning.

The cow gazed benignly at me, some choice penstemon flowers dangling from her rotating jaw. She seemed pleased to see me, and made a gentle lowing noise through her mouthful of light supper.

Much relieved – for who would not prefer a kindly, if hungry cow to an escaped madman? – I rang Mr Roberts's number and awaited rescue.

As I had guessed, Mr Willet was most indignant when he saw the state of my lawn the next morning.

'Never saw such a muck-up in all my borns,' he said, blowing out his moustache with disgust. 'You wants to sue old Roberts. That animal's done pounds' worth of damage.'

'I can't do that,' I protested. 'It's one of the hazards of living in the country. Cows do get out sometimes.'

'Not if the fences is kept proper,' replied Mr Willet sternly. 'Well, if you won't do nothing, you won't, of course, but I shall tell him what I think when I comes across him next.'

'Oh, don't make trouble!' I begged him. 'If I don't mind why should you?'

'Because I shall have the rolling and flattening of this lot, I can see, that's why!'

Against such straight reasoning I could say nothing, but made my way to school.

Here more trouble awaited me. Water had blown through the half-finished dormer window and made a pool on the floor. Joseph Coggs was doing his best to mop it up, but in his zeal was using Mrs Pringle's new duster and I foresaw some ructions.

'Let me have that, Joseph,' I said snatching it from him, 'and get the old floor cloth from the lobby.'

I was wondering if I could tear home, and put the duster to dry out of Mrs Pringle's sight, when the lady arrived, and caught me duster-handed.

'And who,' she boomed, 'done that?'

'It was used in error,' I said placatingly. 'One of the children was mopping up and didn't realize—'

At this moment, Joseph appeared with the floor cloth and Mrs Pringle rounded on him before I could intervene.

'You use my dusters once more, young Joe, and you'll get my hand round your ear-hole! Understand?'

Poor Joe turned pale. Mrs Pringle has hands like hams, and it was no idle threat.

'You can leave the cloth with me, Joseph,' I said hastily, 'and go into the playground until the bell goes.'

I mustered all the dignity I could manage whilst dangling a wet rag in each hand.

'I will see to this,' I said coldly, 'and please don't bully the children.'

Mrs Pringle grabbed the duster and shook it violently. 'You can do what you like with that floor cloth,' she shouted, 'but I'm not trusting you with my nice new duster.'

With that she thrust the damp duster into her black oilcloth bag, presumably to be taken home for its correct treatment, and I was left to mop the floor and curse Mrs Pringle, dormer windows, the wind, and Reg Thorn with equal intensity.

Miss Briggs arrived half an hour late with laryngitis. She had had a puncture, luckily in Beech Green, she whispered painfully, and two of Mr Annett's big boys had changed the wheel for her.

I went into the infants' room with her to supply their wants, and to tell them of their teacher's affliction and the necessity for exemplary behaviour. It was going to be one of those days, I thought grimly, as Wayne switched on his transistor set overhead and filled the air with discord.

As it happened, with Miss Briggs's normally stentorian tones now hushed, it was the quietest day at Fairacre school since her arrival.

The rough weather had done some damage in our area. A tarpaulin had blown from a newly built stack of straw and caught itself in a neighbouring plum tree, bringing down several laden branches.

A branch had crashed on Henry Mawne's greenhouse, and rumour had it that the vicar had gone out in his pyjamas to make sure that his beehives were safe.

In my own garden, the cow had done more damage than the weather, but the television aerial was sloping at an extraordinary angle.

'I can fix that, miss,' Wayne assured me. 'Just got to straighten one of the window catches, and then I'll be there.'

The dormer window, so Reg Thorn said, when I was successful in catching him one morning, would be finished in a fortnight.

'Just a final coat of paint, and we won't be bothering you no more,' he told me with pride. 'How d'you think it looks?'

'Fine,' I said, gazing at the new structure. To be honest, I was not sure about it. It looked heavy and awkward, jutting out from the old roof, but I was so used to the unobtrusive line of the old skylight that anything different was bound to strike me as peculiar. Mr Willet's derogatory remarks too may have influenced me. In any case, the new window must surely be an improvement on the former one which had plagued all the inhabitants of Fairacre school for generations.

Wayne put my aerial to rights as he promised and I thanked him at playtime.

'Don't you mind heights?' I asked him.

'Enjoy 'em,' he said beaming. 'My uncle was a steeplejack. Used to scramble up factory chimneys and walk round the rim at the top.'

To hear about it made me feel queasy.

'No good being a builder unless you've got the stomach for heights,' said Wayne, carrying Reg Thorn's ladder back to its proper place.

The children came out of school to play, and I was thankful that sunshine had followed the stormy weather. Miss Briggs emerged too to take up her playground duty, and Wayne hurried over to talk to her. It was good to see her so friendly and animated, I thought. She would miss the young company when our dormer window was done at last.

The Pringle children were still with us and much as I wanted to know what Minnie's plans were – if any – I was anxious not to appear too curious by asking Mrs Pringle about conditions at her home. However, she appeared one morning with a nasty scratch down one cheek and a large lump on her forehead.

'Good lord, Mrs Pringle,' I exclaimed, 'have you had a fall?'

'No. But someone else has,' she told me with enormous satisfaction.

She settled herself on the front desk, her usual perch when

about to give me all the news. I glanced anxiously at the clock. No need to ring the school bell yet, and although I had still to look out the morning hymn and open the windows, it seemed far more important to me to hear the story behind Mrs Pringle's injuries.

'Well, it's like this. That Minnie wouldn't do nothing about getting Ern back as long as Bert was around and she could see him. I threatened to put her and the kids out in the road, but you know our Min. Water off a duck's back it was, and me going half-barmy with that lot under my feet.'

'But I thought Ern worked at Springbourne Manor. Didn't the Potters wonder where he was when he didn't turn up?'

'That's just it! He *did* turn up! Come on the bus from Caxley each morning, so the Potters never twigged anything was wrong for some time. But, of course, someone tittle-tattled to Mr Potter, and he waylaid Bert, as he sacked for pinching the vegetables if you remember, and got the truth out of him about Minnie and Ern.'

'What happened?'

'He ticked off Bert, and told him not to come between husband and wife, and to keep out of Springbourne or he'd set the police on him. Then he come up our place the other day and had a good talking to Minnie. He told her that Ern would lose his job if she didn't persuade him to go back to live in Springbourne.'

'And did she?'

'Not Minnie! She's a proper soft one! Said Ern might hit her and she was scared, though if he promised to treat her right she might go back. I said to her: "If you won't persuade Ern, then I will, my girl! I've had enough of you and your brats eating me out of house and home, and using my sheets and towels, day in and day out!" So yesterday evening I went to Caxley, and sorted things out.'

She fingered the bump on her head with pride. I was mightily impressed at the thought of even such a doughty fighter as Mrs Pringle facing the formidable Mrs Fowler. She once lived in

Fairacre, and was a tough shrewish woman who frightened the life out of me just to look at her.

'You went to Mrs Fowler's?'

'I did indeed. She started shouting before I'd hardly got the words out of my mouth about Ern. "You let me in and we can talk this over nicely," I said to her, but what she said in return I wouldn't sully my lips by repeating. She made a run at me and that's when I got this scratch, the spiteful cat.'

'Did you retaliate?'

'If you mean did I give her as good as I got, I certainly did. Two handfuls of her hair I tore out, and I blacked her eye.'

Mrs Pringle spoke with quiet satisfaction. It must have been a real battle of the dinosaurs, I thought, and I wondered if the neighbours had enjoyed it.

'She said Ern wasn't there, but down The Barleycorn, and what's more he spent all his time there. Then she slammed the door in my face. I was about to go off to the pub to see if she was telling the truth, when she opened a top window and chucked a suitcase at me, with Ern's things in evidently. Anyway, that's what caused this bump – not that woman.'

At this juncture, Joseph Coggs put his head round the door to say was it time for the bell, and could he ring it?

'Not just yet, Joe. Mrs Pringle and I are having a little talk. I'll call you in a few minutes.'

Joseph vanished.

'Go on! Was he there?'

'He was. I picked up the case and went round the corner and found him in the bar. We just had time to get the last bus back.'

'He came without any trouble?' I asked mystified.

'I *took him*,' said Mrs Pringle.

I gazed at her with respect.

Outside I could hear the sound of children's voices. Were my latest pupils among them? I asked my cleaner.

'They're all going back to Springbourne tonight. Mr Potter's lending Ern the van to fetch the lot, and told him straight that he's out on his ear if he don't treat our Minnie right.'

'And you think he will behave now?'

'If he don't,' said Mrs Pringle rising majestically, 'he knows there's *two* of us can settle him.'

She made her way into the lobby, and I called Joseph in to ring the bell, some five minutes after time.

Meanwhile, I looked out the morning hymn, and settled for *Fight the Good Fight* as an appropriate choice in the circumstances.

10. October

Oddly enough, I heard more about the clashing of the monsters from Amy when she visited me a few days later. Her window cleaner lives next door to Mrs Fowler in Caxley, and he evidently gave her a lively description of the scene.

'He and his wife went upstairs to get a better view from the bedroom window,' Amy told me. 'And whatever Mrs P. may say to the contrary, her language was quite as lurid as Mrs Fowler's. He said their money was on Mrs Pringle right from the start. "She'd got the *motive* and the *spirit* and the *weight*!" was how he put it.'

'Very neatly put, too. They must have made an unholy noise. It's a wonder the neighbours didn't call the police.'

'They were enjoying it so much I don't think they wanted to break it up. According to him, it was pretty plain that Ern was getting fed up at Mrs Fowler's anyway. She used to expect him to do all the odd jobs around the house when he got back from Springbourne, and the food was rather sparse, I gather.'

'I can well believe that! Mrs Fowler had the reputation of being the stingiest woman in Fairacre when she lived here.'

'So it looks as though Ern was ripe for the picking, and Mrs P. plucked him at the right moment.'

'Well, heaven bless the old harridan,' I said. 'Now we've seen the last of Minnie and her brood.'

'For a time, anyway,' Amy said. 'I've no doubt they'll turn up in your life again before long.'

'Heaven forbid! Tell me, how's the dismemberment of the book going?'

Amy looked quite animated. 'I sent two short episodes to *Woman's Hour* and they've taken one. I'm going up to broadcast it, probably early next year.'

'Marvellous! We'll have it on at school in the afternoon. Tell me more.'

'Well, I'm writing an account of our sick room at school.'

'It sounds somewhat morbid.'

'Not really. It's supposed to be rather funny. You've no idea how dreadfully depressing that place was. It's doing me good to write it out of my system.'

'What was wrong with it?'

'Everything! For one thing, it was a symphony in green, of all colours.'

'Very restful, they say.'

'Not when you're bilious, as most of the inmates were. And the greens didn't harmonize, to make it worse. And the only decoration was a past pupil's lettering exercise in the most excruciating calligraphy, quite impossible to read from one's sick bed, but it was evidently that passage from Chaucer about the poor scholar who had twenty books clad in black and red. What with the writing and the spelling, one could feel one's mind giving way.'

'You should have closed your eyes.'

'Even so you were assailed by the most nauseating smell of something the mistress who had attended you burnt on an enamel plate on the floor. It was called Persian tape, if I remember rightly, and if you weren't sick when you arrived you pretty soon were once the Persian tape got going.'

'Were you allowed visitors?'

'Only the odd relative. Anyway, this ghastly place was at the very top of a high building, and most people jibbed at all the stairs. Patients were always in a state of collapse when they finally arrived, with their knees like jelly.'

'Well, I hope you can do justice to it,' I said. 'It sounds as though you have plenty of material.'

'It should do something for my suppressed emotions anyway,' said Amy, with evident satisfaction. 'Now tell me your news. How's the centenary programme going?'

'I'm having Linda and Patrick over here after school tomorrow to try them out with their lines. Miss Clare, bless her, needs no rehearsing, nor Mrs Austen, and Mr Lamb from the post office has promised to tell us something about the famous trip to Wembley in the 1920s. It's not going to be such a formidable job as I first thought, and Miss Briggs is being unusually helpful with the singing.'

'Do you think she'll stay?'

'I'm beginning to hope so. She's much more cheerful since she found that young man, and she's gradually forgetting a lot of the high-falutin' rubbish she was stuffed with at college, thank heaven.'

'Well, good luck with it all,' said Amy, collecting her things. 'By the way, James and I are having a short break in Wales next week to make up for his missing Tresco in the summer, so I shan't see you for a time.'

'Do you know, I thought I might go again next summer to Tresco. I loved it so much.'

'Then book up early,' advised Amy. 'We're going again, but in May, when you'll be hard at work, of course, and we've already staked our claim.'

'It seems rather soon,' I said, 'to book for August.'

'*You do it now!*' replied Amy sternly. 'What a terrible procrastinator you are! I wonder anything *ever* gets done in this establishment. Now mind! Sit down and write to that hotel this evening.'

'Yes, Amy,' I said meekly.

I had written the simplest possible dialogue for Linda as Miss Richards, and for Patrick as the bad boy John Pratt, but even so they seemed to find it difficult to memorize.

'Don't worry if it's not exactly the same,' I implored them. 'As long as you get the meaning across, that's all that matters.'

If anything, this confused them even more. We had a break, and I produced lemonade and biscuits. Tibby entered and received a great deal of admiration from the two, and then we resumed. After two or three attempts, things went more smoothly. Linda seemed to be less self-conscious than Patrick and with practice I thought the little scene should go well.

'We'll try it with the other children one day this week,' I promised them, 'and by that time you'll know your lines so well, it will be much easier to concentrate on the movements.'

They looked doubtful, and I must confess that if these two comparatively bright pupils made such heavy weather of their parts, it did not look too hopeful for the rest of my cast. Again I felt thankful that most of the performances would be in the more capable hands of three or more adults.

They departed clutching their two-page scripts with them, their young brows furrowed with anxiety. Perhaps I was expecting too much from them, I thought, as I waved them goodbye? Fairacre children are shy by nature, and perhaps the idea of displaying their modest talents in front of parents and, even worse, their schoolfellows, was going to prove too much for their nerves.

We could only wait and see.

As so often happens in October, the weather was balmy, the skies cloudless, and that clear light peculiar to a fine autumn bathed Fairacre in end-of-summer beauty.

The hedges were bright with glossy berries. The trees were beginning to blaze in all shades of yellow, bronze and crimson, and the cottage gardens, so far untouched by frost, were still gay with asters, Michaelmas daisies, chrysanthemums and dahlias.

I relish these sparkling autumn days, all the more keenly because one knows that there cannot be many of them before waking one morning to a hoary scene and the knowledge that

winter has arrived. I took the children out for plenty of exhilarating walks on the downs, and after tea each day walked again on my own before the sun set. By six o'clock it was beginning to grow chilly, and I enjoyed lighting a fire and congratulating myself on having the best of both worlds while the fine spell lasted.

On one of my solitary walks, through a little copse at the foot of the downs, I came across Miriam Quinn who was enjoying the fresh air as much as I was, to judge by her pink cheeks and bright eyes. We walked along together in great content.

'This is the breath of life to me,' she said, 'after the office. I look forward to it all day. Caxley's all very well for working, but I simply couldn't go back there to live after Fairacre.'

'You're not proposing to, are you?' I asked.

She looked thoughtful, bending down to remove a briar which had caught her skirt.

'No. I'm staying, and I hope I'm doing the right thing. You know the young Mawnes are taking over?'

I said that Joan had told me.

'Well, I still have slight doubts about whether they truly want me living under the same roof. They've been terribly kind, and pressed me to stay, and as I honestly can't find a thing worth considering elsewhere, I have agreed. In any case, I love it here, as you know, and it would be a dreadful wrench to have to leave.'

'I'm sure they really do want you to stay. Henry Mawne was relieved to know you would be there when David was away on his business trips. I remember him saying how comforting it would be for Irene to have company in the house at night.'

'Really?' Miriam sounded pleased but slightly incredulous. 'I hadn't thought of that. I must say, it's nice to be useful. I have already offered to sit with young Simon in the holidays if they want to go out in the evening. Irene seemed pleased about that, which delighted me.'

'It would help them enormously, I'm sure.'

We walked along in silence for a short time, until we emerged into one of Mr Roberts' fields, and turned towards the village. Miriam seemed to be turning over my remarks in her mind.

'You know,' she said at last, 'one of the difficulties of being single is that there is no one to discuss these little problems with. It's so easy to see just one's own point of view. I'm glad you told me about Henry Mawne's comment. Of course, he's quite right. I'm afraid I've been far too self-centred over all this business – anxious not to intrude, anxious about finding somewhere else, in fact, thoroughly steamed up and not really thinking of Irene and David's side of the problem. That must be one of the bonuses of married life, I imagine – being able to share one's troubles.'

'Except that you've got two people's troubles then,' I pointed out. 'Think how relatively uncomplicated our spinsterhood is!'

Miriam stopped in her tracks and laughed aloud. It was good to see her usually pensive expression replaced by joyous animation. She ought to laugh more often, I thought.

'Perhaps you're right. Anyway, I'm glad we met in the wood. I'm going home in a much more cheerful state of mind. What about coming back to Holly Lodge for a drink?'

'I'd love to,' I said, and we stepped out briskly together.

The vicar called in to school one gloriously sunny afternoon, and we enthused about the weather. He is as devoted to the sun as I am, and when the rest of the villagers are collapsing with heat, he and I gloat together on perfect conditions for sun-worshippers.

He bore a jar of his own honey, and presented it to me with considerable pride. I thanked him sincerely, and enquired after the bees.

'They've really done splendidly. I collected about sixty pounds of honey. It's so rewarding to see it pouring out of the extractor in a beautiful golden stream. To think that those dear bees have made thousands and thousands of trips, all through the summer, to collect the delicious stuff from all our beautiful Fairacre flowers!'

Obviously, our vicar was enraptured.

'Are they still about?'

'Yes, indeed! As busy as ever. I think they are collecting from the bramble flowers and willow herb now. I don't propose to take any more. What they fetch in now will help them through the winter.'

'Is there much for you to do to prepare them for the cold weather?'

'A *great deal*,' said he earnestly. 'They will need some sugar syrup, and I intend to put up the mouse guards at the entrances. They creep in, you know, for shelter, and possibly the honey. Quite alarming for the bees. I shall certainly take steps to protect them from marauders.'

He took a slip of paper from his pocket and consulted it. 'A quarter of mushrooms, half of tomatoes, a dozen large eggs – no, that isn't it.' He turned over the paper. 'Ah! Here we are, on the back of my wife's shopping list, you see. First of all, how is the new window?'

'So far, so good,' I told him.

'That's fine. Really, the old skylight was a sore trial when the weather was rough. We should have a snug winter with this new one.'

I said I hoped so.

'Then the next thing I have here is to fix a date for the centenary service.' He lowered the paper and looked unhappy. 'I rather think I shall have to combine it with a Sunday service in December. My diary has suddenly become horribly full for that month. What do you think? I thought perhaps the Sunday before Christmas might be suitable. It would be the last Sunday of term, and we could have prayers and hymns suitable to the occasion at morning service, and my sermon would be on the subject of our heritage here in the village.'

'It sounds ideal,' I said, 'and the church would be looking festive, too, by that stage.'

'Certainly,' said the vicar looking mightily relieved at my amiability. What did he expect, I wondered? That I might fling myself to the floor, screaming and drumming my heels?

'The crib would certainly be in place, and no doubt some of the Christmas greenery. Perhaps we could arrange for the children to do some of the decorations, as they do for Harvest Festival?'

'That's a nice idea,' I said, but had private reservations about how the flower ladies would react to juvenile assistance at Christmas time.

'Good, good!' said Mr Partridge, making for the door. 'I really ought to have a bonfire, I've so much garden stuff to burn, but I intend to wait until dusk. Nothing is going to detract from this beautiful sunshine if I can help it.'

'A case of "Gather ye rosebuds while ye may",' I quoted.

'Absolutely, Miss Read. Absolutely!'

He looked at the children with his usual benevolence.

'I should take them for a walk this afternoon,' he whispered confidentially.

'Don't worry,' I told him. 'It's at the head of the agenda.'

11. NOVEMBER

It was a relief to be without Minnie Pringle's three children. Not that they were naughty or rumbustious. In fact, they were just the opposite, and sat immobile in their desks contributing nothing and, as far as one could see, taking in nothing.

They were all mouth-breathers, which was hardly surprising considering the revolting state of their nasal passages, and no amount of advice, persuasion or example succeeded in showing them how to blow their noses. They were like their mother in being almost unteachable, but without her demented energy. What they would do when it came to earning a living I shuddered to think. No doubt an indulgent welfare state would give them far more for doing nothing than they were capable of earning anyway.

But if I were relieved to see the back of Minnie's brood, I was really sorry to say farewell to the shepherd's children. Perhaps he had found a better job than his new one with Mr Roberts?

Mr Willet enlightened me.

'Bin pinchin'. Not just the odd egg or swede and that. He done in one of Mr Roberts' sheep, and sold it to that back-street butcher in Caxley. Ought to be deported, but I don't suppose he'll get more than probation when the case comes up.'

'Well, he certainly won't get deported,' I assured Mr Willet. 'Anyway, who'd want him?'

'We don't, that's for sure! And Mr Roberts is hopping mad. Now he's got to start all over again getting some new chap. Can't trust a soul these days, Miss Read. They'd take your teeth off the table if you was fool enough to leave 'em there.'

'At the moment,' I told him, 'my teeth – what are left of them – don't take out.'

Mr Willet looked sympathetic. 'Then you've a mort of trouble ahead of you. I'm thankful to say all mine are national gnashers now, and it's a great comfort to be able to take 'em out now and again to give me gums a nice airing.'

He set out across the playground, and then turned.

'Bring the numbers down a bit though, won't it? Them Pringle kids and shepherd's lot? Bet you'll be hearing from the Office.'

'Oh, shut up,' I begged him.

For the horrid fact was much in my mind, too.

Another cause for relief was the absence of Reg Thorn's men. I had grown quite fond of them both, and found Wayne particularly sensible and friendly. Nevertheless, it was wonderful to be free of that everlasting cacophony from their transistor radio, and from the bangs and thumps as they worked overhead.

Mr Willet still looked askance at the finished product but, as I pointed out, no rain had come through now that it was completed, and we certainly seemed to have more light.

'Hasn't had a fair test yet,' Mr Willet warned me. 'You wait till that old wind gets up!'

Unfortunately, we did not have to wait long. The halcyon October weather broke early in November with lashing rain and a high wind.

I was relieved to see that no water came through, as it certainly would have done in the old days, but there was an annoying drumming sound as the wind caught the jutting framework. I was not too happy about this vibration, and rang Reg Thorn during the dinner hour. For once he was at home.

'I've got to come over to Springbourne this afternoon,' he told me. 'I'll pop in on my way.'

As one might expect, the wind had dropped considerably by the time he arrived, and the drumming was hardly in evidence.

Nevertheless, he clambered up to the window and seemed to make a fairly exhaustive study of the structure.

'Right as a trivet,' he assured me when he descended. 'Good bit of work that! You don't need to worry about a thing. Them boys of mine know what they're up to. By the way, have you heard about Ted Richards?'

I looked blank. 'Do I know him?'

'Young Wayne's dad. He's had a stroke. The boy's off work for a few days, helping out.'

'I'm sorry to hear that. How's the old man getting on?'

'Pretty well. His speech is back, and the doctor says his arm is coming round. Shook the old boy though. I reckon I'll be losing Wayne, and I'll be sorry. He's a good worker, and a bit more up top than some I could mention. Still, his dad comes first, I can see that.'

He stepped back to take a last satisfied look at his creation, and then departed.

I woke in the night to the howling of a terrific gale. I could hear a door banging downstairs, and got out of bed to go and shut it. As I did so a horrific rumbling sounded overhead, and I guessed that a tile had blown loose and was bumping down the roof.

The larder door was ajar and banging every time the gusts came through the small window. I closed both, and returned through the roaring to my bed.

But sleep was impossible. We get these frighteningly strong winds up here on the downs, and a great deal of damage is done to our houses and farm buildings, not to mention trees and gardens. Usually I comfort myself with the thought that I have survived plenty of these rough nights, but this one seemed peculiarly vicious. One thing, it would test Reg Thorn's new window, I thought.

I dropped off again about six, the storm still raging, so that I overslept and had to hurry around to get over to school in time. To my dismay there was rain water on the floor beneath the window. On looking up, I could see that the whole structure seemed to be slanting, but that the water appeared to be dripping to the right of it.

I went outside and bumped into Mr Willet, and pointed out the damage. He surveyed it in silence for a full minute.

'It's the roof timbers, I reckon, not so much the window. It's no good patching old with new and expecting 'em both to thrive. Best get old Reg again, I suppose.'

He came inside with me and surveyed the puddle. Drips from above enlarged it steadily.

'Quite like old times, ain't it?' said Mr Willet, with evident satisfaction.

I rang Reg and left a message with his wife as he was out, of course. Mrs Pringle was mopping up when I returned. She was wearing a new cretonne overall and an expression of extreme martyrdom.

'This is something I could have done without,' she said sourly. 'My leg's proper blazing this morning. I didn't hardly know how to get up the street.'

'I'll get one of the children to do it,' I said.

Mrs Pringle wrung out the floor cloth, and shuffled to her feet. 'Too late! It's done now. And I hope you'll tell Reg Thorn what you think of him when he deigns to turn up.'

I told her that I had telephoned.

'Well, I shall have a word with him whatever you decide to do. Shoddy workmanship, that's what that is.'

'What a pretty overall,' I replied, trying to pour oil on troubled waters. The old harridan looked slightly less gloomy.

'Minnie give it to me when she left. That's one blessing, I must say, to have the house to myself at last. But for how long, I wonder? That girl's still hankering after that Bert, you know. It's as though she can't help herself. Nothing but a prawn of fate, if you take my meaning.'

I said that I thought I did.

'Well, Ern's come round, and seems to be working regular – if work you can call it, leaning on a spade up Springbourne Manor and having cups of tea at all hours in the greenhouse.

He don't know yet about Bert, and I've threatened to tell him, to try and get our Min to come to her senses. Sometimes I wonder if she's right in her head, Miss Read, I do straight.'

I agreed warmly. Mrs Pringle picked up her pail and limped to the lobby.

Later, Miss Briggs and I surveyed the damaged window more closely as we awaited the arrival of Reg Thorn.

'It seems such a shame after all that hard work,' said my assistant.

'It does. By the way, did you know that the dark young man's name was Richards?'

'Yes.'

'Reg Thorn tells me that his father has had a stroke, poor fellow.'

'I know.'

'I wonder if it means that Wayne will have to leave Reg Thorn? He seemed to think so. It is bad luck.'

'Not for Wayne, I shouldn't think,' observed Miss Briggs, and the conversation ended abruptly as the youngest Coggs child approached bearing a dead, and very smelly, starling.

Afterwards it occurred to me that Miss Briggs seemed to know far more about the Richards than I did. Hardly surprising, I told myself, as she talked to the two boys far more than I did, and may well have bumped into them in Caxley.

Reg Thorn did not arrive until school ended. It was still blowing, still cold, and still depressing. I went indoors for my tea, leaving him to discover the worst. Twenty minutes later, having thawed out, I repented, and took him out a mug of tea.

But he had gone.

Rehearsals continued, and I was glad to see that the children seemed much less self-conscious as they began to be familiar with their lines and their movements about the stage – or rather, the schoolroom floor.

The costumes were practically finished, thanks largely I knew to Mrs Moffat's generosity with her time and skill. Nothing second-rate ever came from that lady's needle, and I was confident that our cast would be beautifully dressed.

We ran through the whole programme to time it one afternoon, and were pleasantly surprised to find that the whole thing took about an hour and a quarter. As we were following this with our tea party, we should have two full and happy afternoons, the first for the infants' parents and friends, and the repeat performance the next day for the juniors and the rest of those wanting to come.

The vicar called in one day to give me the good news that the managers were providing our birthday cake, and that Mrs Willet had offered to bake it – or rather two of them, one for each afternoon.

'It's very generous of them,' I said. 'And if Mrs Willet's in charge of the cooking, we know everything will be absolutely superb.'

'It was Henry's idea really. He thought Mrs Willet, as an old Fairacre pupil, might be agreeable, and she just jumped at the chance. She said it would have been a disgrace to ask some Caxley baker to make Fairacre's centenary cake. She's working out the cost, which we're delighted to meet as our small contribution to the fun.'

It was marvellous to see how enthusiastic the whole village was about our celebrations. There was no doubt about it, Fairacre School was the heart of our village, and memories of their own schooldays quickened the adults' response to this tribute to its hundred years. Its influence could never be estimated. I only hoped that it would be able to continue to serve the village as it had always done.

Our numbers were smaller than ever before, and I did my best to push that unpleasant fact, and its even more unpleasant consequences, into the back of my mind.

But I was not always successful.

Joan Benson rang one evening to invite me to a small party for farewell drinks.

'I'd love to come,' I said, 'but "farewell" sounds so sad.'

'Oh, I think I shall pop back from time to time,' she said cheerfully. 'Miriam insists, and so do Irene and David. I must say that now it's arrived, I feel much happier about going than I have all these months.'

'So you've found something in Sussex?'

'I think so. Nothing really fixed yet, but David and Irene have sold their flat, and their buyers want to move in almost immediately. The Mawnes were very sweet and did not want to hurry me – in fact they'd made plans to stay in Caxley, or with Henry and Elizabeth – but it's far better for everyone if they move in here at once, and in any case, I can stay with my daughter until my new abode is ready.'

'We shall all miss you. Particularly Miriam.'

'It's kind of you to say so. Actually Miriam seems much more settled about the move now. I think she's suddenly realized that the Mawnes genuinely want her to stay, and now that she feels she can be useful to them, her attitude has changed entirely. I must say, I feel much happier about deserting her. She so loves Fairacre, it would have been tragic if she had had to uproot herself after such a short stay.'

I wished her luck with her plans, and said that I would look forward to the party on December the first.

Two days later Reg Thorn arrived with three men who, from their somewhat formal attire, were probably from the building department of the County Education Office. They all gazed at the poor dormer window, still hopelessly askew, and a good deal of head-shaking went on and grave looks were exchanged. From my strategic lookout post by the classroom window it seemed that Reg Thorn grew increasingly unhappy during the conference, but of course I could not hear what was being said.

After about half an hour, when we had settled down to arithmetic, one of the three strangers knocked at the door and asked if he could have a word with me. Reg Thorn and the other two men seemed to have disappeared.

'I'm afraid that this is going to be a bigger job than we thought,' he said. 'Mr Thorn will be dismantling the present structure immediately, as it is not too safe.' I must have looked alarmed, for he went on hastily. 'Nothing too daunting! You and the children will be quite all right. But for the time being we propose to put a large piece of perspex over the aperture to keep out the weather while we investigate the roof timbers again.'

Trust our Mr Willet to have been right from the word 'Go', was my private comment, but naturally I kept mum.

'And when will Reg Thorn start the dismantling?' I asked.

'This afternoon,' replied the man. He sounded rather grim, I thought. 'And the sooner the better,' he added.

I was in entire agreement.

Mrs Willet called in during the evening to return a cookery book which I had lent her some time ago, and I took the opportunity of saying how pleased we all were to hear that she was making the birthday cake.

'*Cakes*,' she corrected me. 'It wouldn't be seemly to have half a cake at the second tea party. It's just as simple to make two nice cakes as the one.' She hesitated for a moment. 'Which brings me to the candles,' she continued.

'How do you mean?'

'Well, I reckon we ought to have a hundred candles – those weeny little cake ones, you know – and now I'll need *two* hundred for the two cakes.'

It seemed what her husband would call 'a mort of candles' to me, but I supposed she knew best.

'I've got it all planned out, you see. I'm doing two big square cakes, because it's easier to cut them fairly that way. And if I put ten candles to a row, and have ten rows, it will work out lovely.'

I expressed genuine admiration.

'Oh, it's nothing,' said Mrs Willet modestly. 'I've been baking big cakes in Fairacre for all my married life – W.I. dos and Sunday School treats and that, but I want these two cakes to be the best I've ever done – a sort of "Thank you" to the school. Anyway, I enjoy a good baking day.'

'I bet Mr Willet does, too,' I said.

'Oh, he's a splendid eater!' said his wife enthusiastically. 'Always was. We always said the Willet boys had enough in their dinner basket to feed the whole school.'

I remembered Mr Willet's remark about his recently dead brother who had carried the rush basket to school, and the largesse from Grandma which topped up the original victuals.

'I remember Miss Clare saying once that as long as a person could eat, then there couldn't be much wrong with him. She used to give us lessons about hygiene as we got to the top of the school. Very useful, too, in later life. Sometimes I used to think poor Mr Hope might not have taken to drink if he had had a better appetite. Hardly ate anything, you know. Mrs Hope used to worry about it. But there, he was a poet, poor soul, as no doubt you know, Miss Read, and poets don't seem to need food, do they?'

I thought of Timothy Ferdinand wolfing down Amy's delicious provender at her dinner party, and asking for the veal patties to take home.

'Some don't, I imagine, Mrs Willet,' I said diplomatically, 'but there are undoubtedly some poets who do.'

'Maybe, but what I was going to ask you, Miss Read, was could you possibly buy the candles for me when you go to Caxley on Saturday? I'd like to have them in good time, and I've no plans to go into town just yet.'

I said I would be very pleased to do it.

'And you will get a receipt, won't you?' she begged. 'The managers want to pay every penny, and have told me to make a note of *everything*.'

I promised that I would do so, and she departed looking relieved.

The job of dismantling the offending dormer window went along at a spanking pace. I thought ruefully that it was obviously much quicker to demolish than to build, remembering the months we had endured noise and the ingress of the weather.

To my surprise, Wayne Richards reappeared as well as his former companion. I asked after his father.

'Getting on fine. That's why I'm here for the rest of the week. Reg is in a bit of a taking over this business, and Dad said it would be best to help him out, as the job's got to be done quickly.'

I did not like to ask about his own plans for the future, but he volunteered the information.

'I'm starting in with Dad on a business footing at the beginning of December. Suits us both very well, and there's plenty of work about. He's not one to get in a panic about his health, but I think this last attack rocked him, and he won't do as much as he always has done. About time he eased off a bit, and I'll be glad to take over more of the work. There's only me to carry it on, so I'd better learn the ropes pretty quickly.'

He gave me a flashing smile through the black beard, and mounted the ladder again.

Amy arrived one afternoon in the same week just as the children were going home. She had asked me to look through the article about the sick room and to give her my opinion on it.

The two young men were up on the roof manhandling the large piece of perspex into place.

'Shan't see you tomorrow,' shouted Wayne. 'We'll have this fixed tonight in case we get some rain.'

'Well, thanks for all you've done,' I called back.

Amy and I walked across the playground to my house where Tibby, ever ravenous, gave us a rapturous welcome.

'What's his name?' enquired Amy, slipping off her coat.

'Who?'

'The bearded fellow. Miss Briggs' young man.'

'Miss Briggs' young man?' I echoed. 'That's Reg Thorn's

young man! He's called Wayne Richards. His father's a builder too.'

'He's also Miss Briggs' young man,' said Amy patiently. 'At least, he's the one she was with way back in the summer. The one I told you about.'

'You didn't tell me it was *Wayne*,' I said accusingly.

'I didn't know it was Wayne until two seconds ago,' said Amy reasonably. 'But that's certainly the same fellow. I couldn't forget a beard of that magnitude.'

'Well, I'm blowed!' I said, turning over this interesting piece of knowledge. 'I had no idea this was going on, but it explains quite a lot.'

'How do you mean?'

'Well, the improvement in temper, and the willingness to stay after school – at least, until the boy finishes work. I wonder I didn't twig before, with all this happening before my very eyes, as they say.'

'Why should you? They weren't likely to be particularly demonstrative before you and all those knowing pupils. As two sensible young people they hoped to keep their affairs to themselves, as far as you can in a village.'

'Well, I must say I'm delighted with the news. He's a good fellow, and going to have a steady job with his father. I would have thought he could have done better than our Miss Briggs, though.'

'No doubt she has hidden charms,' said Amy.

'Obviously,' I continued to think about this interesting disclosure. 'One thing,' I told Amy. 'She'll probably stay here teaching. It will be nice to know that I shan't have to start advertising for another infants' teacher yet.'

'Aren't you rushing ahead a trifle?' enquired Amy. 'Give the poor things time to sort out their romance.'

'Who started all this anyway?' I retorted.

12. DECEMBER

Our temporary skylight was a great success. For one thing, it was considerably wider than the original one, as the aperture had been made larger to take the ill-fated dormer window, and so allowed much more light to come through.

As it lay snug and flat against the roof there was no dreadful drumming noise, and from outside, I must say, the line of the roof looked better to my eyes than the somewhat clumsy dormer window. I was beginning to wonder if the powers that be would finally decide to replace the old skylight with another of more up-to-date construction.

The men who had come with Reg Thorn to inspect the damage after the gale, came again after school one day and spent a long session inside and outside the old building.

Their decision was conveyed to me later by a letter from the Office telling me that work on the roof timbers would be put in hand as soon as school broke up. The new window would be finished before the children returned in January, and they were sorry for the inconvenience. They added, rather decently I thought, that unusually severe weather had jeopardized Mr Thorn's work, and that further consultations would be needed to settle the design of the new lights, under the circumstances.

'Mark my words,' said Mr Willet, when I mentioned this to him. 'Reg Thorn will be putting in another skylight. And a durn good thing too. That dormer was wrong from the start, for our old roof. I told you, didn't I, they must have gone into all that pretty thorough when the old place was built in 1880? And they built to last then too.'

Mrs Pringle, who had entered during this conversation, added her mite. 'One thing, it should make Reg Thorn get a move on for once. I take it he won't get paid till the job's done, and he must have lost a packet already. It's an ill wind as blows nobody any good.'

Joan Benson's sitting room was crowded when I arrived on the evening of the party.

It was a pleasant surprise to see David and Irene Mawne among the guests, and Joan was busy introducing the new owners of Holly Lodge to the one or two other people whom they had not met before. Irene's brother, Horace Umbleditch was also there, and it was good to see him again.

The room was looking very festive with a ceiling-high Christmas tree already in place.

'Too early, I know,' said Joan, to the admirers, 'but I intended to enjoy my last Christmas here, and to have all the trimmings.'

I found myself by Henry Mawne and asked when his nephew hoped to move in.

'Just before Christmas, I think, though one can never be certain of these things. The removal people seem to think about the 20th December, and Joan has been absolutely adamant that she will be out by then. We are full of admiration for the way she is coping. She's definitely having the house she went to see a week or so ago and luckily, those people are off on the twelfth.'

'Can she be sure?'

'He's in the army and being posted to the Middle East. That's one thing about the services, once you've got your marching orders, you know where you are. A great relief all round. David's buyers fiddled about until he and Irene were nearly demented, but now that's satisfactorily tied up.'

Miriam Quinn approached and Henry drifted away to talk to the vicar. I asked her if she were going away for Christmas.

'Yes, I'm off to Norfolk to my brother's. I thought it would be more fun for David and Irene to have their first Christmas here on their own. Of course, young Simon will be here, and I believe Henry and Elizabeth have been invited to Christmas dinner. Quite a family affair, and I shall enjoy being with my own folk, too, of course. What are you going to do?'

I told her that I had in mind to invite Dolly Clare to spend Christmas and Boxing Day with me. She would be with me overnight for the centenary celebrations earlier in the month, but if she were willing to come later as well, it would be an added joy.

'Do you know, I've never met her, and would love to.'

'Then we'll fix up a meeting in the New Year,' I promised. 'But we're being called to order.'

Sure enough, the vicar called for silence, and made a graceful little speech, wishing Joan well and welcoming the young Mawnes. We raised our glasses, and drank their healths.

I thought, yet again, how lucky we are in Fairacre to have so many good people united in friendship within our parish bounds.

As our two-day celebrations drew near, excitement began to run high. As well as the entertainment, it was my duty, as always, to provide the annual school tea party. This is paid for from our school funds, raised during the year by such things as jumble sales and bazaars, and I do the ordering.

This time it was obvious that we should need twice as much food, although Mrs Willet's masterpieces should certainly fill up appreciative stomachs. We are lucky enough still to have a baker in Fairacre. He also keeps the village shop, so that I went up one evening to discuss with him such things as scones, buns, lardy cake, and what he calls 'confections' – that is such mouth-watering and fattening things as almond slices, macaroons and madeleines.

Usually I order sliced loaves as well, and spend hours making sandwiches in my kitchen. But this year, with so much else to occupy my time, I decided to give them a miss.

By the time we had finished poring over the order, it was plain to me that we should have to have some more money-raising efforts early in the New Year, as the existing school kitty would be seriously depleted.

And why not, I asked myself? It's not every year that one celebrates one's hundredth birthday! Fairacre School was going to do its friends proud – and enjoy every minute of it.

The two performances and tea parties were to take place on the last Thursday and Friday of term.

Mrs Annett from Beech Green (who as Miss Gray was once my infants' teacher until the neighbouring headmaster snatched her from me into matrimony) brought Miss Clare with her, as our old friend was to stay the night so that she did not get over-tired. I was to return her to her own cottage on Friday evening.

At half-past two, parents and friends came flooding into the ancient schoolroom. We had pushed back the dividing partition, and the action was to take place at the infants' end of the room. The quaking actors and actresses were huddled into the lobby. Miss Clare, serene as ever, did her best to calm their nerves while I greeted our guests, and told them a little of what they would be seeing – with reasonable luck.

I had never seen our little school so packed, and this, of course, was only half our audience. I found it intensely moving to see so many old people, some of whom had been pupils before the First World War and would remember Miss Clare as a young pupil teacher. It was good too to see so many friends, some comparative newcomers to Fairacre, like the Mawnes, who had come to do us honour and to join in this home-spun tribute to our school.

I read the entry from the original log book, and Linda and Patrick took the stage. There was warm applause as they entered, due largely, I think, to the superb costumes which Mrs Moffat had created.

After looking somewhat scared at this unexpected welcome, the two became quite confident, and went through their little scene. The caning went down extremely well, and a toddler in the front row brought the house down by shouting: 'Give 'im some more!' in the most bloodthirsty manner. Obviously, I should have to keep an eye on this juvenile sadist when he came under my care in two or three years' time.

'In King Edward the Seventh's reign,' I said loudly, for hidden Dolly Clare's benefit, 'Fairacre School had a new young pupil teacher.'

Here Dolly entered, smiling, and the applause grew deafening. We had placed the old high chair, in which she had sat for so many years, in front of the audience, and with just one page of notes Dolly began her reminiscences.

Her listeners gave her rapt attention. She confined her memories to the early years of her teaching at the school, and mentioned many children – many now dead, or killed in the 1914–18 war – remembered clearly by the older ones present.

She touched on the clothes worn, the lunches brought, the great distances trudged in all weathers, and the universal poverty which dogged almost all. She also dwelt on the happiness found in simple things: the occasional treat, the annual outing, harvest home, a visit from the bishop, as well as the ineffable joy of country things such as the first primroses, the cuckoo's call and the return of the swallows.

There was no doubt about it. As I had suspected, Miss Clare's contribution, made incidentally without any recourse to her notes, was the highlight of the afternoon, although the following scene, showing the school's part in the war of George the Fifth's reign, obviously moved many of those who could remember those sad times.

Mr Lamb's recollections of the trip to Wembley from the school gave us all a chance to laugh. Some of his contemporaries interrupted his narrative with downright contradictions, but it was all done with such enthusiasm and merriment that his contribution was a resounding success.

Mrs Austen's vivid account of an evacuee's view of Fairacre was warmly received, and probably because she was a woman,

she was not open to the same outspoken comments which had punctuated Mr Lamb's account.

Then it was my turn to give an idea of the school in the reign of our present Queen Elizabeth the Second. I had tried to make it a brief survey and as interesting as possible, but feared it might be something of a comedown after the earlier contributions.

It was a kind audience, however, and genuinely interested, I felt, in the changes which had taken place since the Act of 1944 when the children over eleven went off to Beech Green or Caxley Grammar School, and Fairacre was left as a junior school. The repercussions of the ancient grammar school being obliged to become a comprehensive school were also mentioned, for this fact touched many of the families present.

The children's work was on display round the walls and at one end of the room, and I invited the audience to inspect everything and to see how methods of work had altered over the hundred years. The whole school then clustered on to our temporary stage and sang two songs very sweetly.

Finally, the vicar rose and made a fine speech about the great part this old school had played in village life, and complimented everyone on the work done, not only on the stage this afternoon, but behind the scenes for many, many years. He then asked us all to join in a prayer of thanksgiving for mercies received in the past, and to call a blessing on Fairacre School's future.

While this was being done and heads were bent, I could hear the welcome sound of Mrs Pringle and her band of helpers, dealing with the tea things in the other lobby. Festivity was about to follow reverence.

It was astonishing to see how quickly the mounds of provender vanished. Appetites are keen in our sharp downland air, and I was kept busy filling cups from the tea urn borrowed from the Woman's Institute for the two occasions.

But at last the great moment came when the vicar called for silence, the door opened and Mrs Willet came staggering in, bearing the magnificent cake ablaze with one hundred candles. A great cheer went up and the ancient floorboards quaked under the stamping of stout country boots.

We had asked Miss Clare, as the oldest pupil present, and the youngest child from the infants' room to cut the cake together. My bread knife only just proved equal to severing the beautifully dark, rich mixture, but the two won through eventually and a slice was delivered to everyone present.

It was dark by the time the last of our visitors had gone. The fragrance of the fruit cake still lingered about the empty schoolroom, and far too many crumbs lay upon the floor.

'It all went beautifully,' I said to Miss Clare before we walked across the playground to my home. 'But I don't know what Mrs Pringle will say when she sees the mess.'

'What Mrs Pringle says,' Miss Clare told me, 'can have very little meaning in face of a hundred years of our school's history.'

And with this comforting thought we strolled home to take our ease. There was a sharp nip in the air, and our breath was visible in the dusk.

'A frost tonight,' said Miss Clare. 'The first real one of the winter.'

Sure enough, when I took her breakfast tray into my spare room the next morning, the trees and grass were white with hoar frost. It was a lovely sight, but a pointer to things to come.

Miss Clare protested about being waited on, but I was adamant that she stayed in bed for an hour or two longer. We had a repeat performance to go through in the afternoon, and I knew that there would be a great many friends who would want to talk to her.

As it was the last day of term, too, I should be busy clearing up and trying to remind the children of the date of our return in January, as well as keeping them relatively calm and prepared for their final performance. I found that it was no easy task. Success had quite gone to their heads, and I had never known them quite so excited and noisy. I pushed them out early to play in the frosty playground and to run off some of their excess energy.

Miss Briggs, whose class was suffering from the same *joie de vivre*, joined me in the playground, and we gave them all a further ten minutes of strenuous exercise. If anything, these tactics seemed to rouse them even more, but we ushered the breathless mob indoors, and I suggested that a story might calm them down.

'We have to expect this sort of thing on the last day of term,' I said indulgently. 'And then, of course, there's Christmas looming ahead. Are you going home?'

'Yes,' said my assistant.

'Tonight? Will you want to get off early?'

I wished I could remember if it were Droitwich or Harrogate. Somewhere a good distance away, I knew.

'No. It seemed better to go tomorrow in the light, and anyway Wayne doesn't finish until tomorrow morning.'

I must have looked blank.

'I'm driving home to Leamington and taking him with me.'

Leamington. I must remember *Leamington.*

'That will be nice for you both,' I said, anxious not to appear too pressing, but Miss Briggs was well launched.

'My parents know about him, of course, but haven't met him yet. I expect we'll announce our engagement at Christmas.'

I said, quite truthfully, that I was delighted to hear the news, and that Wayne was a fine young man.

Miss Briggs gave me the biggest smile I had yet seen upon her countenance, and we returned to the noisy rabble within.

Our second afternoon was even more successful than the first. For one thing, all those taking part were more relaxed, and the audience was even larger than the day before. How they all managed to squeeze in I shall never fathom.

Mrs Willet's second cake was as rapturously received as the first, and almost all the school's offerings went too. The few cakes that remained, I put into a paper bag to give surreptitiously to the Coggs family later.

Miss Clare was surrounded by friends, among them Elizabeth Mawne who had not met her before. Their conversation was animated, and I was glad to see my old friend Dolly so lively. I began to realize, more sharply than ever before, that she normally lacked company, and I was glad that I was about to invite her to spend Christmas with me.

Even Mrs Pringle seemed to have mellowed with our festivities, and said nothing about the floor strewn with crumbs.

'I'll see to that tea urn,' she said. 'The W.I. can turn a bit funny if it's not returned pronto, and *clean*.'

At last we said goodbye to our guests, reiterated the phrase: 'Term begins on January the sixth' to those willing to listen, who were few among the general pandemonium, and left the schoolroom to the ministrations of Mrs Pringle and Mr and Mrs Willet, who insisted on helping to put all to rights.

'Well,' I said to Miss Clare, when we sank exhausted one each side of my sitting-room fire. 'I'm whacked! Someone else will have to cope with the next centenary.'

'But it's really been *memorable*!' replied Dolly. 'How glad I am to have seen it – and to have taken part!'

'Have a glass of sherry,' I said, struggling to my feet. 'We need a pick-me-up after all that.'

'Here's to Fairacre School,' said Dolly, raising her glass, and we drank thankfully.

'Have you any plans for Christmas?' I asked, after the first rejuvenating mouthful.

'None. Except that I expect the kind Annetts will invite me there for Christmas Day.'

I said how much I should like her to come to Fairacre for the two days, or longer if she could manage it.

'There's nothing I should enjoy more,' she told me. And so it was happily settled.

'I can honestly say I never feel truly lonely,' she went on, 'but now that I'm such a great age I've no one of my own left. Ada's children lost touch years ago, even before my sister died. Of course, dear Emily meant more to me than anyone in the world, but when she went there was really no one left, except good friends like you. I believe you are in the same boat?'

'I suppose so. No really close relations, though I have a dear aunt, and some jolly cousins, but they are all as busy as I am, and we don't keep in touch as we should. No, I'm like you, very glad of good friends who live near enough to see frequently, like you and the Annetts and dear old Amy at Bent, who wants to meet you incidentally.'

'That will be nice,' said Dolly. She sounded a trifle abstracted, and I wondered if she were over-tired, which would not be surprising. She took another sip from her glass, and then put it carefully on the side table.

'I think I ought to tell you something which perhaps I should have told you before. When I was talking to that nice Mrs Mawne this afternoon, I realized for the first time that you might be worrying about what might happen to you if this school ever had to close.'

'Well, that's been a possibility for years, of course,' I said, puzzled.

'You see, my dear, having no relatives to speak of, I left everything to dear Emily as she had nowhere of her own to live, and only a tiny pension. Not that I had much more, of course, but I did have the cottage to shelter us. When she had gone, I went one day to Caxley to see young Mr Lovejoy and to alter my will.'

Young Mr Lovejoy, I knew, was about to retire as he was now in his sixties. But to Miss Clare, whose family had dealt with the old-established solicitors for two or three generations, young Mr Lovejoy must seem a mere boy.

'He was as charming as ever,' said Dolly, 'and we made out a nice simple little will, leaving some money to the church at Beech Green and the same to Fairacre. My few trinkets I've left to Isobel Annett. Nothing much of value there, I'm afraid, but some are quite pretty.'

'She'll treasure them, I'm sure,' I said.

Miss Clare picked up her glass again. 'And the house I've left to you.'

I felt my jaw drop. I gazed at her, speechless with shock.

'Do you mind?' asked Dolly very gently.

'Mind?' I croaked. 'I don't know what to say!'

'I wanted it to be a surprise for you when I'd gone. I knew you hadn't made any arrangements to buy a place, and I thought you could find a home there while you looked round, if you wanted something better.'

'There is nothing better!' I whispered. My voice seemed to have collapsed completely, and my heart was jumping about like a frog.

'Well, of course, I'd always hoped that you would want to live in it, and be as happy as I have there. I ought to have realized though that you might be worrying about the future. It wasn't until this afternoon, when Mrs Mawne mentioned it, that I saw that I had really been rather self-indulgent in trying to keep my plans secret.'

'Dolly,' I began, trying to control my wavering voice, 'I don't know how to thank you. I'm absolutely overwhelmed, and don't deserve such generosity. I'll try to tell you soon how I feel – but I'm too overjoyed for words just now.'

'Good!' said Dolly comfortably. 'Well, that's settled. Now to more practical matters. What would you like for a Christmas present?'

I went over to kiss her.

'You've just given me one,' I told her.

Later that evening, I took Dolly home, and saw her safely into bed with her hot water bottle and a warm drink. By that time, I had recovered enough to tell her how I felt about her wonderful gesture. It made the future quite different for me, and I was still too dazed to comprehend fully just what it would mean.

I locked the cottage door as directed, and put the key back through the letter box. I still could not believe that one day –

long distant, I sincerely prayed – this lovely house might be mine.

'I shall never sleep a wink,' I said to myself, as I drove back through the frosty night.

But I fell into bed within ten minutes of reaching home, and slept like a log until seven.

I resolved to say nothing about my proposed legacy to any one. Dolly wanted to keep it a secret, and I should respect that wish. But buoyed up with my wonderful news, I set about all the Christmas tasks I had neglected during our celebrations.

Christmas cards were arriving thick and fast. Trees, flowers, robins, skating parties, and every imaginable winter activity glowed from the tributes on my mantelpiece, and I must get down to sending off some of my own.

The card I cherished most was a photograph of a baby seal sent to me by the kind people at the Tresco hotel. The seal had been born on the beach nearby, and no other Christmas card could touch it for its delightful appeal. It took pride of place among the others.

It also galvanized me into doing something which Amy had urged me to do long ago. The first letter of the holidays was to that same hotel, booking a room for a fortnight in August. How Amy would approve!

The frost continued. The ground was iron hard and every morning found the grass and trees covered with hoar frost. Ice was everywhere, and the roads treacherous.

Miss Clare sent a message to say that she had decided against coming to the school service at St Patrick's the next Sunday, because of the weather, but would look forward to seeing me on Christmas Eve for tea at her house. We should miss her at the service, but I was relieved to know that she was not venturing out in this bitter weather. I hoped that by the following Wednesday the thaw would have set in.

Attendance at morning service on Sunday must have delighted Gerald Partridge's heart. Parents, pupils, managers and other friends of Fairacre School turned up in full force, and there were very few empty pews.

The singing was hearty, and I had found time to coach the children in the two hymns chosen particularly for this occasion, so that they added to the joyful noise considerably. The vicar's sermon was a model of sincerity, brevity and gratitude, and Mr Annett had chosen some stirring music for the service. The final voluntary was Mozart's 'Turkish March', and I wondered, yet again, how anyone, Turks or otherwise, could march in step to that dancing rhythm.

But it was a joyous and uplifting ending to our centenary celebrations.

By Wednesday, the murky cold weather had lifted slightly. It was still bitterly cold, but the roads had thawed, and for two or three hours at midday a feeble sun dispersed the clouds.

I drove over to Beech Green and walked up the short path to Dolly Clare's cottage with the most unusual feelings. Pleasure at being there was now mingled with something like awe. That this, one day, might be mine! I could still not fully realize my good fortune, and felt very humble in the face of Dolly's superb generosity. Of one thing I could be certain. The cottage would be cherished as dearly as before, and if ever her gentle ghost reappeared it would be given honour and a warm welcome.

We were at St Patrick's the next morning, admiring the Christmas roses, the holly, the ivy and the mistletoe. Mr Partridge's suggestion that the children might help had not been followed up, and certainly the flower-arranging ladies had made a superb job of their labour of love without juvenile aid.

We walked back through the thin winter sunshine to find that the chicken I had left roasting was done to a turn, and the small pudding was bubbling cheerfully on the stove.

After our modest Christmas dinner we indulged in a glass of port and both slipped off into slumber, awaking just in time to listen to the Queen's message.

We spent the rest of Christmas Day and Boxing Day very

quietly and lazily, going for short walks round the familiar lanes of Fairacre when the sun came through in the early afternoon. But it was always good to return to the fireside and to pick up our knitting, or attempt to solve the crossword puzzle, or sometimes simply to doze. To tell the truth, I was dog-tired at the end of term, and this one had been particularly arduous. Not that I would have missed any of our jollifications for a minute, but I began to realize just how exhausted I was when I could relax at home. Dolly Clare was the perfect companion for this pace of life, serene, undemanding and unfailingly happy.

I managed to persuade her to stay until the Saturday morning, but no longer. She was anxious not to put her good neighbour to any unnecessary trouble.

'She is looking after the cat,' she said, 'and getting in my milk and bread. And no doubt she will light a fire, and generally cosset the house, so I must get back to look after it myself.'

We drove over in the morning, and sure enough a fire blazed in the grate. We settled down to enjoy a cup of coffee before I returned.

'I've lived here for six reigns now,' said Miss Clare, looking about her. 'I thought, when I was telling our friends about my time as a pupil teacher at Fairacre, that I must have closed the door of this cottage some thousands of times and set off on my bicycle along the lane to that dear old school. I've seen the trees and fields breaking into leaf, shading the road later, turning into the gold of autumn and then bitter nakedness, for more years than I care to remember. But always this cottage has been the beginning and end of every journey. The thought that you will do the same after me gives me infinite pleasure. I don't know when I've felt quite so happy.'

'I can echo that,' I told her.

No snow came to our downland country during the remaining days of December, but the skies were ominously grey and the iron cold made one feel that this respite might be short-lived.

On New Year's Eve I was invited to the Mawnes for the evening. I walked through the village in the frosty air to the sound of the bells ringing a practice peal at St Patrick's.

Well, the Old Year had been good to me, I thought. I had seen Fairacre School celebrating a hundred years of useful work, and my personal life had been enriched by friends old and new. And Dolly Clare's incredible kindness had put the final seal upon a memorable year. I had a great deal to be thankful for.

So what would the New Year bring, I wondered, opening the gate of the Mawnes' house? Lights gleamed in the windows. A lantern by the door lit up the welcoming holly wreath dangling its scarlet ribbons against the white paint.

'Come in, come in!' called Henry, opening the door, 'and a Happy New Year to you, and all Fairacre!'